'Malone is the master of twists, turns and the unexpected, with the skill to keep things grounded ... Superb storytelling from a master of his craft' *Herald Scotland*

'A beautifully written tale, original, engrossing and scary ... a dark joy' *The Times*

'A complex and multilayered story – perfect for a wintry night' *Sunday Express*

'A deeply satisfying read' *Sunday Times*

'A fine, page-turning thriller' *Daily Mail*

'With each turn of the page, a more shocking detail is revealed ... There is barely enough time to catch your breath' *Scotsman*

'A complex, nuanced story that is utterly compelling ... I ask again, why is he not more seriously lauded?' Live & Deadly

'Mesmerising, beautifully written and it's just made me so much more of a member of #TeamMalone. Just incredible!' The Reading Closet

'Compelling, provocative, emotive and as always, beautifully written' Hair Past a Freckle

'Every single word in this book has more than earned its place on the page' Chapter in My Life

'It is affecting. It is dark. It is disturbing' Swirl and Thread

'Subtle, sensitivity written, wrought with emotion and has to be one of my most captivating, heart-breaking reads EVER' The Book Review Café

ABOUT THE AUTHOR

Michael Malone is a prize-winning poet and author who was born and brought up in the heart of Burns' country. He has published over 200 poems in literary magazines throughout the UK, including *New Writing Scotland, Poetry Scotland* and *Markings. Blood Tears*, his bestselling debut novel, won the Pitlochry Prize from the Scottish Association of Writers. Other published work includes: *Carnegie's Call; A Taste for Malice; The Guillotine Choice; Beyond the Rage; The Bad Samaritan;* and *Dog Fight*. His psychological thriller, *A Suitable Lie*, was a number-one bestseller, and the critically acclaimed *House of Spines* and *After He Died* soon followed suit. Since then, he's written three further thought-provoking, exquisitely written psychological thrillers, *In the Absence of Miracles, A Song of Isolation* and *Quicksand of Memory*, cementing his position as a key proponent of Tartan Noir and an undeniable talent. A former Regional Sales Manager (Faber & Faber) he has also worked as an IFA and a bookseller. Michael lives in Ayr.

Follow him on Twitter @michaelJmalone1, facebook.com/themichaeljmalonepage and Instagram @1michaeljmalone.

Other titles by Michael J. Malone available from Orenda Books

A Suitable Lie
House of Spines
After He Died
In the Absence of Miracles
A Song of Isolation
Quicksand of Memory

THE MURMURS

MICHAEL J. MALONE

**ORENDA
BOOKS**

Orenda Books
16 Carson Road
West Dulwich
London SE21 8HU
www.orendabooks.co.uk

First published in the UK by Orenda Books, 2023
Copyright © Michael J. Malone, 2023

A catalogue record for this book is available from the British Library.

B-format paperback ISBN 978-1-914585-82-1
eISBN 978-1-914585-83-8

Typeset in Garamond by typesetter.org.uk
Printed and bound by CPI Group (UK) Ltd, Croydon CR0 4YY

For sales and distribution, please contact *info@orendabooks.co.uk* or visit *www.orendabooks.co.uk*.

'Not everything that is faced can be changed –
but nothing can be changed until it is faced'
—James Baldwin

Prologue

A curse is a difficult thing to master. Like weaving a piece of lace from spider silk, moonbeams and a desperate sense of hope. A pause in the wrong place, words too close together, or spend too long on the utterance of a vowel sound, and you risk the magic shifting, the intention being warped and the target changing.

Such were my learnings at my great-grandmother, Jeannie McLean's knee, a woman who lived well into her hundreds – a woman who had the power to defy death itself. It was said that Jeannie was the only surviving child of the last witch to be burned in the whole of Ardnamurchan. It was also said she had watched as the local people had dragged her mother, and her older sister and brother, twins Isobel and Andra, from the house towards a smoking pyre. And then she was forced to listen to their pleas for mercy before they were strangled and their bodies thrown onto the flames.

Isobel and Andra, Jeannie told me, had blue eyes, white-blond hair and a beauty unmatched in the country. In the days before the murmurs started, they were tall, slim and strong.

How could children be so beautiful, people asked? How could they be so clever? For they were both well ahead of their peers in the local school.

They had good, kind hearts, Jeannie asserted, but they had no need of anyone else, such was their connection. And there lay the seed of their destruction.

It was unnatural, the local gossips opined. A boy and girl, related, being so independent of everyone else. They had to be up to something ungodly. They had to be giving in to their most base desires. Why else would they be so indifferent and different to everyone else?

And so the sullen stares became whispers. Hands that had curved over mouths to hide evil conjecture became pointed fingers. Unease grew into a murmuring that wouldn't fade, and suspicion followed them like their own personal haar.

First, it was the turnip crop that failed. Then the oats.

Every ship sent out into the Sound of Mull returned without landing a single fish.

A lamb was born with two heads.

A white-tailed eagle swooped and snatched a child from its mother's arms.

That was nonsense of course, Jeannie said. Who'd ever heard of an eagle doing such a thing? But repeat a lie often enough and it becomes as solid and as unwieldy as fact, she added.

It's a sad truth that the gossip was led by people from our own family – and who else, these self-anointed judges opined, but the McLean twins could make such things happen?

Fire and prayer were the answer.

Fire would cleanse, and prayer would see that the land and sea would turn back to health and prosperity.

And if the twins had to be sent back to hell, so would the wretch who gave them life.

The pain of it all had settled in Jeannie's eyes and informed every look, every gesture. And so, as soon as she was able, she'd relocated to this glen, away from the clan that had treated her and hers so abominably.

Jeannie paused in the telling, her eyes gleaming with the light from the fireplace. 'Of course, they had no idea how wrong they were.' Satisfaction warred with something else in her expression. Another emotion I had difficulty naming, at first. Could it have been humility? 'The twins didn't have the gift.' She paused and looked deep into my eyes as if searching for something. 'I did. And you have it too, I'm sure.'

I felt fear burrow into my heart. 'I do?'

'Don't fret, child. I'll teach you how to use it wisely. For the good of your family.' Her eyes narrowed. 'And to protect you from the sanctimonious.' She grabbed my hand with the power and strength of someone much lesser in years. 'But I shall teach you and you will be wise to it all.'

And here and now, the past had come back to hurt me and mine, and I was desperately glad that Jeannie was long dead and unable to see what had become of her sanctuary.

Having lived a life almost as long in years and pain as the fabled Jeannie, I sneaked back up to the village of Anlochard – carried the last five hundred yards on the strong back of my great-nephew Archie. Now I was knee-deep in the waters of a near-frozen stream that ran through the village down to Loch Suinart, with loam under my fingernails, my white hair loose around my shoulders, and a crown of sage and rosemary on my head.

Pain, Jeannie had warned me, was the key to an efficacious spell. Emotional or physical. Preferably both. Hence, the bone-seeping chill of the river that ran past our erstwhile homes.

With a barely stifled sob and a heart near breaking I took one look over my shoulder at the homes that had housed my family for generations. Flames still licked at the sky from the timber and thatched roofs lit by the factor and his men after they had thrown me and mine out onto the cold moor and destroyed everything we owned.

It was happening all over the country, I knew: lands being cleared of humans for the more profitable sheep and lambs. But I also knew that in our case the motivation wasn't that simple.

A sin other than greed was our undoing, and it came from family – the same family line that pointed the finger and accused poor Jean, Isobel and Andra around a hundred years ago, and that made the betrayal cleave even more deeply through my soul.

Head thrown back, arms wide, throat bare, and eyes staring sightless at the countless stars, I threw words in the old tongue into *the night sky. Words of power and meaning. Words that fired my mouth as they slipped out into the frigid air.*

Words scour, they scald, they lacerate, they leach into the deepest recesses of the mind. They shame. They rob of you the will to live, and to love.

The words I hurled into the night sky were such words. I prayed that they had the ability to reach into the future, causing more harm than any mere fire or sword. The woman I targeted, it was her and hers that set off the whispering – the murmurs that started the agony for my family. And maddening, agonising, unceasing murmurs would be the instrument of my revenge.

Chapter 1

Annie – Now

She was underwater. The world reaching her ears through a muffle, gurgle and splash.

At first, it was nice. The water just how she liked it. She was on her own. No annoying sibling or parents demanding anything.

Then.

Pressure and a weight on her head.

Strong.

Firm.

Determined pressure.

She kicked furiously. Screamed, 'Help!' But as she opened her mouth it filled with water. She spat it out. Panic sparked bright, increasing her need for oxygen.

Desperately trying to scream while not taking in any more water. 'Help.'

Shaking her head, fighting to get away from the pressure. Fighting to get a hold of the fingers holding her head. Struggling to get purchase that would help her push up out of the water. But her heels slipped furiously against the floor of the bath.

And no matter how much she fought, and struggled, and screamed, she was stuck. Always stuck.

Lungs desperate for air.

Breathe, breathe, BREATHE. But she couldn't open her mouth because it would fill with water again.

In silent desperation she pretended she'd drowned. Went limp. Waited for the hand to move. Then she could shoot up out of the water onto dry land.

But the pressure never let up.

Until, blessed relief, she shot up from her pillow, hair sweat-plastered to her forehead and her quilt wrapped so tightly around her legs it took several moments to get free.

That Annie had the dream on the night before the next big change in her life, having not had it for a long time, made her query her choices. Was she doing the right thing? Going for the right job? Was the dream some kind of warning?

'Did I nearly drown as a kid?' she'd asked her brother Lewis after the first dozen times the dream visited her.

'Pff,' he snorted. 'I can barely remember what I had for dinner last night, and you expect me to remember something like that?'

'Godssake,' she countered. 'Surely you'd remember something like your favourite sister nearly dying?'

'Only sister.' He grinned.

'Well, what the hell is this dream all about then?'

If she'd had parents, she could have asked them, but they both died when she was in her teens. Her mother in a car accident – that she was also supposedly in; no memory of *that* either – and her father ten months later, of a broken heart.

'Great that he loved his wife, and all that,' she'd said to Lewis during a teenage Buckfast session in the local park. 'But suicide? Really? Couldn't he have loved his kids a wee bit more? Save us having to live with those losers.'

Those 'losers' were the McEvoys, childhood friends of their father – church elders, who applied to adopt them when their father died, to save them going into the system. A fact that Mrs McEvoy reminded Annie of after every teenage huff.

They were good people, Annie was able to freely acknowledge when she grew up, realising that her petty rebellion was a complication of her grief and anger at being left so young without parents. They could have had so much worse, and Mrs McEvoy had become a friend to her now, as an adult.

As she finally shook off her duvet and sat on the edge of the bed, ready to get up, her phone pinged an alert. It was said lady wishing her good luck on the first day of her new job.

Teenage rebellion had not only led Annie to distrust her carers – and get her belly-button pierced – it had fuelled her anger and a resolution that she didn't want to take an active part in the world. Consequently, education was for stiffs, and work was for the enslaved. And while Lewis got himself a good degree and a well-paid job, as an accountant, for God's sake, she huffed and puffed from one arts course to another. She was self-aware enough to know that she needed to keep busy, and doing something in art would satisfy that need without kowtowing to The Man and becoming a good little sheep.

But whether she agreed with it or not, she was living in a material world, and that meant she had to have some stuff – like a roof over her head, some clothes, and possibly even a television. And that meant earning a living. Selling tie-dyed T-shirts and leggings from a stall was not going to bring in enough to give her independence; that required regular income, and that meant an actual job.

Mrs Mac – as she now affectionately called her – had advanced her a small loan against future earnings, meaning that for the first time Annie could rent a place of her own.

'It's not that we want rid of you, dear...' Mrs Mac said while all but wringing her hands against the thought that Annie might feel unloved.

'But it is time to grow up,' Mr Mac said with his trademark gruff honesty. An honesty that was always delivered with a half-grin and a twinkle in his grey-blue eyes. Such was his charm, Annie had always felt unable to be offended by the man, even as she railed against his wife.

What neither of them said was that it was time she grew up, like her brother. And she appreciated that. All through her school years that was the attempt at encouragement her teachers had thrown at her. *They were twins for goodness' sake, how could they be so different?* He was a top student and athlete. If he wasn't her brother she would have hated him.

That the McEvoys realised this and never compared the two siblings was one of the reasons why Annie grew to love them.

Annie looked down at her phone, at the message from Mrs Mac wishing her good luck, and with a little lift in her heart replied with a simple thank-you – and:

Feeling a wee bit of first-day nerves, tbh.

Mrs Mac came straight back with:

You worked for this – you deserve it – now go and do what you were born for. Love you, doll.

She wasn't one for displays of affection, but Annie pictured Mrs Mac in her living room right then, among her china ornaments and doilies, wiping away a tear as she typed out the message on her new tablet, and then doing that thing she did every time her emotions threatened to spill over. A little cough, a shake of her head and an upward tilt of her chin, as if that was enough to reset her brain.

Annie fetched her breakfast, and while she spooned cereal into her mouth she watched the TV news.

An item snagged her attention. A man and woman stood side by side, in the background a small hotel, and beyond that a glimpse of mountain and loch.

'It's been fifteen years,' the woman said, her expression an essay in grief.

Annie stilled her spoon and bit her lip.

'She just disappeared,' the man said as he put an arm over the woman's shoulder. 'Surely somebody out there knows something.' In response the woman moved even closer to the man.

Annie noticed the woman was holding a framed photograph of a teenage girl. She held it up and the camera zoomed in on it while the mother spoke.

'We've never given up hope that our girl is still alive,' she said. 'If you're watching this, honey, come home. Please. Come home.'

That face, Annie thought; it was so familiar. Who was that girl, and how did Annie know her? She became aware of a pressure just behind her right eye. Pain built and bloomed across her forehead. She screwed her eyes tight. Not today, please. Not today.

She looked at the screen again, diving into memory and finding nothing. Who was that girl, and why did Annie suddenly feel certain that her parents' prayers would never be answered?

Chapter 2

Annie – Now

All the way to her new job, Annie couldn't stop thinking about the girl in the photo, and the unending grief her parents must face. Five minutes into her journey she fished her phone out of her bag and searched for the story. The news channel she'd been watching had a page given over to it.

Mossgow, it said, was a small town in the Scottish Highlands and a scene of a possible tragedy...

Annie's heart gave a twist. Mossgow. That was where she, apparently, grew up, but she had little recollection of the place. The accident with her mother had wiped almost everything from her memory, although the landscape behind the girl's parents did stir something in her mind. She scrolled through the article, hoping that if she read it a few times it might unravel more solid memories. But nothing more presented itself.

God, that poor girl. Her poor parents. To have lived with that for fifteen years and still be functional. Annie guessed that it was the hope that kept them going, but again, somehow she knew, or could sense, that there simply wouldn't be a positive outcome.

She realised her stop was next, and putting her phone back in her bag with a mental promise to phone Lewis and pick his brain, she stood and shuffled towards the door.

When the bus stopped, she jumped off and made her way up the hill to Heartgrove House, arriving only slightly out of breath and warmed through from the climb. It was a modern, red-brick, two-floor structure with large windows and a high sloping roof. Despite the builders' best attempts at softening the look with a large, curved drive and plenty of trees and shrubs, the purpose of the place was evident in the safety doors and signage. This was a functional building and no amount of dressing up was going to offer a disguise. It was a care home for the elderly. The fact that current Annie was determined to work in this sector would have had teenage Annie squirming with disbelief.

The lobby was full of large-leafed plants, eighties-style red-and-yellow wallpaper, a small reception desk and a row of chairs against the wall, which gave a view out of the glass door and down the driveway.

Sitting there, a chair's space apart, were two old men. They both looked past Annie and down the hill as if they were losing patience with whoever was going to visit them.

One had a particularly lost expression on his face. He was wearing a light-blue cardigan over a vanilla-coloured shirt, with grey trousers. His face was well lined; one eye drooped and shone with fluid, and his hair was sparse and white over a freckled scalp.

'Morning,' Annie said to the men.

'Whit's guid about it, hen?' the man she'd been studying asked. 'I'll no' be happy until I'm away wi' fae this damn place.'

'Och, you're an arsehole, Jimmy. The lassie was just trying to be nice,' the other man said.

Where Jimmy was dimmed with the need to escape, this man was wreathed in smiles. He was wearing similar clothing to the other man, except his cardigan was green. Glasgow's age-old Celtic and Rangers rivalry evident even in a place like this.

'Don't give me your "glass half full" bollocks the day, Steve. I'm no' in the mood for it,' Jimmy replied.

Steve looked across at Annie and rolled his eyes. 'He's lovely guy really, hen. His son's late coming to pick him up, so he's worried he's no' getting out the day.'

'Aye, Steve,' Jimmy said as he reached down to the floor, moving in increments towards a stick that lay there. 'Talk about me as if I'm no' here. That's how you win friends and influence people, eh?'

A car horn beeped and both men perked up. But Jimmy's energy quickly faded when he realised it wasn't for him.

"Sake,' he said under his breath.

Annie heard someone approaching and turned to see Jane Anderson, the woman who'd interviewed her.

'Morning, Annie, I see you've met our star turns, Jimmy and Steve,' Jane said with the energy that Annie remembered from her interview. An energy that Annie found herself instantly warming to, thinking this would be a woman she could work with. 'Gents, this is Annie, a new member of our staff.'

'Hello, darling,' said Steve with a chuckle. 'I'm awfy sorry, but Jimmy appears to have got out the twisted-bugger side of the bed this morning.'

Annie thought it was because she'd moved her head too quickly from Jane to Steve, but her head spun. Lights flickered until her vision dimmed altogether. Her head buzzed with pain. Fear twisted in her gut.

She had to leave. She had to get out of here. Her breathing reduced to gulps.

Annie screwed her eyes shut tight, held a hand out to the wall to steady herself.

'Here, Annie. You alright?' Steve asked.

'I'm fine, thanks,' Annie replied, fighting down her mounting panic. What was going on? What was wrong with her? She closed her eyes and flashed them open again to send Steve a smile of thanks, but with horror she saw that instead of the kindly face she expected there was nothing there but the bleached bones and vacant eyeholes of a skull, and a low hateful voice murmuring in her head that the old man was about to die.

Chapter 3

Then

The light hurt the girl's eyes. She blinked hard, trying to see where she was. But her head was so sore. And she was tired. So very tired. She could barely focus.

She slept. Woke again. A flash of memory.

She was in a car.

Too fast.

'Mum!' she screamed.

A tree loomed. They were approaching it far too quickly.

Mercifully, sleep tugged at her consciousness, pulling her back.

The girl dreamed. A series of confused sensory impressions. Hot water. She was in a bath. Under the water. Pressure on her head. Unable to breathe. She kicked. Her heels drumming against the floor of the bath. She was only small. The person holding her head down so much stronger than she was. Then shouts. Screams. Release, and a deep, lung-filling breath.

Sleep.

And the dream.

But this time the car reached the water. And went under. And the water was cold. So very cold.

'Mum!' she screamed again.

A face – with a terrible light in its eyes – changed into a skull.

The girl woke again.

Again, the light. It scoured her eyes, her brain. Sleep tugged, but she fought it. Where was she? Tentatively, she sought feedback from her senses. Her head was on a pillow. Her body was being pressed down onto a mattress. She moved her feet. Her arms.

Sheets were tucked in so tight it was like she'd been restrained. Cushioned shoes squeaking on a hard floor. The swish of trousered thighs. Then a kind-faced woman leaned over her. She felt a light touch on her shoulder.

'You're back with us, dear.' The woman sounded pleased. 'We thought we'd lost you there.'

'Where...?' The girl found that the question escaped her lips in a croak.

'Let me get you a glass of water.'

'Don't leave...' Panicked, she managed to release an arm from under her covers and reached for the woman. Nurse?

The warm skin on hers was reassuring. Something tangible to help her align her senses. Help her feel this world was real.

'It's okay, honey. I'm just here. Getting you some pillows so you can drink without getting the water all over you.'

The light wasn't so painful now, so the girl swivelled her head round to follow the progress of the nurse. Who moved to the side and returned, as promised, with a couple of pillows.

'Here' she said before carefully propping the girl up in the bed, just enough to slide the pillows under her head and shoulders.

Head elevated now, she groaned as pain shot in.

'You're our little miracle.' The nurse beamed. 'Just some bruising, as far as we can tell,' she added. 'You're going to be just fine.'

The girl detected something unspoken in the nurse's tone. Someone else was not so fortunate?

'Who...?'

Out of sight, she heard more movement. Someone approaching in a rush.

A man. His face tight with anguish and concern.

'You're alive,' he said. Strangely, his voice was familiar, but his face wasn't. 'We thought you were dead too.' He reached the bed, and pulled the girl into his arms, his body convulsing with movements that were like hiccups.

Too. The word rang in her mind like the pealing of a bell.

Body limp in his arms and mind ablaze with confusion, the girl watched the show as if removed from herself. She sent a mute plea for help over the man's shoulder towards the nurse. She had no idea who he was. But strangely, the one thing she knew was her name. Four syllables announcing her identity.

She was Annie Jackson.

Chapter 4

Annie – Now

Annie was on a seat in her new boss's office. Jane offered her a drink of water. Everything was coming at her through a dissociative fog, as if her senses were somehow coated in cotton wool.

'You really have taken a funny turn,' Jane said. 'Perhaps you should go home, Annie. You don't look well.'

'No, no,' Annie replied. She shook her head. And immediately regretted it as pain lanced through. 'I'll be fine,' she groaned, holding a hand to her forehead. She had no idea if she would be fine. Ever again. What on earth happened? The old man's face had changed into a skull right in front of her eyes. Her head was bursting with the pain that had begun at the same time as the vision – or whatever it was. But what she was trying hardest to ignore was the voice that sounded in her mind at the same time.

He's going to have a massive stroke, it murmured. *If he doesn't get help quickly he'll die.*

Then, in her mind's eye, like a lost reel from a movie, she'd watched the old man in a room, wearing pyjamas and stumbling towards a door. The door was ajar, and beyond it Annie could make out the white porcelain curve of a sink, topped by a mirror. The man reached out desperately. For what, Annie couldn't tell. Then he was on the floor, mouth open, eyes staring.

A stroke. The old man was going to have a stroke, and she knew this with the same certainty she knew how to breathe.

What the hell was going on?

'Is Steve okay?' she managed to ask, squinting against the pain that was drilling into a point between her eyes.

'He'll outlive us all, that man...' Jane's answer clearly one of habit. 'Why are you asking? Did he say something?'

'No,' Annie replied. 'No. It's just...' How could she say what she'd seen? They'd rush her out of the door and tell her never to come back. They'd think she was deranged. 'Sorry. This sudden headache ... I've never had anything like this before.' She took a long, slow breath, marshalling her resources. She couldn't afford to mess up. Not on her first day on the job.

'That drink of water,' Annie said, 'and a couple of paracetamol, and I'll be right as rain.'

Jane looked relieved, and as if she was allowing herself to be persuaded. 'We are a bit short today. Holidays and all that. And we never really recovered staffing levels after the pandemic. So if you're sure you'll be okay?'

'I'll be completely fine.' Annie worked a smile onto her face. Opened her eyes wide, hoping that would sell the lie. 'See. I'm better already.'

'Excellent,' Jane replied. All bustle now, she got up from behind her desk and made for a door just off to her left that Annie somehow knew was to the bathroom.

'My office is being redecorated, so I'm using one of the bedrooms for the moment,' Jane said when she returned, as if she'd read the question in Annie's eyes. She handed Annie a glass.

'Thank you.'

Annie sipped, trying to disguise her discomfort. A sudden chill enveloped her entire body. She recognised this room, yet she'd never been in it. She hadn't been in any of the bedrooms, but she *knew* this was the double of the one she'd 'seen' as she'd watched in her mind's eye while Steve clutched at his arm, collapsed and fell to the ground.

Chapter 5

Annie – Now

Gradually, by attempting to focus on what was in front of her, Annie managed to get control of herself.

Sandra was the other woman on the shift and was asked to show her the 'tea and toast' ropes. She was about the same age as Annie, and at a guess she was around six feet tall, had no chest or hips to speak of and had her long, black hair pulled tight to the back of her neck in a ponytail. The hairstyle served to exaggerate Sandra's sharp chin and cheekbones, and Annie got the impression that Sandra couldn't have cared less.

Annie fancied that the other woman sized her up in a millisecond. The line of her mouth sagged with disappointment.

'Where have you worked before then?' Sandra asked.

'Here and there,' Annie answered brightly, refusing to show Sandra that she was put off by her tone. 'A few shops and cafés. Mostly retail.'

'Mostly retail.' Sandra's eyes joined her mouth in a sag. 'At least you'll be used to being on your feet all day.'

Then she turned and started walking away along the corridor. 'The kitchen's this way,' she announced over her shoulder.

Another woman in the same uniform was already hard at work in the kitchen. She turned to face them when she heard their approach.

'Hiya,' she said and gave a little wave. 'I'm Joy.'

She was a small woman, arranged as if from a composite of parts. Her face and upper body were tight and wiry, but her hips were wide enough to almost fill the doorway at her back. Her white hair was cut short and her eyes were circled with enough kohl to bleed into her wrinkles.

Sandra stepped away. 'Can I leave you with Joy ... while I go and...?' Without explaining what she was about to do she left.

'Right.' Joy clapped her hands. 'You're about to make yourself very popular. Our ladies and gents love their elevenses, so they do.' She swept a hand across the ranks of brown cupboards, double sink, tall aluminium urn and a machine that looked like one of those toasters provided at a buffet breakfast in a hotel. 'Everything you need is here. We just need to fill the trolley with cups and saucers, load up the industrial toaster behind me, get the urn boiling and we can serve up.'

※

As soon as they entered the Sun Room, a large conservatory full of soft chairs and coffee tables, all heads turned to face them. There was an audible 'ooo' when those waiting realised there was a new member of staff in the room.

'Everyone,' Joy said, 'this is Annie. She's new, so be gentle with her.'

A round of soft laughter, and then voices that ranged from the querulous to the brisk sounded out.

'Hello rerr, Annie.'

'Welcome, dear.'

Annie felt a hand in hers. Looked down to see a woman in a purple cardigan propped up with a number of cushions. Her hand was so light that Annie felt it was almost imaginary.

'You look just like my grand-daughter, Lucy. Lovely girl.' The woman paused. 'Frances,' the woman added, holding a trembling hand to the middle of her chest.

'Frances likes milky tea,' Joy said with a little edge, suggesting to Annie that they didn't have enough time to pause over every resident.

✳

Soon it was time to set up for lunch, and after that had been served it was not long before they had to get things ready for afternoon tea and visiting time. And after that, dinner. It felt like Annie's whole day had been taken up by doling out food and drink. How tragic, she thought, that for many of these people the highlight of their day, every day, was to be served teas and coffees.

One old lady stood out. Her skin was remarkably smooth, her white hair lacquered into place, bright-red lipstick lining her smile, and her eyes were shining. She was wearing a light-blue twinset with pearls and a navy skirt. Thin limbs folded into her chair, she looked lost among the cushions, but her head was up as if ready for a photo shoot. There was a frailty to her that had Annie annoyed at the waste of her own youth. She wanted nothing more than to sit with the woman and listen to her story. To validate a life well lived.

'Welcome to the nut house,' the lady said to her, the glint in her eyes suggesting that though the body was struggling with the effects of old age, her mind was as sharp as ever. 'My name's Margaret.'

Instinctively, Annie reached forward and lightly touched the back of Margaret's hand. 'Enjoy your tea,' she said before moving on to the next person.

What frustrations must this woman be feeling? Like everyone else here, she may have had a career, or businesses, or organised her family, thrown herself into hobbies – and done the multitude of things we do as we try and live a fulfilled life. But here she was, the best part of her day spent with a hand out, waiting for a hot drink to be placed in it. Nothing on the horizon but a long, silent prayer for a quick and peaceful death.

✳

Back in the staff room, standing with her coat on, ready to go home, Annie was a mess of indecision. What on earth she should do about Steve? All day, she hadn't been able to rid her mind of the image of him on the floor in his bedroom. But if she told anyone what she knew, or thought she knew, she'd be carted off to the nearest psych ward.

Another thought occurred to her. This place was essentially an end-of-life station. Would Steve be the only one, or would she get more of these visions?

Just thinking of it, and that strange voice in her head, her heart began to race, and her hands were sweating. God forbid that she'd spend the next few years seeing things like that and knowing when and how people were going to die. It would drive her crazy.

❋

Upstairs, after having checked at reception for his room number, she exited the lift, took a left and walked down the corridor until she located Steve's room.

She placed her head to the wood and paused to listen. The faint burble of a familiar theme tune sounded from the other side of the door. Steve liked his soaps then, she thought. Would he want to be interrupted?

Annie took a step back. What was she doing? The old man would think she was crazy. Was she crazy?

She was certainly beginning to worry that might indeed be the case, but there was no shaking her certainty. If she did nothing, Steve would die.

Chapter 6

Annie – Then

Just a few days before the accident that was to change her life forever, Annie was in the back garden chatting with her best friend and neighbour, Danni. They always met up after school at the far end of the garden, under the wild cherry tree that grew there. Cross-legged on the grass, their conversation would invariably begin with: 'I hate this place.' Danni usually said it, and 'this place' referred to Mossgow, a town a couple of hours south-west of Fort William on the banks of Loch Suinart. Annie guessed that most preteens who lived in similar-sized places in the Highlands of Scotland would rather be anywhere there might be bright lights and more interesting people, but the kids of Mossgow were doubly troubled, because the place held a church of historic importance and a religious community, meaning adherence to the rules of said church were strictly observed and a complete kill-joy.

'I'm telling you. It's like we're living in a cult,' Danni said, eyes large.

Annie made a dismissive noise, Danni was always going on about cults. As far as she could understand it, the area was selling itself as a place of religious retreat and hoping that would attract visitors.

'Well, anyway.' Danni tossed her hair. 'It's like they want us to die of boredom before we grow up,' Danni said. 'Save on having all those teen pregnancies.' The girls shared a giggle. 'I have a cousin in Edinburgh,' Danni said, for the millionth time, 'and she has an actual computer and a TV *in her room*. She watches TV for hours, and says I have to get Destiny's Child's new album.'

A voice cried out into the garden.

'Danni. Mum says it's time to come in and do your homework.'

It was her brother, Chris. He and Annie had exchanged a small kiss the previous night. Her first kiss, and she hadn't yet managed to talk to Danni about it.

Danni read her reaction and smiled knowingly. 'Well?' she asked. 'What?'

Danni laughed. 'Don't play the innocent with me. He's my brother. He tells me everything.' She tossed her head. 'Well, not everything, because that would be gross. But...' she stared into Annie's eyes '...is my brother a good kisser?'

Annie felt her face heat. 'It was okay.'

In truth it was better than okay. It was thrilling, embarrassing, fraught with feelings of failure and the possible promise of an exciting time. Her head had been so full of conflicting thoughts since, she worried they might drive her out of her mind.

She leaned forward and asked, 'What did Chris say?'

'Danni,' Chris shouted. 'Dad's home.' Annie could hear a warning there: Danni needed to comply, there and then, and go back into her house.

Danni sighed and looked to the sky. 'You can tell me about it later.' She winked, then she jumped to her feet and without a word clambered over the fence that separated their gardens, something she did with such ease, it scandalised her church-elder father, Dennis Jenkins.

Next it was Annie's turn. A voice from her back door. 'Kids?' Annie's mother.

Her mother was out of bed? She often took what she called her 'turns' and stayed in bed for weeks at a time. Annie wasn't stupid. She'd heard about depression and was sure that was the source of her mother's intermittent incapacity.

Her mother was standing, arms crossed, just outside the back door; there was something in her stance that sent a shiver of warning through Annie. Something was wrong.

'Annie!' her mother repeated. 'Lewis!' she called to Annie's twin brother, who was playing keepie-uppie with a football.

She and Lewis raced to the back door. Everything, or almost everything, they did was in competition. They charged inside and made for the sink. Lewis stopped so abruptly that Annie ran into the back of him.

'Ouch,' he complained.

'Idiot,' she replied.

'Kids,' their mother said. Annie turned to her, recognising the strain in her voice. 'I want you to meet someone.'

By the door to the hall stood their father, wearing the same tight smile as their mother, and beside him stood a woman. She was like a slightly older version of their mother. Same height and build. Same face but with more lines, and a light in her eye that was almost completely missing from their mother's.

'Meet your aunt Sheila,' their father said, a forced brightness in his voice.

Annie and Lewis looked at each other. A look that asked: we have an aunt Sheila?

Chapter 7

Annie – Then

They were in the dining room. Mother and Father at either end of the table, Lewis and Annie to their mother's left, and Aunt Sheila facing them.

The table was heavy with food, as if her mother was keen to show off to her sister that she had made a success of her life. See: the food I can provide at the drop of a hat. There were dishes high with mashed potato, green beans, carrots, corn, French fries, chicken wings, sausages, burgers. Annie knew her mother had raided the chest freezer. Meat was a rare treat in their house, usually only served on Sundays, or hot summer's days when her father took a notion for a barbeque.

Without waiting for the command to begin eating, Lewis's arm hand shot out as he helped himself to the sausages. They were his favourite and Annie knew he wanted to make sure he got the most.

'Lewis,' Dad chided. His eyes shot to the cross on the wall. 'You know we wait to say grace.'

Lewis sighed.

Annie nudged him with her elbow. Snorted in appreciation of her brother being publicly reproached.

'Say grace, please, Annie,' Mum asked.

Annie looked from her mother to her father. Then to her aunt, who was smiling across at her. But the smile halted, became stuck as if there was a shadow lurking behind it.

'She looks like her.' Sheila stared at Annie, nodding her head. 'Mum would have been so pleased.'

Like *who?* Annie wanted to ask, but the words were frozen by her certainty that her mother wouldn't want the question answered.

She instinctively liked her aunt. She was like her mother, but softer. Life for this woman wouldn't be about absolutes, she was certain.

'Grace, please, Annie?' Mum said.

Stifling a sigh, Annie ducked her head and recited the prayer by rote.

'Always so fast,' Mum said when she'd finished. 'Try to show some genuine appreciation at your good fortune.' She made a slow waving movement with her hand across the food.

'Kids,' Sheila said. 'Always with an empty belly.' She laughed. A sound Annie rarely heard from her parents. 'To be fair, it does all look delicious. Thank you for inviting me to stay for dinner.'

'It is good to see you, Sheila, after all this time, but some kind of warning would have been nice,' Mum replied, and Annie could read a guardedness there. Just what had gone on between these two, and why had Sheila never been mentioned to them? Annie was desperate to ask, but felt, strongly, that she couldn't.

'You're right,' Sheila said. 'I shouldn't have imposed on you like this, but I was worried. We didn't exactly part on the best of terms.'

Annie watched as her mother inhaled and corrected her posture so that she was sitting perfectly straight. Her head had a slight tilt to the left. A challenge. She didn't like something about Sheila's statement.

'You did a good thing, Ellie,' Sheila added, a note of affirmation in her voice. 'The *Christian* thing. I'm grateful for that, and I'm not here to cause a fuss.'

Annie exchanged a quick look with Lewis. What on earth was happening here? She couldn't shake the thought that it involved her and Lewis.

And 'Ellie'. Annie had never heard her mother being called anything but Eleanor. It brought another version to her mind;

of her mother as a young girl, jeans dirty at the knee, face smudged. Where that image came from she had no idea, because that was far from the version she'd known all her life. Her mother rarely had a hair out of place, and Annie was sure she had an invisible shield around her that any particle of dirt wouldn't dare cross.

'Have you left the army then, Sheila?' Annie heard her mother ask, and even to her it felt like a clumsy attempt to change the subject. Nonetheless, it was very cool that her aunt had been in the army. It meant she'd got to see a lot of the world. Most of the people she knew had barely left Mossgow.

'You wanted a fresh start.' Sheila bluntly bypassed her sister's conversational thread. 'You wanted to protect ... them...' Sheila inclined her head in the direction of the children. 'And I get that. But there are *other* people involved.'

'Not now, Sheila. Please,' Eleanor replied. Annie recognised that firmness of tone and waited to see how her aunt Sheila might respond.

'Try the chicken, Sheila,' Dad said, with a look to his wife. 'Same butcher. And the...'

Whatever her father said next was lost to Annie. The room spun. Sounds stuttered. Lights flashed at the back of her eyes.

She shook her head. Shut her eyes. Opened them again.

What was that?

'You okay, Annie?' Sheila asked.

'Yes ... I'm...' Annie looked towards her aunt. But the woman speaking was no longer there. Annie's vision shifted. Light fluttered furiously. Her aunt's face wavered. Lines crossing it as if Annie was viewing her through a broken screen. Her face reformed, and Annie could see through the skin and muscle and veins to the bones of her skull. A voice began in her head, its words unintelligible, strung together without pause. A harrying, urgent voice, the sibilant 'S' loudest of all, linking the words like the long coil of a serpent. The face shook again, and then the benign version of her aunt once again looked back. Her eyes full of concern, and a certain knowing.

Annie gasped. Fear a charge under her skin. What was happening to her? She scanned the other faces in the room. They were all completely normal, and all of them were looking at her with worry.

Pain pierced Annie's head as if she'd been speared, right through the space between her eyebrows.

'You okay?' Aunt Sheila asked again, her voice softened with tenderness.

Through the stream of words issuing in Annie's mind, one word was more prominent. Two syllables. A diagnosis. A word of dread. A word that even she knew, as a preteen, was one to shrink from.

And she just knew, somehow, that it was true.

Annie made herself look up, across the table at Sheila, and spoke with terrible certainty. 'That's why you've come. You've got cancer.'

Chapter 8

Annie – Now

Resolve strengthened, she raised her hand and knocked on Steve's door. She heard him call something, then his footsteps. Swithering at the wisdom of her approach, she took a step back. Turned to walk away. The door opened.

'Annie, isn't it?' Steve asked, his face warm with a smile of surprise. 'What can I do for you, hen?'

'I just wanted to check in on you before I go home.' Feeling unable to explain why, Annie took another step back, her eyes darting to his shoulders, feet, the carpet at his feet, anywhere but at his face. *What* was she doing?

Annie forced herself to glance up, and directly into his face. She gasped. Turned away. Then realising his face was normal she looked back into his eyes. They were framed with concern. 'You okay, Annie? Want to come in for a wee blether?' He opened the door a little wider.

Annie could see the TV in the background. It had been paused on the face of a well-known actor in a long-running TV series.

'Sorry. You're watching your programme. I'll just...'

'Don't be daft. It's not often I get visited by a lovely young woman.' He stepped back, and then stopped. 'You don't mind that all the old codgers around here will be gossiping about us?' He laughed. ''Mon in and have a seat.'

Annie stepped inside and sat down in one of the armchairs positioned either side of the TV.

'What's on your mind, doll?' Steve asked as he sat too. He raised an eyebrow. 'And I mean what's *really* on your mind?'

Annie cringed at her stupidity. Steve might be old but he wasn't daft, and he could clearly see that she was hiding something.

She met his gaze and wondered how much, if anything, she should say. She scanned the room and recognised all of the items from her vision. What she'd seen as the bathroom door was shut.

Something about the directness of his look snagged in her mind. She considered his almost military bearing. There was something about Steve that reminded her of the few cops she met in her life.

'You weren't in the police were you?' she asked.

'Why? Has there been a murder?' he laughed. 'Aye. Did my full service, hen. I guess it leaves its mark on you, eh?'

His answer made Annie consider carefully what she was going to say next. She opened her mouth to speak.

'Here,' Steve said. '*Has* there been a murder?'

'No,' Annie replied. 'It's just ... I got this feeling when I met you this morning...' God. She was going to sound like a fool. She reviewed the vision she'd had. The bathroom door had been open. The sink in full view. On a shelf above it were some items.

'I've never been in this room, right?' she asked.

'Far as I know,' Steve replied as he sat back in his chair.

'That's your bathroom door, yeah?'

'What's this about, Annie?'

'Humour me. Please.' Annie leaned forward, hoping the earnestness in her face would convince him to bear with her. She closed her eyes and, despite her fear, took herself mentally back to her vision. 'You have Boots shaving cream and an orange-handled razor on a shelf above the sink. Oh, and a glass with a green-handled toothbrush sticking out of it.'

Steve got to his feet, eyes wide with confusion and alarm. 'Annie, hen, you need to explain yourself.'

Annie held a hand up. 'I got this ... this impression this morning. I saw you. Here.' She looked around herself. 'It was a vision. A warning. Or something. You fell on the way to the bath-room. It was the middle of the night. A stroke.' Annie felt her fear of the skull face and her worry for Steve mount. 'And I know, I just ... *know* ... if you don't get immediate help the damage will be so bad you'll never recover.' She paused, almost too frightened to say the words, as if casting them into the air might see them pass into truth. 'And you'll die.'

Chapter 9

Annie – Then

Annie was on her bed, lying on top of the covers, with a damp cloth over her eyes. Terrified to lift it off because she might see the same skull superimpose itself over her aunt's face. Because then the voice would come back. That insistent voice full of ill portent and certainty.

Was her aunt really going to die?

Her bedroom door opened.

'Jeez, you're a weirdo.' It was Lewis. She heard his footfall on the carpet as he walked inside, and then she felt the bed give as he climbed on. 'What was that all about?'

'Leave me alone,' Annie demanded. In her mind's eye she saw him cross-legged, staring at her like she was a strange exhibit at the zoo.

'Lewis,' the shout came from downstairs. 'Don't be bothering your sister when she has a headache.'

'That's not a headache,' he snorted.

'Just go, will you?' Annie said.

There was a moment's silence.

'Seriously, though, you okay, sis?' Lewis asked. 'That was freaky.'

The concern in his voice was so surprising that Annie pulled the cloth from her eyes and sat up. She groaned as the pain pulsed through her head. Screwing shut her eyes against it she asked Lewis, 'What did you see? Did you hear anything?'

'Hear what?' Lewis asked. 'You went pure white and stared at Aunt Sheila like she'd just grown a horn out of the middle of her forehead.'

For a moment Annie felt like jumping off the bed and checking herself in the mirror. Maybe that was where the pain was coming from? Maybe she'd grown a horn herself.

'It was scary,' she said. Pleading. 'You've got to believe me.'

'What was?' Lewis replied. He edged further away from her. 'You're freaking me out, Annie.'

'Aunt Sheila's face. It became like this ... skull. And I heard a horrible voice, and I knew, I just knew, she was going to die.'

'Fuck,' Lewis replied.

Annie didn't know whether to be more shocked at Lewis's language or the fact that he clearly believed her.

'Cancer, you said.'

Lewis climbed off the bed as if he was worried that whatever Annie had was catching. He sat in the chair at her desk. Elbows on knees, he leaned towards her. 'Did you see Aunt Sheila's face after?'

'After what? My head was so sore, and Mum was staring at me as if I'd just taken a crap on her favourite piece of china.'

Lewis laughed. A note of joy that rang through her terrified mind and settled it a little.

She reviewed her mother's face in that moment. Tried to read what her thoughts might have been. No. That wasn't a look of disgust. It was a look of fear. But mingled with it a terrible truth. And a decision made.

'The strange thing is...' Lewis began. 'No. *One* of the strange things is that Aunt Sheila just nodded. She wasn't weirded out by you at all. It was like none of it – the word popping out of your mouth, the way you were shaking your head – none of it was a surprise to her.'

'Just leave me alone, Lewis. Please?'

'It was like...' he continued, as he walked to the door. 'It was like she was expecting it.' And with that he left.

A few minutes later there was a knock at her door.

'Leave me alone,' she groaned.

'Mind if I come in?' It was her aunt Sheila.

Annie didn't reply. She turned over and faced the wall.

Sheila entered her room. Just a couple of steps. In her imagination, Annie could see her standing there, looking around. With that skull face of hers. She shuddered.

'Nice space you have. I never had a room to myself as a kid. Longed for it, to be sure, but with three girls in a two-bedroom house that was never going to happen.'

Annie sat up so quickly her head spun. 'There were three of you?'

'Yes,' Sheila replied, her mouth settling into a line of sympathy. 'Your mother's been keeping you in the dark, eh?'

'What else hasn't she told me?' Annie replied, looking everywhere but at her aunt's face.

'Is it okay now?' Sheila asked. 'The voice? Has it gone?'

Annie shot a glance up at Sheila, prepared to look away just as fast. But, with relief, she noted it was just her new aunt Sheila looking back at her.

'Do you know what's happening to me, Aunt Sheila?' she asked. 'And why did I not know I had an aunt? Two aunts?'

'Your mother had her reasons,' Sheila replied. 'It's not for me to say.'

The door behind her opened wider and her mother came in.

'No, it isn't, Sheila,' Eleanor said.

Sheila squared up to her sister. 'She needs to know, Ellie.'

Annie watched as her mother's face grew pale and her mouth tightened. 'And she will. When the time is right.'

Please don't talk about me as if I'm not here, Annie wanted to say, but instead she just stared at these two women, these *sisters*.

'I wanted to see them. Just once. Before...' Sheila began.

'Well, you have. And now you need to go.' Eleanor pushed her chin out, but not before Annie read a stab of pain and concern in her mother's face.

'But Ellie,' Sheila said, holding her hands out. Almost pleading. 'She needs to know.'

'I'll be the judge of that,' Eleanor replied.

'Yes,' Sheila said quietly. 'You always were good at that. Judging.'

The two sisters looked at each other for a long moment. A library of secrets weighted in that look.

'Just go,' Eleanor said.

Sheila stepped across the room to Annie and then did something the adults in Annie's life rarely did: she leaned forward and hugged her.

'What we don't understand scares us,' Sheila whispered. 'Learn,' she urged. 'Try to understand. Only then will you be able to work with the family gift.'

'Gift?' Eleanor said so loudly it made Annie jump. 'How dare you. It's a damned curse. Leave us, Sheila. Leave us and never come back.'

Sheila held up a hand. 'Okay. Okay,' she said.

Then she stepped closer to her sister and pulled her into a hug. But Eleanor's hands were limp by her side, as if the hug was the price she had to pay for her sister leaving.

When Sheila stepped back her smile took in both Eleanor and Annie.

'Regardless, it was lovely to see you again, Ellie. And Annie, you're going to grow into a wonderful human being.' Her eyes were shiny with suppressed tears. Then, without another word, she turned and left the room.

Once she was gone, Annie's mother visibly relaxed.

'What's going on, Mum?' Annie asked. 'Why didn't I know you had two sisters? Why are you telling her to leave already? It feels like I don't even know you anymore.'

'I care for you, Annie Jackson,' Eleanor said, and Annie in all her twelve years had never seen her mother look so vulnerable. 'Please understand: I've only ever done what I've done to protect you. To try and keep you safe.'

For a long while after her mother left the room, Annie tried to puzzle through everything that had occurred – everything she'd just learned – and couldn't help but wonder who her mother really was.

With a sigh of exasperation, she threw herself back onto her pillow. And regretted the movement when pain bloomed once again between her eyes.

She placed her forearm over her face, squeezed her eyes shut, and considered her mother's words.

'I care for you, Annie Jackson,' she'd said. *Care for you.*

Not love.

Care.

Chapter 10

Annie – Now

Steve leaned forward, elbows on his knees, steepled fingers propping up his chin. That he hadn't taken her by the elbow and escorted her to the door, Annie thought was a bonus. It meant he was at least considering what she was saying.

But his next words put that interpretation to bed.

'You need to leave.' Steve got to his feet.

Annie jumped to hers. 'I ... I ... Please listen to me, Steve. Something's going to happen and you're going to fall – a stroke or something – and you'll die.'

'How did you know what was in my bathroom?' His eyes bored into hers. 'Have you already been in here?'

'No,' Annie asserted. 'I just saw this picture in my mind...'

'Annie, hen, before you dig yourself any further into this strange wee hole you've prepared for yourself, you need to leave.'

'But Steve. I'm not making this up.'

'What's your angle? How on earth could you benefit from telling me stuff like this?'

'You've got to listen to me.' Annie was becoming desperate. 'If you don't...' A crushing pressure built behind her eyes. She felt a swoop and pulse in her stomach, pressure in her throat as if she was about to vomit. She swallowed it down and again saw Steve in her mind's eye in a tangle of limbs on the floor.

'Jesus, Annie. Have a seat. You've gone awful pale.'

She felt his hand on her shoulder as he guided her to a chair. But she couldn't look at him. The voice started up again, building in pitch and repeating the words *die die die diediedie*. She shook her head, as if that might dislodge it, but the movement only caused pain to bloom across her forehead. 'Water, please? A glass of water.'

'Right. Aye. Sure.'

Moments later a cold glass was thrust into her hand. Still keeping her eyes covered she took a sip.

'Any warning signs?' Annie asked after a moment. 'Anything going on ... anything with your health that might suggest a stroke is possible?'

'I'm not going to entertain ... whatever this thing is. Please, once you've had your drink just go.'

'I'll stay with you,' Annie rushed to say. 'I don't mind. I can sleep here, on the armchair, and keep an eye on you. I know that when it happens there has to be some kind of speedy intervention or you're...' She couldn't finish her sentence.

'Enough,' Steve said. 'You need to go.' He leaned forward, his arm outstretched. 'C'mon.'

'But...'

'We'll just pretend this never happened, Annie. I won't complain to the bosses, and you'll get to keep your job, but if you ever pull this stunt again, or I hear you talking to any of the other old biddies in here like that I will kick your arse into touch. Am I understood?'

Annie looked into Steve's eyes and could see the determination there. She backed towards the door.

'Please,' she tried one more time as she reached behind her for the door handle. 'If you feel any sense of being unwell...'

'Goodbye, Annie.'

She left, and Steve closed the door behind her. She walked along the corridor, legs trembling, before movement became too much and she had to lean against the wall.

What was she going to do? Steve needed help, but he clearly wasn't going to listen to her.

And there was something else that was slowly becoming clear

to her: there was a familiarity here. She couldn't shake the thought that this had happened to her before, but she couldn't recall when, and what had happened next, only that something bad…

There was a weight on her head and shoulders, a souring in her mouth and a painful twist in her gut. And over-riding all of that, a sense of something wrong. Something very wrong indeed.

A scream sounded in her mind. Sharp. Discordant. Full of anguish and pain. Then the scream subsided and became a jumble of words full of brittle consonants and harsh vowels. She felt her thighs give and she fell to the floor.

Hands over her ears, she begged, 'Leave me alone. Leave me alone.'

Laughter then. A high and strangely happy sound, as if her pain was its reward. And to earn that shilling it would drive every last ounce of sense from her mind.

Chapter 11

Annie – Then

After Sheila left, her parents had gone into their bedroom. Lewis and Annie stood as close to their door as they dared, trying to listen to what was going on inside.

'Can you hear anything?' Lewis whispered to her, his face so close to hers she could feel the heat from his breath.

'No,' she whispered back.

The voices inside the room grew steadily until there was a loud 'NO' from their father, and the door was pulled open so fast and so hard that Lewis and Annie almost fell inside.

'Go to your rooms,' their father said, his face red in a way Annie had never seen before.

Annie could see beyond him. Their mother was by the window, arms tight across her chest as if they might fend off the world.

'What's wrong?' she asked. Seeing her mother standing there looking so small and scared, tears running down her face shook her, the room spun. Fear built. If her mother was frightened, something terrible was going to happen.

'Go to your room, honey,' her dad replied.

'But, Mum...'

'Please...' Her father placed a hand on her shoulder. 'C'mon.' Her dad spun her round and guided her back to her room. 'Have a lie down. It's nearly bedtime anyway. And in the morning we'll tell you everything you need to know.'

✳

The weak streetlight coming in through the chink in her curtains was enough for Annie to see Lewis as he crept into her room. Annie could hear the swish of fabric as he dragged his quilt with him.

'You awake?' he asked.

'Sssh,' she replied, propping herself up on her elbows. 'Mum and Dad will hear.'

'Want me to leave?' he asked. Annie could see in the half-light that, without waiting for her answer, he had placed a pillow on the floor to the side of her bed and was preparing to lie down – a 'camp out' was what they used to call it, when one or other of them would go into the other's room and chat into the small hours, often falling asleep there. When they were smaller they would crawl under the covers, but of late Lewis had taken to bringing in his quilt as if tacitly acknowledging they were both getting too old to do that.

'What do you think about Aunt Sheila?' Annie asked as Lewis settled in.

'Seemed nice,' Lewis answered. 'Like a relaxed version of Mum.'

'And what about this other sister Sheila told me about? Why did we never hear about her?'

'Our parents are weird,' Lewis replied. 'Do you think she's dead?'

Annie thought that one through. 'Maybe. But why never tell us about her? Or Sheila?'

'Maybe she joined a cult, got pregnant by the cult leader and then they all committed mass suicide.'

'Ewww,' Annie replied. 'You're sick.' She paused in thought, considering Danni's assertions. 'Maybe we're the ones in the cult. The folk in our church are, like, intense.' She thought about the minister who preached from the pulpit every Sunday. Saw the hook of his nose, the sweep of his thick, black hair. The strange light in his eyes.

'Nah,' Lewis replied. 'Our church is just your regular buttoned-up Scottish Presbyterians.'

'Dad says he'll explain everything in the morning. Do you think he will?'

'He usually does what he says,' Lewis answered. 'But this is big, and this is Mum's stuff. I guess it will be down to her.'

'Did you hear how she talked to Sheila? Mum was so rude.'

'Sounded frightened to me.'

'Really?' Annie mused, and heard the music of Sheila's voice slip into her mind: *What we don't understand scares us.*

Annie listened as her brother's breathing slowed. It was okay for him, falling asleep like the world hadn't shifted, like a massive secret hadn't been thrown into their laps.

Secrets.

With a huff, she turned and lay on her back, staring at the ceiling. Reviewing the events of the day before. Her mind replaying the looks on the faces of the adults, the weight of their combined knowledge, a load that held their mouths shut fast.

Then the moment when Aunt Sheila's face blurred, shook wildly, and then transformed into a skull.

Annie burrowed under the quilt as if that might shelter her from her fear.

What we don't understand scares us.

She didn't want to be afraid.

But that face. The voices. And the knowing. Why had no one mentioned her aunt's cancer? Annie had announced to everyone at the table that Sheila was dying. And no one took her seriously.

Why would they? It was ridiculous.

But deep down, with a certainty that was both unshakeable and terrifying, Annie knew that this was the truth. What she didn't know was how long it might take to kill her aunt.

※

Next morning, after a largely sleepless night, she and Lewis were in the back of the car, being driven by their mother to Sunday service. Under the noise of the music coming from the radio, Annie whispered her plan to Lewis.

'I'm going to find out where Sheila's staying and go see her.'

Lewis shot her a warning look. 'Mum will kill you,' he hissed as he glanced at their mother.

'Don't care. This family's messed up, and I need to know what's going on.'

'You're messed up.'

Annie ignored him. Then she set her resolve, and shifted in her seat so she could see her mother's eyes in the rear-view mirror.

'Where's Aunt Sheila?' Annie asked.

'She's gone,' Eleanor replied. 'Just put her out of your mind.'

'But she's dying,' Annie replied. 'Don't you care that your sister is dying?'

'You are never to say that again,' Eleanor said taking her eyes from the road and glaring at Annie in the mirror. 'Utter nonsense. Where you get these fanciful ideas from I'll never know. Ridiculous.'

'It's not ridiculous. I know it,' Annie shouted back. 'And she didn't deny it either, did she?'

Eleanor, completely mindless of the traffic around them, pulled the car harshly to the side of the road. She braked so abruptly Annie felt her head shoot forward.

'Jesus, Eleanor,' her father said from the front passenger seat.

A car horn blared at them before someone drove past.

Eleanor twisted in her seat so she could look Annie in the face. 'You are never to talk like that again, you hear me, girl? Never again. Your aunt hasn't been part of this family for a long time, and that is how it is going to stay.'

At her side, Lewis was making a 'calm down' motion with his hands. Annie glared at him. Always the peacemaker was her brother, between her and her mother, but this time he was wrong. Very wrong.

'But—' she began.

'But nothing.' Eleanor turned away from her. 'Crazy talk. My daughter is full of crazy talk,' she muttered angrily. 'What will people say? What will the pastor say?' Then louder. 'You are never to speak like that again, am I understood?'

'But—'

'Can we go now?' her father asked. 'We're going to be late.'

'Am I understood?' her mother demanded, ignoring her husband.

'Yes, Mum,' Annie replied, ducking her head, feeling a slow churn of resentment that her mother's will would beat hers. Again.

※

After the service, in which the pastor had gone on at length about 'everyday kindness', Lewis shared a joke with some friends their age on the steps of the church, while Annie stood limply by his side.

An elderly couple walked out of the church doors towards them. Mr and Mrs Holding. They lived two doors down the street from them. Mrs Holding was always baking cakes and giving them to her and Lewis. Annie's mother said it was because her own grandkids lived too far away and she was trying to compensate.

As they passed, Mrs Holding smiling a hello, Mr Holding's face began to fade. Lights entered Annie's vision. Her mouth grew dry. Her heart thumped a warning.

A low voice started in her mind, like an incantation. *Die, die, die, hesgoingtodie.*

Annie looked away, pushing her gaze towards anything that wasn't human. Then she screwed her eyes shut.

Was it happening again? Part of her wanted to look back at the old man to see what might unfold, but a bigger, more frightened, part held back.

He's going to die, the voice repeated.

Her mind presented her with an image: Mr Holding sitting up on a chair, eyes shut. Sleeping. No.

Not sleeping.

Dead.

She wanted to scream. Instead, she stamped her foot on the ground. Hard. 'Go away. Go away,' she said in a strangled whisper.

'You okay, weirdo?' Lewis asked. But she could see in his eyes that she was spooking him.

She felt a hand on her shoulder. 'Right, kids.' It was Dad.

Annie looked up at him, then back inside the church to see if her mother was on her way too.

She was still right at the front, with the pastor and Mr Jenkins from next door. His kids were fun but there was something about Dennis Jenkins that chilled Annie. Whenever his eyes lit upon her it felt like he was measuring her worth, trying to work out if he might have a use for her.

As for the pastor, he was easily the creepiest man she'd ever seen. Standing about as if he was both waiting for a sainthood and an open, empty grave.

Groaning to herself, Annie watched her mother, her nose almost up the pastor's backside, head tilted, expression moulded to suit a saint-in-waiting. Then all of their heads swivelled down the length of the church, towards the door – and her.

Something cold twisted low in Annie's gut.

What was her mother telling them?

But she knew, of course she knew.

The pastor walked down the aisle, closely followed by her mother, who was all but wringing her hands.

Run.

But a hand on her shoulder stopped that impulse. It was her father.

'Dad, can we go home?' she asked.

'In a moment, honey,' he said. 'Looks like Pastor Mosley wants a word.'

For an awkward moment they all stood in a huddle just outside the door. People who would have normally stopped and spoken to the pastor walked straight past, eyes down, as if they sensed there was serious business going on.

'When should we come back for her?' her father asked the pastor.

'An hour should do it,' he replied.

'What's going on?' Annie asked, feeling herself shrink under Pastor Mosley's gaze.

'Come back inside, Miss Jackson,' he said, his tone that of a man who thought his word was law.

Mosley was a tall man, slender to the point of emaciation. His back had such a stoop that from the side he resembled a human question mark, but his hair was all black, his face unlined.

He smiled at Annie. A smile that revealed his teeth but went nowhere near his eyes.

Those teeth.

Annie shuddered. They gave her shivers. They looked like they were too large for his mouth, the top row too long, and resembling, to her mind anyway, a row of coffin lids.

'But, Mum,' Annie protested.

Her mother didn't look at her. It was as if she couldn't. Her eyes and the curve of her mouth now slumped with shame.

'Lewis, c'mon,' Eleanor said, and her mother, father and brother left her on her own with the pastor.

'Just in here, by the door,' Pastor Mosley said. 'Take a seat at the end of the pew.'

Wanting nothing more than to run and run, Annie nevertheless did as she was told.

The pastor got to his knees by her side, and still he loomed over her.

'Let us pray,' he said, and placed his hand on her head.

He closed his eyes. His mouth moved. A smell escaped his lips, reaching Annie's nose and almost making her gag. The pressure from his hand was too much. Too heavy. Annie wanted to move, get away, but she daren't.

For what seemed an eternity, but would have only been an hour, as prescribed, they remained in that position. The smell became almost unbearable, the weight of his hand like a torture, and the words issuing from his mouth a gravelly whisper.

Occasionally an intelligible syllable or two would take shape in the bowl of her ears, vowels and consonants formed in quiet urgency. Followed by the odd spot of saliva that landed on her cheek like a cold spark of disgust:

'...soul ... torment ... forgive...'

The last words he saved for when his eyes were open and staring directly into hers:

'...into the gates of Hell.'

Chapter 12

Annie – Now

Waiting for her bus home, all she could think about was Steve and his refusal to listen to her. And why would he? It sounded ridiculous. But still, she *knew* it was the truth.

Once she arrived home she threw herself onto the sofa, suddenly feeling exhausted with the full weight of everything that had happened.

Her phone rang. It was Lewis.

'Wanted to check in, sis,' he said. 'See how your first day in the new job went.'

'Thanks, Lew,' she replied, wondering how much to tell him. 'It went okay.'

Lewis rushed to fill the pause: '*My* day went great.' There was a high and happy tone to his voice. 'Something exciting has happened. Go on, ask me...'

'Okay. What happened?' Annie was relieved she wouldn't have to tell him what had gone on in her own day.

'Have you been following online what's going on up at our old church in Mossgow?'

'No, not really.' Annie only had vague memories of their time living in the Highlands. She remembered a round, white church, and she had vague memories of the neighbour's kids, Danni and Chris, and that was about it. Her childhood, pre-crash, was a mostly empty space in her mind.

But that was the second time she'd heard the name of their childhood home that day. What was going on? Coincidence or something more?

'You need to check out the old church on YouTube. It's gone global, and they want me to do their accounts.'

'Right.'

'You don't get it. Fair enough,' Lewis sounded disappointed that she wasn't caught up in his excitement. 'The short version? Our old pals Danielle and Chris Jenkins have grown an online congregation in the millions, raising a crazy amount of money, and they want me to come in as their accountant. This is an amazing opportunity for me.'

Annie rubbed at her forehead. 'God, I'm sorry for not realising, Lewis. That sounds great.'

'No worries,' he replied. 'But you really need to check them out online. So slick. They took advantage of the whole Covid lockdown thing, put all these videos on YouTube and Insta etc of Chris preaching.' Annie had a vague memory of Lewis telling her that their old neighbours' son was now the pastor at the church of their childhood. 'And the Americans fell for his schtick; the accent, the scenery, the history of the place ... It's huge. It even made it into the *Herald*.'

'Wow,' Annie said, finally catching up with Lewis's excitement. 'Sounds like this could be the making of you.'

'Yeah, it could well make me one of the partners in the practice.'

'You've worked so hard for this. Well done, Lewis.'

'I'm a shit brother,' he said after a long second. 'It was your first day and I'm all me, me, me. How was it? Really?'

'It was okay.'

'Shit,' Lewis said. 'As bad as that?'

'It was fine. Honest.'

'Your voice sounds shaky. You okay?'

The sympathy and concern in his voice made her lose control. 'Oh for godssakes,' she managed through her tears. 'Why do you have to be so nice?'

'What's happened? If you hate the job, resign. I'm sure Mrs Mac will understand.'

'It's not that. The job was fine.'

'You're holding back. What happened?'

Annie paused. Could she tell him? Lewis was her rock, her biggest supporter, but even he would struggle to believe this story.

'Annie,' he insisted. 'Tell me. What's going on?'

Slowly and carefully, deliberately using simple, unadorned terms, she told him everything. And then waited to see how he would react.

There was a silence so long and so deep that Annie wondered if their connection had been cut.

'Lewis?' she said.

'Oh, Annie,' he replied, and in those three syllables was understanding. And something else entirely.

'You believe me?' Relief softened Annie's body. She could feel it flow from her forehead to her neck to her shoulders and down to her thighs. 'You don't think I'm talking shite?'

'You know how we always used to talk about "pre M.D." and "post M.D."?'

Annie felt herself nodding. As a way of discussing their childhood, while minimising the pain of doing so, she and Lewis used this shorthand to mean life before Mum died and life after Mum died.

'Yeah?' she replied. Where was he going with this?

'And of course, you know, there's stuff pre M.D. that you simply don't remember?'

'What are you telling me, Lewis?'

There was a long pause. Then, as if he'd come to an inevitable decision, Lewis said, 'I'm coming over.'

'Could you not be so bloody vague. Just tell me what you think I need to know.'

There was a clinking noise, and in her mind's eye Annie could see Lewis in his hallway picking up his keys. 'I'm on my way,' he said. 'But know this: I'm sorry. Really sorry.'

Chapter 13

Annie – Then

Annie jumped to her feet and fled the church as if her coat was on fire.

Her father was waiting in the car for her outside. 'You okay, honey?' he asked as she got into the front passenger seat.

'Fine,' she replied, before clipping in her seatbelt, crossing her arms, and staring out of the side window. She didn't want to look into his eyes, see that he was also ashamed of her.

She could feel his gaze on the back of her head.

'Mum only wants what's best for you. You know that, don't you?' he said.

Annie grunted. Clenched her jaw against the shame and humiliation that burned through every cell of her body. And tried to ignore both the ache in the back of her neck and the light feeling on the top of her head. It was a strange, unsettling combination. She could still hear the susurration of the pastor's urgent prayers, like an echo in her mind, and she shuddered.

The car moved off, and Annie looked back at the church as it receded from view. It was such a small building to have inspired so many people to come and live and work in a relatively remote region of Scotland. Its importance to the Church overall emphasised almost every week, either at Sunday school or during R.E. in the proper school.

Annie knew, because she was told every week, that although the present church was built in the late 1600s the site itself had been the focus of religious groups for almost a thousand years. Its grisly history always got the kids to sit up and pay attention. The monks who initially built here had all been murdered by Vikings. And some witches were reputed to have been executed here and their bodies burned; and then several hundred years later, during the Reformation, more priests had been murdered and hanged from the church rafters to be found on the Sunday morning by an already dwindling, and, Annie imagined, terrified, congregation.

There was even a patch of earth in the field just beyond the church where, despite the efforts of the groundsmen, the grass would never grow. This was reputed to be the spot where the witches were burned and their bodies buried.

The church had apparently been built in its round shape so that there was nowhere for the Devil to hide. All the adults she knew raved about the building – its historic importance, and *blah* – but it made Annie feel deeply uncomfortable. There was something about the small windows and the heavy, dark wooden pews inside that felt oppressive. As if all that history and death and forced adherence to the rules of the church led only to pain and suffering for everyone concerned. When was the last time she saw someone look happy in the place? Inside the building it was grimaces and silent nods all round. Only when people reached the door would they seem to take a deep breath and actually smile.

'What's happening to me, Dad?' she asked. 'Am I going mad?'

'Aww, honey.' He lifted a hand from the steering wheel and placed it on her knee. He shifted his line of sight from the road to her face, just long enough for her to register his concern. 'No, you're not going crazy. Some people just go through strange phases when they hit their teens, that's all.'

'Dad. Please,' she said as she crossed her arms. 'A phase? I know that Aunt Sheila has cancer. She's going to die soon. And why are she and Mum strangers, and who's this other sister we know nothing about?'

'Let's go into town,' her dad said, abruptly changing the subject. 'Some father-daughter time in that coffee shop you love. The one with the giant empire biscuits.'

She looked at him, and eyes steady on his she made her decision. He wasn't going to tell her anything, but she knew someone who might.

'I said I'd go and meet Susie,' she lied. 'Can you drop me off at the pool?'

'But you don't have your swimming costume or towel with you.'

'We're not going for a swim, Dad.' She looked over at him for the first time since she got in the car. 'Susie's got her period,' she lied, wondering at how easily it flitted from her lips. She was definitely going to hell. 'We'll just sit in the café and drink juice and stuff.'

'Okay. When should I come back and pick you up?'

'S'okay. I'll walk home.'

'Right. Well, don't be late for your dinner, or your mother will have my guts for garters. Five o'clock. On the dot, okay?'

Annie looked around. The pool was five minutes away. And her target was just beyond that.

'Can you drop me off here, please, Dad?' She used her best, compliant-daughter voice. 'It's a lovely day,' she added, aping what an adult would say. 'The walk will be nice.'

He pulled into the kerb, and she had her seatbelt off and her hand on the door before he'd even come to a stop.

'Five o'clock,' he said to her as she jumped out.

She pushed the door shut, bent over and smiled and waved through the window. 'See you later.'

She began walking in the direction of the pool until he had driven out of sight, then she doubled back. Her target wasn't the pool. It was somewhere else entirely.

※

Mossgow was barely even a town, she always thought. It had one street with some shops on it, a couple of hotels that offered half-decent steak pie and chips, the primary and secondary schools, and four churches. Four churches in a place as small as this told you all you needed to know, thought Annie. The one they attended as a family, the Church of the Everlasting Christ, was the smallest, but around it everything in the area had been constructed.

Where she lived were the posh houses with generous gardens, spread the length of the loch road, and backing in under the shadow of the mountain was an ugly sprawl of local-authority housing.

That mountain was more like a hill with a few trees, a rocky outcrop and illusions of grandeur, and this, along with the white church, was the source of the town's weak claim to fame. There was a monument on the rounded summit, little more than a six-foot column of stone with a brass plaque commemorating a little-known skirmish from the Wars of the Three Kingdoms.

This combination of politics and religion did nothing to interest Annie, but from the little she remembered of her school lessons and the annual town fair, it occurred sometime in the 1600s, and had something to do with some bishops, an Irish rebellion, and Royalists fighting Covenanters, and ended up with Oliver Cromwell occupying Scotland. It was this connection to Scotland's part in the Reformation that led the original church elders to set up a base here. And so the Church of the Everlasting Christ was born.

Now, though, her mind was much more set on the family puzzle: just who was this aunt who had turned up, who was the sister who might have died, and why was none of this ever talked about?

To be fair, they talked about little that had any depth or importance, but how had she grown to be this age without knowing about any of her mother's family?

And today it was going to end. She was going to find out where her aunt was staying before she fled back to die in the comfort of the place she'd called home, and ask her to tell her the truth.

Hopefully, the skull face would remain hidden, the murmuring would be silent and she would be able to listen to the answers.

At the thought of the skull shape that her aunt's face had formed the day before, and the voice that came with it, Annie quailed. Did she want to go through that again? It was horrible. And scary. But if she wanted to know the truth she had no choice, for there was no way her mother was going to suddenly open up.

That meant finding her aunt Sheila. Which was where the town's smallness was in its favour. Most visitors came on religious retreats, and there was accommodation for that built by the various churches, but there were only two hotels. And if Sheila wasn't at one, she would surely be at the other. Unless she'd left town already.

The Lodge on the Loch was the largest of the two hotels, and by Annie's thinking the most obvious. As the name suggested it sat facing out on to the water and was only a short walk from where she was now.

A cold wind bowled in off the sea, carrying with it a spit of rain that sparked on Annie's forehead. She looked upward for a clue to any change in the weather, but saw nothing but a clear cerulean blue stretching to the horizon. With a churn in her stomach and a determined hitch in her step, Annie burrowed into her coat and set off, determined to uncover some long-held secrets.

※

The Lodge was the go-to place for any special family occasions – any that didn't include a religious ceremony. Annie and Lewis were last here for their twelfth birthday and it was with that sense of familiarity that she walked up the three wide stone steps to the front door.

She pushed the door open and walked inside. Wood panelling and red tartan carpets. Did the people who work here ever get tired of them? She walked up to the reception desk and viewed the row of animal-head trophies that lined the wall behind it. Surely, the employees would get sick of those. Creepy. Who would want to work at that desk with those staring at your back all day?

'Can I help you?' the girl behind the desk asked. Her name was Jenny Burns and she was two years ahead of Annie at school. While they were at school Jenny wouldn't so much as glance in Annie's direction, but here, where she was at work, she had to be all professional and polite. That would have normally given Annie a little thrill, but today she was feeling more than a bit scared that her aunt would be here and she would be faced with that skull thing again.

Annie's head began to throb, nausea rose in her stomach and a tremble began in her legs, and from there spread, slowly but surely through the rest of her body.

She was afraid to look.

Please, God. Not again.

'Can I help you?' Jenny asked, her tone containing only a suggestion of the politeness her father, the manager of the hotel, would expect.

Annie took a tremulous breath. Looked up and into Jenny's face.

Jenny sat back in her chair, her face pale as she reacted to the fright on Annie's. 'Oh God, you look like you've seen a ghost.'

Annie screwed her eyes shut. Opened them again, and saw the bones of Jenny's face imprint themselves over the skin. A series of images formed in her mind. Each of them flickering into the next. The moment she thought she could make sense of one, it blended into another, her mind like weak hands seeking soap in a too-warm bath. Then she saw a red car. A tree. A pool of water, and hair floating like seaweed on the surface.

She gasped.

'Don't go in the red car,' Annie whispered.

'What?' Jenny asked. 'The what?' Jenny looked scared. Her face reddened and her fear flipped into anger. 'Weirdo,' she hissed. 'You should go home, Annie Jackson, you're giving me the creeps.'

Annie bent over the desk, fighting to control her breathing. And trying desperately not to be sick. What had she just seen?

She looked back at Jenny's face, and there was nothing there but an indignant teenager. 'Should you be out on your own?'

Jenny's anger sparked a reaction in Annie. She may be cowed by her mother but she wasn't going to be bullied by this girl. Annie straightened her back.

'My aunt is staying here. I think,' she said, through gritted teeth. 'Sheila...' God, what was her name? She hadn't thought to check that out. She would just go with her mother's maiden name.

'Bennett. Sheila Bennett. Do you have a woman staying here with that name?'

'I'm not sure I can pass on that kind of information,' Jenny replied, clearly puzzled, but also pleased with herself.

'She's my aunt. My mum's sister. There will be no problem if you contact her in her room and tell her I'm here.' Annie added some steel to her tone. 'Seriously though.' Despite herself and the tremors she could still feel in her mind, Annie leaned over the desk. 'There's this red car...'

Jenny screwed up her face in confusion, her mouth opened, and Annie could tell she was about to tell her where to go; but a man appeared from a corridor. He had a round face, like his daughter, and a large belly, which was straining against a tartan waistcoat the same colour as the carpet. He had a name badge on – James Burns – and under that the title *General Manager*.

'Everything okay here, girls?' he asked.

'I'm looking for my aunt,' Annie replied. 'Sheila Bennett. We were supposed to meet today,' she lied.

'Ah. Okay,' Mr Burns replied. 'Ms Bennett's your aunt,' he added as if, to himself at least, a mystery had been solved. 'I didn't know you had family staying over?'

Annie became aware of movement behind her.

'Annie. You made it.'

She turned to see Aunt Sheila. She was wearing a red knee-length overcoat and her long, dark hair was pulled back from her face into a ponytail. With relief, Annie noticed that it was her real face – with eyes, nose and teeth – that was smiling at her. Then her aunt spoke.

'Let's go for a bite to eat in the bar, okay?'

'Sure, that would be...' Annie looked at her aunt's coat, her quickly summoned white lie obvious.

'Thank you, Mr Burns,' Sheila said to the manager. 'Jenny.' She nodded at the receptionist, and Annie detected a little warning in her aunt's eyes.

Jenny ducked her head and coloured a little.

Sheila took Annie's arm. 'Hungry?' And without waiting for an answer started marching towards the double glass doors that led from reception to the bar. Once inside, Sheila aimed for a table by the window, put her coat over the back of a chair and sat down.

Annie, feeling very unsure of herself, sat down opposite her aunt, tucking her hands up inside her sleeves.

'I'm sorry, I didn't mean to surprise—'

'Oh, don't apologise, Annie,' Sheila said. 'It is so nice to see you.' She beamed. Then her smile faltered. 'Does your mother know you're here?'

Annie bit her lip and slowly shook her head.

'Okay,' Sheila replied. 'We'll take a leap at that bridge when we come to it.' She leaned forward and grasped Annie's hand, still hidden in her sleeve. Even through the material Annie could feel the heat. 'I'm so sorry you had to see that the other day.' Sheila's eyes grew sombre. 'Was it awful? Did the voices start as well?'

'You know about that?' Annie asked, all thoughts of Jenny and warning her about the car completely forgotten in her need to get answers about her family. 'It doesn't surprise you? You understand what's happening to me? You know about this ... whatever it is?'

Sheila sat back in her chair and looked out of the window.

Annie followed her gaze to the low sea wall and the dark, smooth rocks draped in bladderwrack beyond, uncovered by the low tide.

'It's pretty here,' Sheila said, absently. 'I can see why your mother would be called to come back...'

'Come back? We left, and we came back?' Annie asked, wanting to shout at her to explain everything. 'It feels like I know nothing about my family at all. Where are we from?' She could feel herself growing agitated. Why would her mother and father keep all these secrets?

'There are good reasons why your mother has kept you in the dark, I'm sure. She wants to protect you.'

'But from what? I'm not a kid anymore.'

Sheila smiled. 'Jeez, you remind me so much of me when I was your age. I bet you like to beat the boys at everything, yeah?'

'Aunt Sheila, tell me, please. What the hell is going on with my family? And how did I see your face like that, hear that horrible voice and know you...' Annie paused. Could she say it out loud? Would it upset her aunt?

Sheila held a hand up. 'Sorry. I'm being flippant, and you deserve answers.' Her face crumpled with sympathy. 'I just don't know that I'm the one who should be telling you them.'

Annie crossed her arms and pushed back into her seat. 'God, I hate being part of this family. We're nuts. Completely nuts. My dad is a total wimp, and my mother's the bitch from hell.'

'Whoa, sweetie. That's quite the rant you've got going on there. Something tells me you're better than that.'

Annie sagged in her chair. 'But I just need to know.' Again she thought of her aunt's face, and felt a charge of fear. 'Don't I deserve to? There's something totally weird going on here.'

'But—'

'Will I see you like that again? Will I see other people like that?'

'Have you had any other ... experiences?'

'I saw something in the church this morning ... an old man.

But I looked away before it ... I couldn't face it.' And Jenny. She didn't want to go there again. The old man in the church and whatever would happen to him felt like the natural order of things; but Jenny ... That was so wrong it was terrifying, and she couldn't trust herself to mention it in case her fear became too apparent.

Sheila's hand hovered over her heart. 'Oh, Annie.' She paused. 'Have you seen me like that again? Can you see my proper face just now?'

'Right now it's just a normal face,' Annie replied. 'Is that how it works? A one-time thing?'

Sheila shook her head. 'I have no idea. My sister – your aunt Bridget – never talked about it much.'

'Bridget.' Annie mouthed the word as if tasting it. 'Your sister had this? Anyone else?'

'My grandmother. Your great-gran. There seems to be no real pattern to it. But whatever it is it seems to only move down the female line.' She was wearing an expression of deep sympathy. 'We hoped it would skip your generation.'

'What happened to your sister? To your gran?'

Sheila grew pale. 'I don't ... Bridget called it "the murmurs".'

'Aunt Sheila, please. I need to know.'

'There's some things you're better off not knowing, honey.'

'God, you're just like her.' Annie slammed a hand down on the table in frustration. Several people turned to see where the noise had come from, and Annie felt her face heat with shame. This was just so frustrating. 'Where is this sister? Maybe I could talk to her and she could help me understand.'

'She's...' Sheila faltered.

Annie read Sheila's expression and her deep pause. 'She's dead, isn't she?' She shivered. 'Is it this thing I've got? Will it kill me?'

'Aww, honey,' Sheila reached across the table with both her hands and grabbed Annie's.

'Well, tell me. This is driving me nuts.' She pulled her hands from Sheila's grip. 'Please?' she added, hating that she sounded so pathetic.

'Your aunt Bridget ... Your mum was devastated when Bridget...'

Annie became aware of a presence at her side, almost at the same time as she saw Sheila's face blanch.

'Stop this now, Sheila.' Annie recognised her mother's cold tone. 'Haven't you done enough damage?'

Chapter 14

Annie – Now

A knock at the door alerted Annie to Lewis's arrival. The door opened and he shouted, 'Only me.'

Footsteps. And then he was in her living room, a plastic bag in his hand, which held, judging by the smell, some Indian food.

'Hungry?' Lewis studied her face, then held the bag up. 'I'll stick this in the oven. We can eat later. Looks like you need answers first.' He was wearing a dark-grey suit with the knot of his blue tie loosened.

'Too right,' Annie said as she stepped out from under the folds of her blanket. 'How could you end a call like that?'

'This isn't easy for me either, Annie. I've been holding on to this shit for years.' His face was tight. He put the bag on the table and rubbed at his forehead. 'Dad made me promise not to tell you.'

'Tell me what? And when did Dad become more important to you than me?' Annie demanded, her face almost pressed up against his.

'Just ... let me explain, eh?'

'Explain what?' Annie could see the strain on Lewis's face, but couldn't have cared less in that moment.

'Sit down,' Lewis said firmly. 'You need to hear this. Properly. You need to take a breath and listen.'

'Okay. Okay,' Annie said. 'This better be fucking good.'

Lewis sat beside her. Closed his eyes. Opened them and looked into hers.

'Lewis, you're scaring me.'

'The day Dad died?'

Shit.

'Yes?' And Annie was back in that moment, when a screaming Lewis had run out into the garden, his eyes mad with fear, shouting something unintelligible, until the words hit her mind – their father was hanging in the attic.

'He told me this when you came back from the hospital after your and Mum's accident. But he repeated it that day. The day he died. You'd lost your memory in the accident and that was a good opportunity to offer you a revised edition of your life that would be more ... beneficial.'

'A revised edition?' Annie said. 'Beneficial? What the hell does that mean?'

'The thing you described to me about the old man in the care home? That happened to you before.'

'It did?'

It did.

A sense of memory pushing, probing, sending light into the dark recesses of her mind. Her mother a shadowy figure in the kitchen. A visitor. Her mother's reaction. Whoever the woman was, she had not been welcome.

'There were a couple of times it happened. Do you remember that Mum had a sister? And then there was a girl – Jenny Burns – and a red car...'

A girl getting into a red car.

A pool of water, hair on the surface like kelp.

A woman's face.

A woman's face transforming into nothing but bone.

A voice, low, guttural, unceasing, and harsh enough to scour off a layer of skin.

A knowing.

Something, long coiled, slowly relaxed. A serpent's slide into wakefulness. Like frost furring a metal pipe, she felt the cold grow up from her stomach.

'Oh my God,' Annie said, hand over her heart. Fresh pain burst across her forehead. She screwed her eyes against it. 'The girl? The woman. Do you remember them?'

Lewis nodded.

'The woman was family? Our aunt? I said she had cancer. Did she die?'

'Don't know. Her and Mum had a falling-out and she left. Then when Mum died Dad was so full of his own pain, I guess that we didn't ever look for her to find out.'

'So, I somehow knew this aunt had cancer. What's wrong with that?' Apart from the feeling of dread and horror when it comes to you. 'Why should that be kept from me? I needed to know this stuff so that when today happened I was in some way prepared,' Annie insisted. 'All you did was make it worse for me.'

'If that's the case, I'm doubly sorry. But Dad was determined that we had to protect you. From yourself. Being asked to do something like that, just before he offed himself? Can you understand how that might feel like a promise I couldn't break?'

Lewis was twisting his fingers together in that way he did when he was anxious about something. Usually, if she noticed it, Annie would rein in her own upset, but today that wasn't going to happen. Things had been kept from her. Things that would have helped her make sense of the horrors she was experiencing, and she needed answers. And she needed them to make sense. Taking a deep breath to force calm into her mind, to help her take in this new information, she stared into her brother's eyes.

'Tell me. Tell me everything.'

Chapter 15

Annie – Then

Having marched into the Lodge restaurant and told Aunt Sheila what she thought of her, her mother now stared at Annie.

'And you, young lady: I can't tell you how disappointed I am that you would go behind my back...' She was speaking just above a whisper, jaw tight.

'But, Mum, what do you expect when—' Annie began, but her mother cut her off by pulling at her sleeve.

'We're going home,' she said. 'Now.' Her tone brooked no dissent, and Annie allowed herself to be guided out of the room.

As they walked through reception Annie looked over her shoulder at the desk to see if Jenny was there, but she wasn't. Her stomach surged with fear. She couldn't explain whatever had popped into her head when she saw Jenny earlier, but the feeling that the girl was in some sort of danger had only grown stronger.

'Is Jenny...'

'C'mon,' her mother said impatiently, prodding her on the back of her shoulder.

Out in the car park, Annie got into the back of the car, but as her mother was about to climb into the front, Aunt Sheila appeared.

'Sheila, please, just leave us alone,' Annie heard her mother say.

'It's been too long, Ellie. We need to talk. We don't...' Sheila paused. 'I don't have long.'

There was a moment's silence.

'That's not fair, Sheila. You can't play the cancer card. Not now.' Annie winced.

'What else would you have me do?' Sheila demanded. 'You

moved more than a hundred miles away and refuse to even talk to me when I call?'

'That's your doing, Sheila, and you know that fine well.'

'I know nothing of the sort. It was you who decided to move away, take the kids with you and cut yourself off from your only family. Not me.'

'How convenient. Change the truth so you can take the moral high ground.'

'Oh, Ellie.' Annie watched as Sheila stepped towards her mother, hands out, wearing an expression of sadness, but her sister batted her hands away and took a step back.'

'Don't "oh Ellie" me.'

'Please, Ellie. I don't have long.'

'Emotional bribery. Nice.'

'For goodness' sake, take that stick out of your arse and feel something for once.'

'Feel something? You knew that my religion was important to me. That I had purpose and meaning for the first time. It was too late for me to follow Daddy to the missions, and this was my chance to make a difference, but you spat all over that.'

'No. Mosely spat all over that.'

'He did no such thing. You believed a sick, demented girl over a man of, of, of ... substance. Of the cloth.'

Annie was scandalised and fascinated at the notion of Pastor Mosely being wrong in some way. She'd known it somehow – every time she encountered the man.

'For chrissakes, Ellie. The man's a fake. A dangerous, abusive snake. How you can't see that is beyond me. How Brian allowed you to follow him up here is—'

'Nonsense. Utter nonsense. And don't bring Brian into this. He's a supportive husband. As for the pastor, he's a good, good man, and what's more, I'd follow him to the ends of the earth. How you can accuse him of such...'

Sheila's chin dropped. 'You're in love with him.'

'Oh for goodness—'

'You're in love with him. Have you? Has he ever...?'

'How dare you? That's why I had to get away. You people wouldn't listen to me. Bridget is deluded. She's deranged. You can't believe a word that comes out of her mouth.'

'He as good as raped her, Ellie. She was a vulnerable young woman, and he took advantage.'

'Shut up. Shut up. Shut up.'

Sheila paused, her face grew pale. 'You haven't left Annie alone with him, have you?'

Annie heard a dull thud as her mother stamped her foot in frustration. 'For...' Silence. 'Just go, Sheila. Just go.'

Sheila closed her eyes, and Annie could see her hands bunched into fists by her sides, as if she was fighting for control. After a long moment, she opened her eyes, looked at her sister, defeated, and then looked towards the car.

'Can I say goodbye, properly, to my niece?'

Before her mother could answer, Annie jumped out of the car and ran to her aunt. Sheila pulled her into a hug. 'Look for Bridget,' she whispered. 'Look for her and she'll tell you everything.'

Annie took a step back. Nodded. But just how she was to look for Bridget she had no idea.

'Back to the car, please, Annie,' her mother said, a question in her eyes, suspicious about whatever had passed between the two of them.

As Annie did as she was told, she heard Sheila ask her mother:

'Remember the cottage? The little white cottage up by the loch?'

'The cottage? What cottage?'

'Before Gran became unwell she brought me, you and Bridget up here a couple of times for our holidays?'

'I ... eh.' It was clear to Annie that the sudden change of topic had confused her mother.

'I wondered if you knew what you were coming back to when you brought the kids up here,' Sheila said.

'Sheila,' her mother said, 'you're making no sense at all.'

'This area,' Sheila looked around, arms out. 'We have history here. It marked us. Pastor Mosely aside.' Her tone was acid when she said his name. 'It's not a coincidence you brought a daughter of yours here. You were drawn...'

'Sheila, have you gone crazy? I know Bridget has had her issues, but it sounds like you've been infected now too.'

'You've blocked that out as well.' Sheila paused. 'No matter,' she said, shaking her head. 'As the eldest daughter, the cottage came to me. I'm leaving it to Annie. If this thing continues, send her there. It will give her peace, I hope.'

'Sheila.' Eleanor warned, and looked back to check if Annie was listening in.

Annie turned away.

'My lawyer will be in touch,' Sheila said, a firm message in her tone.

'Okay, Sheila.' Annie could hear the relief in her mother's voice that the meeting was about to end. 'I'll look out for a letter.'

There was a moment's silence

'You don't remember at all, do you?' Sheila asked again.

'The cottage? No.' Her mother edged back towards the car, blocking Annie's view of her aunt.

Then she changed direction, stepped closer to Sheila and gave her a quick hug. Whatever she said in that moment was inaudible to Annie, but when her mother stepped away, Annie was granted a quick view of her aunt's face and could see the love and emotion there.

'Just. Please...' Sheila said. 'And the pastor?'

'Goodbye, Sheila,' Eleanor said firmly, all but jumped inside the car, and they took off.

They'd driven about a hundred yards up the lochside towards their house when her mother suddenly pulled the car to the side of the road, her hands over her face, and silently wept.

Chapter 16

Lewis – Now

Once he'd finished filling in what he could of her missing years Lewis asked her, 'Do you remember anything at all about Aunt Sheila?'

Annie shook her head. Opened her mouth, and closed it again as if the words were trapped inside. Her eyes had been fixed on Lewis's face while he spoke, but now they were roving around the room. Not focusing on anything. Moving quickly from one object to the next.

'I'm so sorry,' Lewis said again. He felt awful. How could he not? His sister was in pain, and he had played a large part in causing it. But what else could he have done? His father killed himself not long after he swore Lewis to secrecy. How on earth was he supposed to deal with all of that?

He was back in that moment, again. Looking up the attic stairs. Asking, 'Dad?' Knowing, somehow, that something was terribly wrong. And then, as he inched up the stairs, a pair of feet came into view, suspended in the air, one clad in a blue slipper, the other in only a sock. It took some moments for realisation to arrive. How could someone's feet be up there suspended in mid-air?

Hanging.

In the face of all that, how could he have betrayed that last request?

'We need to protect Annie,' his father has said only that day, the gravity of his words floating in the grey of his eyes. 'This ... thing has driven most of the women in your mother's side of the family mad. We need to shield her from that.'

Lewis remembered shaking his head. He just wanted everything back to the way it had been. His mother alive. His father smiling, joking, always gently joshing to get Lewis and Annie to behave.

Not this.

This man with the pallid skin and the dead eyes, and the heavy grip on his shoulder, demanding, 'Promise me.'

'Dad.'

'Promise me.' The grip on Lewis's shoulder intensified. 'Annie seems to have forgotten everything. And that's a blessing. Make sure it stays that way, son.'

Now, Annie spoke, plucking him from memory.

'Sorry?' he asked.

'I've just had a thought,' Annie said. 'Maybe this aunt is still alive. People get cancer all the time and survive.' She sat upright, a hopeful expression pushing through the fear. 'If the things I see don't always come true, what repercussions might that have for Steve?'

But then her thinking skipped on. Her eyes were back on Lewis. Hard, judging eyes.

'Hey,' he said as he jumped to his feet. 'Don't look at me like that. That's not fair. Dad made me promise this just hours before I found him hanging. I was only a kid myself. You didn't see him. I protected you from that at least. And then … it was just impossible. And when would you have had me tell you, eh? While we were at school when you were having a shitty time? When you were off doing your art-school crap? Just before you started your new job?' He sat back in his chair. 'Tell me. When would have been a good time to betray my father's last fucking wish?' He knew his anger was misplaced, but it still felt good to express it.

'I feel let down, Lewis. I can't help it. And sure, that was a shitty thing Dad did to you, but, still, I'm having a hard time processing that a massive part of my life has been kept from me.' She crossed her own arms – a mirror image of him.

After a moment she attempted a smile. 'Jesus, they really did a number on us, didn't they?' she said.

'Hungry?' He answered her smile with one of his own.

'I could eat.'

A truce had been established.

'Good, 'cos I'm bloody starving.'

Lewis went into the kitchen. He heard Annie follow, after a beat. As if she didn't want him to think he'd won her over so easily.

Annie took a seat at her kitchen table, and Lewis plated up. They concentrated on the food for a time, eating mostly in silence, apart from the occasional appreciative noises as the flavours hit their tongues.

But it was not long before Annie pushed her plate away and fixed him with a stare. He could tell she needed more answers.

'Protect me from myself,' she said. 'You said that Dad wanted you to protect me from myself. What did he mean by that?'

Lewis paused in his chewing. 'I was never quite sure about that, to be honest. I was aware that you'd said spooky stuff about people's health that a twelve-year-old girl shouldn't know about.' He pursed his lips.

'You're holding back,' Annie said, sitting back in her chair. 'If you're still protecting me, you need to stop. I need answers, Lewis.'

'Please.' He screwed his eyes shut and leaned back. 'Please don't do this, Annie.'

'Lewis.' She stared at him, waited till he looked at her, held his gaze and refused to let go.

'Okay.' He held both his hands up. 'You need to stop giving me the evil eye.' Then a thought occurred to him. 'Hey, you haven't picked up anything about me, have you?'

'Yeah, you're about to get a fork through your right eye if you don't tell me everything right now.'

'Okay. Don't say I didn't warn you.' He took a deep breath. 'There's a curse. Or to be more accurate, Mum believed there was a curse that only affects the female side of the family. Apparently, she was terrified to have children in case one of them was a girl.'

'A curse?'

'Yeah. These premonitions you had as a youngster – Mum was terrified of them. They drove her grandmother mad, apparently.' He bit his lip. 'Do you really want to hear this? It's not nice, Annie.'

'I'm done with nice,' Annie replied. 'Tell me.'

'Mum's mother made her visit her grandmother in the local loony bin pretty much every weekend. She took it as a warning not to ever have kids of her own.' Lewis's mind was focused on the imagined horror. 'How fucked up was that? She watched her grandmother incrementally lose her grip on reality. In the end even a breeze against her skin was enough to send her screaming into a corner of her room.'

Chapter 17

MOIRA MCLEAN – A MEMOIR

Around a hundred years before our homes were set on fire, only a few miles as the crow flies from Anlochard, sisters Mary and Jean lived with their grandmother in the village of Mossgow.

The girls knew each other's every thought, every gesture. They finished each other's sentences with the ease that other people breathed. They were wild creatures running through the gorse and heather, twigs and leaves caught in the unruly tangle of their auburn hair, catching rabbits and pigeons, gathering herbs, and helping to bring in the sheep.

Health and vitality shone from their eyes and the satin blush of their skin, and it was whispered all through the neighbouring glens that one day both girls would catch the eye of great men and rise in the world.

But the girls had no use for men, as yet. Their world was in the fresh loam of the earth, the oaks sturdy against the winds, and the star-scattered sky. When you have those elements as your companion what need do you have for mere men?

The girls were able to run so free because their mother had died in childbirth and their father was often at sea. It pained him to set eyes on his girls, so alike were they to their sadly deceased mother. They were attended to by their mother's mother. A woman who held fast to the old ways.

From time to time they would sit at their grandmother's hems and listen to her stories of ancient times, of warriors brave and damsels fair. And learn which of those tales to pay attention to, and those that were nary but lies.

'*Tell no one,*' she ordered, '*for the King of Scotland himself, James the Sixth, orders our persecution. It is said he has written a book, a* daemonologie, *that describes the many ways in which witchcraft works and orders that any found be tried, and if found guilty, strangled and then burned.*'

How she knew this neither girl could guess, because they had no access to such things as books. But her warning was delivered with passion, and the girls took heed.

It was the old woman's lessons about the earth and its bounty that held them fast. Which herbs would help a child quicken in the womb, and the leaves that would stop that child from taking seed in the first place.

'*Here,*' the old woman said, her palm full of dark, rich earth, a green shoot sticking up from it. '*Terrible times are upon us. The knowledge of how to observe nature, and work with it and use it for our benefit is being lost to us...*' she paused, her lips in a thin disapproving line '*...in favour of science. And it is up to us women to cherish the old knowledge, pass it down the generations and hang on to it for the betterment of our people.*

'*Mark my words: one day the things men now consider to be scientific*' – she narrowed her eyes – '*will be seen as barbaric by more clever people than the ones that surround us presently.*

'*They seek a cure for peoples' ills by sticking foul leeches on their skin. And all the while...*' she paused and looked from one girl to the other, her eyes large '*...every secret they ever wanted to know was right here, in front of their faces.*' She pointed at the shoot. Held a trembling finger under one dainty leaf. '*Learn my lessons well, girls. Hold them fast to your heart and share them only with the deserving and the desperate.*'

Old Mother McLean held a hand over her own heart. '*Never forget that the minds of many men and women be tainted. That if they so decide, you will be found guilty of the most nefarious acts, using the words of our own fell king to justify themselves.*'

She leaned back, looked up at the gathering clouds, and sniffed, *her face souring as if she smelled blood. To the girls it appeared as if she had momentarily swooned. Her head swaying on the thin stick of her neck. Then her eyes shot open. 'There will come a time your gifts and knowledge will place you in grave danger.'*

She blinked hard, as if a new piece of information had landed in her mind. And the girls sensed that whatever came out of their grandmother's mouth next was going to be dire news indeed.

'You will both bear twins, and twins will be a feature of our line long into the future.'

The girls looked to one another, feeling relief.

'But there will be a young man by whom you'll have those children, and you will have a falling-out of the most serious nature.' She wiped a tear from her cheek with the back of a wizened and trembling hand. 'One of you will betray the other, and her very body will be thrown to the flames.'

Chapter 18

Annie – Then

Monday morning, the day after Annie had met with Aunt Sheila in The Lodge on the Loch, she went to school as always, elbow to elbow with Danielle Jenkins. As they walked, Annie swore Danni to secrecy and then told her everything about Aunt Sheila's visit – her skull face, and then the visit to the hotel, and what she'd said to Jenny Burns.

Danni was completely captivated by Sheila's transformation and Annie's diagnosis.

'Do you think you're psychic or something?'

'Shh,' Annie prodded her friend with her elbow, and looked around. There was no one who could overhear, but, still, those kind of things were looked down on, especially in this community. As far as Annie could tell they'd moved on from the days of burning witches, but only just. 'Promise you won't tell anyone. Promise.'

'Okay, okay,' Danielle said. 'You can trust me, Annie. But, wow, this is unreal.' 'Unreal' was Danni's favourite word. 'Have you seen anything else?' She looked around, her hair whipping about her face. 'What about that old man over there? That woman in the grey coat?'

'Jesus, Danni. I wish I hadn't told you now.'

'Sorry,' Danni said.

'Pinky swear. Not another word,' Annie demanded.

'What are we, eight?' Then, reading the thunder on Annie's face: 'Okay. Pinky swear.'

They were approaching the school gates when Danni asked again, 'But did you see anything else?'

A jumble of images inserted themselves into Annie's mind:

'Jenny Burns. I saw her at the hotel and .... there's a red car. A woman's hair in the water, rising and falling with the waves, and ... Oh no...' Nausea rose quicker than she could stop it, and she turned her head to the side and vomited on the pavement.

A group of children from the year below them were passing as it happened.

'You're gross,' one of them said, face a mix of glee and disgust.

'Annie,' Danni exclaimed, while she kept a respectful distance. 'You okay?'

'Just get me inside. Into the loos. Quick.'

*

After they'd cleaned Annie up, the two girls made their way to their first class of the day, registration and religious education. The rest of the morning passed in the usual way, and while her teachers and all the other kids behaved as they always did, Annie looked on, wondering if her life would ever be the same again. To everyone else it was just a normal day, but she was forever changed. Death was no longer an abstract. It was touchable. Heartbreakingly real.

She moved through her morning as if on an axis, the world spinning around her, everyone she came into contact with in her imagination only ever moments away from the grave.

At dinnertime, she queued to be served soup and a sandwich purely out of habit. The moment she sat at her table she was sure she'd offer it to whoever was closest. There was no way she could eat without vomiting it all back up.

There was a buzz of expectancy in the hall. Everyone stopped speaking and turned to face the stage at once.

'What's going on?' asked Annie, looking at Danni.

The headteacher, Mrs Dalrymple, was climbing the steps to the stage. A grey-haired man in a black suit just behind her. As they approached the middle of the stage, Annie became aware of a cluster of girls, wet-faced and red-eyed, directly in front of them.

Annie gasped. Saw the red car in her mind.

The headteacher held both hands up. She was speaking, her words reaching Annie's ears in a jumble of sound, almost drowned out by the beat of Annie's pulse in her neck.

'Anyone ... knowledge of Jennifer Burns ... Detective Sergeant Campbell ... strictest confidence.'

Annie became aware of movement. Danni was at her side, her face hot with need.

'Annie,' she urged in a harsh whisper. 'You have to tell them.'

'What's happening?' Annie asked, hand searching for something to hold on to. Something to root her in the moment. Something that would tell her she was real. She was breathing. This was not a dream.

'Annie,' Danni said. 'Wake the hell up. It's Jenny Burns. She's disappeared.'

Chapter 19

Lewis finished his dinner in silence, while Annie, unable to face the rest of hers, pushed her plate to the side.

Lewis smiled at her. 'Has what I've told you unleashed any more memories?' he asked.

'Some,' Annie replied, before pausing to let one unspool in her mind. 'This aunt? I can see her. I visited her at her hotel, you know.'

'I remember,' Lewis said. 'Mum was furious. When Dad came home from church on his own and told Mum where he'd dropped you she guessed where you were really going and ran out to follow you in her car.'

'Why didn't she want me to know about this thing?' Annie asked. 'I'd had one of these vision thingies already. Surely it would have been better to get my aunt to talk me through it rather than continuing to deny it.'

Annie was back in that hotel, in the village of her childhood, anxious to hear whatever her aunt was about to say next when her mother turned up, the fury pulsing from her in waves. 'You're right. I'm remembering it. Mum was so angry,' she said. 'Don't think I'd ever seen her that mad.'

'Did Aunt Sheila actually manage to tell you anything?'

'Don't think so...' Annie paused. Another memory was leaking through. A heavy hand on her head, and she saw a man with the strangest teeth – she remembered thinking the top row were shaped like coffin lids – was talking to her. 'Who was Pastor Mosely?'

'Shit,' Lewis said. 'I was hoping you'd lose that particular memory.'

'And I thought you were going to tell me everything,' Annie snapped. 'C'mon, Lewis. What the hell happened with him?'

Chapter 20

Annie – Then

Annie's mother barely spoke to her for the whole of the week following Aunt Sheila's departure, and as the days passed Annie dreaded the coming Sunday service and another bout of being prayed over by the pastor.

But that dread was surpassed by another. Her sense that Jenny Burns' disappearance had something to do with a red car.

One evening, up by the tree in her back garden, Danielle persuaded her to climb the fence and come in to her kitchen to tell her dad what she'd seen. Annie quailed at the thought. People would think she was deranged. She didn't want to go admitting this stuff to anyone.

'Dad's a bit of a big deal locally,' Danielle bragged. 'If anyone knows what you should do about all of this it would be him.'

A bit of a big deal. Who talks about their father like that? It sounded to Annie that her friend was copying what the adults around her might be saying. Besides, Annie barely knew the man. Despite having lived next door to him, she doubted that they'd ever exchanged more than two words.

'You've got to talk to someone,' Danielle continued. 'Jenny's mum and dad will be going out of their minds. Don't you think you should say what you know? Try and help?'

Minutes later, Annie was in the Jenkins' living room, hands clasped before her, fingers twisting as she told Mr Jenkins what she knew. It felt odd to her that she was explaining this to her neighbour when she hadn't even mentioned it to her own parents, but Danielle hadn't given her much of an option. She'd dragged her in front of her father and before Annie knew it she had no choice but to talk to him.

Danielle's father wasn't particularly tall and he had a bit of a belly, but he had an aura about him, an air of importance. Chris and Danielle took their good looks from their mother, Annie thought, harshly. There was something about their father's eyes that always made Annie feel uncomfortable. A coldness. In Annie's limited dealings with him she could hardly recall him even smiling.

His expression was inscrutable as he heard Annie out.

'It was horrible,' Annie finished. 'I can't get the picture of Jenny and the red car out of my mind.'

A silence almost thick enough to spoon filled the room.

'Go to your room, Danielle,' Mr Jenkins said in a low voice without looking at her.

'But, Dad, this could be important. Jenny's vanished and Annie might—'

'Chris,' Mr Jenkins insisted, his tone brooking no dissent, 'take your sister up to her room.'

Annie hadn't even noticed that Danielle's brother was there. He emerged from the gloom of a corridor. There was a grimness to his expression in the half-light. And something else. Fear. He put a hand on Danielle's shoulder. She shrugged it off, but she allowed Chris to lead her away.

Annie was struck by the change in her friend and her brother. She didn't think they were that easily brought to heel. But then, nobody really knew what other peoples' lives were like behind closed doors. She was twelve and she already understood that.

Chris paused to stare at her, an unreadable expression in his eyes. And then, for the briefest of moments, hostility sparked from him.

Annie wanted to shout, 'It's only me. Why are you looking at me like that?' But the moment passed and the siblings disappeared, the house swallowing them up.

'Annie,' Mr Jenkins' eyes settled on hers. 'We are a Christian family. This is a Christian town. We do not tolerate witchcraft.'

Witchcraft.

His eyes were shadowed under the bush of his eyebrows, his mouth a stern line of disapproval. No, not disapproval – loathing.

Annie stepped back, a hand over her heart. What was happening? 'Mr Jenkins,' she felt the need to speak. 'I don't ... A witch?' She suddenly felt small. And in danger. She looked to the door, assessing how quickly she could leave.

'All this talk of visions and seeing people's deaths. That is witchcraft, Annie Jackson. If I were you I'd keep my mouth shut. And may the good Lord strike you down if you ever talk like that again.' He stood up, menace exuding from him, and gripped her forearm with a power she'd never experienced. 'And from today you and Danielle are to stop being friends. Am I understood?'

Mute with fear she could only nod.

He let her go. Slowly. His finger tracing a cold line down the inside of her forearm, lingering and light at the line where wrist met palm.

Chapter 21

Annie – Now

Annie woke with a start. Her first thought was of Steve. How was he? Had he survived the night?

The clock on her phone read 07:23, so, with anxiety building, her pulse a heavy rhythm in her neck, she called the care home.

The line was engaged.

Damn.

She waited five long minutes and dialled again.

Still engaged.

Shit. She would have a shower and try again after. Hair wet, she called and was still unable to get through.

She dressed.

Tried again.

With relief she heard the line being connected and her boss's voice filled her ear.

'Hi, Jane, it's Annie,' she said. 'I just wanted to check in on Steve. Is he okay?'

'Annie...' Jane replied. 'But how did you know to call?' She sounded shaken. Then, trying to resume some form of professionalism: 'We found him in his bathroom. On the floor. We called for an ambulance ... but before they arrived he was dead.'

Chapter 22

Annie – Then

It was Sunday, just three days after Mr Jenkins had all but called Annie a witch, and all through the service Annie sat with her hands clasped in her lap, head bowed, terrified that she might look up at someone, only for the murmurs to start and tell her how horribly they were going to die. Proof perhaps that Mr Jenkins was right.

Too soon, the service was over and everyone left the church. Annie made to go with all the other people, but her mother put an arm out to hold the whole family back, and the pastor made straight for them, confirming Annie's worst fears: that her mother had been in touch and arranged another prayer session.

Mouth dry, she watched him approach. She read the look that passed between Mosley and her mother, and flinched at her mother's reaction. Eleanor Jackson, in Annie's mind, was a fearsome woman, one who was in charge of her own thoughts and actions, and those of everyone else around her. To see her grow pale and bow her head like that? The only thing that Annie could surmise was that her mother was deeply ashamed of her.

'The devil has her,' Mosley said. 'But not for much longer.' He beckoned her father, her mother and Lewis closer. 'We all should pray. It will take a group effort, but if we all place our hands—'

'Mum, Dad,' Annie protested. 'I want to go home. Please?' She hated how feeble she sounded, but the condemnation from her family and the pastor combined was a weight she could not bear.

'Ssh, Annie,' her mother hissed. 'This is for your own good.'

Annie felt her eyes fill with tears. She tried to blink them away.

Tried to show that she was the strong one; she was stronger than all of them put together, but a single tear betrayed her. It slid down her face, fell from her chin and landed on the back of her hand.

'Look at me, dear,' Mosley said. He put a hand under her chin and pushed it up. She recoiled from his touch but was unable to fight it. 'Look at me.'

She opened her eyes. The vast space of the church dimmed as if the moon had temporarily banished the sun. The pastor's face wasn't there. She watched, breathless, as it flickered in the half-light and changed into a visage of bleached bone, lipless, with a gaping hole where his nose should have been. A strange light shone from the eye sockets, and she knew he was staring. Demanding her attention.

The jaw fell open, and words issued. Deep and guttural and accusatory:

'Remove thyself, demon.' He gripped her chin, forbidding her the option of looking away.

'Mum. Dad. Please,' Annie cried. Panic squeezed her lungs, she tried to get to her feet, but a hand on each shoulder held her down.

Anne became aware of other voices. But these were all in her head. A congregation taking voice to declaim her. A choir of discord murmuring about her descent into hell. Fear clutched at her heart.

One voice became louder than all the rest. Demanding her full attention. It spoke to her. Through her. The murmurs became a shout.

'You're going to die, Pastor Mosley,' she said, unable to stop the impulse to do so, while pointing at his heart. 'It's going to stop and you're going to die.' Then she screamed and screamed.

*

Annie was lying on a pew, head on her father's lap, and she could just make out a clutch of people gathered around a body on the floor. All that was visible was a pair of long, thin legs clothed in black.

'Looks like a massive heart attack,' Annie heard one of them say. 'Probably died even before he hit the ground, poor guy.'

Pastor Mosely?

For a long moment she knew little. Recent memory nothing but a black spot in her mind.

'What happened?' she asked her father at last, and tried to sit up. Her head spun so fiercely she had to lie back down.

'Careful, sweetheart,' a woman dressed in green was now saying. 'We need to make sure you're okay.' She smiled. 'How many fingers am I holding up?'

'Two,' Annie replied. 'What happened to the pastor? Is he okay?' Panic clutched at her. Had she killed him? He was dead because of her, wasn't he? She felt herself tremble. Tears building. A scream she dared not issue.

Oh my God. Who was she?

What was she?

'Hey, sweetheart,' her father patted her shoulder. 'You're okay. Everything's okay.'

Except it wasn't. And her father's tone did nothing to add to the weak certainty of his words.

'If you sit up, do you still feel dizzy?' the paramedic asked.

Annie blinked hard, wanted to shout at her: what does that matter? A man died. But of course she said nothing. She was a good girl after all. Or she was trying to be.

Her father helped her sit up, and as he did so she got a better view of the pastor. His eyes were open, staring. His mouth partly open as if he was about to reprimand her again.

Annie screwed her eyes shut. She couldn't look at him any longer. Proof that she was bad. That something was wrong with her.

'C'mon,' the paramedic shot a look of reprimand at Annie's father. 'A child shouldn't be allowed to look at that poor man.' Then she offered Annie a reassuring smile. 'Let's get you out of here. Can you stand?'

Between her and her father they guided Annie out of the church and onto a bench just outside the door. A group of people were gathered there – all familiar faces, all people she'd known most of her life. But they shrank from her now, as if she carried some dreadful disease.

One woman approached her and her father. Mrs McClymont, who lived at the end of their street. Her father, who rarely said a bad word about anyone, had previously said that she was 'one of the less pleasant people in the area'.

She was wearing a navy blouse under a heavy wool coat, a crocheted beret sitting precariously on top of her tight, slightly purple curls. Her mouth was a tight line of disapproval, tinged with fear when she leaned over Annie, and whispered something.

Annie recoiled from the old woman's words.

'What did you just say?' her father demanded. Mrs McClymont ignored him, simply walking away as if he didn't exist. 'What did that woman say to you?' her father repeated.

Annie shook her head. 'Nothing. It's nothing.'

'It's not nothing,' her father replied. 'It looked like it was pretty nasty.' His eyes darted from her to the old woman's retreating back. She could see that he was undecided: protect his daughter – support her in this strange and frightening moment – or go on the attack. Her father was not made for the latter. She'd barely ever heard him speak harshly.

'Dad, just leave it,' Annie said. 'It's just ... Can you take me home?' She desperately wanted away from this place, away from the hard stares, and the caustic whispers. Everyone looking at her like that, as if she had somehow caused the pastor's heart attack, as if she was evil made flesh.

Without another word, her father took her by the arm and

guided her through the silent, watching crowd and down the path to the car. Lewis was already in the back seat, tucked against the door as if afraid that any part of him might touch any part of her.

'God, school's going to be a nightmare tomorrow.' He shot her a look of blame from under his fringe. 'Weirdo.'

She couldn't argue with him. What happened here this morning would spread around the town like a contagion. Her name would be on everyone's lips.

'Leave your sister alone,' her father said. 'She's been through...' His words tailed off as if he was struggling to articulate exactly what had happened. He put the key in the ignition and started the car.

'Where's Mum?' Lewis asked.

'She'll find her own way home, after...'

As one of the church elders her mother would be involved in ... whatever people have to do when someone important died. Annie stopped listening. She simply craved the four walls of her bedroom, the softness of her bed and the darkness that might comfort her once she was tented under the covers.

When her father stopped in front of the house, she jumped out of the car, ran upstairs and dived under her duvet. She wished fervently that she could be anyone else right now – live in someone else's head, because this was just too much.

Moments later she felt a weight on the edge of the bed as someone joined her.

'Talk to me, honey.' It was her dad. 'This might all feel difficult right now, but believe me, in a week's time everyone will have moved on to something else.'

'Go away, Dad,' she replied. She wasn't stupid. She doubted even he believed his words. This was way bigger than the usual feeble gossip that worked its way around the town. Someone had died – an important person in the town. And she had caused it. Or as good as.

Annie suffered under the weight of her thoughts for several

hours, refusing to come down for dinner and ignoring her father when he said he'd leave some food for her on her desk.

Eventually the house quietened as everyone went to bed.

Then, through the wall between her and her parents' bedrooms, she heard the strained voices of an argument.

Her father was shouting, and there was something desperate in his voice that stopped Annie's heart for a moment.

Silence.

Then her mother sobbing, with her father's deep hum of consolation woven through.

She hated that she was the cause of their upset. She should just run away. Try and find wherever her aunt had gone and join her, because she was the only person who understood. If she stayed here she'd only suffer more stares, or worse. Words thrown with the intent to wound. It had already started with old Mrs McClymont.

Annie could see the dry, tight line of the old woman's mouth as she spoke those words, feel the spray of saliva that came with them, and feel the shame that they caused burn all the way to the furthest parts of her mind.

'Horrible girl,' the old woman hissed. 'Once upon a time you'd have been burned at the stake.'

Chapter 23

Annie – Now

Steve was dead? Feeling like her heart was souring behind her ribs, Annie didn't answer Jane's question – 'How did you know to call?' – and simply cut the connection.

The murmurs bloomed in her ears, an unending susurration, a plea to enter madness, and stay there.

Laughter took over, then died to the pitch of static.

No, she screamed, no. That lovely old man couldn't be dead.

She replayed Jane's voice in her head, saying that he'd died before the ambulance could get there. If only he'd listened to her. She wasn't crazy. She could have saved his life.

She wandered into the kitchen and sat at the table, trying to process what had happened over the last twenty-four hours. First day in a new job and she'd known an old man was going to die, tried to warn him and failed.

She lived in a city with a population, at a guess, of more than half a million people. She worked in a care home. If this was her life now, could she face knowing such things and being presented with them daily? Or even several times a day?

How many people would she come across on her travels? Her bus to work cut right across the city; how many deaths might she be faced with? Her heart quailed at the thought.

Then she considered how her grandmother reportedly reacted to it. How on earth could she herself go through something like that and not go mad?

Chapter 24

Annie – Now

The curtain of the living-room window twitched, and then Mrs Mac appeared at her front door, opening it before Annie could reach it.

'I saw you walking down the path,' Mrs Mac trilled, her arms wide. She was wreathed in smiles, so happy to see her that Annie couldn't help but feel a little lift. 'You're early,' she added. 'You're normally not here until closer to five.'

They hugged, and Annie held on for a little longer than was their custom.

'Aww, honey.' She felt Mrs Mac's cheek move against hers as she spoke. Then she pulled back. 'You okay? How were your first few days at work? Did you make any friends?'

'Hey, Mandy,' her husband said as he appeared behind her shoulder. 'Let the lassie in before you bombard her wi' questions.'

Mandy McEvoy laughed. 'What am I like?' she said. 'C'mon in. The kettle's on. The biscuit barrel is full.' Mandy had a little yellow Tupperware biscuit barrel in the cupboard above the kettle, which she seemed to think it her duty to keep stocked for any prospective visitors.

Minutes later, warm mug in hand, wiping crumbs from her chin, Annie had appraised the couple of her first few days working in the care home.

'I'm thinking your colleagues could be nicer,' Mandy said, leaning forward on her chair, elbows on her knees. 'Especially that Sandra one. Sounds like she would be worth the watching.'

Worth the watching. A Mrs Mac catchphrase if ever there was one. Her way of keeping tabs on the world and preparing Annie for the shocks she might find there. The more mature Annie could appreciate that where she and Mandy might have had a spiky start to their relationship, her adoptive mother had always had her best interests at heart.

Annie gave a distracted 'Hmmm' to the question, which had Mandy raise her eyebrows.

'Something on your mind, Annie?'

'I don't think I can go back,' she replied. And started to cry.

'Hey,' Mandy said, and came over to sit beside her on the sofa. 'What's wrong?'

Annie wiped her eyes and chewed on her inner cheek, wondering what exactly she should say to them – an exercise she'd been working on all the way over from her place to theirs. How much could she say without sounding like a crazy person?

'Lewis was over yesterday,' Mandy said, her face in a *we already know* expression.

'What ... what did he say?' Annie asked, while cursing her brother. She knew from experience that whatever was on his mind didn't take long finding its way onto his tongue.

'The premonitions,' Dan said starkly, but apparently without judgement. She studied them both. Saw nothing but acceptance – and something else too. Relief?

'You knew,' she said suddenly. 'You knew this would happen.' She jumped to her feet.

'We didn't know,' Mandy said. 'Not for sure. But your father was Dan's best friend.'

Dan nodded, an old grief casting itself across his eyes. 'And he shared his worries about you,' Dan continued. 'Before he died.'

'What did he say?' Annie asked, still standing. She was so angry she was almost tempted to scream her defiance before running out of the house – something she'd often done as a teenager. 'You guys knew this might happen and didn't warn me?' She knew she was being irrational but she couldn't help herself. She needed to strike out. Hit something. 'You're as bad as Lewis.'

'It's not exactly an easy subject to broach,' Mandy said. 'You would have thought we were crazy—'

'But you let me think *I* was crazy,' Annie interrupted.

'No,' Mandy said. 'If it happened we were prepared to offer support. And if it didn't happen we hadn't warned you about something that would have sounded, frankly, as nutty as squirrel shit.'

Part of her mind could appreciate the dilemma they were in, but the larger part didn't want to let them off the hook just yet.

'Before he died?' Annie repeated. 'When, exactly, and what did he say?'

Dan was sitting opposite her, his shoulders slumped, twisting his fingers, his gaze fallen to the carpet. 'I had a lot of time for your dad. He was a quiet man. And quietly proud of you two.' He lifted his eyes to meet hers, and his look told her that he wasn't going to apologise for honouring his dead friend's wishes. 'I struggled to believe what he was saying, to be honest ... But at his funeral I met one of his old neighbours. Mrs McClymont.'

'Mrs who?' Something tugged at Annie's mind, and she heard a voice: *Once upon a time they would have burned you at the stake.*

Pain burst across her forehead, and she held a hand against it. 'You okay?' Mandy asked.

Annie screwed her eyes shut against the drill piercing her skull, gritted her teeth, and then looked at Dan. 'Go on,' she said.

'You were not long out of hospital, after the crash, and you were still living up north at the time, but he came down to Glasgow with you two in the back of the car, and while Mandy took you to the shop for some sweets and ice cream...' Annie's mind presented her with the memory of that very occasion. She'd had mint chocolate chip. Lewis had a ninety-nine. The flake had dropped from his cone before he'd managed to get a bite out of it...

'He didn't say how much he was struggling or I would never have let him out of my sight. I had no way of knowing that he was planning for what might happen after...' He paused.

'After he killed himself. You can say it,' Annie added, and felt her mouth sour as the words spilled out.

'You're his daughter, so you've every right to feel whatever you feel when you think of your father, but know this: he loved you. He clearly just couldn't see a world where that was enough to stop the pain he was in.'

'Anyway,' Annie shook her head as if to throw thoughts of her father from her mind, and regretted it when a fresh burst of pain bloomed across her skull. 'That day...?'

'He explained what some of the women in your family experienced, and that your mother was terrified ... He couldn't stress enough the terror she felt that it was going to happen to you too. So...' He bit his lip, before continuing. 'So he said that if anything ever happened him, he would want us to look after you, that he wanted to put that into his will, should we agree to it. He warned us. He said that we should be wary – not of you, Annie. But of things you might say. About people dying.'

'And none of that seemed weird to you?' Annie demanded.

'Of course it did,' Dan replied.

'Was that not a bit of a suicide red flag? Preparing you as a standby parent?'

'He knew we'd wanted kids but were never able to have them,' Mandy said, with a quick look at Dan. 'And it made sense that after his wife died he was worried about something happening to him too. We thought it was pretty sensible for him to prepare for the worst.'

Even in Annie's tumultuous state of mind, she could see the sense in this. 'And the mention of the curse and premonitions? That didn't come across as the ramblings of a madman?'

'He was very convincing,' Dan said.

'And that was that. That was all he said?'

'Pretty much,' Dan answered. He looked off to the right as if considering something.

'What?' Annie asked.

Dan and Mandy shared another look. Then nodded at each other.

'What?' Annie demanded.

Dan sighed. 'He also left something with us. For safekeeping, he said.'

'Something? What kind of something?'

'We don't know. We never looked inside,' Mandy replied.

'But he did say we'd know when the time was right,' Dan added.

Mandy twisted in her seat and picked up something from the floor beside her armchair. Then held it out with both hands. A black leather briefcase with gold clasps. An item Annie, in a flash of new memory, could see her father carrying out to his car, going off to work.

She put one hand over her heart, as if it might stop the clamour of its beat.

Chapter 25

Annie – Now

Mandy McEvoy put the briefcase on the pouffe in front of her and leaned back. Then stretched forward again and gave the top surface a wipe with her sleeve.

'Should have given it a wee dust,' she said.

Everyone simply stared at it for a long moment.

'Is there a combination?' Annie asked, but made no move towards it.

'No,' Dan replied. 'I checked it the day your dad brought it to us. It opens without. But...' he added hastily, 'I didn't look inside so...'

'God. I don't know if I want to...' Annie tucked her hands into her oxters.

'Why don't you take it up to your old bedroom?' Mandy suggested. 'And have some time on your own.'

Annie felt her throat tighten with emotion and regretted her short temper. She really didn't deserve this wee woman in her life. Mandy McEvoy had been nothing but loving and supportive since she'd moved in. Forthright and occasionally blunt when needed, too.

'Why wait till now to give me this?' she asked.

'When was the right time?' Mandy asked, in an echo of her brother's answer the day before. 'You were, frankly, a bit of a nightmare for a few years. Then, when you got your act together, it was like one milestone after another. Dan and I would say to each other, "Right, next time we're all together," but then something else would happen.'

'Sorry, love,' Dan added. 'It just never seemed to be a good moment. And then when Lewis told us about, you know...'

Annie shook herself and quickly reached for the briefcase, flicked the locks, counted from five to one, and opened it up. 'Let's see what we have here,' she said, disguising her apprehension with a flippant tone.

The briefcase contained a jumble of papers. Annie thought she might be here for some time going through them all. On the top was an official-looking document. Her parents' marriage certificate. She read her parents' names and dates of births. No surprises there.

Which was disappointing. She needed something, anything, out of the ordinary. She'd always felt separate, distinct from everyone around her, and when she heard the click of the briefcase locks, she felt a surge of hope in her gut – hope that this case might hold some answers to the questions she'd never been able to form from the smoke constantly swirling through her brain.

A little blue cardboard box caught her eye. She plucked it from its place, and read its little tag: *Lewis's first tooth*.

She shifted the papers around, looking for a little pink box. But there was nothing. She shifted more. Saw nothing and felt a flare of disappointment. As part of her watched on, another part grew increasingly upset that there was nothing so personal of her young life in this briefcase.

She lifted the whole thing up and emptied it onto the coffee table. Spread the papers around, to give her a better view of the contents.

Nothing. No little box that suggested an infant tooth of hers might be there.

Typical, she thought. Lewis always was the golden child. And her? What was she?

The world shifted, circled, and the hollow feeling in her gut grew. Annie had the terrible feeling that she belonged to no one and nowhere.

In truth, she remembered little of her mother. Whenever she'd sought her out in her memories she'd got nothing back except for the sense that she wasn't wanted.

She felt the knowledge of this, and the sadness it elicited. And felt a surge of resentment burn and coil around the corner of her heart where a mother's love should lie.

Chapter 26

Annie – Now

The McEvoy back garden was a broad expanse, the width of the generous house, edged with flowering shrubs and small trees. Near the back door was a flagstone patio surrounded by planters bearing flowers in vivid colours.

In the middle was rust-coloured fire bowl and four raffia chairs. Annie sat in one and closed her eyes. The breeze was warm and carried with it the scent from the honeysuckle hedge.

Just then a raucous chorus filled the air, and she looked up to see a flock of around twenty jackdaws swooping around the neighbourhood, their cries accusatory, demanding. She watched them until they settled in the tops of the trees in the nearby woods.

The house had become too warm, the air stifling, so she'd refilled the case and carried it out to the table on the patio. Turning her attention from the birds back to the case, she opened the lid once more.

She spotted the corner of a black, shiny packet, and recognised it as the kind that had once been used when people took their photographic film to a shop or a chemist to be processed. With her heart stammering at what she might find, she released the folder from the pile and delved inside.

The first few images were of her and Lewis as infants, both of them aiming exaggerated smiles towards the camera. They were on a beach somewhere, wearing swimsuits, and they had buckets and spades in their hands. Lewis's happiness looked genuine, his eyes big and sparkling, his chin up as he pulled back his lips to display more cheese in his grin. If he'd been a pup he'd have had three tails.

Perhaps it was years of wondering just who her parents really were that made Annie think her own grin by comparison was too forced. If Lewis was an overeager pup, the look in her eyes was like an old dog waiting for a kind word. She searched the rest of the photos for clues as to where and when they might have been taken, but there was nothing in any of them that chimed loudly enough to spark an actual memory.

The door opened behind her, and Dan and Mandy appeared at her side with a glass of water.

'How you getting on?' Dan asked.

'Want us to leave you alone?' Mandy asked, hands clasped before her.

'Guys, you don't need to worry about me. I'm okay,' Annie lied. 'Just a little discombobulated by all of this.' She dredged up a smile from somewhere and repeated, 'I'll be okay. I'm not the flake I used to be as a kid.'

She delved into the case again, came back out with another photo. Her father as a young man, with a lustrous beard and moustache.

'Good God,' said Dan as he sat in the seat beside her. 'I'd forgotten he'd gone through that phase in his early twenties. Big bushy beards with a neat short back and sides were all the rage in those days.'

Annie stared into the eyes of her father as a young man, looking for some sort of connection. And she remembered that Dan had tried, many times, to talk to her about her father, but each time she rebuffed him, thinking: if he wasn't man enough to live and look after his kids, he didn't deserve her attention. She looked over at Dan now, and noted the sadness in his face.

'Dad was your friend, eh?' she asked.

Dan nodded. 'I loved the guy like he was my brother. We grew up together. Lived in and out of each other's houses.'

'Sorry,' she said, and reached across to hold his hand. 'I was just always so resentful of him killing himself and leaving us, I didn't stop to think about the relationship you guys might have had, and your loss.' She knew Dan and Mandy were her and Lewis's godparents and that was why they'd stepped in to look after them. Other than that she knew little about what their connection with their father might have been. If she wanted clues about her past, where better place to start than these two. 'I know I never used to be interested in learning about those days, but anything you can tell me about my parents' – she looked from Dan to Mandy – 'would be appreciated.'

Mandy sat down on the other side of Annie. 'You sure, pet? It might not all be stuff you want to hear.'

Dan looked off into the distance as if mentally flicking through the photographic stills of his own memory, choosing which moments might be pertinent to this conversation.

'Your dad met your mum when they were both fifteen,' he began. 'She was the year below us at high school, and from the way he went on about her – constantly, by the way,' he grinned, 'it was love at first sight for him. It took your mum longer to warm up to him.' Dan studied her face for her reaction, and added, 'I'm sure we've told you all of this stuff.'

Annie nodded. They had. But now, faced with all of this knowledge about her past, it felt important to her that it was repeated, to help her understand better who she was and where she came from. 'I don't know why,' she replied. 'But it helps.'

Dan crossed his arms and sat back in his chair. 'Not that she was reserved or anything, it was simply that at fifteen Brian was just a kid. Girls tend to mature earlier, don't they? It was kinda like she was waiting for him to grow up before she really threw her lot in with him. But when she did, they were inseparable. In fact, the three of us were – for a time. Went everywhere together.'

'Did you find being the third wheel uncomfortable?' Annie asked with a smile.

'Ha,' he laughed. 'It really wasn't an issue. We were so innocent back then. They were definitely a couple, but they included me in everything.' He made a face. 'Well, in pretty much everything. But then – I can't remember when, exactly – they had a bit of a break. It drove your father nuts. He couldn't bear being without her.'

'What caused the split?' Annie asked.

'I never really got much of the detail,' Dan replied. 'But it was around the time that one of your mother's sisters took unwell—'

'Wait,' Annie interrupted. 'There was the sister that came to visit us just before the crash. Was it her?'

'There was?' Mandy asked with a look to Dan. 'She did?'

'Yeah, Lewis told me. But Mum chased her away.' Annie shook her head. 'We didn't really understand why. But my recall about that time is very patchy.' She exhaled through pursed lips, frustration building.

'That must have been Sheila,' Dan said. 'Your mum's other sister, Bridget, was the one who was hospitalised.'

'Really? Why?'

Dan and Mandy shared a silent look.

'Come on, guys. No more secrets, right? I need to know this stuff.'

Dan held his hands up. 'All this is only just making sense to us, so please, bear with us. Your parents kept us in the dark. Mostly. But your dad did open up one night, some time before you all moved up north. He was worried about your mum. As I said, they split up for a little while, just before your mum fell pregnant, but he heard from a neighbour that Bridget had been carted off in an ambulance. That she tried to kill herself.'

'Oh.' Fear buzzed under Annie's skin. Is this what might happen to her? 'Do you think she was like me? With these visions?'

'That's the only thing that would make sense,' Dan replied. 'I met Bridget a few times before it happened. She was a very quiet young woman. Withdrawn. Wouldn't ever quite meet your eye when she was talking to you, if you know what I mean.'

Annie digested that. *Wouldn't ever quite meet your eye.* She was starting to do that: avoid eye contact in case the person she was looking at turned into some kind of monster and the voices started up. And Bridget tried to kill herself, and was hospitalised because of it.

Shit.

She fell back into her chair. Crossed her arms. Every part of her trembling. What was she going to do?

'Hey,' Mandy put an arm over her shoulders and pulled Annie into a hug. 'We're here for you, Annie. Nothing bad's going to happen to you.'

'Yeah,' Dan said, and put a hand on her knee. 'We have no idea what you're going through, but we're here for you, morning, noon or night, okay?'

Annie gave them both a weak smile and managed a nod.

'Did Dad ever confirm that Bridget really attempted suicide? I mean, if it was just gossip from the neighbour...' Even as the words tumbled from her mouth Annie knew she was grasping for an out. She knew in her heart that the neighbour's whispers must have been true.

'We never found out for sure. When your parents got back together your dad kinda clammed up on the subject. Wouldn't tell me anything. Then, after they got married, and your mum had you guys, they moved up north. And we didn't see that much of them – for years, actually.' Annie could see that this still hurt a little, that his oldest friend had abandoned him. 'The odd family occasion: weddings and funerals and the like. And we were asked to be both your and Lewis's godparents. And then we had no further contact until that day your father came to visit. Just before ... he died.'

Annie thought about this aunt who had been hospitalised as a young woman. What had happened to her? If she was still alive she would probably be not much older than Mandy. And if she was still breathing, was she still in the hospital? Was she still being visited by the visions, or had they medicated her out of them?

These were questions that she might never know the answers to, and if she kept thinking about them they might drive her crazy. In an effort to distract herself, she dived back into the briefcase, and started going back through the stack of photos in the black plastic wallet.

Among them was a photograph of her mother. And her two sisters.

There was no mistaking the fact they were sisters. They looked so alike: same dark hair; thin, long nose; heart-shaped chin. And she could pick her mother out straight away. She was the middle child, and in the middle of the photograph. There was an impish twist to her mouth as if she'd just whispered a rude joke to her sisters, trying to get them to lose control in front of the camera. The younger sister, that would be Bridget, was caught mid-laugh, mouth open, head angled back, while the older sister looked like she was able to chew down on her impulse to laugh and was making herself a promise to get Annie's mother back later.

Seeing the girls together in this moment, and noting an obvious chemistry between them, saddened Annie. How different might life have been if this family curse hadn't afflicted Bridget? Could she have had a normal life, full of the joy of sisterhood that these young women displayed?

It would have been so nice to have had women like this in her life when she was growing up.

'God,' she said. 'Look at them. They're so happy.' And without any further thought she came to a decision. 'When I saw Aunt Sheila, I *knew* that she was dying of cancer. I remember that much, and with Steve at the care home, I also knew he was going to die. What if Sheila is still alive? We don't know if my premonition about her came true. And poor Bridget, she was carted off to a mental institution. Where is she now? She's still only going to be in her early fifties.' She felt her determination strengthen. 'Whatever happened to my aunts, I'm going to find out.'

Chapter 27

Annie – Now

A week later, Annie was sitting in Lewis's car, listening to the metronome of the windscreen wipers. As she'd told Mrs Mac she would, Annie had tendered her resignation at the care home and had been at a loose end all week. But Lewis had been his usual busy self. This was the first day off he'd had since Annie was given the briefcase.

She stared out of the window at a building that looked like it had been transported from the set of a Stephen King movie. There was a long, curved drive that stopped before a rank of wide steps. Above that a moat of red stone chips and then a mansion house four floors high, with rows of tall windows either side of a double oak door. The stone of the house was an air-pollution-stained, blond sandstone, the roof a steep pitch of grey slate. A large sign at the gate read *Oswald House* with a silhouette of a nun's head covered in a cowl replacing the 'O' of house.

To the left a row of poplar trees braced against the wind, and behind them a pair of giant sycamores waved their skeletal branches as if imploring the chill to lessen. At their foot a small figure in dark-blue overalls swept up piles of brown leaves, only to watch them swirl in the wind and disperse.

'Very tasteful,' Lewis said as he leaned across her to look at the sign. 'Are we going in or what?' As soon as she'd told him what she was planning, he'd insisted on coming with her. 'How did you find out about this place?' he asked.

'There was a letter among the piles of stuff in Dad's briefcase.' At the bottom of the briefcase she'd found some correspondence from a couple of hospitals. This one was the nearest, so it made sense to start here. The letter was nothing more than a fund-raising plea, but the fact that it was addressed to her grandmother, Elizabeth Bennett, and was clearly from a mental-health institution of some sort, meant it might help her find out what happened to her aunt.

Lewis looked around. They were in the north of the city, just by Victoria Park. 'I've been through this area hundreds of times, and I had no idea this was even here.'

They'd driven past ranks of very typical Glasgow tenement buildings, through a maze of more genteel houses with well-tended front gardens, and past a couple of boarded-up Victorian schools. Then at the bend of a hill, on a dead end, had found the building they were looking for.

Annie had found out online that this building had been gifted to the city by the Oswald family, part of the Scottish merchant class that made their fortune from the slave/sugar/tobacco trade with the New World. They'd originally built it for one of their daughters, who had then 'gone to the colonies' – whatever that meant – and never returned. Unused and unloved, and beginning to fall into disrepair, the good sisters of the Magdalene had offered to buy it, but the family generously declined the cash and offered it to the nuns on the understanding that they would house and minister to the unfortunates of the area. They started with the insane and the addicted, then moved to unwed mothers and their bastard children. The babies would be adopted by childless couples, and the young women thereafter returned to the families. Later, in more enlightened times, it had become variously an orphanage, an old folks' home, and more recently, it appeared to be a convalescent home for those women who without it would have fallen through the cracks and ended up homeless on the streets.

Annie stared at the building, at the ranks of windows, looking for clues of life beyond the glass, but all she could see was a reflection of the dark-grey, leaden sky.

Annie allowed herself a little bit of excitement at the thought their aunt might still be living there. Being orphaned as a teenager made her hanker for something else, a life where she could connect with people who shared her genes. 'If she was sent here before we were born, that means she's been here for around three decades. If she's still alive, that kind of institutionalisation doesn't create a well-rounded person.'

'Meaning, you think she could still be nuts.'

'If she was *nuts* in the first place, Lewis,' Annie said pointedly. 'Or if she was driven out of her mind by this *thing*.' She crossed her arms against the thought of what that might mean for her. 'And can we stop saying the word "nuts" for people who're suffering from a mental-health condition?'

'Understood,' Lewis replied, and reached over to give her knee a reassuring squeeze. Then he asked, 'Did you phone and let them know we were coming?'

Annie shook her head, trying to ignore the swirl of emotion in her gut. 'It's way more difficult to fob someone off when they're standing in front of you,' she replied.

Chapter 28

Annie – Then

The morning after Pastor Mosley died, the family sat at the break-fast table, and no one spoke other than to request milk, pass the cereal, the butter, or in Lewis's case, more toast. Every now and again he shot a questioning look at Annie, as if to say, *Everyone is acting weird this morning*.

Annie didn't have the head space for him, on top of her parents and her worries about what might happen at school that day, so she refused to react to her brother's attempts to engage her. Perhaps he was trying to show support, she thought at one point, but the most she could offer in response was an upward twist of one side of her mouth before focusing once again on the cornflake box.

She was sure she would be the sole topic of conversation that day, and in her mind's eye she saw her fellow pupils in small groups, foreheads almost touching as they speculated about her, and Pastor Mosely's death. They'd only break off their whispers to stare at her as she walked past. Some would surely hurl insults at her. Even the teachers would be wary of her.

'Do I have to go to school today?' she asked.

'Yes,' her father said.

Her mother broke off from whatever thought was all but pinning her chin to her chest to say to Lewis, 'You and your sister's lunches are in your boxes in the fridge. I couldn't sleep' – she shot a look in Annie's direction – 'so I got up early and made them.'

'I'm not going to school,' Annie said. 'I don't feel well.'

'You've just got to rip off the plaster, Annie,' her father said. 'Get it over with.'

'You're bloody going.' Mum stood up so quickly her chair fell back and crashed to the floor. She leaned forward, eyes red and puffy, narrowed to pinholes of fury. 'I had to speak to the congregation last night. I had to tell the church elders that my...' she paused as if choosing the right word to describe her relationship with Annie '...daughter was not cursed. I had to...' She broke off, her chin trembling. Then she managed to get her emotions under control, blinked hard, and stared Annie down. 'I had to deal with that lovely man's death. You are going to school if I have to drag you there by the hair.'

Annie burst into tears, and ran from the table. On her bed, sobbing, she replayed her mother's words. Her face. The anger. Did her mother blame her for the pastor dying? It wasn't her fault. She just heard the words in her mind – she just knew it was going to happen. She didn't cause it.

Did she?

Her bedroom door swung open. It was Lewis. 'Hey, sis,' he said. 'You okay?'

Annie turned to him, just as her mother joined him at the door. 'Brush your teeth. Be in the car in five minutes.' She turned and walked away.

Lewis made a face of apology. Things must be bad, thought Annie, if Lewis was siding with her so obviously.

He sat on the bed beside her. 'If anybody gives you grief they'll have me to deal with, 'kay?'

'Okay,' Annie replied. 'But I didn't...'

'Whatever.' Lewis waved a hand. 'You said the words. He died. Don't you see? Everyone's completely freaked out.'

✳

Lewis was only partly correct. The kids in her year group were all over her, wanting to know every detail; what she thought, what she heard, what she said.

'And did he die straight away?' Kenny Dunlop asked, his eyes all but bugging out of his head.

Everyone around her stiffened as they saw the headteacher approach.

'Class, everyone. The bell ran five minutes ago,' Mrs Dalrymple said. The children started to disperse. 'Annie Jackson. A moment.'

Annie looked down. Studied the floor. Just what she needed, the headteacher making an example of her.

Mrs Dalrymple gave Annie a little smile. 'Everything might seem a little overwhelming just now, Annie. But remember that nothing bad, or good, for that matter, lasts forever. You know where I am if you need me.' Then louder. 'Run along. You don't want to keep Miss Cairns waiting.'

Reassured, and relieved at this small kindness, Annie picked up her pace and made her way to class.

Everyone stared when she walked in.

'Why's everyone late this morning?' Miss Cairns asked, looking at Annie with a quizzical expression. One person who clearly hadn't heard what had happened. 'Sit down, please, Annie. We have a lot to get through this morning.'

Annie made her way to her usual seat by the window. From there, halfway down the rows, she tried to gauge who in the room had heard about the pastor and her. Judging by the number of people who initially met her look, but then looked quickly away, it was pretty much everybody.

'Any questions?' the teacher asked, after speaking at length about something Annie had paid no attention to.

'Miss.' A hand went up near the front. Benny Higgins, the class clown.

'Yes, Benny.'

'Can you stop someone's heart with a word?'

It was as if the whole class held their breath.

Annie's face burned.

Miss Cairns scanned the room. 'What on earth is going on?'

A long, slow creak as the door opened.

'Miss Cairns?' It was Mrs Dalrymple. 'Can I speak to Annie Jackson, please?' Mrs Dalrymple found Annie in her seat with her eyes. 'Bring your bag, Annie. You won't be coming back.'

Excited whispers chased Annie out of the room. She couldn't get through the door quickly enough.

'Nothing to worry about, Annie,' Mrs Dalrymple said. 'Your mother is here for you. She reconsidered and thought you might need a day off school to process...' Mrs Dalrymple smiled. Actually smiled. And there was concern and warmth there. 'Process everything. You can come back when you're ready. No rush. Okay?'

※

Her mother was standing on the other side of the external door. Annie could see her through the glass, head bowed. Her heart gave a sour twist. All she wanted in that moment was her mother. A hug. A quiet word. A sign of affection. But looking at her she knew that none of that would be forthcoming.

Biting her lip, Annie pushed the door open and stepped outside. Silently, her mother turned and started walking.

'Where are we going?' Annie asked.

Nothing.

'Where are we going?' she repeated.

'Get in the car, please, Annie.' There was something about her mother's tone that was unlike her. A nagging feeling followed Annie all the way across the tarmac playground to the car park, where the little silver Ford sat on its own. There was something off about her mother. More off than normal. If she could just work it out, decipher her mother's mood, perhaps she could make everything better between them.

It was only when she sat in the passenger seat, and her mother automatically said, 'Seatbelt,' that she realised what it was. That tone: it was defeat.

Her mother had given up on her. She'd never loved her anyway – Annie knew that. Not in the way she loved Lewis. They were both cared for in the same way – her mother was too concerned with looking the part not to feed and clothe her – but in the small things the difference was evident. The way her mother would linger over Lewis's words. The way she'd reach out and lightly touch him whenever their paths crossed in the house. The way her eyes lit up when he gave her his attention. Every time Annie noticed this difference in her mother's affections, something in her broke.

'You've never loved me, have you?' Annie said into the silence.

To her gratification her mother gave a little flinch. Most people would have missed it, but Annie had so tuned herself into her mother's moods and movements that it yelled out to her like a pealing bell.

Her mother started the car up, checked her mirrors, then moved off.

'God, at least talk to me,' Annie yelled. 'What is wrong with you?'

'Leave God out of this.' Her mother flashed her a tight-lipped expression. 'Don't add blasphemy to your list of transgressions.'

'Would you prefer I say "fuck"?'

Her mother briefly shook her head as if dislodging Annie's words from her ears. 'You're trying to shock me,' she said. 'And it won't work. I only ever wanted the best for you, Annie.'

'You should tell your face that then.' Annie was almost shocked at her own words. She had never before talked to her mother in this manner. 'Maybe if I was a boy you'd love me. Maybe if I was more like Lewis.' Annie hunched down into her seat. 'I don't know where the words came from, okay? I hear this voice thing. Murmuring. And I need to say what I hear. I can't help it. I don't know how I knew the pastor was going to die. I don't want this. It's horrible. It's scary. I just want someone to scrape it out of my head.' She began to cry. And as she gave into her tears, a part of her noted her mother's lack of reaction them. 'What's wrong with me, Mum?'

They were on the loch road now, a stretch of grey water on their left, and Annie was aware that her mother was driving a little faster than she normally would. The car crested a hill, and Annie saw the bridge ahead. Under the bridge flowed a river that fed the loch. When the tide was out she and Lewis had spent many a sunny afternoon there, clambering over the rocks. What she would give to be in one of those simpler moments right now.

They were gaining speed now, when normally they would be slowing down. Trees and bushes rushed past. The bridge was close. Too close. The water rushing towards them.

'Mum,' Annie screamed. 'Mum!'

Chapter 29

Eleanor – Then

When they told her she was pregnant, Eleanor smiled, just like everyone expected, but emotionally she retreated. She couldn't love this baby. Wouldn't. Being a mother was difficult for Eleanor. It was not something she planned for, or hoped for, and as she performed the expected emotions, part of her mind was considering a termination.

I'm too young.

I want a career.

There are too many people in the world already.

She rehearsed all the possible reasons why she might want to cleanse herself of the tiny cluster of cells growing inside her, but never gave voice to the real reason. The fear that kept her awake at night: that her child might be a girl and might therefore inherit something that might ... She swallowed, took a breath, and realised she couldn't even think the words let alone say them out loud.

'It passes a generation,' her mother had said, a wan light in her eye, her mouth a tight line of uncertainty.

'Not always,' Eleanor replied. 'Your mother and your grandmother—'

'Enough,' Delia Bennett interrupted, before getting to her feet and standing in front of the fireplace, where she moved an antique clock a centimetre back towards the wall.

She was a slight woman, never wearing an open blouse, in case her prominent collar bones became visible. There might not have been too much of her but she always planted her feet squarely on the ground and tilted her head up as if offering her jaw as a target.

After straightening the clock, Delia straightened her back, turned to her daughter and seemed to force lightness into her voice.

'I take it your husband is looking forward to being a father?'

'I haven't told him yet,' Eleanor admitted.

Delia nodded in understanding. Then looked towards Eleanor's stomach. 'Good job you carry a little bit of extra weight there. You can delay having that conversation for a little while longer.'

'Mother,' Eleanor remonstrated, 'must you always make these little digs?'

'Not a dig.' Delia looked to the ceiling as if something there, a smudge of shadow perhaps, had caught her eye. 'A fact.'

That morning there had been a conversation at Eleanor's work. About mothers and how they were treasures. Utter nonsense. The truth was that Eleanor simply couldn't imagine herself in that role, or carrying it off. Unless of course the child was a boy.

Eleanor couldn't love her daughter. Wouldn't.

Because she feared what might be coming.

※

Sleep became like a foreign land – a place she visited with increasing irregularity, until a combination of exhaustion and guilt at keeping Brian in the dark led to her blurting out the news of her condition one morning when, with concern cushioning his tone, he asked her if she was okay.

'Well … that's … wonderful news,' he said when she told him – his smile on standby as he tried to assess her mental state.

'But what if I'm a shit mother? My mother's terrible at it. What if I carry on the tradition?' She started to cry.

'Hey.' Brian stepped in close and held her to him. 'The fact that it's even a concern for you will surely mean you won't. Besides' – he kissed her on the forehead – 'you're too loving a person to be anything but a wonderful mother.'

She pushed him away. Steeled herself against what she was going to say next. 'What if I got rid of it?'

'You wouldn't ... You don't want to. Do you?'

Eleanor forced herself to meet her husband's gaze. Bit down on her lip. 'But what if I do?'

Brian's face whitened. She knew he wanted kids. He rarely talked about it – and she thought that was because he sensed her reserve – but she could see it in the way he hovered over the children of friends and extended family. The way his eyes sparked just that little bit brighter when actors in a movie were presented with their new-borns.

He moved closer again. Eleanor stepped back. Brian cocked his head to the side, and held his hands out. 'You're the one who has to do all the hard work, so I can't force you to do anything.'

'But what if it's a girl? What if it has this...? What if she's driven mad?'

Eleanor crumpled at the concern in his eyes. Brian reached for her and pulled her into his arms. Then he held a hand against her abdomen, fingers splayed wide.

'There's a child in here. A mini you or a mini me.' His smile was tentative. 'Give me your hand.' Without waiting for her to move, he took it and placed it where his had been. 'Just beyond this thin wall of skin and muscle there's a life. A future. We have no way of knowing how that life is going to turn out. If you want to end it now, I'll stand by you. But can you really imagine yourself killing the possibility that we'll have a healthy child we can care for and love?'

His eyes searched hers, and she could see how earnest he was. He wanted this child more than anything, but his love for her meant he would stand by her decision.

She felt something deep in her womb stir. Of course the foetus was too small for any movement to register, but her imagination provided the necessary spark, and in that moment Eleanor knew there was no real decision to be made. She couldn't do it. Her fear of the unknown was a lesser thing than the guilt that would arise should she end this little life.

※

Eleanor had a difficult pregnancy. She was exhausted all the time, barely ate, barely slept, and for the last six weeks it was like someone had turned up her internal body temperature; it was the middle of winter and yet all she could tolerate were dresses made of the thinnest cotton, and if it was raining a knee-length coat with the lining removed.

And all the while, her mind ran on a loop:

Could she face what might be in her near future? It wasn't that she didn't care, she told herself almost every night in the cold dark, hand hovering over her distended belly. It was that she cared too much.

From what her mother had told her about the curse, it sometimes skipped a generation. But, she'd warned, as far as she could see there was no real pattern to how it moved through her line. It had visited both her grandmother's generation and the one before that.

Might it be that after Eleanor's grandmother, it had missed her mother's generation before landing with Bridget – and that might mean her offspring would escape?

Being harassed by her own fears every moment of every day changed her. Even she could see that. But Brian put up with every harsh word, every cutting silence, massaged her swollen feet and ankles every time she asked, and poured her a bath every night with a forbearance that made him seem almost saintly.

And then even that saintliness irritated the hell out of her, so she found herself, no matter how tired she was, shuffling around the city block they lived on at all times of the day and night just to get away from him.

Problem was, everywhere she went, there she was: a too-warm body, a cold, petrifying heart and a mind full of dread.

On one walk, on a cold, crisp Sunday morning in late January, she thought she found the answer to her problem.

It was the same walk she took most days, but on this day as she passed the entrance to the Church of the Everlasting Christ, the sound of a voice blasting through a briefly opened door caught her attention.

From her position on the pavement she couldn't make out the actual words, but the passion and good intent coming from the speaker carried out into the winter air and reached something in her dulled and fearful heart.

As if on automatic, she found herself climbing the three steps to the church's front door. She stretched out to pull the door open, but a voice interrupted her. She looked down in the direction of the noise. There, on the ground, wrapped up in a dirty blue sleeping bag, was a young man with old eyes and sunken cheeks.

'Sorry?' she said.

He screwed up his eyes. 'You look like you've got stuff going on.' He offered her a smile. 'But ken this, the storm will run out of rain. Eventually.'

Glasgow, thought Eleanor; comedians or philosophers on every street corner. Eleanor rarely carried her handbag when she went out for her walks, but she always took her phone, and a little cash. She pulled it out and handed a note to the man.

He beamed. 'A tenner? Thanks, missus.'

Eleanor turned back to the church door and grabbed the handle.

'Boy or a girl?' the young man asked.

'Sorry?'

'Do you ken what you're having?'

Eleanor's hand hovered over her belly. She nodded. And without another word pulled open the door.

Singing began just as she stepped inside the foyer. She could see into the main body of the church, and the man in black right at the front, facing the gathering, arms open wide, giving full voice along with the rest of the congregation. Such as it was. Eleanor counted the back of three heads on one side of the aisle, and five on the other. Still, the noise they made was impressive.

The pastor saw her. His lips twitched in a sign of welcome, and he waved her in.

Grateful that not one head turned to look at her, she sidled in and sat in the back pew.

The singing stopped and the pastor began speaking. And it was as if his words were meant for her ears alone:

'Give your problems over to the Lord. Only he can save you.

'You carry your burdens with you like a heavy rock. They weigh you down. Your back is breaking under the strain. Give them over to the Lord.

'It's like there's a giant black box in front of you. You do nothing but stare at that black box. It takes over your life. Closes out everything else. Every possibility of joy and happiness gone. Lift your eyes from that black box. Give it all over to the Lord. He will set you free.'

*

After the service had ended, after everyone had left, Eleanor remained sitting where she had landed, pulse a slow beat in her neck, her mind as calm as it had ever been. Perhaps this was the answer? Hand it all over to a higher being and just do her best with what was left?

She heard slow footsteps, looked up and saw that the pastor was approaching her, slowly, as a rescue officer might approach an abandoned kitten.

He sat down at the end of the pew opposite her.

'It's always lovely to see a new face in here,' he said. He held a hand over his heart. 'I'm Pastor Mosley.'

Eleanor looked into his face. He wasn't a conventionally handsome man; his black hair needed a trim, his nose had a large bump in the middle, and his mouth was slightly cast to one side as if partly frozen in a half-smile. But his eyes. His eyes were a promise to the world – what you see is what you get, and what you get is honesty, passion, non-judgement and devotion.

She felt all of that with just one look.

'Eleanor,' she replied, hand over her heart.

'You look like a former congregation member of mine.' He paused, eyes wide. 'You could well be sisters.' He smiled. 'Bridget Bennett?'

'Bridget comes here?' That was news.

'Haven't seen her for some time.' He smiled. 'A kind but tortured soul.'

Eleanor nodded. Wondering what exactly Bridget had told him.

'I haven't heard from her in some time.' He paused, and in that pause Eleanor heard a request for information. He was hunched in his seat, hands clasped before him, and from the expression of care on his face, Eleanor read that he would dearly love to know that her sister was well.

She told him everything. Well, almost. She detailed the curse and the impact on past generations of women, but made no mention of her fear for the child and that she had considered ending the pregnancy. The shame of that dark thought was too much for her to share with a man such as him.

While she talked, he listened. His attention never wavering, his eyes expressing only compassion and understanding.

For the first time in her life Eleanor felt that someone was actually listening to her. That she was understood. And in that moment she realised she was so grateful that Pastor Mosely only had to lead her to the edge, and she would jump.

Chapter 30

Lewis – Now

The woman who answered the door to them wore what Lewis could only describe as a beatific smile. She might have reached Lewis's shoulder if on tiptoe and she was wearing a dark-blue skirt and a matching cardigan. Her auburn hair was cropped short, and a crucifix nestled under the collar of her buttoned-up white shirt.

'Do you have an appointment?' she asked, her voice so gentle her words reached them like a lullaby.

'Sister…?' Lewis asked by way of a delay tactic. They hadn't worked out exactly what they were going to say.

'Theresa,' she replied, and then looking from Annie to Lewis she added, 'And who's asking?' This time her eyes lingered on Annie's face, as if studying her. 'Do I know you, dear? Have we met before?'

'I don't think so,' Annie replied. 'My name is Annie Jackson, and this is my twin, Lewis.'

'My.' She clasped her hands to her bosom. 'Twins is it? And how can we help you both? We try to work to an appointment system, Annie, and Lewis.' At this she gave Lewis a little bow of acknowledgment. 'Unless, of course, you have a family member staying here. In which case there are official visiting times.'

The nun's saintly expression seemed to hide a level of suspicion, and Lewis wondered if they might have to pass some sort of test before they got inside the giant door.

He smiled; the one that always made Mrs Mac crumble whenever he wanted permission or forgiveness. 'Would it be possible to come inside, Sister Theresa. It might take a bit of time to tell you why we're here.'

There was a moment's thought from the nun. 'Where are my manners,' Sister Theresa said. 'It's not the warmest today, is it?' She stepped back and beckoned them both inside. When she shut the door behind them it echoed in the large hall with a note of finality.

'Give me a moment,' Sister Theresa said, motioning them to stay where they were. Then she pulled open the door facing them and left.

Lewis shivered and looked around. Despite the large radiator against the wall, the reception area was almost as cold as the outside. At best it offered a respite from the biting wind. It had a tall ceiling, and the bare brick walls were painted industrial vanilla. The wall on the left was adorned with a two-foot-tall crucifix, the plaster Christ wearing a particularly pained expression. And to their right there was a windowed hatch with a reception desk behind it. Just then Sister Theresa appeared at the desk and smiled.

To the left of the hatch Lewis noted a photograph that must have been at least three feet wide and showed a large group of people standing in front of the doors they just entered. There were three rows of them; some of them were in the uniform of nuns, a few wore the starched white clothing of medical staff, and a small group at the front were wearing striped pyjamas. Not one of the latter were looking at the camera; instead they were looking down at their feet, or their hands, but one woman, right in the middle, was looking up into the sky with an expression of wonder as if it was the first time she'd seen it without the limiting edge of a window.

Above the photograph, the wooden frame bore a small plaque with the name of the establishment and the year – *2022*.

Lewis looked back at the row of nuns and noted that not one of them was smiling, and was reminded of an old university friend who spent a portion of her childhood in an orphanage run by such an order, in a different city. This friend was released into the community, as she described it, just ten years before this photograph was taken, and the tales she told of the women who looked after her were very mixed indeed. Ranging from moments of kindness to moments of cruelty. Often both from the same woman.

'We get a photo of everyone once a year on our open day. Invite the local press, local dignitaries, and some businesses, to try and boost our funding,' Sister Theresa explained when she saw where Lewis's eyes had moved.

'Not many patients,' Annie said under her breath.

'What was that?' Theresa asked.

'It's very quiet,' Annie answered. 'I was expecting more ... bustle. Where are the patients?'

Lewis looked towards a double set of doors, each with a glass insert, that the nun had just walked through, and tried to work out what might be beyond them. Annie was right. It was eerily quiet.

'The ground floor is for admin staff and the day rooms, and at the back we have the dining room and kitchen. The thick walls of this space make it feel like a little sanctuary from all of that activity. And believe me,' she laughed, 'it gets rather busy out there. But you good people aren't here to talk about how busy or quiet we are.' She clasped her hands in front of her as if summoning a moment of prayer. 'How can we help you?'

'How far back do the annual photographs go?' Annie asked.

'Looking for someone?' Sister Theresa enquired, her saintly smile back in its place.

Chapter 31

Annie – Now

Sister Theresa's helpful demeanour had faltered the moment Annie stated what they were after.

'Bridget Bennett, you say?' Her expression was stiff, and her eyes never left Annie's face. Annie looked away, towards Lewis.

'Yes, Bridget Bennett. Our long-lost aunt,' Lewis answered.

'I can't help you,' Sister Theresa said softly. 'Not unless you've got a court order in your pocket.' She nodded at Annie's coat, leavening her words with a half-smile.

'We're orphans,' Annie replied. 'Our parents died when we were preteens, and we just found out that our mother had a sister who was committed to this place back in the nineties. It's been so long since we had family, we're keen to find out what happened to our auntie Bridget.'

'Sorry, I can't help you,' Theresa repeated. Then set her mouth into firm line. 'I don't know anyone of that name, and besides, it's before my time.'

'We might have a long-lost relative who may actually be still alive. Can't you understand how important that might be to us?' Annie appealed.

'That's as may be,' Theresa replied. 'But I don't know who you are, why you really want this information, and what you are going to do with it. Our priority is our residents, and we will not allow any harm to come to them.'

Annie briefly considered showing her some identification, but then discounted that. They had a different surname, and had nothing that might prove their link to Bridget.

'We don't wish to cause any harm either,' Lewis interjected. 'And wouldn't it be a good thing for someone who's been in here a long time to finally have family, and some visitors?'

'If she's alive that is,' Annie said. 'We don't even know if she is.'

'Again, I'm sorry.'

'We know she came here sometime in the nineties. But then her trail goes cold.'

'I can't tell you anything,' Sister Theresa said patiently.

'Her name is Bridget. She'd be about fifty years old now. She'll be delighted to know she's got family out there who want to know about her,' Annie persisted, hearing the desperation in her own voice.

'There are proper channels,' the nun said. 'And this is not one of them. You can't just turn up and demand to see someone.'

'"Demand to see someone",' Annie jumped in. 'That means you know her and she's here.'

Sister Theresa tutted. 'It means nothing of the kind. You're testing my patience, dear.' The mask had slipped. 'I think you should both go.'

'Okay. We'll leave,' Annie said. 'But there may well be a lonely woman within these walls who finally has a way out of that loneliness. Are you going to deprive them of that?'

'As I said' – Sister Theresa's voice was back in lullaby mode, as if sensing that she'd regained control of the situation – 'there is a proper way of doing things. Please get in touch with our head office and put your request in writing. And in due course you will have your answer.'

Annie wondered what the limits of this curse might be. If she touched Sister Theresa, what might be revealed to her? Might she get a hint as to what the nun knew?

She allowed herself to be guided out of the door by the nun then quickly turned and reached out to her. She caught hold of Theresa's hand, felt the warmth and the soft plumpness of her skin. But nothing else. No flash of knowing.

But then Sister Theresa jumped back, pulling her hand from Annie's as if the surface of her skin was blistering in pain. Before the hard blink, and a forced return to a look of benign grace, there had been something there in her eyes.

Recognition.

And fear.

Chapter 32

Annie – Now

Straight away after leaving Oswald House, Annie and Lewis agreed to drive into the centre of the city and the Mitchell Library, to search out the local newspapers that might hold the previous photographs of patients and staff mentioned by Sister Theresa.

Annie always got a little thrill stepping inside the doors of the establishment. She loved the grandeur of the domed Edwardian baroque building – the modern extension not so much – and when she'd heard that it was bequeathed to the city from the man who launched a thousand libraries, Andrew Carnegie, she thought she couldn't love it more. Every time she passed she would mentally travel back to the times when as a young woman trying to negotiate the world around her, she was mainly hiding from it within the pages of a good book.

They aimed for the reference library on the second floor, and the newspaper microfiches. Annie approached a young woman working behind the clear plastic screen at reception. She had long, dark hair and a welcoming smile.

'We're looking for some old Glasgow newspapers,' said Annie.

'Do you know which ones, and the period?'

'Starting from 1990, I would think,' Annie replied.

'And it would have covered the Scotstoun area of the city,' Lewis added, teeth flashing.

Annie noticed the librarian's smile when she took in her brother.

'Not an area of the city I know very well,' Lewis added. 'We've always lived over in the south of the city.'

'Could it have been the *West End News*?' Annie asked.

The librarian switched her attention back to Annie and gave them directions towards the ranks of drawers behind them, and which ones they should be looking for.

'Then, just get yourself sorted out with one of the microfiche readers. If you've any problems, let me know.'

They both thanked her and followed her instructions.

Annie stopped at a cabinet and read the date on the handle. 'Try this one?'

Moments later they were perched in front of a screen, scrolling through news from a time before they were born.

They were both silent as the images moved slowly by, until Lewis remarked, 'Not much has changed, eh? Folk drinking too much, Rangers and Celtic fans at each other's throats. Oh, and look, at least that's historically interesting.'

The front page from November of that year was the news that the then prime minister, Maggie Thatcher, had resigned.

Annie noted the date and considered whether they might need to go to earlier that year.

'Aye, right enough,' he agreed when she suggested it. 'If it was an open day, people are more likely to do that in the summer months.'

More scrolling.

Then an excited 'Stop' from Lewis.

On the screen was a similar image to the one that they'd seen in the entrance hall to the big house.

Annie carefully scanned the faces, paying particular attention to the people in the front row. All of them had a similar look to the first photograph she'd seen: a vacancy that suggested not all was well in their internal or external worlds; or that they'd been medicated before being brought out in public.

'God,' Lewis said, his tone in tune with her response. 'Those poor sods.'

'That's your worst nightmare, eh?'

'Aye. Drugged, and locked up in an institution.' Then a pause. 'Thank heavens for the McEvoys. Fuck knows where we might have ended up without them.'

Annie nodded. Shared a smile of thanks with her sibling. Then she turned back to the screen. 'Anyone there who might be Bridget?' she scanned the line of patients. None of them were Bridget's age when she was hospitalised, and she could see no family resemblance in their faces.

'You didn't think it would be that easy, did you?' Lewis was replying, when Annie gasped.

'Look.' She pointed.

'Is that Sister Theresa?' Lewis asked.

'God, she looks so young,' Annie said as she studied the face of the woman they'd been speaking to at Oswald House. Sister Theresa was standing at the far right of the row of nuns, hands clasped in front of her. She was wearing a similar uniform to the one they'd seen her wearing earlier; the cardigan, white blouse, and dark, long skirt – but she was wearing her headdress further back on her head, displaying some hair and allowing her fringe to hang free. Her chin was tilted down, but her eyes were looking up through her hair.

Then just as the thought occurred to Annie, Lewis voiced it: 'Didn't Sister Theresa say that the nineties were before her time at Oswald House?'

Annie nodded. She definitely had. 'The question is: why is she lying?'

Chapter 33

Annie – Now

They sat in silence for some time, examining the photo, disappointed that Bridget wasn't present.

'Maybe this was taken before she arrived?' Lewis suggested.

'Let's try the following year,' Annie replied.

She loaded the film for 1991 onto the machine and began the slow trawl through the newspaper copy, stopping on any images.

Ten minutes of this and nothing.

Another ten and they were up to June of that year.

'Stop,' said Lewis. 'Go back a little.'

Annie wound the tape back.

'There.'

It was a smaller image this time, and further into the newspaper, with some copy that said the Oswald House open day had been a huge success and raised £1,912.23 for the ongoing management of the house.

'That wouldn't have got them very far,' Annie thought out loud. 'See anyone promising?'

Without a word Lewis pointed. His finger hovering over a face. 'Can the image be enlarged?'

Annie fiddled with a little knob in the middle of the control box and the image grew to fill the screen.

'There,' Lewis said, his voice little more than a croak of hope.

A young woman right in the centre of the crowd stared into the camera, her mouth slightly open, her eyes lidded, long hair thin and dull.

For Annie, it was like looking into a distorted, sepia mirror.

And there, close enough to hold Bridget's hand, was Sister Theresa.

Chapter 34

Annie – Now

Who are they?

They're every woman burned, every man flayed and skinned, they're every trauma visited upon every human – they're pain, they're torture, they are the scream echoing in the distant dark, the whispered taunt in your ear.

They're the baited breath, the hammering pulse, the cold, beaded sweat, dry mouth, and the bunched yet frozen muscle ignoring the command to run, run, RUN.

They are vengeance and they will never stop.

Annie lifted her head from her pillow, aware of a tremor of fear in her heart, feeling as if she'd been awake all night. But she had slept for some of it, she was sure, it was just that the voices came and went, and images of bodies being thrown onto fires populated her dreams, making her feel like she'd spent the whole night in a state of fear.

Minutes later, or it may have been hours, she came to, as if from another dream, and became aware that she was shuffling back and forth across the floor of her living room, head bowed, hands over her ears, terrified that the voices might start up again.

Her phone rang, making her jump into reality.

'Hello, dear.' It was Mrs Mac. 'Just checking in to see how you got on yesterday with Lewis.'

Annie relayed what she and Lewis had learned. As she spoke she felt her spirits rise slightly, and the fear of the murmurs recede. A little. Perhaps finding out about her aunt could be her way through this? If she could meet her, talk to her, see how she dealt with the curse, or even learn more about it, and where it came from, that could help her handle it. Annie had never been one for running away from her problems, and as terrifying as this was, she didn't want to start now.

'I'm thinking I need to go through official channels and submit a request in writing,' she added, thinking she would do just that the moment she ended the call.

'Seems like the logical choice to me too, Annie,' Mandy replied. 'I recall something I came across in the papers not long ago, that the Scottish government had set up a scheme – a redress scheme they called it – to offer people compensation for the abuse they might have received as a child in a home.'

Annie was mystified as to why this was relevant, and said so.

'It means they'll be inundated with paperwork.'

Annie felt a pang of disappointment.

'But it also means, people – and by people I mean people from other political parties – are watching them, so they'll have to respond, and have likely set up a team of folk to do it.'

'Right.' Sister Theresa's face popped into Annie's head. 'And that probably means if they have a head office it will be getting dealt with there.'

'Aye,' Mandy McEvoy agreed. 'And that nun won't be able to ignore you. If that's what she was doing.'

Chapter 35

Eleanor – Then

'Your hair,' Pastor Mosely said to Eleanor after service one Monday morning. They were standing at the sink drying dishes. Mass came first, and then the soup kitchen for the homeless. This was his way of ensuring attendance at his church. Feed the soul, and then the body, he'd said to Eleanor, when she'd volunteered to do more work for him and the church.

Eleanor braced herself. Her hair was the one thing she spent any time on. Her one luxury. She wasn't too bothered about fashion, as long as she looked presentable, that was enough for her. But her hair reached almost to her waist, and was a lustrous length of auburn that she religiously brushed one hundred times before bed.

'You don't like it?' she asked, hand hovering over her heart.

'It's beautiful,' Mosely smiled, and in his smile was a sense of loss, as if it reminded him of someone important to him. 'Shines like a beacon of health.' He paused. 'It's your one vanity, is it not?'

'I suppose so,' Eleanor replied, as she tucked a strand behind her right ear. 'I was wondering how I would manage it after the birth.'

Mosely nodded approvingly and Eleanor understood this was a test. He'd pronounced it a vanity, and she recalled his words from the pulpit that morning:

'Proverbs says charm is deceitful, and beauty is vain,' he'd said, 'but a woman who fears the Lord is to be praised.' Then, back ramrod straight, both hands on the top lip of the stand that held his huge, ancient Bible, he'd sought her out in the congregation, wearing the same calm smile he was wearing now as he spoke to her.

✳

A few days later, she'd turned up to help again, this time by doling out boxes of tinned food at the food bank. Her hair was shorn close to her head. She'd wept as she took the electric cutter to it, head over the sink as chunks of hair floated into the basin and covered the bathroom floor. But now, having had a day to get used to it, she wondered why she hadn't done it before. Her head felt so light.

When Mosely saw her his eyes brightened, and he smiled in that way that made her feel understood and approved of. Heart warmed, she asked how she could be of help that day.

Later, when the last of the people in the queue for food had been served, they'd drunk some coffee and shared one of the last pastries. They chatted for hours about life and the weather, and shared their concerns about the people forced to supplicate for a bite to eat.

'I've been watching you, Eleanor,' he said.

'Oh, yes?' She felt a little charge in her heart. An excitement. He sounded as if he were addressing an intimate; an equal. 'The good Lord has seen fit to offer me a new challenge.'

'Yes?' Eleanor recognised a sadness in his demeanour now, and her heart twisted a little with the expectation, this time, of bad news. Was he leaving her – them?

'It seems a congregation up north, a little town a few miles from Fort William, has need of a new face. A new vision.'

'Oh.' Eleanor felt her breath go. Her mood swooped from the heights of elation, to the weight of disappointment.

'I was wondering...'

But now, again, a lift in her heart. He wanted to somehow include her.

'Once you've delivered...' he looked at her extended belly '... whether you and your family might relocate? I will have need of you.' He smiled, and then, for fear of any impropriety, she thought, he added quickly: 'Need of people like you. Good church-going people.'

'My.' Eleanor held a hand over her mouth, her mind crammed with possibility. She would get to do good work. She would be able to move away from the constraints and the constant reminders of her deeply flawed family.

More importantly, she got to keep Pastor Mosely in her life.

Chapter 36

Annie – Now

Stark images, feelings, sensations, presented themselves in her mind. A dream fog, a kaleidoscope of impressions, muffled sound, heart-charging fear. A hand on her head. She couldn't breathe. She was walking along a corridor without end, her feet sticking every time she placed them on the floor. It took all her effort to lift a knee and place a foot.

Breathless.

She was underwater. Kicking. Then a light probing, flickering. A crush against her chest. A kind man's voice. 'We'll get you out of here in a jiffy.'

A wall of water looming.

The squeal of tyres.

And she was back in the corridor, thighs heavy with effort, forcing one step at a time. Water lapped at her feet. A door to her right opened, then every door in that side of the corridor silently followed.

Through each doorway a head appeared. Distinct faces, yet all of them complete strangers. Sightless eyes all in a row, their focus on her. Diseases listed themselves in her mind. Accidents. Countless ways of dying. All of these people were going to stop living, and there was nothing she could do about any of it.

One terrible event after another. The weight of that realisation suffocating, crushing her.

A certain knowing: she'd fail them all.

She screamed.

Her ears rang with it when finally she lifted her head from her pillow, emerging from her dream exhausted, and wondering if she'd ever be able to sleep again.

A rattle at her flat door. Firm. Officious. She wearily scrambled out of bed and into her dressing gown. As she walked to the door she tied the cord at her waist, feeling a tremble of anticipation. Could this be the postman delivering the letter she was waiting for?

Breath ragged, she looked down at the solitary envelope on the door mat. An A4-sized white rectangle with her name in type on the front.

Shit.

Did she really want to know what was in this package?

She crouched and picked it up. It was heavy.

She carried it through to the kitchen and placed it on the table. Her mobile was there. She called Lewis straight away, staring at the envelope as she said hello.

'It's arrived, hasn't it?' he said, without so much as a hello back. 'When can you come over?'

❋

When Lewis arrived, his tie undone and the top button of his shirt open, he looked every bit as trepidatious as Annie felt.

They both stood at the kitchen table and looked down at the envelope as if it might scald them should they touch it.

'It looks like a fair old package,' Lewis said. 'There's way more than just a letter of reply in there.'

Annie ripped it open and pulled out a wad of paper. A covering letter was loose on the top. She started to read. '"Dear Ms Jackson, thank you for your letter enquiring about a former patient of ours, Bridget Anne Bennett."' The word 'former' tolled in her mind. '"We can confirm that she was a patient at our establishment, Oswald House, Glasgow, from the 23rd of April 1992. Sadly..."' She looked over at Lewis. 'Shit.' She coughed, and then continued to read. "'…Bridget passed away on the 15ᵗʰ of December, 2004. The inquest…'" She looked over at Lewis. 'There was an inquest? Why the hell would they need an inquest?'

'Maybe they have to do one when there's no obvious cause of death?'

Annie continued reading: "'…found that Bridget withheld symptoms of her condition from the staff until it was too late.'" She looked at Lewis again. 'What symptoms? And why would she do that?' She thought of her family curse. Would it include knowing about your *own* death? She shook her head; that was too much to think about right now. She read on: "'By the time medical staff were able to intervene and prescribe treatment, her cancer was too far advanced. We did everything we could to make her last few weeks as peaceful as possible.'" She skim-read the next few lines. Then: "'Please find enclosed a copy of her death certificate, social-work reports, a summary of the inquest findings, and some other materials relating to this case we feel may be of interest to you. We would like to offer our sympathies that your letter of enquiry hasn't resulted in a more positive outcome. Please accept our condolences for your loss, and we remain yours in servitude…'"

'God,' Lewis said, mouth hanging. 'Poor Bridget.'

'She hid how ill she was…'

Lewis's face lengthened. 'But why would you…?' By the realisation on his face, Annie judged that she'd formed the same reason as her brother. She said it first.

'Bridget didn't want the anyone to intervene. Maybe she didn't know for sure that it was cancer, but whatever it was, she knew she was going to die – and she wanted it to happen.'

Chapter 37

Annie – Now

Annie stepped back from the table. Wrapped her arms around herself. The mood from her dreams and this new information coalescing in her mind like a heavy, grey mist. Unable to stop herself, she began to cry.

Lewis pulled her into a hug. 'Hey, sis,' he said, his tone warm. 'Once they realised what was wrong they did what they could to help her. Bridget's last days would have been...' he struggled to find the right words '...less traumatic. They would have helped her manage whatever pain she had.'

Annie pushed her brother away. 'You don't get it,' she said between sobs. 'That's not why I'm upset.'

Lewis looked at her, hands out. 'What is it then? What's upsetting you?'

'That could be me,' she shouted. 'Carted off to a loony bin because of this ... thing.' She sat down at the table, head in her hands. 'Can you imagine having such a curse? And life in that kind of place dragging you down so badly that dying in pain becomes preferable?'

'Jesus, Annie.' Lewis sat beside her and placed his hand lightly on the back of her neck. Then her head. With a shot of panic she realised that the weight of it was too similar to the feeling she'd had in the dream, so she pushed him off.

'Sorry. I...' She'd never seen him so lost for words.

Slowly, carefully, Annie focused on her breathing, on her bum on the seat, the ticking of the kitchen clock. Anything and everything that was solid. Definitively real. She would not give in to this. She could do this. She wasn't Bridget. She'd learn to deal with whatever these premonitions would bring.

Wouldn't she?

※

Lewis left for work, but returned at lunchtime with some sandwiches and coffee.

As they ate, Annie picked their earlier conversation up, trying to show Lewis that she was back on an even keel, that she was able to deal with whatever this curse might mean for her.

'What about the church up in Mossgow?' she asked. 'They still raking in the cash?'

'God, yeah,' Lewis replied. 'Have you been watching them online?'

'No, thanks,' Annie said, making a face. People preaching religion was very much not her thing. 'I'm struggling to imagine me being friends with someone who went on to be a pastor.'

'Far as I can remember, you only had a wee snog. Which is just as well. You were a little younger than he was.'

'What do you remember about him? Was he good-looking?' Annie asked, suddenly curious about this boy from her past. If he was her first kiss, that would have been quite the moment for her, particularly as he was older than her. She imagined that her friends, whoever they were, would have been jealous.

'We were kind of buddies. Played football. Usual boys' stuff. But he disappeared whenever his big cousin, Conor, was about. Like he was embarrassed by me.' Lewis gave a shrug. Ancient history. He was not the kind to bear a grudge, and besides, if there was a deal in the offing for his firm he wouldn't want childhood resentments to get in the way. 'His sister and their mother was nice, but the dad was weird. He gave you the willies.'

Something stirred in Annie's gut. 'Can you remember why?'

Lewis shook his head. 'At the time I just put it down to him being a grown-up, and one that tended to ignore us most of the time.'

'How did you reconnect with Chris?'

'Social media. How else?' He paused. 'Out of the blue. Maybe around a year ago I got his message: *Hi, are you the Lewis Jackson who used to live in Mossgow...* or something like that. We got chatting—'

'You never mentioned it to me,' Annie interrupted, feeling strangely left out.

'I must have. I tell you everything.' Lewis grinned. 'Anyway, social-media algorithms and all that stuff – the next day a clip of him preaching up at the old church appeared on my timeline. You should have seen him, Annie – a natural.' He reached for his phone, paged through a couple of screens and then typed something. 'I've something to ask you,' he added. 'But first, take a look at this.'

'Something to ask me? What?'

'Watch this first,' Lewis insisted. He propped his phone against a mug. 'Then I'll explain.'

Music sounded from the phone, harps and violins playing something that sounded like a Highland lament. Annie expected to see a man in a kilt running into battle; instead the image shown was that of a still loch, an atmospheric sky, a small mountain that was vaguely familiar, then the church. A voice spoke. Welcomed them to that week's service, before the camera panned in on the doors, they opened and to the sound of someone walking, the viewer was escorted inside the church, to a pew in front of the minister. A young man she'd last seen when she herself was only a child. And kissed, apparently.

'That's Chris?' she asked.

Lewis nodded.

He had short, blond hair, wide shoulders, a trim beard and an open and honest gaze that Annie felt herself respond to.

'Wow. He's ... hot,' she said.

Then he began to speak. He spoke of tests and troubles, and overcoming them, using homespun wisdom that she'd heard a million times. He was delivering the familiar and the useful in a highly palatable way. Annie's troubles momentarily forgotten, she managed a laugh. 'Wonder how many marriage proposals he's had.'

Lewis grinned again. 'They arrive every week.'

'Yeah,' she said. 'I can see why this is popular.' She paused. 'And they're making how much?'

Lewis held a hand up. 'Not allowed to give specifics, but it's in the six figures every month.'

An image of the small, white church repeated itself in Annie's mind. Then a patch of earth beyond the building, and she suddenly knew that nothing would grow there because that was where the witches were burned, and then buried.

The knowledge made her gut twist, and she felt her mouth sour. She fought to ignore the feeling and present a neutral expression to Lewis.

'You okay?' he asked, frowning.

'Fine. I'm fine.' She screwed her eyes shut. 'Think I've got a sore head brewing.'

Lewis looked as if he didn't quite believe her. 'Right.' He made a face of sympathy. 'Anyway, my question.' He paused. 'Fancy a wee trip up to Mossgow?'

'Oh.' That wasn't what Annie expected.

'They're filming a special – some kind of anniversary for the church – and they thought it might be cool for some of the old residents to be in the audience.'

'Not a chance,' Annie said. 'Who's going to want to see us?'

'You'd just be in the congregation. Part of a reunion thing.' He sat back in his chair. 'But I got the impression that his sister Danielle was driving the invite. I think she wants to reconnect with her old pal.'

'She does? Why doesn't she reach out via social media like everyone else?'

'Maybe she did and you missed it.'

Maybe she did. Annie was a touch haphazard around social media.

'In any case, I'm not sure I want to go back there,' Annie said. And again her mind was full of the image of the church, that patch of earth, and a feeling of unease. She shuddered. Shuffled some papers. 'Can we get back to Bridget?'

'Okay, let's hear it.' Lewis sat down in front of her.

Annie had been reading and taking notes most of the time Lewis was away. The act of writing things down on a notepad helped her create a little mental distance from the information she was working from. She thought for a moment, assessing the best way to get the information across to Lewis.

'There's all sorts of material in here, and you can read it later if you want, but the essence is that Bridget tried to kill herself three times before going into Oswald House ... that they knew of.'

'Holy moly,' Lewis said. 'Poor woman.'

'Aye,' Annie agreed. 'Her mother, our grandmother, had her sectioned.' Sectioned. Such a cold, flat word on the page. Two syllables that did little to illustrate the emotional pain felt by all those involved.

Lewis slowly took that in, and Annie could tell his thought process was much the same as hers had been. How would that have felt, as a mother, having to do that to your daughter? And how would it have felt, as a daughter, to have your mother do that to you? If, that is, Bridget was capable at the time of such a thought.

'She was placed in Inversnaid Hospital for treatment, which included several drugs, and electric shock therapy. Once she was deemed safe, she was transferred to Oswald House for, I guess, the remainder of her life, or until she appeared able to function without trying to top herself.'

'Wait,' Lewis said, looking concerned. 'Electric shock treatment? Really?'

'Or electroconvulsive therapy, as it's more properly known.'

When Annie had read this she had mental images of the treatment 'patients' received in Hollywood movies. A search on the internet had reassured her that this form of treatment had been refined with modern medicine and was deemed to be highly effective, and, more importantly, safe, when people failed to respond to drug regimens. She explained this to Lewis.

'Still,' he said. 'Seems barbaric.'

'Don't know that I'd fancy it.' Annie wrapped her arms around herself. 'But if it stopped the visions, I might give it a go.'

After a beat, Lewis asked, 'Any good news?'

'Not really.' Annie made a face and pushed at some of the papers in front of her. 'There's lots of reports here of meetings, and assessments of her treatment. They didn't just leave her to rot. They seemed to have people actually looking into her treatment and giving her some standard of care.'

'That's something, at least. Any mention of visitors?'

'Yeah,' Annie nodded. 'I found something about Mum.'

Lewis sat up straight. 'And?'

'It doesn't go into any detail, just that "the patient"' – Annie made quotation marks in the air with her fingers – 'was perceived to be in a low mood after her sister Eleanor came to visit.'

'Not like Mum to bring everything down, eh?' Lewis said, raising his right eyebrow.

'What do you remember about Mum?'

'Bits and bobs,' Lewis replied. 'My over-riding impression was that she was hard on you.'

'She was, wasn't she?' Annie said, feeling pleased and *seen* that Lewis noticed. 'What do *I* remember?' Annie paused as she tried to encapsulate the morass of emotion that surged through her every time she thought of the woman who gave birth to her. She struggled to find the right word. 'Absent. That she was mostly absent.'

Chapter 38

MOIRA MCLEAN – A MEMOIR

It is true that envy can take hold of even the most pious and kind hearts. It's also true that love can play its part in driving even the closest people apart.

Mary and Jean were friends as well as sisters, rarely more than an arm's reach away from each other. But the tale of their separation began with the attentions of a young man – the son of the clan chief no less. And he was a Campbell.

In the normal course of events his family would have arranged a pairing with a woman of means. But the young Mr Campbell had a mind of his own.

Such was the chatter around the shire about the girls' fabled beauty that he came calling one afternoon, on one of those rare days that the girls were apart. Jean had been called to assist with the widow Flora Maclain. And while she was gone Mary answered a knock at her door to find a most becoming young man standing there. Her father was away on one of his travels at this point, many of the men of the village being reduced to piracy following the loss of Castle Mingary and surrounding lands to the McNeils from across the Sound of Mull. Local gossips were of the opinion that the young Mr Campbell chose his time propitiously, that he knew the father would be gone and therefore the girls might be more open to visitors.

The young man claimed to have a cough. She made a tea containing scurvygrass, and while the brew slowly simmered they found themselves talking about life in the surrounding glens.

The next occasion Mr Campbell arrived at their door was under the pretext of needing something to help with a rash. The young lady *at home that day was Jean, but Mr Campbell had no idea he was speaking to the other sister.*

Jean herself was well aware that he believed he was dealing with her sister. But finding the young man to have such a handsome countenance, Jean had no intention of disabusing him of this notion. She found herself responding to the young man's gentle humour and ready smile. There was a kindness in his eyes that was missing from the menfolk in her own family.

That evening, when Mary returned, Jean told her everything, and for a time both women were silent. That they each loved and cherished the other was a given, but they both felt themselves enamoured of the young Campbell.

There was nothing else that would suffice, but that the young man would have the choice of it. At his next visit they would ensure that both were present. They would tell John that he had been separately wooing twins.

John arrived in due course, and with alarming alacrity, Jean thought, he chose her sister Mary. What was it about her that failed to win his heart? she thought. What was it about her sister that won it?

From them on, whenever the lovers were together, Jean made sure she was about and she would study their interactions for particulars that might help her win the young John for herself.

But there was nothing there of ready evidence. It appeared they simply had a spark – a blending of mind and soul that from Jean's perspective could only have come from some sort of alchemy. Was her sister Mary practising the dark arts?

This troubling thought caused Jean no end of consternation, and she devoted herself to discovering the truth.

Chapter 39

Eleanor – Then

Eleanor understood the look Pastor Mosley gave her. He was about to impart some wisdom, so she instantly dropped what she was doing and prepared to listen.

'I sense you're troubled, Eleanor,' Pastor Mosely said as he picked up a large box of cornflakes and added them to a grocery bag that would go on to feed a needy family. She'd told him that she answered to Ellie but he had simply smiled in that understanding way of his and said her given name was so lovely, why shorten it?

She held a hand to her growing belly and shook her head. It was a slight movement. Could she admit to him that her mind was in turmoil?

'I have this life growing inside of me,' she began. 'But I don't know if I have the strength to carry it through.' To her surprise, tears sprang into her eyes and slid down her cheeks. She hadn't realised she was that upset until he had spoken.

He guided her over to a seat in a quiet corner of the hall. 'To question such things is only human. And you are human, are you not?'

'Sometimes barely that,' she answered. 'Feels like I'm nothing but a womb on legs. I'm just here to provide nourishment to this … succubus.'

She started to cry again. Until the words hit the air she had no idea that this was the way she felt. And, how unfeeling, unhuman, was she that she would have these thoughts? And how was this man always able to illicit such honesty from her? 'Listen to me,' she said. 'I'm awful.'

She bent her head and gave in to her emotions. While she cried the pastor simply sat by her side and patted her hand. Once she'd calmed a little he began to speak again.

'Usually the things that upset us so greatly are linked to troubles we had as a child. What parallels do you see between this situation' – he looked down at her belly – 'and your life as a young girl?'

'My own mother,' Eleanor replied after a long pause. 'I never felt loved. Only tolerated. My mother had three daughters, when she only wanted sons. Of course, now I know why – this family's curse. But growing up I felt that I was such an unlovable child. And that little girl is still here.' She tapped on the side of her head, then her hand faltered over her heart. 'She still cries out for that motherly affection while knowing it will never arrive.' She paused to wipe her face with a sleeve. 'And I worry that this is the kind of mother that I will be to my own child.' The next few words formed in her mind only. She couldn't speak them. She feared her child would contain within herself the seed of the family madness. And knowing what Bridget had done to herself to try and escape, she was terrified that a daughter would live a life so full of fear and shame that she'd also be driven to terrible acts to silence the voices.

She remembered holding Bridget's hand while waiting for an ambulance. And if she hadn't come home early from work that day – well, she didn't like to think what might have happened.

The moment she'd opened the door to their childhood home she knew something was wrong. There was an energy, or, more, a lack of energy that something in her brain picked up on. Her mother would be at work, and so would her older sister, Sheila. Bridget at that point was unemployed, so Ellie expected her to be cross-legged on the sofa in the living room, eyes focused on a novel, a curtain of dark hair hiding her face. When she was sure of who'd entered the room and was ready to see them, Bridget would lift her head, eyes focused in that off-centre way of hers, and nod. Give a quiet smile, followed by an enquiry about how their day had been. If Ellie was ever to reciprocate with a question about Bridget's day, it would be ignored, another question being asked instead. No one kept themself to themselves like B.

The sofa was empty. So was the kitchen and the entire downstairs.

'Bridget?' Ellie remembers shouting up the stairs. Nothing. Certain something was off, she'd bounded up, two stairs at a time, and gone to the bedroom she shared with Bridget.

It was empty.

Slow, tremulous steps – now she was certain something was wrong – took her to the bathroom. She pushed the door open to reveal a sight she would never forget.

It revealed itself to her in moments.

A head of dark hair at the foot of the bath, face to the wall, as if framed there by shame. An arm, still clothed, sleeve pulled back to the elbow, lying along the lip of the bath, while bright, life-stealing blood dripped down the white wood of the bath surround.

Mindless of the pool of blood, Ellie had fallen to her knees by her sister. Screamed in her face. Pushed at her shoulder. Shouting, screaming, 'Bridget. Bridget!'

A knife was on the floor. A kitchen knife. And next to it a small, plastic bottle lay open on its side.

How Ellie knew what to do was anyone's guess, but some kind of instinct took over. She grabbed a towel, wrapped it round the bleeding wrist, then she grabbed Bridget by the chin with one hand, and with the other she stuck fingers down the back of her sister's throat until she vomited.

Then, fearful about having to leave Bridget, she'd torn downstairs to the house phone and dialled 999.

A calm, professional voice told her someone would be right there. Ellie ran back to wait by her sister's side.

'What did you do, Ellie?' Bridget asked, her voice a desperate croak. And in the pleading of her eyes Eleanor could see that this was no cry for help; but rather her sister now found the idea of living more terrifying than the fact of dying.

Ignoring this plea, Ellie spoke in soothing tones. 'You're going to be okay. We'll sort this. You're going to be fine.'

Bridget shook her head, a movement that seemed to take minutes not moments. 'You don't understand. No one ... understands.'

'You can't die, B,' Ellie said. 'You can't. I won't let you.'

Her sister's voice growing ever weaker as the sound of the siren grew stronger, she prayed that the medics would arrive before Bridget's last breath.

Only when the paramedics had taken Bridget away did Ellie phone her mother, and with her mother screaming in her ear, she noticed her hands were covered in Bridget's blood. She ran to the kitchen, turned on the tap and scrubbed at her skin until it was pink and raw. A fevered action that fed her nightmares for the rest of her life. Then she waited for her mother to come home and take them to the hospital.

And in that agony of waiting her mind replayed the answers from Bridget to her question, 'Why?'

'The murmurs,' Bridget replied. 'The knowing.' She closed her eyes, looking momentarily at peace. Then a new fright made them shoot open. They looked into Eleanor's eyes, pleading. Begging something.

Forgiveness? Why would Bridget want Eleanor to forgive her?

'It's the faces,' Bridget looked away. Exhausted. 'Of the soon-to-be dead. So many faces. And the murmurs of their dying.' She looked back to Eleanor. 'Why did you stop me, Ellie? I don't deserve...' Whatever she was about to say next died on her tongue. She screwed her eyes shut. Opened them again, searched Eleanor's face for understanding. 'You should have let me die, Ellie.'

Chapter 40

Annie – Now

Lewis pushed his chair back from the kitchen table. Stood up, and stretched his back.

'Does any of this help you?' Lewis asked, nodding down at all the information they'd been sent.

'A little,' Annie replied after a moment's thought. Why was she doing this? Why was she interested in this woman she'd never met? As she continued to speak she allowed her thoughts to voice themselves, hoping that hearing the words aloud would help her make sense of what was going on in her head.

'I'm looking for a way to deal with this thing,' she said, 'other than staying at home all day, avoiding other human beings so I won't have the fear of these horrible whispers telling me about some poor stranger's imminent death.'

Lewis grimaced in sympathy.

'It's the certain knowledge, and the murmuring voices that come with it.' She held one hand over the other to disguise the trembling. 'But I'm also getting more and more curious about our family.'

They sat in silence for a long minute.

'What else would help?' Lewis asked, and she loved that he was so willing to support her.

'Bridget died. But what happened to Sheila? We know – well, I *knew* –she also had cancer. Lots of people survive that with good treatment. Is she alive? If so, where is she?' she paused. Made a face. 'I'm just trying to get a sense of what I'm up against, you know? It drove my aunt and my great-gran crazy.' She felt a wobble at that thought. A desire to hide from the rest of humanity for the remainder of her life. She set her jaw. She would not give in to her fears. 'One of the things that I noticed from reading the notes is that in the last year of Bridget's life there was little mention of her "episodes", as the nuns called them, but prior to that it was mentioned regularly. Maybe the medications she was on dampened the part of her brain that provided the premonitions?'

'I should read one of the notes about her episodes,' Lewis said.

'Why would you want to?'

'So I can get a sense of what you're going through.'

'Isn't what I tell you about what happens to me enough?' Annie bristled, and then held up a hand. 'Sorry.'

'No.' Lewis took the hand. 'I do hear what you're going through. And I'm trying to understand it. It's just that the words of a medical professional might give me a different perspective.'

'What, and tell you that I am crazy?'

'You're not crazy, okay?' He sat back in his chair. 'If you don't want me to read it, then that's fine.'

Annie reached forward, leafed through some papers, and handed one to Lewis. 'Here. This looks like an excerpt from a book.' She made a decision. 'I need some fresh air. I'm going out for a walk.' She grimaced. 'Ignoring anyone I might meet. Read it while I'm out. And...' She thought back to their visit to Oswald House. 'That nun we met. We know she lied to us. See if you can find anything in here that might tell us why.'

Chapter 41

Inversnaid Mental Hospital. 18th August, 1994
Patient: BB
Interviewer: Dr Lindsey Patricks

BB initially presented well. She was happy to drink the tea I provided for her and was willing to engage in small talk. This was our third session in as many weeks, and the first in which it appeared that she was not reluctant to be here. The pattern, well established, was for her to sit wordlessly when she was guided in by the nursing staff and to ignore any offer of a beverage that I might make. As an aside, the nursing staff who brought her over to the office were all well experienced, and most of them had seen all manner of behaviour from their patients, but I had noted a reserve from them when they brought BB to me, and what I can only describe as a rush to be away from us as soon as they arrived. As if they didn't want to spend any more time with her than was necessary.

On this occasion, once BB was seated on the soft chair in front of me, I ventured to ask her how she felt she was cared for by the nursing staff.

'They leave me alone, I leave them alone,' she answered, while looking down at the coffee table in front of her.

'When you say leave you alone, what do you mean?'

'Look it up in the dictionary,' she said.

'Are they unkind in any way?'

She shook her head. I left a silence. She neglected to fill it, so I changed the subject.

'I believe your doctors increased your drugs last week. How has that made you feel?'

'Sleepy.' A half-smile flitted across her lips, as if this mental state was a welcome one.

'Have you had any more episodes?'

'Episodes' was a word we landed on that aided discussion. Bridget was apt to use more colourful words, such as 'visions', which offered a validity to her experiences that I was careful to avoid in order that it didn't impact on the tone of my research.

'It's been a good week,' she replied.

'What do you mean by that?'

'Death has been absent from my thoughts,' she replied after a long pause. Her words struck me as odd – she was rarely this formal in her speech. She was of course referring to her belief that she could tell the imminent death of someone in her presence.

I told her she looked relaxed and it was nice to see her so. She didn't reply.

I determined that this might be a good place to recommence talking about her episodes and I asked her when they started.

'Just after my first period,' she replied.

'What else was happening in your life around that time?'

'Nothing. School. My mother was a pain, but what's new? My sisters had their friends and didn't bother with me, so I was left pretty much to do as I wanted.'

'In what way was your mother a pain? And where was your father?'

'Dad died,' she replied with a faraway look. 'Or Mum would never have got away with making us visit our gran in the loony bin so many times.' She smiled here. A first full smile, but it didn't reach her eyes. 'Ironic, eh?' She looked around the room. 'It was an attempt to scare us.'

'Scare you? Why?'

She declined to answer verbally. Gave me a look to say, *isn't it obvious*? 'This is nicer. More modern. The place she was in was like something out of a Dickens novel.'

I noted that this must have been quite the experience for a young woman.

She pursed her lips. Exhaled. And I could see that she was back in that moment. A scared little girl. 'It's been worse since,' she said. Then she looked me in the eyes for the first time. 'Much worse.'

I was able to observe that when she looked at me she inhaled as if experiencing some trepidation at the thought: that she was forcing herself to look me in the face. Then she relaxed at some internal signal, and said, 'You're okay. You're not going to die anytime soon.'

I asked her why she found it difficult to look directly at me.

'Because that's when I see it, and hear it. If something bad's going to happen to a person, their face changes, and I see…' she shrugged as if she was sure I wouldn't believe her '…through the skin, right down to the bones, and the voice, the murmurs, tell me how they are going to die.'

I will summarise one of the first manifestations of BB's episodes, which is detailed in her hospital file, dated April 1992. BB caused quite a fuss in the ward, and the noise of her screams and her physical thrashing necessitated sedation. It seemed that a young nurse, by the name of Tracy Dobell, was serving up BB's daily medication when BB became agitated. It was reported later that BB appeared to be terrified – that was the word used by the member of staff, 'terrified' – of Tracy. Screaming that she should keep away. Tracy fought to console BB. Took her by the hand and waited to see if she would calm down, but she became worse, even more agitated. And a distraught Tracy noted in the file a few days later that BB was so hysterical her words at times were unintelligible, but what she could make out was that BB was warning her against going on holiday. Over and over, Bridget said to her, 'Don't go, don't go, don't go.'

As it happens, Tracy had that morning booked to go on holiday somewhere in the Mediterranean with her fiancé in the summer. (How BB could have ascertained this we have no way of knowing – a cynic might suggest that perhaps she overheard Tracy talking with another member of staff.) In any case Tracy was so disturbed by what BB said that she cancelled her trip, despite the fact she would lose a substantial deposit.

Instead, her and her fiancé hired a car and decided to tour the West Highlands of Scotland.

There was a break in the script in order to display a photograph. A young man looked out from the page, his image in the manner of police mugshot. Above the image a newspaper headline cried out: 'Edward Trainer Found Guilty of the Murder of the Young Nurse, Tracy Dobell'.

*

As soon as Annie returned, Lewis waved the pages of the excerpt in the air. 'This is fascinating. And then there's this.' He reached for his laptop and turned it so Annie could read the screen. It displayed a page from the BBC website:

> Convicted murderer Edward Trainer was released today after serving the full term, without parole, of the sentence he was given when he was found guilty of murdering his fiancée, Tracy Dobell, during a holiday in the Highlands. Mr Trainer has maintained his innocence throughout his term, which is why he never received parole. He has expressed his relief to be out of prison and his frustration that the real killer of 'the love of his life is still out there, probably murdering other innocent young women'.
>
> Ms Dobell's mother is distraught that their daughter's convicted killer is being released. In a recent interview she said, 'This man is a danger to our daughters and he is still of an age

when he could cause more damage, while my daughter didn't get to have a life. She was an amazing young woman, caring, and by all accounts a wonderful professional. I miss her every day. Her father and I will never recover from this and to see this man getting out of prison is forcing us to relive all that trauma. He should remain in prison for the rest of his life.'

They both sat in silence as they absorbed what they'd learned.

'Jesus,' Lewis said. His vision drifted off out of the window, and then he turned to Annie. 'That poor woman. Just to help me get my head around this, and what you have to put up with: how much of this woman's murder would Bridget have seen?'

Annie held her brother's gaze, thought of the detail that she experienced when learning about someone's fate. She took a long, slow breath, and then answered, 'Enough.'

Feeling uncomfortable with the sympathy in Lewis's face, Annie looked back at the laptop, and read some more.

'Wait,' she pointed at the screen. 'This was last year. He got out just last year.' Her eyes narrowed. 'He's the one live person we know who can report on how Bridget actually was.'

'Well, only second-hand,' Lewis said. 'And why? What are you thinking?'

'I wonder if he'd be happy to talk to us...'

Chapter 42

Eleanor – Then

Eleanor paused at the huge doorway, took a step back onto the red gravel that surrounded the building like a moat and looked up at the rows of windows. The glass gave nothing away, blinking blankly back at her in the crisp winter sunshine, no sign of life beyond their frames. She shivered. This didn't auger well for her visit to see Bridget.

She was on the point of turning away and trekking back to the gate and the bus stop, but the door opened.

A nun appeared.

'Hello, dear,' she said. 'Visiting hours are about to start if you want to come in.'

'Thanks,' she said, and swallowed. What was she doing here? Bridget wouldn't want to see her. Instead of thanking her for saving her life, she was probably cursing her.

'Reception is just inside. Let them know who you're coming to see and they'll direct you to where you need to go.'

'It's okay,' Eleanor replied. 'My mum was here the other day and she told me where I could find ... her.' Strangely, saying Bridget's name out loud to this perfect stranger felt disloyal. Like an acknowledgment of her sister's failings.

Here, from what her mother told her, was a mental-health facility. The local hospital had seen to Bridget until she was no longer at risk, and she'd stay in Oswald House, her mother had said, her long fingers twisting the gold chain she always wore around her neck, until she was no longer a risk to herself. However long that may be. Her words were laced with shame and a sense of inevitability. She'd witnessed what the curse had done to her own mother, and now, to prove her fears, it had also sent her daughter insane.

'That was why I took you to that damned place to visit my mother so regularly. To scare you out of having children of your own. And yet...' she had bit her lip '...here we are.'

The institution Eleanor and her sisters had visited with their mother was not unlike Oswald House. Similar-shaped building, same colour of stone, and rows and rows of windows.

Each time they went, the girls would hang around the doorway, reluctant to enter the room, afraid that whatever afflicted their grandmother would be carried to their brains on her breath.

On most visits their grandmother was an unresponsive shell, sharp points of cheekbones, chin, elbows and knees arranged under a blanket, eyes as blank as a powered-off TV screen.

Eleanor understood now that her grandmother had been heavily sedated, but at the time the vision of this woman, deathly still, and staring sightless at the space directly in front of her, was chilling to a little girl. Who wouldn't see that, and knowing this woman was related to them, wonder if that might be their own future?

There were a couple of occasions when the drugs hadn't been administered in the correct dosage, or at the correct time perhaps, because they wore off halfway through their visit. On one such visit, their grandmother began weeping, begging for the voices to be silenced. 'The murmuring. It never stops,' she said. Then she rose from her chair and reached for Eleanor. 'You, girl,' she beseeched. 'Get them to stop.' Eleanor remembered her grandmother gripping the collar of her sweater.

'Mum,' Eleanor cried. 'Mum. What's she doing?'

A nurse appeared and tried to pull her grandmother away, but she hung on tight.

'Mum,' Eleanor shouted, and tried to tug her clothing out of her grandmother's grip.

The old woman fell to her knees. 'Get them to stop!' she screamed.

Released from capture Eleanor turned, fled the room and ran down the corridor to the first exit she could see, her grandmother's screams chasing her all the way.

Now, here in Oswald House, Eleanor picked her way through corridors and upstairs, following the directions to Bridget's room the nun at reception had given her. And as she went deeper into the building, a memory of what her mother had said to her earlier that day grew louder in Eleanor's mind.

She'd looked down at Eleanor's extended belly, her mouth a ruthless, tight line. 'God forgive me but you should get rid of it.'

'Mother,' Eleanor exclaimed, while holding a hand to her abdomen, unable to admit she'd had the same thought.

'Or wait until you know what it is, and if it's a girl...'

'Mother,' Eleanor repeated. 'Please do not talk about my baby like that ever again.'

'...drown it,' her mother said, and jumped to her feet as if trying to distance herself from the violation of her words. 'You can't bring another child into the world, Eleanor. Our line has to die out. You know it makes sense.'

❋

Sheltering her bump behind both hands, as if the very air in this building could contaminate it, she found herself on the second floor of Oswald House, at the nurses' station, being pointed in the direction of Bridget's room.

She approached the open door slowly, as if nearing a bed of bracken and a wounded fawn. Peering round the door frame she took a good look at the room where her sister might spend the rest of her life.

It was a decent size and a standard hospital bed jutted out into the middle, Bridget a long, thin line under the quilt, her head off to one side. A small chest of drawers sat in the far corner, a TV set on the surface. Other than that and the bed, the only pieces of furniture were a pair of striped, pink armchairs. A door to her right must be the bathroom.

'We're just getting her used to the medication,' the nurse who'd told her where to find her sister had said. 'So don't be alarmed if she's not too responsive at the moment. She may well be sleepy.'

'Hey, Bridget,' Eleanor said, and even to her own ears her voice sounded brittle. She cleared her throat and stepped across the room to one of the chairs. 'It's me,' she said. 'Eleanor.' She sat, knees tight together, every muscle prepared for judgement, and flight.

Bridget's head lay to the side, her mouth slightly open, and Eleanor recalled the first time it became apparent that her sister was 'infected', as her mother called it, with this ability to see the death of those around her.

She'd been around six – Eleanor herself was approaching ten – and Bridget had been singing about Mary Queen of Scots getting her head chopped off.

'That's a horrible song,' their mother protested. 'Where did you learn that?'

Eleanor and Sheila, who liked the nice little tune and had thought nothing of the words, both stepped back from the vehemence in their mother's voice.

'It's a nursery rhyme, isn't it?' Sheila answered on Bridget's behalf. She was always the first to stand up to their mother. 'You sing it while you hold a dandelion and then you pop its head off.'

'Like Daddy,' Bridget said, as if the truth had just been revealed to her. She was standing in front of the coffee table on which stood a pair of framed photos of their father. One was a group photo. He was the one white face in a sea of African faces. 'Like Daddy got his head chopped off.'

They all looked at Bridget in horror. She stood stock-still in front of the photo, her mouth open, her eyes bright at the horror of whatever her mind was now presenting her with.

'Bridget,' their mother scolded, and swept up their now hysterical sister.

Afterwards she'd simply brushed it off as the mental workings of a highly imaginative child. But Bridget was persistent, or at least her imagination was, and from then on she regularly woke up having had a nightmare about their father having no head.

Finally, in an effort to stop her night terrors, their mother gave them the unbridled facts. While helping in a French mission in Algeria, a group of fundamentalist Muslims had attacked and decapitated all of the holy men who worked there.

Quite how Bridget had ascertained this fact was not at the time available for discussion. When pressed on the matter by Sheila, their mother fudged an answer, saying she expected that she'd overheard her talking with a friend.

But you don't have any friends, Eleanor remembered Sheila saying, with the same brutal honesty their mother would use. This earned Sheila an early night without supper.

Eleanor was plucked from her memories by the sight of Bridget stirring in the bed.

She opened her eyes, and a smile formed itself on her lips as if in slow motion. 'Eleanor,' she said, the word falling from her mouth in a series of too-long syllables. 'Look good,' she said, her eyes almost slipping down her face. She swallowed, made a visible effort to rouse herself, looked towards Eleanor's stomach. 'Showing ... wee bit ... now.'

Eleanor was swamped with relief that Bridget appeared to be friendly towards her and clearly didn't hold her attempt to save her life against her. She pointed at the control at the side of the bed.

'Can I prop you up a wee bit?' she asked.

Bridget nodded. Her tongue edged out from between her cracked lip, slid slowly from one side to the other and moistened them. 'Please,' she managed.

Once the bed had risen enough for Bridget and Eleanor to look at each other comfortably, Eleanor sat back down.

'Friends?' Eleanor asked.

Bridget's cheeked bunched in a smile. 'Course.' She hiccupped a laugh. 'Silly.' Then she looked again at Eleanor's small bump. 'How long?'

'I'm thirteen weeks,' Eleanor said.

Then Bridget asked the question Eleanor was dreading. 'Do you know? Boy? Girl?'

Eleanor shook her head wordlessly, trying to convey that she didn't want to know until the very last minute.

Bridget then surprised her. Tears sprang into her eyes and trailed down the pale silk of her cheeks, and her hand strayed to her own stomach and hovered over it, her mouth open in a long but silent cry of anguish.

Chapter 43

Annie – Now

It was a week or so since Lewis had uncovered the story of Edward Trainer, and Annie had a photo of the man in her hand as she watched people exit the building she was parked in front of.

When she had said to Lewis what she planned to do, he immediately tried to argue her out of it.

'Are you mad? This guy's a convicted murderer. Why on earth would you want to meet him?'

'Tracy Dobell is the only person, apart from that stupid nun, that we know of who met Bridget. The only one who experienced her having one of her visions. I need to talk to him to find out if she told him anything about it.'

'You do? Really?'

'Yes. Really.' Part of her quailed at the prospect, but a bigger part of her was driven to know. 'I'll be perfectly safe. You'll be with me.'

'But you'll have brought yourself to his attention. An actual murderer. Not a good idea.'

'It will be fine. We'll just rock up at wherever he's living, talk to him when he's out and about in public. Appear sympathetic.' She made a face as she thought how difficult that might be. 'And find out what he knows.'

'Wherever he's living' was where they presently sat. Clearly realising Annie wasn't going to be persuaded out of her plan, Lewis had made some investigations and traced Trainer to this down-at-heel bed and breakfast in Ayrshire, between Prestwick and Troon, facing a beach. A grand entrance suggested it had seen better days, but even from the car park they could see that the paint was flaking from the window frames, there were a couple of windows on the top of the second floor that had been boarded up with cardboard, and the guttering held a number of plants.

'Thank you for all of this,' said Annie. 'I know you were struggling with the whole notion of me wanting to talk to Trainer. How did you find this place?'

'I found an article in the *Herald*. After Trainer's release a journalist traced him here, took a snap and published it along with an exposé of our' – he performed air quotes – '"rotten criminal justice system".' He paused. 'I saw the photo, looked at the building behind Trainer, did an online search for comparisons, and voilà.' He held a hand out, palm up in the direction of the B&B.

'Get you, Miss Marple.'

'If accounting doesn't work out for me, maybe I'll get a job tracking down released murderers.' He paused, looked meaningfully at his sister and added, 'I also looked into Trainer's background.'

Annie tore her gaze from the front door. 'And?'

'Most of the papers covered the trial. It was big news, back in the day.' He raised both eyebrows. 'They never found her body, you know?'

'Really?'

Lewis nodded. 'A murder case without a body? That suggests a shit-ton of circumstantial evidence was used to help put him away.'

'Did the papers manage to provide details?'

'Several witnesses came forward to say that they'd seen them arguing that morning. And various other times during their holiday. Our Mr Trainer is a man with a temper, apparently. There were broken objects in one of their hotel rooms. Crockery and the like that hotel staff said had clearly been thrown. Old girlfriends testified that he was shouty and would throw things but that he never actually harmed any of them. The prosecution used that to suggest his anger then escalated to murder.' He blew at his hands, and rubbed them together. 'Shit, it's cold even before we leave the car.'

'Anything else in this shit-ton of circumstantial evidence?' Annie asked.

Lewis nodded. 'Blood in a hotel bathroom, in the hire car, and on a piece of Trainer's clothing. He said that she was prone to nose bleeds. But there was nothing in her medical records to back that up.'

They both sat in silence, Annie thinking about the man she was about to engage in conversation. Until now he was an abstract, but hearing all of that from Lewis made her rethink what she was doing. Should she approach him?

Before she could make her decision the main door opened, and a man came out.

'That's him,' Annie said, and jumped out of the car. A man resembling the image she'd downloaded from the internet stood before the main door, shrugged his arms into his sleeves, buttoned up his coat, and turned to his left, without raising his eyes from the ground.

'Annie.' Lewis joined her on the pavement at her side of the car. 'What's the plan?' he asked in a low tone. 'You can't just walk up to the guy.'

'I'm thinking we can follow him. See where he goes, and once there are other people around, we approach him.'

Lewis looked up to the sky and shoved his hands into his pockets. 'Fucking freezing,' he announced. Then under his breath, 'I must be mad,' before taking several steps in the same direction as Trainer.

A man coming towards them nodded to Trainer as he passed him. Then carried on up the steps to the building, pulled open the door and went inside.

Lewis stopped for a moment and stared at the door as it swung shut.

'What is it?' Annie asked Lewis, impatient to be following their target.

'That guy...' Lewis screwed up his face in puzzlement. 'He looks like someone I used to know. Remember Conor Jenkins?' he asked. Then answered his own question. 'Course you don't. He's Chris Jenkins' cousin.' He shook his head. 'Nah. Couldn't be. No way that guy would end up in a place like this.'

'Lewis, would you come on?' Annie urged, walking away. 'We don't want to lose Trainer.'

He jogged to catch up with Annie, and a few minutes later they were walking along a wide tarmac pavement, windblown sand in wet, rust-coloured drifts heaped against the low beachside wall, on the other side waist-high marram grass scratched up from the dunes, before a stretch of sand, and a dull, calm sea. Looking ahead they only saw more of the same.

'Come to the seaside for the views,' Lewis said with a small laugh. To his right, beyond the wall, the tide was in, and the water was a murky, lazy grey. The clouds were low over the sea and nothing was visible on the horizon. 'I usually like this part of the coast.' He cocked his head. 'But it's like the Isle of Arran has vanished.'

'What do you make of him so far?' Annie said in a hush.

'Big coat. Head ducked down. Fairly sensible in this cold weather.'

They walked in silence for a time.

A couple with a dog passed them. The dog stopping to sniff Annie's hand.

'Lovely day,' Annie offered the couple.

'Aye,' the man said. Then added, 'But the rain's no' far away.'

And on the couple and their dog marched, moments later overtaking Trainer. Annie saw him respond, nodding his head in greeting as the couple walked by.

Ahead, Annie could see a low building, with large windows facing out to sea, a pair of tables with chairs just outside the door. Someone was hunched over on one of the chairs, in a thick, padded jacket, hands wrapped round what Annie guessed might be a cup of coffee. A blue sign at the side of the path suggested there were also toilets ahead.

'Need a pee or a coffee?' Lewis looked at Annie, eyebrows raised. 'I'm hoping Trainer pops in.'

He didn't. He walked straight past.

'Bastard,' Lewis said.

'Bet he stops on the way back.'

'In that case, why don't we just wait here? He's going to have to come back this way, isn't he? No point in me freezing my nuts off when I could be in there with a nice, hot java. And, if your man is of a suspicious nature, it makes it look like the coffee was our reason for being here.'

Annie nodded and they went inside, feeling a welcome blast from the heater at the door as they entered. Annie took a seat at a table by the window while Lewis put their orders in at the counter.

The order soon arrived, and they settled in to wait for their target's return.

Twenty minutes later, and not one more person had come into the café , or indeed had walked past outside. The girl behind the counter had settled into her chair, head down as she studied her phone.

Then, an icy blast as the door opened and someone entered. Trainer.

The girl looked up, offered a half-smile. 'The usual, Eddie?'

'Please.'

'Sitting in?'

'Please.'

Annie studied the coffee server for any kind of reaction. She seemed perfectly relaxed and only mildly more interested in Trainer than she had been in Lewis. She couldn't have any idea who he really was.

There were only three other tables in the small space, and Trainer took a seat at the one furthest from her and Lewis. Out of the corner of her eye she watched as he took off his coat, placed it over the shoulder of the chair and sat down. Once seated he reached around to pull a small paperback from the inside pocket of his jacket and placed it on the table in front of him.

'Good book that,' she heard Lewis say. She recognised the cover, it was a book she'd enjoyed herself, a massive bestseller about a young girl growing up on her own among the marshlands of the American Deep South.

Trainer nodded.

He was smaller than she'd imagined, his face was puffy and pale, his dirty-blond hair washed through with grey. Lines scoured his face, and he looked a good deal older than the early fifties suggested by the report on the BBC.

'*Where the Crawdads Sing*,' Lewis added. 'It's a movie now, I believe. Not sure I want to risk seeing it. The movie is never an improvement on the book.'

Trainer's eyes flitted across the room at them, skimming over their faces before returning to rest on the cover of the book. 'Aye,' he said, and opened it, placing the bookmark he'd been using squarely by the side of the book. This seemed an oddly precise movement, and Annie wondered what it might say about him.

Once Trainer had been served his coffee and cake, Lewis tried to engage him in conversation again.

'We heard about this place and had to try it,' he said. 'Coffee's pretty good, even if we're off the beaten track.'

Annie noticed Trainer close his eyes, briefly, before answering. 'Yeah.'

Lewis sent Annie a look and a shrug, as if to say, what next? Annie exhaled and said under her breath, 'For God's sake.' She got to her feet and moved across the room. Ignoring Lewis's spluttered 'Annie!' she sat on the chair to Trainer's left.

Immediately she sat down he reared back in his seat. 'I don't speak to reporters.'

Annie held a hand up. 'I'm sorry to bother you. I know you just want to read your book and drink your coffee in peace...'

Trainer stood up, lifted his book and made to put his coat back on. He then looked over at the waitress as if expecting her help.

Hurriedly, Annie spoke. 'My name is Annie Jackson. My aunt was a patient of your fiancée's. She was...' she waved her hands about, trying to come up with the right words '...some kind of psychic and warned Tracy about going on that holiday.'

Edward Trainer just stood there, staring down at Annie, his expression unreadable, but she could tell his mind was elsewhere; somewhere in the past.

'I know this might sound weird, and I'm sorry if I'm intruding, but I read the social-work reports, and Tracy was one of the few people we know of who experienced my aunt's gift, and I wondered if she told you about it. Sorry, I'm babbling, but I'm desperate.'

Trainer was quiet for a long moment. His eyes moved from the far distance to Annie's face. She dared to meet his gaze, terrified of what she might find there, but saw nothing other than a lost and lonely man looking back.

Now that she was close to him she could see that he carried his own cloud with him; sadness coloured every inch of his skin and cast the light from his eyes in melancholy. But there was a guardedness about him, an attempt to protect himself from those who might fear, or indeed, pity him. Life in prison had hollowed him out, left nothing but a husk.

He swallowed, looked into her eyes and said, 'You've got it too, then, eh?'

'Excuse me?' Annie asked.

'This psychic ability you talked about. You've got it too.' It was a statement. He'd read her perfectly.

Suddenly frightened, she took a step back. Whatever else he might be, he was no fool. But then what he'd actually said fully sank in, and she realised it had come as no surprise to him. 'Wait. She told you?' she said. 'Tracy told you and you remember.'

'That's all I have left,' he said, his eyes sinking deeper into his face. 'Memories.'

'If you could tell us everything you remember about what Tracy told you, that would be great,' Lewis said as he sat down beside Annie. Trainer gave him a guarded look. 'I'm Lewis. Annie's brother,' he added.

Trainer looked back at Annie and sat down. 'This thing,' he said. 'It tells you when and how people are going to die?'

Annie nodded.

'How does it work?'

She was impatient for him to tell her about Tracy, but wanted to keep him talking, so took a breath and said: 'It starts with a sound in my ears. A low kind of murmuring. Then the face I'm looking at goes funny, kinda *shivers*, if that makes sense. Then I see the bones of their skull, and hear this hateful voice, which goes on and on and on.' She shivered. 'And I just know that person is going to die. And how.' Annie crossed her arms, feeling sick at the thought of the next visitation from her curse.

'Is my face doing anything?' he asked, hope temporarily lifting his expression.

Annie shook her head, slowly. 'There's nothing coming to me.'

'Right,' he said in a small, disappointed voice. He sat back in his chair. Faced Annie. 'What do you want to know?'

Chapter 44

Edward – Then

Edward was at the kitchen sink, peeling potatoes, when he heard the front door close as Tracy arrived home. He was expecting her usual chat about how her day had been, but when he turned around to greet her, she burst into tears.

'Tracy, what's wrong, honey?' Edward asked. He knew that working at Oswald House was tough on her, but she always managed to lighten her tone as she told him what went on, playing down any upset she might have felt. Not this time though. This day, she was inconsolable. And scared. Trembling when he took her in his arms. He could smell the hospital on her hair as he tried to calm her. After a long minute of tears, he took her by the hand into the living room, sat her down and asked her to begin again.

With her free hand she wiped the tears from her face. 'God, you'll think I'm such an idiot, but it was so scary. This woman was terrifying. She kept saying over and over again, "Don't go, please don't go."'

'Don't go where?' Edward asked, mystified. 'And who is this woman? What exactly did she say?'

'Bridget. She's a patient. I've mentioned her before. We get on so well...' Edward smiled. Tracy thought everyone was lovely. 'She just seems so lost.'

'And?'

Tracy sucked on her bottom lip, in that way she did when she was thinking. It was so endearing, Edward had to resist the temptation to lean across and kiss her cheek. 'She'd not long been there when whispers began about her, among the staff and patients, that she was a wee bit touched.'

'Touched? Couldn't they say that about everyone in there?'

'Well, yes,' she replied. 'But not in the way they meant it. Fey is a better word. She's a little fey.'

'What? She acts all shy and innocent, or do you mean she sees ghosts an' shit?'

'The latter. Sort of.' Tracy exhaled. Swallowed. 'She can tell when someone is going to die.' She started crying again. 'And how.'

Edward pulled Tracy into a hug and waited until the tears subsided. 'I've got an open mind about stuff, but really? She knows all that?' He felt his chest tighten, and his gut sour. If something happened to Tracy he didn't know what he would do. He shrugged off that thought. It was crazy. 'Ridiculous,' he added. 'Nobody knows that kind of stuff.'

As if fending off his next objection, Tracy looked into his eyes and said, 'She knew we were due to go on holiday. How did she know that?'

'Maybe she overheard you talking to one of the other staff members?'

Tracy shook her head. 'I don't see how that's possible. I might have mentioned it to someone in the staff room, say, but we don't have time for small talk when we're dealing with the patients. At that point it's all about them.'

He was finding this very difficult to believe, but he could see that Tracy had been swayed. He laughed in an attempt to bring levity to the situation. 'You know it sounds crazy, right?'

Tracy gave a little smile of acquiescence. 'Yes, but...'

'Did she say how you were going to die?' He then made a ghostly 'oooo' sound, waving his fingers in her face, trying to get her to laugh.

She looked at him. But she wasn't seeing him, she was back in the room where this happened. 'It was terrifying, Eddie. You had to be there. She was going crazy. Screaming at me, "Don't go, don't go." We had to sedate her, that's how bad it got. She held my hand as the drugs began to work. Wouldn't let me go.' She tucked each hand under an armpit as if keeping them out of reach of anyone else. 'Then she said – and I'll never forget the look in her eyes – she said if I was to go on holiday with the man with the blond hair' – she looked up at Edward's head – 'I'd never come back.'

Chapter 45

Annie – Now

Trainer started sobbing, at which point the waitress came out from behind her counter and faced up to Annie and Lewis.

'If you're tormenting this poor guy you should just leave. It's like he can't even come here in peace. There's always somebody having a go at him.'

'We're not...' Annie began.

Edward lifted his head from the table, wiped the tears from his puffed-up eyes and waved at her. 'It's alright, Emma...'

'Okay,' Emma said with reluctance, and backed away a couple of steps, sending Annie and Lewis a warning look, before turning to go back behind the counter.

'Every day of every month of every year since, I've gone over that conversation with Tracy. If only I had listened to her,' Trainer said.

'But who in their right mind is going to believe that shit,' Lewis said softly. 'It's happening to my sister, in front of my eyes, and I'm struggling to follow it, so it's understandable you had a problem believing these claims.'

'Yeah, but still, she insisted that we cancel our trip to Cyprus and stay at home. So I talked her into going on a tour of the Highlands. It was totally selfish. I'd saved up for two weeks in the sun and if I wasn't going to get that I wanted to get away somewhere.'

'You can't blame yourself.' Annie could see that these what-ifs were haunting this poor man. She reached for his hand but then remembered that 'this poor man' had been convicted by a jury of his peers of the rape and murder of the woman they were talking about, and she stilled her movement.

He offered her a tentative smile of understanding – as if to say *I wouldn't want to touch me either*.

'The holiday was going really well, you know, until the second week. We were somewhere near Fort William, and I wanted to go to Mallaig, via the Glenfinnan memorial, or go through the Great Glen to Inverness. The scenery in that part of the world is spectacular.' He shook his head slowly. 'We'd hired a car – couldn't afford one of my own in those days – and got a puncture, and the spare tyre was flat as well. So I left Tracy in the car and walked down the road – this was around the time mobile phones were becoming popular but I still didn't have one. I was resisting that whole notion of always being within reach.' He shook his head. 'Idiot – if I'd had a phone maybe...' He screwed his eyes shut. 'Anyway, I left Tracy there in the car, thinking that would be the safer thing, away from the traffic, you know...' He paused as if swallowing that irony. 'And I walked back down the road. We'd seen a garage.' His bottom lip trembled. 'By the time I got back with the pick-up truck she was gone.' Trainer wrapped his arms around himself and seemed to disappear into his thoughts – the should-haves and could-haves. He might have been ten thousand miles away from them rather than ten feet.

They all remained quiet, the silence only broken by some customers coming in, and the coffee machine grinding out the orders.

'Eddie.' Annie said his name softly, leaning towards him, hating to pull him out of his reflections, but needing to know. 'Did Tracy know Bridget prior to that incident with her she told you about? Do you know if she had regular contact with her?'

Trainer looked at her as if he'd never seen her until this moment, then his eyes shifted, something uncoiled and he was back in the room. 'Sorry.' He scratched at his forehead. 'Yeah, she had spoken about her before, and she talked about her some during that earlier part of the holiday. Seemed she liked her.' His smile was a wan thing. 'She liked everybody.' He shrugged. 'She felt really sorry for her. Said there was something broken there,

Like she was a lost little girl. But then she'd become angry. So fucking angry. So she had to be sedated.'

'Did Tracy ever say if she got a handle on why Bridget was so angry?'

'The unfairness,' he replied. 'For the most part she was quite lucid. Normal, even, Tracy said, until the anger took over. They were not that far apart in ages, I think, so that made Tracy feel there was some kind of bond, you know? Until the whole "don't go on holiday" thing.'

Annie sat with that for a moment. Bridget's anger. Who wouldn't be angry in that situation? Dumped in a mental hospital. Annie felt a burn of hostility towards her grandmother. How could she have left her daughter there? Surely the threat of suicide could have been handled in a better way.

'For a time that was one of the highlights of her day at work – the wee chats she had with Bridget.'

'What did they talk about?' Annie asked.

'Life in general. Boyfriends, what was on TV. How they wished they got on better with one of their sisters. Tracy's oldest sister and her were always arguing.'

Annie's stomach swirled at the mention of a sister, and guessed that might be her mother. She opened her mouth to ask more about that, when Trainer spoke.

'Anyway, that friendship would have ended,' he said. 'Because a few weeks before our holiday, Tracy moved jobs, to a maternity hospital. But she did go back to see Bridget at Oswald House one more time.'

'Yeah?' Lewis asked.

'Yeah, and she regretted it. Said it was like talking to a different woman. She kept turning away from her, hiding her face. Tracy couldn't figure out what was wrong, you know? But she wanted to know if the change of holiday plans would mean she was safe. That's why she'd gone back.' He shook his head. 'I told her she was crazy – that she'd only be scared again. I mean, what good would it do?'

'And did Bridget offer any other advice? Did she see ... did she start screaming again?' Annie asked.

'No. She barely spoke, apparently. Tracy said she was weirder than ever. Acted like they'd never met, and when she did speak she talked about herself in the third person: "If Bridget told you not to go on holiday, don't go on bloody holiday," she said. Maybe she was more than a bit unhinged after all.'

Chapter 46

Annie – Now

Most of the way back home to Glasgow, the siblings sat in silence, each of them digesting what they'd learned and wondering where to go next.

'Do you think he did it?' Annie asked Lewis as the M77 unspooled in front of them.

'The jury found him guilty.'

'Yeah, like juries never get it wrong.'

'They saw the evidence, to be fair.'

Annie looked across at her brother. 'You don't think he did it either.'

'We're meeting him twenty years after the fact,' he replied. 'He's had a lot of time to perfect his act.'

'Or he's innocent and broken down by guilt about leaving her alone, and the horrors of the prison system.' Annie looked out of the window. 'The waitress was very protective of him.'

'Maybe she wanted to fix him? There's all kinds of stories about women who fall for men on death row in the US. This could be one of those situations.'

'I do feel for the guy,' Annie admitted. 'But I'll be keeping my distance. You know, just in case.'

'What now then?' Lewis took his eyes off the road to look into hers. Annie let out a long, slow sigh.

'We know Bridget died, but we still don't know what happened to Sheila. Did she go back to wherever she was living after that visit to see us and Mum?'

✳

Lewis dropped Annie off at her flat, before going back to his office to catch up on some work.

Once inside, Annie sat in front of the pile of papers on her kitchen table and wondered if any of it had actually helped her understand who she was and how this curse might impact on her ability to have any kind of normal existence. As she was tidying up the pages, she picked up the large envelope they came in and realised there was still something inside. Holding it up, she felt whatever it was slide around. Curious, she tipped it over, and out fell a small bundle of letters, held together by a purple silk ribbon.

With trembling fingers she pulled one of the silk ends, and the knot of the ribbon released.

The first letter was from her grandmother to Bridget. It gave her grandmother's address as King's Park, and in the letter she explained her sorrow, but there was a stiffness in her prose that suggested a woman struggling to explain her real feelings. She begged forgiveness and hoped that Bridget would recover and be back in the bosom of the family as soon as was humanly possible. She then went on:

> In honesty, and you know how I value this aspect of communication, I don't hold out much hope. Your grandmother was similarly cursed, and it broke my heart to see her so damaged. She wasn't much of a mother to me because of it and I truly hope that I've learned from that experience and been more of a mother to you in turn. My advice, darling, take the drugs – ALL the drugs, otherwise this is a condition that will ruin your life.

Annie had to curb her impulse to tear this letter up and throw it in the bin. How cold could her grandmother have been? She tried to imagine herself in Bridget's predicament: torn from her family, being kept among society's most damaged individuals, and receiving a letter like this from someone who should have been able to offer emotional support and sustenance. What a horror show.

Why would Bridget hold on to this? Maybe because it was contact of a sort? Or did she use it as a reminder not to pin any hopes on her mother?

The next letters she picked from the small pile were from her own mother. The handwriting was precise, each letter of each word in its own little space. In her mind's eye she saw her mother, stiff-backed at a table, pen in hand, carefully choosing each word before committing it to ink. There were four letters, spread over six months. They all started, 'Bridget'. No 'Dear Bridget', just 'Bridget'. The first three weren't terribly interesting. Lots of apparent concern. Promises to spend more time visiting. Complaints about their mother.

The fourth letter was where the curtain was pulled to the side and Eleanor allowed herself to be more open:

I pray this letter finds you well and that the terrors are easing in your mind.

Prayer is such a comfort, I'm finding. I've joined a new church, and the pastor here is a man of conviction, a man worth following. I listen to him speaking and feel awe that a human mind can produce such comfort and guidance in so few words, and with such ease. It would take me years to learn such economy. I thank God every day that He brought the pastor into my life.

In any case, I'm writing to explain why you will see (even) less of me from now on. I'm moving away. Pastor Mosley has been transferred to a small town close to Fort William called Mossgow, and I feel that now I'm about to have my own child I should do what I can to protect them from this family, and move. I have a very real fear that I will have a daughter and she will inherit our family curse. But I'm certain with the pastor's guidance and the care of the good Lord, if it does manifest itself in her we will be able to curb it with a life dedicated to prayer. I'm sure you understand why I need to do this. But whenever I'm in town I'll be sure to pop in.

I had considered whether I should skirt over the name of the pastor. Given your current state of affairs that might be the kinder option, but on reflection I feel you should be taken to task. You made terrible accusations against a good and kind man that might have ruined him, and I can't in all conscience ignore that. I hesitate to say you should be ashamed of yourself, but I hope you have plenty of time to reflect on the damage you might have caused.

It was signed, simply, *Eleanor*.

Annie felt a trail of moistness running down her cheek, and wiped it away with a thumb. She hadn't realised she'd been crying. The cold approach of her grandmother explained a lot about her own mother. And for Bridget to have received such communication from her sister as well as from her mother, she must have truly felt abandoned.

And what on earth might the accusations have been against Pastor Mosely? That certainly seemed to have set the sisters at odds. There was no point in speculating though; in Annie's experience the truth was always stranger than any fiction she might come up with.

She went back to the letter, and a word her mother used snagged in her mind.

'Child'.

She'd written about her pregnancy in the singular. Hadn't she known she was going to have twins? Perhaps she hadn't wanted to pay much attention to any prenatal scans, delaying finding out the sex of the baby until the last moment?

As she tidied the pile in preparation for retying them with the silk ribbon she noticed a hard edge among the envelopes. She teased them apart to find a postcard in among them. Where had this come from? Had it been tucked inside one of the letters?

On the front was a standard image of a stretch of golden sand and the sea. It could have been anywhere. On the back, on the right, was Bridget's name and the address of Oswald House. On the left a simple hand-written message. *Sorry you're there, not here.* Under that was a single initial. *B.*

Chapter 47

Eleanor – Then

Eleanor enjoyed the little intellectual challenges Pastor Mosley would set her during their conversations, despite the fact they often made her feel uncomfortable. If we don't challenge our thinking, he'd said to her, how are we ever to develop?

This particular Sunday he suddenly asked, 'Do you understand the concept of shared responsibility?'

Her answer to the pastor's question was a shake of the head. 'Surely, I'm only responsible for the wrong stuff that I do?' she argued.

He nodded as if pleased she'd considered a response. 'Yet, all of us share the punishment for Adam's sin in the Garden of Eden. Accepting responsibility for yourself has its power, but similarly, looking to atone for the sins of those close to us brings understanding, and humility, and that humility allows you to see the world with clear vision, and purpose.'

This sounded like gobbledy-gook to Ellie; how could taking on responsibility for someone else's wrongdoing give her purpose?

'Suicide is a sin in the eyes of the church, is it not?'

Ellie nodded.

'And you yourself argued that you could have been a better sister?'

Ellie barely responded, feeling the weight of her shame.

'Some argue that the moral responsibility is solely on the shoulders of the actor concerned, the person who did the thing. But no one acts entirely alone. The Bible says, "May the iniquity of his fathers be remembered before the Lord and let not the sin of his mother be blotted out." We carry sin with us. The good Lord suggests that none of us exist in a vacuum. All kinds of actions result from a stray word here, a thought there, so how much more important is a neglectful parent, or a sister who turns a blind eye...'

As he said this, his eyes were staring, seeing her laid bare, or so she imagined. She was stripped of artifice, all of her beliefs and faults written on her face available to him to scrutinise and criticise.

She closed her eyes, clenched her fists, braced herself for the further criticism that was surely coming.

'Your sister bears the greater sin, to be sure, but all of you must acknowledge the part you had to play, and learn from it, only then can you move on. Only then can you embrace the next stage of your life and prepare for the sins to come.'

Then, he put a gentle hand on her cheek, from there to the back of her head, and pulled her to him. The skin of her face now on the course wool of his jumper, the warmth of his body apparent, she felt the depth of his forgiveness, and surprised at the weight of her relief, she wept.

Chapter 48

Annie – Now

Even on that pillowed bridge between sleep and wakefulness Annie was aware of the harsh jitter of her anxiety. *There is only now*, the dream voice told her. *We know this with a certainty as deep as any pit we've visited in hell. Yesterday and tomorrow all blend into one experience of existence. Action born of reaction. This moment and the then-moment, a continuous chain of thought, of knowing. That's why, when the girl is born, when she's given to her mother, she sees the woman she becomes, in them and from them and between them, and knows, knows, knows her mind is pliable, as are, were, all the ones before, during, and after, all at once. Pliable, pitiful, wearing their fear like a straitjacket, and we'll be there, by her side, waiting, whispering, murmuring, until all she knows is teeth and strain, and terror, and tearing and cold, cold, sweat, and a heart that burns with a begging prayer to stop, stop, STOP.*

The moment of waking was almost a blessing, after the voice that inhabited her dreams, but when she shuffled through to the bathroom and caught sight of her face in the mirror she was shocked at how fatigued she looked.

Days had become weeks had become months, and it was now approaching summer. Annie was still haunted by her experience in the care home, but she had bills to pay and was a frequent visitor to job sites online. She'd applied for work as a school assistant, a cleaner, and call-centre worker, among others. Mrs Mac had told her not to worry, that they'd help out, but she felt she'd taken enough from the Macs and was intent on making her own way in the world.

Every time she stepped outside the house was a trial. A middle-aged woman in a supermarket – her face a blur of light and bone, before it settled into the terrifyingly familiar skull. Moments later her death diagnosis murmured in Annie's mind: *blood cancer*. She had mere months left.

Despite her mounting fear, Annie reached for the woman as they passed in the corridor leading out to the car park, and tried to express as much sympathy as she could through her eyes. The woman reared back from her and demanded, 'What's your problem?' before marching off in speedy indignation.

Each time after that, when her curse expressed itself, she would settle for a small smile and then she would move on, trying to ignore the feeling of helplessness that scoured her mind and soul.

Her sleep was spare. Exhausted when she fell into bed, she'd sleep for about an hour, then terror would seep into her dreams and rush her awake. She would lie trembling under the covers until, frustrated at always feeling scared, she'd get up, wrap herself in her quilt and sit on her sofa and try to distract herself with old sitcoms on a streaming service. Often she would judder into consciousness, unaware that she'd fallen asleep, but always the fear was there, a solid mass pushing against the tired and heavy thump of her heart.

The letters and the postcard migrated from the kitchen table to the coffee table perched in front of her sofa. Occasionally she'd leaf through them all once more, always stopping at the postcard and that little handwritten *B*.

There was a puzzle here and she just couldn't work it out; tiny sparks of the question reached into the synapses of her brain and fizzed into nothing. What did it mean?

Nothing.

Probably nothing.

But still.

There was a thick scribble of black ink on the back of the postcard obscuring what Annie guessed was the name of the place where the photo had been taken, so no clues there, but Lewis was convinced it was somewhere in Scotland. Annie wasn't so sure. The sand was so golden and the sky and water so blue; it had to be somewhere warmer, surely.

One day, she decided to go for a walk in the local park. Their birthday was coming up, and while out there she'd try and work out what to get Lewis. He always did something very thoughtful for her, like that time he got her tickets for the Barbra Streisand concert in London; she'd been a fan of hers since forever. The most thoughtful she'd been for him was when she bought him two pairs of underwear instead of the usual one.

Boys are rubbish to buy for, she'd tell him. Beer, football memorabilia, or underwear, that's all you need or are interested in, He would just shake his head and reply: aye, when you've no imagination.

So this year she would outdo him. She'd think of something special; something *extra*. But what?

The problem was that every time she had a spare moment to think her mind would stray back to those letters and that postcard. Poor Bridget. What a miserable existence. The photographs in the local newspaper, of the crowd of staff and patients during their open day, being, as far as Annie could tell, the only highlight.

The one photograph they'd seen, which had been taken not long after Bridget had been admitted to the place was such a sorry one. It told a story of nothing but misery, and in that sadness Annie felt her family's collective guilt. Might it ease that feeling if there was a nice photo?

She could at least try the Mitchell Library again, go through the microfilm newspapers one more time. All ideas of a walk forgotten, she got herself ready and made her way back to the library.

✳

As she walked up the steps to the grand library building she caught a movement behind her. She turned in time to see a man, hunched in his jacket, disappear around the corner. Something about his gait triggered a memory. She'd seen him before somewhere.

Could it be Edward Trainer?

Surely not. What would he be doing in the city? He was supposed to be down on the Ayrshire coast. No. She shook her head. She was imagining things.

Up on the third floor she loaded the microfilm viewer with the year after the last one that she and Lewis had examined. And with a pulse of disappointment she noted that Bridget was absent from that photo session.

The following year, with a shot of excitement, she found what she was looking for.

There they were: Bridget and Tracy, side by side, angled towards each other, and although they were only visible from the chest up because of the row of people sitting in front of them, Bridget fancied that they were holding hands.

Her aunt was posting a shy smile to the world. It was tentative, softened perhaps by a cocktail of drugs, but enough of it reached her eyes to suggest there was genuine emotion there; a touch of happiness, perhaps. She'd found a friend, an ally, and she was no longer completely alone.

With a shake of her head, Annie sat back in her chair. She was seeing what she wanted to see. Wasn't she?

Taking a closer look, Annie realised again how similar herself and Bridget looked. They could be sisters.

Might there be other photos that highlighted the similarity even more strongly?

She'd start from the year before Bridget died; look for an image that was more recent.

When that year's image was loaded on to the screen Annie had to search it for a time before she found Bridget. She scanned each row quickly, and then, disappointed, started again, much more slowly this time. It was on the fourth pass through when she saw what she'd come for.

Then she realised this was what had pulled her back to examine the photographs. The idea of looking up a more cheerful image of Bridget that would rid her of her sad feelings was in fact her mind sending out a tenuous explanation, because deep down, so deep she was unwilling to accept it, she expected to find something else. Something there, something in that building, pulled at her, demanded her attention. Somehow she knew there was a mystery waiting to be solved at Oswald House, but had refused to pay attention.

Instinct, Annie mused, was something that had been all but bred out of the modern human. But one thing her curse had taught her: not everything that is out there suffers an explanation. She'd allowed her mind to pull at the thread, and without questioning what it demanded she'd found what she was looking for.

Heart beating a heavy, speedy rhythm she looked around the library, surreptitiously pulled her phone from her bag and dialled.

'Lewis,' she whispered when he answered, fighting to keep control of her breathing. 'You need to come over to mine. Tonight. I've got something you need to see.'

＊

A few hours later, Lewis was bent at the waist, hands on her kitchen table, eyes ranging across the lines of faces on the photograph.

'What am I looking for?' His gaze moved from the image Annie had printed out to her eyes.

Annie pointed. 'There. Tell me who you see.'

He bent over. Stared. 'Bridget looks different. Older.' He paused. Stood up, his mouth open in stupefaction.

'That's not Bridget. It's … it's—'

Annie couldn't wait for him to say it. 'You remember her face, don't you? From when she came to see us that time before the accident. It's Aunt Sheila, isn't it?'

Chapter 49

Annie – Now

'What in the actual fuck is going on?' he asked.

'Look at the date.'

He read, and then performed a mental calculation. 'That's around the time you were in hospital, or more accurately, in your coma after the crash.'

Annie nodded. 'I think Aunt Sheila came to visit us first, knowing she didn't have that long to live. Then she went and swapped places with Bridget.'

'Wow,' Lewis said.

'Her last gift was to give Bridget the chance of freedom, knowing her life ... would soon be over.' Annie's throat tightened as she spoke, the last four words issued as if she was being choked. 'I'm not grasping here, am I? There's the cancer. We know Sheila had it. And it's on Bridget's medical notes. What are the chances that two sisters had breast cancer at exactly the same time?'

Lewis nodded slowly. 'I agree. It's quite a thing to do, but when you put it like that, it makes sense.'

'And then there's the postcard signed *B*,' Annie added.

'What postcard?'

Annie showed it to Lewis.

'Holy shit.'

'And, there's the nun.' Annie had had the whole day to work this out. As one connection dropped after the other, she had become more and more impatient for Lewis to arrive so she could tell him her theory. 'Sister Theresa. Why was she so antsy? Because she lied to us. She must have known this swap had happened.

Perhaps she worked it out after the fact, or maybe she was in on it, but that would explain why she acted so strangely when she saw us. She didn't want the truth to come out.'

'Wow,' Lewis repeated. 'How sad this all is. And what a character Sheila must have been.'

'I keep thinking of that day she came to see us. You said Mum wanted nothing to do with her. Practically threw her out of the house.'

'She would have had her reasons,' Lewis replied, and judging by his tone he was struggling to reconcile their mother's actions with what they knew about her sisters. 'I don't remember much about Sheila, to be honest.' He looked out of the window. 'I remember the shock when Mum introduced us to her. Like, who even was this woman?'

'I don't get it, though. How could one sister be so giving and the other be so cold? And what did they fall out about? You'd think the worry of having their other sister in an institution would have given them a reason to support each other,' Annie said.

She studied the image more closely. Their aunt was looking off to the side, and Annie wondered if that was part of her act, to keep her real identity secret – to shift in her seat, to try and blur the image so she wouldn't be recognised by someone reading the paper? But from that side view they could see that there were real similarities between the sisters, Sheila even had the same length of hair that they'd seen Bridget wear in all the other photos.

'If we're seeing what we think we're seeing, Bridget got out. So where's she now?' Lewis asked. 'Is she even still alive?'

'Who knows,' Annie answered. She placed a finger on the postcard and slid it closer. Looked at the light-blue water, the golden sands, the warm haze of the sun spread across a clear sky. 'Unless the good Sister Theresa is happy to fill us in, this is our only clue.'

Chapter 50

Edward – Now

Eddie Trainer could no longer recognise himself. Every time he passed a mirror since he'd been released from prison, he had to stop and stare. His skin was the colour and consistency of putty; his hair – once his only vanity – had gone from blond to a washed-out grey-blond. Nothing matched up to the internal image of himself he'd clung to while inside. He was a shadow of his former self.

He'd learned many lessons while serving at Her Majesty's pleasure. Chief among which were the ones that helped him to survive as a marked man – as all killers of women and children were. He quickly discovered that in the prison system men who were convicted of such crimes were targeted by all the other criminals – as a way to boost their own credentials. It was also true that prison openly embraced the law of the jungle, so displays of strength and a willingness to be brutal dimmed the target on his back a little.

How the first guy to attack him got into his cell was anyone's guess. Anyone with a contact in the guard changing rooms that is. The thing is this man – a boy really – was as skittish as a week-old foal, and when he lunged for Edward he tripped over himself. As he fell his head hit Edward's knee and he lost grip of the shank he'd been about to use to perforate Edward's stomach.

Edward got to the shank first. There was a stand-off, with both men breathing heavily, facing each other, each of them wishing they were somewhere, anywhere, else, but knowing this had to be endured.

All the frustrations of Edward's treatment by the judicial

system and every fear he had ever faced built and built, and then shot through him like an electrical charge. Energy he'd never experienced before sparked in every cell of his body. Adrenaline fuelled a savagery he hadn't known himself capable of, and he found himself pinning the lad to the floor, his knees on the other guy's shoulders, the shank millimetres from piercing his eye.

'Try this again, and you lose an eye,' Eddie told him. 'Understood?'

Ashen-faced, the boy nodded, and when Eddie released him he ran from the cell.

That ended any attacks on his person for a time, until a new cycle of miscreants were jailed, and his name was highlighted once more. He met the next attack with the similar lack of restraint he'd shown the first time, and again, for a time he was left alone.

Problem was, the parents of his deceased fiancée had turned their daughter into a *cause célèbre*, constantly campaigning for action on violence against women and promoting their efforts through the media. Meaning his name was never allowed to fade from the public's minds. Meaning every time Mr and Mrs Dobell hit the news there was someone willing to use his name to boost their own.

Edward therefore learned he was a natural fighter, and while he was a man who otherwise kept mostly to himself, he saw each attack as a way to vent his own hatred for the system.

That wasn't the only thing he learned while he was inside, however. And that was why he was standing, staring in the mirror, in the bathroom of Annie Jackson's flat, while she slept soundlessly on the other side of the wall.

Chapter 51

Annie – Now

Annie woke with a start, her dream world holding fast to her mind. She'd had that dream. The one where she was drowning. One moment she was aware she was inside a submerged car. Then she was stretched out in a bath, a strong hand holding her down. Kicking desperately against the walls of the bath. The dream would usually then have her in a hospital bed, then upside down in a car, dangling from the seatbelt, knowing that someone else was in the car, and they were dead.

Her mother.

And each time the grief was there like a block of granite squeezing the air from her lungs.

This time the dream stopped at the hospital bed. And there was someone watching over her. The light from the window behind them obscured their features. Their shoulders were hunched, their arms out towards her, hands grasping at the air as if desperate to touch.

She could sense the pain from this shade. And the hunger. It couldn't suffer its own hurt any longer and was desperate to pass it on to someone else. Suffering was all it knew and all it wanted to share with those around them. That's what gave it energy and purpose.

It moved.

Reached for her.

She shrank back.

It was close.

Closer.

Its breath was like a physical extension. She could sense it touch her forehead, wrap itself around her face. She gagged. Felt a little vomit in her mouth and forced herself to swallow it down. The smell was worse than anything she'd ever encountered. It was rotting vegetation, decaying meat – it was evil held in vapour.

Closer still. One of its chill fingers under her chin pushing it up, and she knew with dreadful certainty if their eyes met she would die.

Then the murmuring started. A low, incomprehensible chorus of threat.

No, no, no.

She fought the movement. But every muscle in her body refused her command. Up the finger pressed. She fought back, refused to allow this thing to tilt her chin any further.

As if her ears were becoming more attuned to the hated voice, certain words became clear to her.

Mine. You're mine. You're mine.

No, she screamed. No.

But its strength was colossal, and she knew she had no chance to fight it. Her chin was rising. Their eyes almost level.

She screamed.

And woke up.

Annie pushed herself up in bed. She rubbed at her forehead and realised it was damp with sweat. It was just a dream. Nothing more than a dream. She forced a slow exhalation, hand over her heart, trying to slow her racing pulse.

A fragment of dream prompted her to look around towards the window. A small gap in the curtains sent a slice of light through the dark, splitting the carpet in two. There was no one there. Now. But the space felt more like an absence of something, a void, rather than being simply empty.

It was just a bad dream.

Painfully aware of the weariness in her limbs, she swung her legs out of the bed and padded through to the bathroom. While she was washing her hands, she looked up at the bathroom mirror, expecting to see evidence of her fatigue bouncing back at her. Instead, she noted that the mirrored cupboard door was smudged in the centre. She placed a finger to it and smeared it a little. What could that be? She'd no idea where the notion appeared from, but it occurred to her that someone had been standing there before her.

With a shake of her head, Annie dismissed her thoughts. She was being ridiculous, but the impression stuck with her, and she measured herself up against the smudge – someone taller than her had leaned their head against the glass as if the sight of their own face was too much to bear.

Chapter 52

Annie – Now

Annie had a couple of nights straight with the same dream. The voices, the finger hard under her chin, her face being drawn inexorably up, the burning certainty that if she met this thing's eyes she'd lose her mind.

No matter how tired she was, she decided after a morning coffee, and checking her inbox for any replies to her job applications, she had to get out of her flat, and she made her way into the West End of the city, walking towards Kelvingrove Park. The sun was beating down on her neck and shoulders, but the towering clouds gathering on the distant horizon promised a change in the weather. It was Glasgow after all.

She loved this part of the city, especially in the summer, when people were enjoying the warmer weather. The chatter of passers-by, the hum of traffic. Fresh produce from a fruit shop arranged in boxes in front of the window, vivid primary colours promising a taste and health bounty, coffee shops with tables outside, each chair taken, people chatting with the freedom that the city was famous for. But all this energy around her failed to work its magic on her tired mind.

Walking past one shop, someone almost collided with her. They rushed off, mumbling something. She took a few paces forward, a nagging feeling built, and she stopped.

She knew that person.

Eddie Trainer?

She turned and scanned the crowds behind her. And with a sense of relief realised she was mistaken. There was no one around her that even resembled the guy.

This was the second time now she'd thought she seen him here in Glasgow. She was allowing her poor state of mind to scare her.

But only a few minutes later, when she was in front of one of her favourite shops, a little patisserie, looking over the array of treats in the window, she caught a reflection of someone standing off to the side. Someone watching her. He was facing the traffic.

He turned his head. Looked straight at her.

Edward Trainer. It *was* him.

And had it been him at the Mitchell Library previously? Was he following her?

Heart a heavy thud in her chest, she turned. Walked away.

She stopped two shops down, and looked into the window of a sportswear shop.

Yes. There he was. He'd stopped again.

He *was* following her.

She began walking, adding more urgency to her step. Took a left, almost knocking over a small child who had strayed away from their mother's hand.

'Sorry,' Annie offered the woman. And she was about to ask her for help, ask her if there was a man just behind her, when the woman swore at her.

'Watch where you're going, eh? Nearly knocked the wean down.'

'Sorry,' Annie said again, and walked on. This was a street she didn't know. Mostly residential, with fewer people passing.

There was a shop at the far corner, a brightly coloured sign advertising that it was a general store. A couple of older men were standing chatting at the door. On the verge of a run, she made her way there. Ducked inside the shop and had a quick look around. There were two aisles of shelving, packed with goods. At the far end was the till, and behind it a couple with broad smiles. Behind them an array of cigarettes, alcoholic drinks, and a coffee machine. There was a large window that gave a clear view out into the street. At the window there was a small bar and two high stools.

Annie made her way to the window bar, noted the small menu on a card and stood, pretending to read it as she searched the street outside. Looking right and left she could see no one who might be Trainer.

'Help you?' the woman behind the counter asked. 'Want to try out our new coffee machine?'

'That would be lovely,' Annie said, tearing her eyes away from the street outside. 'A cappuccino?'

'You alright, dear?' the husband asked.

Annie nodded. 'I'm okay, thanks.' She looked back out onto the street, and still saw no one. She realised her legs were shaking and had to prop herself against one of the stools. What an idiot. There was no one there. She'd worked herself up for nothing. 'Nothing a nice coffee won't fix,' she said as she met the concerned gaze of the shopkeeper.

Movement from beyond the window caught her eye. There, across the street, a man was standing in the doorway of a block of flats. He stepped back, further into the doorway when her head turned.

Trainer.

Chapter 53

Annie – Now

Without thought, without even speaking to the shopkeeper, Annie left the shop, and completely mindless of the traffic, she charged across the road and faced up to Trainer.

'What the hell are you doing?' she demanded. She was angry. Very angry. Her life was an unending supply of other peoples' misery, and just when she'd been able to push some of that to the side for a few moments, this arsehole decided to follow her. She wasn't having it.

'Well?' she said, as a flustered and blushing Edward Trainer stepped out from the doorway and held his hands up, as if her temper was a gun and it was aimed at his chest.

'Sorry, I—' he began.

'You what? Like to follow defenceless females?'

'I only wanted to talk to you.'

'And that's how you arrange a chat in your world, is it? Stalk someone?' Annie felt a hot cleansing; a release. She'd had so much pent-up emotion over the last few months that a chance to vent on someone was incredibly welcome.

'You alright, hen?' The shopkeeper from across the street appeared at her elbow. 'This man bothering you? Want me to call the police?'

A small group had gathered. Half a dozen faces all glaring accusingly at Trainer.

'I'm sorry,' he yelped. 'I just needed some help and thought you might be able to...' He turned side on to the circle of people, his head shrinking down into the folds of his baggy jacket. He was so abject that Annie's anger softened.

But one of the men stepped forward, fists bunched by his side, looking for an excuse to vent his anger, it seemed. 'You bothering this lassie, ya arsehole?'

Trainer's expression hardened – the other man's anger had caused a reaction, one that in the right circumstances he would be more than happy to meet, Annie sensed. *This* was a form of violence he was more than comfortable with.

Shit, she thought, this could break out into a proper fistfight. She should put a stop to it before things escalated. She took a step closer to Trainer and held her arms out wide.

'How did you find me, and what exactly do you want, Eddie?'

'Your ... *thing*,' he answered raising his eyebrows.

Annie realised he was trying not to spell it out in public. Jesus. She really didn't want to discuss it with this man, but she could see he was not only determined, he was desperate, and unlikely to take no for an answer.

'Right,' she said. 'This nice man here has a coffee bar in his shop.' She indicated the shopkeeper. 'We can go there...' She looked at the man. He nodded, while narrowing his eyes at Edward in warning. 'And we can quietly discuss what it is you want.'

'Thank you, thank you,' Trainer replied, almost bowing.

'But if the answer is no, you have to accept that, okay?'

Relieved, or perhaps disappointed that the street drama was at an end, the group dispersed and Annie walked across the road with the shopkeeper, Trainer a couple of steps behind.

'The name's Davie,' the shopkeeper said as they stepped inside his shop. 'You sure about this?'

'Annie,' she replied automatically. 'I think I'm safe.' Then she thought about the two different versions of Edward Trainer she'd seen in that doorway. The one who was all but cowering, and the one who'd just looked like he'd happily meet violence with violence.

Once inside, she made for the stool at the window. Trainer

stood a respectful distance from her and when Davie asked what he wanted he requested a glass of water.

Davie left them, returning a minute later with their drinks. Annie gave him a nod of thanks and taking a sip of coffee, she wondered if she should message Lewis and tell him to get here as quickly as possible.

'Thanks for giving me your time,' Trainer said.

'Didn't give me much of an option, Eddie,' Annie replied.

He ducked his head in apology. And Annie noted a run of sweat down the side of his head. 'You should take your jacket off,' she said.

'I'm fine,' he replied.

'Let me save you some time,' Annie said. 'You want me to try and find out where Tracy's body is, don't you?'

Trainer's glum yet hopeful expression answered her question.

'I'm not sure this thing I have is capable of working that out, Eddie.'

'I'll pay you,' he said.

'Again: not sure I can do it. You'd be paying me for nothing.'

'You could try though?'

'Why should I? I don't know you, and frankly I don't want to. Why should I put myself in that position?'

'Because there's a body out there, and a killer who may well have murdered other young women. You'd give peace to Tracy's father and possibly save other lives.'

Annie gave that some thought. The pleading look in Trainer's eyes suggested he was being honest, or as honest as he could be. But, she reminded herself, he had been found guilty. Was this some kind of ploy to clear his name?

'Wait. You mentioned Tracy's dad. What happened to her mother?'

'She died yesterday,' Trainer replied, his face full of sadness. 'Can you imagine? She died without knowing the truth about her daughter's death.'

'Don't put that on me,' Annie said. 'Don't you dare.'

Edward held both hands up. 'It's just the truth, and to be honest, it's what prompted me to come here today.'

'Yes, how *did* you find me, Eddie?'

His pale smile was by way of an apology. 'Social media. You liked a post from Tracy's mother a few weeks back. I clicked on your name and saw that you'd also liked a cake shop round the corner. So I kinda hung about there until you showed up.'

'I don't know whether to be worried or impressed at all of that,' Annie said, not quite believing him. She'd only turned up here on impulse this day. He could have been waiting here for weeks in order for her to eventually show. Something about this assertion didn't quite add up.

'Please,' Trainer said, hands up. 'You have nothing to worry about. If you want to help, then wonderful. But if you don't then you'll never hear from me again.'

'That's a promise?'

'A promise.'

'Not that I'm guaranteeing anything, mind, but how do you suggest we go about this?'

Trainer's chin came up, a light attached itself to his eyes and Annie quailed at the thought she'd just raised his hopes.

'I don't know how your gift works, but maybe if I gave you something of Tracy's to hold? A photograph of us? Something more personal, like jewellery?'

Annie had no idea if that might prompt a vision. She hadn't fully investigated the capabilities of this curse – simply because she was so scared of it. Might it operate in the same way psychic people on TV claimed it did? Could she even try what Eddie was suggesting? She screwed her eyes shut against the thought that doing as he asked might set off the murmurs. She twisted away from him and faced the window.

'I don't know, Eddie. It's bad enough knowing how the people around me might die, without deliberately looking into an actual violent death.'

Trainer's face closed down a little, and Annie felt a pang of guilt, then chastised herself for being so soft. As she looked over at him she saw that he was momentarily distracted. She followed his line of vision and saw a woman outside the shop looking in. She was holding her phone up to the window.

'She's filming us. Do you know that woman, Eddie?'

The woman appeared to be about the same age as Annie – slim; long, sleek, dark hair; perfectly applied make-up, wearing dark jeans and a bright-yellow off-the-shoulder top.

Annie realised the phone was aimed at her, not Trainer, and got to her feet. 'Who is she, Eddie?'

'It's okay,' Trainer replied, hastily. 'It's not what you think.' He waved at the woman, beckoning her into the shop, but she merely waved in reply, turned and walked off.

'What on earth is going on?' Annie demanded.

Eddie looked more than a little shame-faced. 'She's a ... journalist,' he replied as if reluctant to admit it.

'A what? What on earth are you doing talking to a journalist, Eddie?' She thought of some of the lurid headlines that Lewis had told her regarding Trainer. And then quailed at the thought of her image being front-page news alongside him. 'They haven't been kind to you.'

'They got in touch yesterday, when the news broke about Tracy's mum, looking for a comment. Wanting to sensationalise the whole thing over again, but I gave them a different angle...' He suddenly looked less sure of himself than he'd been so far.

'What did you tell them, Eddie?' She felt a chill, knowing before Eddie spoke what his angle would have been. 'No, Eddie. Please, no. You didn't tell them about...'

'I'm desperate, Annie,' he said, pleading, hands clasped in his lap as he leaned towards her. 'I couldn't take any more headlines about me being this horrible murderer. My family read that stuff. I need to clear my name and you're the person to help me.' Then in a small voice he added, 'I hope.'

It occurred to Annie then how Trainer had really found her. The social media story he'd told her was a lie. He was in cahoots with this journalist, and it would be easy for someone with their skill set to find her.

'The journalist tracked me down, didn't they? After you told them,' she hissed. 'You bloody told them about this curse of mine, didn't you?'

He blushed and nodded. 'I couldn't help it, the words just blurted out.'

'Oh, piss off, Eddie. You've been planning this.'

'No, no, I swear. Yes, I wanted to find you.' He had the decency to blush all over again. 'But the newspaper thing ... they tracked me down.'

Annie looked away from him, then back, fury a white-hot muscle working in her jaw. 'What exactly did you tell them?'

'How a little girl, years ago, warned a school friend not to go in a red car, and she disappeared that very day.'

'How did you find that out, Eddie?'

'Did you know that Jenny Burns disappeared around the same time, and not that far away from Tracy?' His demeanour had completely changed, as if this were an important message.

Annie was thrown. 'Sorry? What's the link here?'

'I saw Jenny's dad on telly,' Eddie replied. 'So I decided to go up there and talk to him. To Mossgow. His daughter went missing around the same time Tracy did.' He repeated. 'And in roughly the same area. That had to be more than a coincidence. Then I found out that there were other missing girls in the Highlands over the years.' He held his hands out. 'They have to be linked.'

Annie exhaled sharply. 'You're making these connections because you're desperate to...'

He rubbed his thighs, and Annie couldn't decipher if he was excited or nervous. She was finding it difficult to get a read on the man. Did he believe all this stuff, or merely want her to believe it?

'I stayed the night in his hotel,' he went on. 'Ended up chatting with him in the bar, and talked to him about his daughter.' He looked into Annie's eyes. 'He told me about a certain Annie Jackson and her warning about the red car.'

Something shifted in Annie's mind. Mists swirled, information leaked out. A low whispering began in her ear. She shook her head. 'No.' In her mind's eye she saw a small red car, and felt that same raw terror she'd felt as a child, as if her memory had lost the words, but her body remembered the tune.

Eddie's eyes shifted, stared into the middle distance. 'You remember a guy called Conor from your time in Mossgow?'

Conor? Annie had a vague recollection of Lewis talking about someone called Conor recently. He thought he'd perhaps seen him that time they were outside the halfway house.

'Lewis knows Conor, but I remember next to *nothing* about my time in Mossgow,' Annie replied quickly.

He ducked his chin. 'Sorry ... just ... There's a guy called Conor who lives in my halfway house. His family were, or are, not sure which, from Mossgow. He said to watch out for the pastor. Dodgy as fuck, apparently.'

So it was Conor that Lewis saw, Annie thought. Then a partial memory leaked through. The pastor. A man with horrible teeth, his hand on her head, pressing down. She'd foretold his death. She couldn't remember how or when, but she knew she'd said the words.

'Can we not—?' she shuddered.

'It can't be a coincidence, Annie,' he interrupted. 'It can't be. You have to help me. You're a link between the two missing girls.'

Chapter 54

Annie – Now

It was Sunday, just after noon. Two days after she caught Trainer following her. Two days in which she'd spent most of her time fighting to ignore the murmuring in her ear and flashes of a red car presenting itself to her mind.

She was looking out of her window at the people walking along the pavement below her first-floor flat, envious of the seeming normality of their lives. Wondering what it might be like to just walk, talk, work and breathe without feeling constantly on edge. Without constantly wondering about what had happened to Bridget, and how she could learn more about this aunt who might hold the key to understanding and living with this curse.

Perhaps she should just go over to Oswald House and confront Sister Theresa? Put her on the spot and see what she said?

Or maybe a call would be better. She reached for her phone, looked up the telephone number for the place and dialled before she could change her mind.

'Can I speak to Sister Theresa, please?' she said when someone answered.

'I'm sure I just...' the person speaking said in an absent tone. 'May I ask who's calling?'

'Annie Jackson.'

'One moment.'

She was put on hold.

Thirty seconds became a minute. One minute became two. Then three. Then four.

What was taking so long? If she didn't get to speak to the little nun, maybe she should write back to the people who'd sent her the file on Bridget and tell them what she suspected. See what their response was.

The voice interrupted her thoughts: 'So sorry to keep you on hold, dear. I must have been mistaken earlier. I've just been informed that Sister Theresa is on retreat ... somewhere. In Ireland. Somewhere in Ireland.'

On retreat. Somewhere. You're a terrible liar, thought Annie. Certain she was getting the runaround, she replied, 'Tell Sister Theresa – when she comes back from her retreat, of course – I'll be back in touch.'

The moment she cut the connection her phone rang. It was Lewis.

'What did you do?' he asked as soon as she'd picked up.

'What are you taking about, Lewis?'

'You've gone viral, sis,'

'What do you mean, viral?'

'Front-page news. The *Herald*, and you're being discussed all over social media.'

'What?' Annie felt her stomach twist.

'What were you thinking, having a coffee with Trainer, on your own? He's a convicted murderer, Annie. God only knows what he has planned for you.'

'He kind of ambushed me, Lewis,' Annie replied, recognising the concern in her brother's voice. She was surprised that it rankled. 'And we were in public at all times, so calm down.'

'How the hell did he find you?'

'Not the point, Lewis. And I don't need your protection, okay?'

'Okay,' Lewis replied, his tone now mollifying. 'What about this article though? It shows you and Eddie – quite cosy together, by the way. You're drinking coffee in a shop window, and it says you're going to help him find out what really happened to Tracy Dobell.'

'I need to see this. I'll call you back.' Annie cut the call, went on to a search engine on her phone and, breath on hold, she typed in her name.

The first hit was the headline from the newspaper: 'Psychic Helps Convicted Murderer'.

Shit.

And there was a large photo of her with Trainer.

She clenched her jaw. Felt a surge of fear. Was she incredibly stupid to have put any trust in the man? Everybody would see this. Everyone would recognise her. She would be a marked woman.

Annie Jackson is to all intents and purposes an ordinary woman. But she holds a terrifying secret. Annie, through a process she finds impossible to understand, can intuit when and how someone is going to die.

It appears that if you are dying, or about to, and you meet Annie, your face transforms into a skull and she hears a terrifying voice that tells her how and when you are going to die.

And that is why she's sitting in this Glasgow café with convicted killer, Edward Trainer. Many of you will remember that Mr Trainer was convicted just over twenty years ago of the murder of his fiancée, Tracy Dobell. Trainer has never admitted guilt and indeed maintained his innocence even in the face of a reduced sentence.

Annie Jackson is with Mr Trainer because she has agreed to try and use her gift to work out what really happened on that fateful day in 2001 when his car broke down in the Highlands. He went for help, and Tracy remained with the car to protect their belongings. When he returned, Tracy was gone. A story he has stuck to ever since, despite all the circumstantial evidence that helped convict him, and offers from the authorities to reduce his long sentence.

Tragically, Tracy Dobell's body has never been found, and

her mother recently died without ever being able to properly grieve her daughter. Edward Trainer has since uncovered the cases of a number of girls and young women who have gone missing over the years in that part of the West Highlands. One of them foretold, apparently, by a preteen Annie Jackson when she was only twelve years old. It has entered local legend that Annie warned Jennifer Burns, fifteen, not to go into a red car. Only hours later she disappeared never to be seen again.

Annie herself has not lived a life without tragedy.

Below this statement sat a grainy image showing a car being winched out of a loch. Annie studied the image, expecting it to upset her, but she felt nothing but a detached enquiry – so that's what happened. And, despite herself, she was impressed that the journalist had found all of this out when she herself had known nothing.

This is Annie's mother's car, after they tragically lost control at an infamous local accident hotspot. Annie's mother, Eleanor Jackson, died in the accident, but Annie washed up on the banks of the loch, and made an almost full recovery.

Her only complication? Severe memory loss. Everything that happened to Annie before that time has been erased from her mind, and that is why her gift is so important.

Two young women tragically ripped from the bosom of their families. And one young woman with a terrifying gift who may well hold the key to unlocking both mysteries.

Chapter 55

Annie – Now

Feeling a sense of betrayal and anger so intense it almost made her dizzy, Annie sought the name of the journalist, looked up the number of the newspaper and called them.

She wasn't available.

'I've got a tip about a big story. Huge,' she lied.

'In that case,' the switchboard person said coolly, 'leave me your number and I'll get her to call you.'

That wasn't happening, Annie thought. That would only lead to more pieces about her. She hung up. Called Lewis.

'You okay?' he asked, and the obvious concern in his voice almost had her in tears.

'I'm so fucking angry,' she replied.

'I'll be over in thirty minutes.'

*

Half an hour later, Lewis appeared. 'What are you going to do about this newspaper article?' he asked.

'Stew a bit more, and hope that it blows over? There's not a lot I can do.'

Lewis shook his head and looked into space for a moment. 'And this swap thing. I still can't get over it. The audacity to dream up such a thing.'

Annie nodded. How would Bridget have felt – suddenly released after years in an institution? How would life have changed on the outside in the meantime? Would she have been able to navigate all of that? And what about the murmurs? She no longer had access to her medication, so would they have come back with a vengeance?

Her mind presented her with an image of someone like her, just a little older, lost and alone, wondering where she should go, and all the while beset by that incessant, viperous voice.

'Aunt Sheila must have been an amazing woman,' Lewis continued, completely unmindful of how Annie's mind was unspooling.

Bridget, the murmurs sang, and laughed. *Poor little Bridget, all alone.* The laughter built and shifted, became a loud buzzing, saw-toothed with a tone of menace.

'What about this red car?' Lewis asked. 'And the Mossgow link? Do you think Trainer has a point?'

Annie shook her head. Set her jaw. She focused on Lewis. He was her big brother. He would keep her safe. She forced herself to engage in the conversation. 'I'm not sure,' she managed. Concentrate, she told herself. 'But he did say something interesting. He came across Conor Jenkins in the halfway house.' The words stumbled from her mouth, like a half-remembered response to a question she'd been asked years ago. 'So you did recognise him that day when we were there. Apparently Conor had stuff to say about our old pastor.'

'Like what?'

'Just that he was dodgy.' With a trembling hand Annie tucked a strand of hair behind her right ear. 'What do you remember about Conor?'

'Bit of an arsehole. If he was chocolate he'd have eaten himself. Didn't have him pegged as a future hardened criminal, to be fair.'

'Remind me.' Keep talking, Lewis, she thought. Maybe it will drown out the voices in my head. 'Who was he again?'

'He's Chris and Danielle Jenkins' cousin. His parents owned the big hoose up in Mossgow. New landed gentry or some such. He was away at private school, mostly.' To illustrate what he thought of that Lewis pushed up the edge of his nose. 'Toffs. Thought they were way better than us.' He sat back in his chair. 'Chris played football and all that with me now and again, but whenever his cousin Conor was in town he didn't want to know.' He shrugged. 'I get it now. We were only kids, and he didn't want to be seen with a boy a few years younger than himself. It did used to annoy me, to be honest, to be suddenly surplus to requirements.'

The souring that had started in her mind and body with the newspaper headline, and continued the moment they started talking about Bridget built to a sudden headache, like a thunderclap. Annie bent forward, holding a hand to her head and moaned. 'God, I'm so fed up with this shit. I'm sick and tired of being sick and tired. I'm fed up being afraid. I've had enough of these bloody voices, the dead people...' She slammed the heel of her hand against her forehead – three rapid hits.

Bridget's dead, Bridget's dead, Bridgetsdeadbridgetsdeadbridgetsdead.

'Hey,' Lewis reached towards her, his tone an attempt at soothing her.

Annie let out a scream. But it felt like it came from another woman. She leaped up and ran into her bedroom.

Once there she slumped to her hunkers in the far corner, started rocking and crying, and rhythmically hitting her head off the wall. Part of her mind looked on as if from a distance, wondering who this weeping, terrified person was.

'Annie,' Lewis said, appearing in the doorway. Tentatively, he approached, arm out, reaching as if to offer some kind of help, but at the same time he seemed to be keeping himself as far from her as possible. As if she was some kind of wild and dangerous animal.

Witch, witch, witch, witchwitchwitchwitchwitch.

He forced a strained smile, but it was too late. She'd seen what it was disguising.

Fear.

Her brother was not only afraid for her, but of her.

Chapter 56

Annie – Now

Annie was in a car. A red car. Jenny Burns was in the seat beside her. Driving. How could she be driving? She was too young. She was talking ... No, her mouth was moving, but there were no sounds coming out.

Speak up, dream Annie said. Sounds like you're underwater.

Jenny's face shivered. That was the only way Annie could describe what she was seeing. Her body was completely still, but her head shivered.

A skull took its place, strands of hair flowing around it like seaweed.

They were now waist-deep in cold water. Water so cold she could feel it numb her legs, her arms, her mind. The car was filling up fast, water rushing in. It reached her chest. Her chin. She tried, in vain, to lift herself higher in her seat. The water was now past her nose, her eyes, her hair. Over the top of her head.

Annie thrashed against the restraint of the seatbelt. But it was held fast. She pounded at the window, her arm slowed by the weight of the water.

Terror filled her mind. Stole the last atom of oxygen from her lungs.

Annie clamped her mouth shut. Her lungs felt close to bursting. The pain, the anxiety was overwhelming. She needed oxygen. Now. She tried to bang on the window. Wrestled with the seatbelt. Survival her only thought. Air. Clean air. She desperately needed air. But she was in a car. Submerged.

'I love you, Annie.' The voice pealed in her mind. A soothing. She turned.

It wasn't Jenny Burns in the car, it was her mother. Her face was full of acceptance. She was going to drown, and she was taking her daughter with her. They would die together and she was okay with that.

'No, Mum. No.'

Annie tugged feverishly at the seatbelt. Nothing. She pounded on the window at her side. Her mother placed a hand on hers. Her eyes, even through the murk of the water, sending messages of love and support, and telling her to relax, to let it happen.

'I love you, Annie,' she mouthed. Allow death in. It was for the best, she was saying.

Annie shook her head furiously, while her oxygen-deprived lungs screamed for air, demanded she open her mouth and allow the reflex action to happen. Except she knew if she did, her lungs would fill with water and she would drown.

'Please, Mum, no. Do something. I don't want to die.'

Hair slowly waving around her head, her mother's voice sounded in her mind, but her lips weren't moving. Her words overlaying the building sound of the murmurs: 'It's okay, honey. Let it happen. It's time.'

Annie sat up like she'd been launched from a rocket. Her heart was a ferocious drum beat, her mouth was dry, and she could feel her hair sticking to her damp forehead. She glanced around, searching and listening for something tangible that would ground her in the present, waking moment.

She'd forgotten to close the curtains when she'd settled on to the sofa the previous evening, and weak morning light filled the room, lending everything a tone of sepia, rounding off corners. It was such a welcome shift from the urgent sense of threat in her dream that she sagged back into the seat.

What was all that about? Was this her curse trying to warn her? Was it just dream, or something more? Memory? If it was a memory ... had her mother really tried to kill her? For that was the only interpretation that worked.

Annie felt herself tremble at the thought, and crossed her arms tightly over her chest. If only her memory would come back she would know what had actually happened. Was this part of her gift? Was there a lesson in the dream that she needed to take note of? Might Jenny Burns be in the very same waters that killed her mother and almost took Annie's own life?

Where was her phone? Annie sat up, and looked around the room. There on the coffee table. She reached for it. Checked the time. It was 6:45am. There were some missed calls from Lewis. She recalled the meltdown she'd had the previous evening, and was sure he'd tried to call to make sure she was okay.

His eyes, full of fear as he tried to soothe her.

No. She couldn't face talking to him right now, but Mrs Mac, she knew, was always an early riser, so she brought up her contact details and pressed the little green phone symbol. Mrs Mac answered straight away, as Annie knew she would.

'Annie? What's wrong?'

Annie could have reached through the phone and hugged Mrs Mac. A jumble of thoughts and questions raced through her mind. The dream was fading, but the fear attached to it still had its tendrils buried deep in her mind.

'How did I not drown?' she asked.

'What's that, Annie?' There was a rustle of bedclothes, a male voice and Mrs Mac told her husband to go back to sleep. 'What's wrong, dear?'

'The accident that killed my mum – why didn't I drown? Was there an inquest, or whatever you call it? How did I get out of that car and my mother didn't?'

'Have you had that nightmare again? The one where you're both in a submerged car?'

Annie couldn't have been more surprised. 'I've had this before?'

'Oh, yeah. You regularly came through to our bed in the middle of the night talking about this dream. You've not had it for such a long time I thought you'd grown out of it.'

'Did they have an inquest?'

'Yes, but it was such a long time ago.'

'How did I survive? Do you know? I have this horrible feeling that it was deliberate. That because of this curse, my mother tried to kill herself, and me.' Then, once more, she recalled her dream of being in a bath, a strong hand pushing her under the soapy water.

'And I don't think that was the first time.'

Chapter 57

Annie – Now

Lewis was standing off to the side, in the McEvoys' dining room, his hands bunched into fists, face pale.

'How can you say that?' he demanded.

They were at the Macs' for Sunday dinner. As usual the table was set like it was Christmas, and the Macs were fussing over them like they hadn't seen them for a year.

Annie had outlined their findings so far, and their theory that Bridget and Sheila had swapped places. As she talked, Lewis kept sending her worried glances: *Are you okay?*

She had batted off his concerns with a tight smile. No she wasn't okay. Her brain felt like it was fractured, and she was constantly on edge. She felt she had to show that she was coping, when in truth she was terrified that the men in white coats were just out of view, preparing a powerful sedative.

Later, Mrs Mac was in the kitchen plating up while her husband was pouring them drinks, when Annie told Lewis her theory about her mother trying to drown her. He made a face. Dismissive. Disbelieving. Like he thought she was a nutter. She felt the back of her neck heat up.

'Hang on,' Annie said. 'It's the only thing that makes sense.'

'The only thing that makes sense to a woman who's barely slept and who claims she knows when someone is about to die.'

'Piss off, Lewis,' Annie hissed. 'You believed me the last time we spoke about what I sense, but now I'm talking about your precious mother you've gone all aggro on me? In case you hadn't noticed, she was my mother too.' She paused and added with as much spite as she could muster, 'Golden boy.'

Lewis's face tightened and Annie knew her jibe had hit home.

'You've lost it. For your own sanity you need to rein this in now.'

There were footsteps behind them, and Mrs Mac was in the doorway holding a tray laden with food.

'Right, kids. Whatever you're arguing about you can park it. We're about to eat.' Her tone brooked no dissent.

Lewis and Annie sat in their usual places at the dining table, glaring across at each other, while Mandy put the food out for them.

Dinner passed in a near-amicable fashion, or as near as the siblings could make it, but Annie could tell that Lewis was seething. Too bad. Eleanor Jackson was her mother too, and it was just too bad if Lewis couldn't understand that her dreams were of a different kind of mother altogether.

But were they dreams, or were they memories? She couldn't help but have a sense that they were a bit of both.

After dinner, Mr Mac and Lewis would usually do the dishes while the women sat in the living room and watched TV. But, as Annie expected, Lewis was so annoyed he left, making some excuse about an early morning at work.

Annie took Lewis's place with the dishtowel and helped dry the dishes and put them away in the cupboards, and realised it was an opportunity to quiz Mr Mac.

'What do you know about my accident?' she asked, part of her mind impressed that she was carrying off this act of normalcy.

'What do you remember about it?' He stopped what he was doing for a moment.

'Nothing, really. There are fragments of dreams that I've had over the years since, but I don't know if they're just my mind's attempts to fill in the blanks, or if they really happened.'

'All I recall,' Mr Mac began. 'Is that the police were content that it was an accident. Sadly, it wasn't the first time someone had gone off the road at that spot and ended up in the water. I think what made it worse for you guys is that the weather was so foul that day. Wind and rain. The visibility was terrible, so no one saw what happened.'

'Did they ever work out how I managed to survive when my mother didn't?'

He shook his head, his features melting into sorrow. 'All I know is that you washed up on the bank, and a passer-by spotted you before hypothermia set in. Your mother was still strapped into the driver's seat when they found the car.'

Annie had been so convinced earlier she was right about her mother's intentions, but now she wondered if she was allowing the horror of her dream and the dark of night to twist her perception. 'Do you think my mother had it in her to do something like that ... deliberately?' Even as the words spilled from her mouth Annie realised that she was striking out, randomly, seeking impossible answers to a challenging question.

Mr Mac searched her eyes, his own full of care. 'Is anyone capable of that kind of action?'

'You're fudging, Mr Mac.'

He dried his hands. Put one on each of her shoulders and looked down at her. 'You're searching for something I can't give you, Annie.'

'And what's that?'

'Certainty.'

Annie stepped back out of his reach. 'You could say: no, Annie, your mum was lovely. You were lucky to have her in your life.'

'Your father was my best friend. I loved him like a brother, and even he would attempt to qualify that statement before he said it.'

Chapter 58

Annie – Now

Next morning, Annie's mobile rang. It was Lewis.

'Phoning to apologise for being an arsehole?' she said.

'Only if you apologise first for talking shite.'

Realising she would get nowhere with this, she changed tack. 'What do you want?'

'Danielle and Chris Jenkins are in town. They want to meet us for lunch or dinner.'

'You rushed away from the Macs last night saying you were very busy today. Was that just to get away from me?'

'No, it happened to be true. And it happened to be about the Jenkins. I knew they were coming in to town and I wanted to double-check some work I did for them before we met.'

'And why didn't you tell me about this invite yesterday?'

'You weren't included until now. Chris just asked if I would bring you along. He wants to relive old times, apparently.'

Annie pushed into her memory to try and recall the time she and Chris supposedly kissed. Nothing. Then she thought about seeing her old neighbours on their religious video podcast, their carefully cultivated air of Christianity, and tried to compare that to how they were as kids. She came up blank.

'Do we have to bring stepladders so we can climb up and polish Chris's halo?' she asked.

'Just one thing, to save on any awkward moments, you should know that both their parents are dead.'

'Oh? Was it recent?'

'Mr Jenkins had a stroke about ten years ago. Became wheelchair bound – and then died in a nursing home at the start of the Covid pandemic.'

'Well, that's shitty. What about their mum?'

'I think the strain of looking after a sick husband did for her. Cancer.'

Annie grimaced. 'Thanks for the heads-up. I'll make sure not to mention their parents.'

And, she thought, she also would also have to avoid eye contact with everyone she came across and pray that the murmurs remained just a hateful hum in her head. Anxiety became a churn in her stomach. She thought of her breakdown the other day. What if she lost it and made an idiot of herself in public?

'It'll do you good to get out in new company,' Lewis said as if he sensed she was about to change her mind.

✳

They were all seated in a huddle in a café in the West End of Glasgow wearing too-large smiles.

As Annie watched the Jenkins siblings chatting to her brother, she became aware that other customers in the place kept stealing glances at their table. And there was an unmistakeable glamour to their visitors. They were both tall and slim, and beamed a rare vitality. Chris was wearing a navy suit, and a white shirt without a tie. He had a trim beard and a set of teeth that any dentist would be proud of. His sister, Danni, was a little more casual. Shoulder-length dark hair, a light-blue, knee-length raincoat, and under that a pair of dark jeans. The only bright colour on her was her pink lipstick, which as far as Annie could tell was the only make-up she wore, while still managing to look cover-girl ready.

'So nice to see you,' Danni said to Annie in an 'us girls together' tone, reaching across the table top and gripping her hand. 'Gosh, it's been so long.'

'Yeah.' Annie faked enthusiasm as best she could.

'You have no memory of me, do you?' Danni asked frankly.

Annie shook her head. 'Sorry.' She could tell by the directness of Danni's gaze that little got past her. 'We were friends, yeah?'

Danni smiled. 'Every night after school we used to sit under the tree at the far end of your parents' garden, chatting for hours.' She held her arms out, palms up. 'If your younger self could see what we'd become as grownups you'd be, like, *no way*.' Annie felt herself warm to the other woman's straightforward manner and honesty.

Annie looked at her menu. 'Crushed avocado,' she read out loud. 'The folk who lived here just twenty years ago would have been happy with a bacon sandwich.'

Chris laughed, and studied her carefully. She felt herself react – a little flutter in her chest and the need to make sure her hair was sitting just so. She resisted touching it.

A waitress approached the table and took their order. The food arrived quickly, and they ate, while talking about inconsequentials. Lewis took the lead, and was way too loud for Annie's liking. She wanted to take him by the elbow and tell him to calm down. Instead, she settled for a couple of meaningful glares. But in response Lewis became even louder, bordering on the obsequious as he talked up the Jenkins' siblings latest online Sunday sermon.

'The way you talked about the Bible and stoicism, and how those kind of attitudes might benefit today's youth? Masterful,' he said.

Annie couldn't help but roll her eyes.

'You don't quite agree, Annie?' Chris asked with a half-smile.

Shit. She didn't think she'd been that obvious.

'I'm not dismissing the notion,' Annie said, suddenly not giving two hoots about what these people might think of her. Who were they anyway? As far as she was concerned, complete strangers, and she owed them nothing. 'Generations past, perhaps, took that stoicism too far, closer to denial really. And the current generation have swung too far the other way and are too easily offended. But,' she went on meaningfully, 'I was rolling my eyes at my brother's sycophancy.' She looked over at Lewis, whose face had flushed. 'Sorry, Lewis. Just saying.'

Chris and Elaine laughed.

'Nothing like a sibling to give it to you bluntly,' Danni said. Then she leaned across the table and took Lewis's hand, and looked into his eyes in a way that made Annie wonder if they'd slept together. 'You've got the gig, Lewis. You don't need to try so hard.'

Lewis's answering laugh failed to reach his eyes, and Annie felt a pang of guilt that she'd caused him some discomfort.

'I'm sorry, Lewis,' she said. 'You were just getting a wee bit too pompous there.'

Lewis gave her a look that suggested he'd get her back.

'In any case,' Chris said. 'Let's give the church stuff a rest for now.' He looked at Annie with frank appraisal. 'The years have been good to you, Annie. You're looking well. Do you remember much about your time in Mossgow?'

Annie felt that little flutter again. Was it just her imagination or was there real interest in Chris's gaze? He was a good-looking man. She usually fell for guys who took much less care of their appearance, but his eyes were shining, and so very blue.

'No,' Annie replied. 'It's all pretty much a blur. It's like my life began in the hospital after the accident.'

'What about that newspaper headline?' Danni asked.

'You caught that?' Lewis asked.

'We live in the Highlands,' Chris replied with a smile. 'Not Mars.'

'That's not what I—'

'This thing about the red car,' Danni said. 'I remember you saying that at the time.'

'You do?' Annie sat back, aware that she was sounding defensive.

'I didn't get the chance to ask too much about it. Events kind of took over, if you know what I mean.' She made a face and Annie knew she was referring to her accident and the death of her mother. 'And there was the thing with the pastor.'

Annie closed her eyes, exhaled, wished she was anywhere but there. Her breath shortened. Vision paled.

'I'm sorry,' she stood up. 'I need to...' She looked around, feeling the room shrink. 'I don't feel so well.' She should have known that this would come up. God, she was so stupid agreeing to meet these people for lunch. Her past was not up for debate. It was done. Over.

She turned, made for the door, almost knocking over a waiter who was carrying a tray full of food.

Pulling the door open and all but breaking into a run, she stumbled into someone who was standing at the window, peering in. Hearing their grunt of surprise she stepped back.

'What the hell, Eddie?' she asked. 'Are you following me again?'

Chapter 59

Annie – Now

Lewis appeared at Annie's elbow.

'Trainer? What the fuck?'

Lewis made a grab for him, but Trainer turned and fled. Lewis chased after him, and both men disappeared round the corner.

'Lewis,' Annie shouted after them. 'Don't...'

Chris and Danni came out of the café.

'Are you okay?' Danni placed a hand on Annie's arm.

'Who was that?' Chris asked, looking as if he might join in the chase.

'Please,' Annie said. 'I'm fine.' She could feel her face heat and her heart jumping in her chest. What on earth was Trainer doing standing outside the café? He must have been following her again. But why?

'Who was that?' Chris repeated.

'Oh, no one,' she answered. 'Just some guy...'

Lewis reappeared from round the corner, his face a flustered red. 'He's the guy from that news article who was convicted of murdering his fiancée twenty years ago.' Lewis answered Chris's question while staring accusingly at Annie.

'Where's he gone?' Annie asked, bridling at Lewis's glare.

'Ach,' Lewis waved his hand, as he bent over, trying to catch his breath. 'He disappeared across the road, and...' He took a quick couple of gulps of air.

'You don't think I'm still encouraging him, do you?' Annie asked, more than a little pissed off at Lewis's attitude. 'I've not heard from him since the article in the *Herald* came out.'

'You shouldn't have given him the time of day in the first place.'

'I was just being polite,' Annie replied.

'To a bloody murderer.'

'What the hell is your problem, Lewis?' Annie demanded. 'I'm the one he's following.'

'And Lewis is just acting like a concerned brother,' Chris Jenkins intervened, in a soothing tone. 'I might be the same if a dangerous individual was mooning after Danni.'

'Hmmph.' Danni made a dismissive noise. 'I'm sure Annie can take care of herself. As can I,' she added pointedly.

Chris laughed, his expression warm and fond. 'Looks like we're not going to win this argument, Lewis.' He put a hand on Lewis's shoulder. 'Why don't we all go back inside and finish our lunch?'

'Annie was about to go home, though,' Danni said while looking at her for clarification. 'Want to stay a little longer?'

Annie paused, thinking that her heart wasn't quite beating as normal. She didn't believe Eddie Trainer wasn't a real danger to her, and, stealing a glance at Chris she did feel that company would be a welcome distraction. 'Sure,' she replied. 'Sorry for running out earlier. I just get all—'

Danni held a hand up. Smiled. 'No need to explain. Let's go back in? Fancy a coffee and some cake?'

Annie allowed herself to be persuaded, and they all went back inside.

'Another reason we wanted to see you,' Chris said, after they'd finished their coffees and he'd asked the waiter for the bill, brandishing a black credit card, 'is that we plan on filming a special up at the church.'

'It's a big anniversary concerning the history of the area,' Danni added.

'Some *made-up* anniversary for the history of the area,' Chris grinned. 'The US market has exploded for us, and we want to grow that.'

'And we thought it would be cool,' Danni continued, 'if some of the old gang were in the congregation for the filming.'

'Yes, Lewis did mention something – I don't have to say anything, do I?' Annie asked. 'You're not going to use my thing with the red car, or Pastor Mosely?'

'Good grief, no,' Danni answered, alarmed at the thought. 'This is about the church's history in the area, the martyrs and all that. The last thing we want to focus on is anything to do with ... well, you know...' She left her sentence hanging.

Annie was relieved. She could see that her connection with the otherworldly would go against the Jenkins' work and religious teachings.

'So, you'll come?' Danni exclaimed, clapping her hands with joy. 'Oh, that is so cool. Thank you, thank you.'

'But I...' Annie began to protest.

'Of course, she will,' Lewis added, as if sensing Annie was going to say something else. 'We both will.'

❋

Outside, on the pavement just as they parted company, Danni took Annie's arm and guided her away from the men.

'I'm so glad we reconnected,' she trilled. 'I've missed you.'

'Oh,' was all Annie could say. The pleasure was so naked in Danni's eyes, that she hesitated to say something similar. She didn't have any memories of Danni, but she did enjoy her company, and felt relaxed with her fairly quickly.

'Let's keep in touch,' Danni said and pulled Annie into a hug.

'Yes, let's,' Annie replied, feeling her heart lift. Something positive in her life would be welcome.

The two men said their goodbyes, Lewis hugged Danni, and Chris approached Annie for the same. When he touched her arm she felt her head go numb, then pain flickered at the edges. As she stepped back from him she saw his face shiver, and the skin pull back as if peeling from the muscle. The murmurs built, but as quickly as they arrived they faded. What was going on? And why now? Why hadn't she had this response when they hugged earlier? Was she ever going to understand this thing?

She blinked, and he appeared in front of her just as he had been all afternoon; bright-eyed, skin glowing with health, and teeth gleaming and unblemished.

'You okay?' he asked her, his arms still spread for a hug. Annie stepped back again.

'Headache,' she said. She waved a hand then clumsily patted his shoulder. 'I'm fine. Honest. Just the beginnings of a migraine or something.'

***

On the way back to her flat, Annie and Lewis barely shared a word, but she could tell he was seething. When they arrived at her door she told him he could go.

'I'm just making sure Trainer isn't waiting for you.'

'Well, as you can see, he's not, so thank you.' Annie smiled at her brother and put the key in the lock.

'Don't spoil this for me, Annie,' Lewis said. 'The work I'm doing for the Jenkins is a big deal. The fees will be huge and put me in contention for making partner.' His eyes were pleading.

'And how do you think I could ruin it?'

'I saw how you were with Chris at the end there. You looked like you were in pain. Was it your curse? Do you think he's going to die?'

'Are you more interested in your old pal's ability to help you make partner, or in his possible demise, Lewis?'

He shook his head. 'Of course I don't want the guy to die, for fucksake, but...'

'I don't know what I saw there,' Annie admitted. 'It was less clear than it usually is. As if...' She thought for a moment. 'As if he has a big decision to make, and one of the outcomes...' She shook her head. 'I can't make sense of it.' She assessed her brother, at the need in his expression. 'Whatever it is, I'm sure the Church of the Everlasting Christ won't blame the new accountant.'

'That's not...' Lewis's face had flushed.

'Goodbye, Lewis.' Annie stepped inside, not bothering to hide her disappointment in her brother, and closed the door behind her, unwilling to listen to any more of his poor attempt at explaining what he himself couldn't quite admit. She loved her brother, but this was a new side of him that she couldn't quite take to. All through their meeting in the café he'd been so sickeningly respectful that she'd wanted to slap him. Where had her irreverent brother gone? Was he so desperate to go up in the world?

He was earning a perfectly decent salary, with a nice flat in a good area, a posh car, and a wardrobe full of expensive suits. What else did he need?

Her mind full of her brother and the meeting, she walked into her living room, went over to the window and looked down on the street. He was walking over to his car. She saw him put a hand in his pocket, extend his arm and open the door with the remote.

For a moment she was tempted to run down to him and apologise for her judgement. Perhaps she was being too harsh, she thought, as she assessed his heavy body language. He only wanted what most of the people around her were after: some form of financial security. Who was she to judge him?

She lifted a hand to knock at the window, to send him away with a wave and a smile, but too late. He was quickly inside his car and moving into the traffic.

Her phone rang. Not recognising the number, she answered. 'Hey.'

She recognised the voice straight away, and her heart gave a little jump.

'Chris,' she said. 'How did you get my number?'

'Three guesses,' he laughed. 'You don't mind, do you?'

'No,' she sat, tucked her feet under her. Bit her lip. Tried not to feel too flattered. She pushed her hair behind her ear, then slipped it back into its previous position as if he could see her. She cursed herself for being so stupid.

'Just thought I'd take a trip down memory lane with the girl I grew up next door to.' His voice was low, quiet, as welcome on the ear as a lullaby. 'You have beautiful eyes, Annie Jackson.'

'Well,' she answered, flustered. 'I bet you say that to all the girls.' Jesus. How corny was she?

He laughed. 'Sorry. That was cheesy. But true. I'd like to see you again, Annie.'

'Well, as you know, I live in Glasgow,' she replied. 'And it's not exactly convenient for someone who lives a three-hour drive away.'

'They've got these new inventions. Cars. Time passes very quickly in them.'

'Not that quickly.'

'Agreed,' he laughed again, and she realised she enjoyed the sound. Wanted to make him laugh some more. 'But it's a detail you don't have to concern yourself with too much. I'm in Glasgow a fair bit these days. Would be nice to hang out. Just you and me.'

As she thought about it she realised the idea wasn't too terrible. In fact the more she thought about it, the more attractive it was.

'You're not outside my door, are you?' she laughed, half-hoping he would say yes. And then her heart gave a little twist of fear when she recalled another person she might find outside her door: Eddie Trainer. It seemed every time she turned round, there he was. Should she be concerned about the level of his persistence? What did he want from her, really? Might all of this stuff about looking into the death of his ex be some sort of twisted ploy?

Chris interrupted her thoughts: 'Sadly, no. I've launched myself into that three-hour drive you just talked about.'

'Oh,' she replied, noting a faint feeling of disappointment.

'I'll text you,' he said. 'I'll be back down in a couple of days.'

They ended the call and she curled up on her sofa, her mind

full of her conversation with Chris. It was a surprise – both the fact that he was interested in her, and that she was interested in him. She hadn't had a boyfriend for some time and was frankly not that interested in having one anytime soon.

Could Chris, and Danni for that matter, be good for her? She needed, desperately, to have some element of positivity in her life, because she knew she was on the verge of spiralling into a very bad place indeed.

That thought was accompanied by a little reminder. A faint, echoing sound of wicked laughter.

Fearing it would build and keeping on building, she picked up her phone, brought up YouTube and went through a couple of Chris's sermons.

He was all wide shoulders and flashing eyes. Strong chin, shiny teeth, and so very earnest. And, she had to admit, handsome.

The laughter in her head faded.

Would it bother him, she wondered, that she didn't have a religious bone in her body? If anything, she was anti-religious and thought those who needed to belong to such organisations a bit desperate to find meaning and purpose in their lives, and would be better off volunteering at their local foodbank.

But, she thought, she could have a nice time while it lasted. It wasn't like the man had asked her to marry him.

How would the murmurs be when she was with him? There seemed to be no pattern to their harrying voices, other than when she was in the presence of someone who was dying, and then they jumped into overdrive; but other times they could either be a faint but distant presence, or like a furious dog barking at a gate.

How would they be if she was doing something that might benefit her emotionally? Would they work to sabotage that?

She recalled the moment she and Chris touched. The electricity sparking as the skull face sizzled, then paused. And her explanation to Lewis that she thought Chris had a momentous decision to make; one that could be life-altering.

She threw herself back in the sofa. What was she like? Idiot. Seeing things where there was nothing to see. When it had happened with Chris the usual nausea and headache hadn't arrived. She must have misread the signals.

That was it, she decided. She was too used to terror coming from this curse of hers, and what she'd actually experienced with Chris that afternoon was simply the excitement of a possible romantic connection. It was the first time she'd had physical contact with a male since this change in her. Indeed, her first contact with an attractive man in a very long time.

Annie had always fought to do what she wanted in life despite the presence of fear or any dissenting voice in her head. Of course what she was dealing with in the past were just the run-of-the-mill doubts and fears that most people had to live with. But this was on a different level entirely.

No. She would not give in to the murmurs. She would not let them win. She added some imaginary steel to her spine, sat up, chin forward. She would face this thing down, and if a new romance was actually possible, she was going to allow it into her life, and try to enjoy it – whatever this curse threw at her. Whatever the consequences. She was determined she wasn't going to succumb and end up in some institution, doped and stupid on tranquilisers.

Like Bridget.

She scrolled through her recent calls and stared at the number for Oswald House. Bridget had never known happiness. Annie owed it to her aunt to find out what had happened to her.

Chapter 60

Annie – Now

Six long days after he'd texted and phoned to let her know he was interested, Chris called, said he was outside her door in the car, and did she want to go out for dinner?

'Kinda presumptuous, aren't you?' she said, trying to hide the smile in her voice.

'Sorry,' he said in a quiet, hesitant voice. 'I've mucked this up, haven't I?'

Hurriedly, she reassured him. Asked for half an hour to get changed, which lasted forty minutes, because she didn't want to appear too keen. And then they drove across town to the West End and a restaurant that was pricey, but served delicious food.

Then it was back to hers.

Feeling brave – she hadn't done this for such a long time – she asked him up for a coffee. One thing led to another. Coffee wasn't served. In fact, she didn't even get to put the kettle on, so hungry were they for each other.

On the sofa, clothing shoved aside, her mind reminded her again of the moment when she'd seen Chris's handsome face turn, sizzle into a skull and then just as quickly reform.

As if sensing the change in her mood, Chris eased himself off her. 'You okay?' he asked.

'Yes. Fine,' she answered, pushing her hair off her face, realising her raised pulse wasn't only to do with sexual excitement.

'You don't sound so sure.' He was looking down at her, arms extended, holding himself up so easily a distracting thought had her wonder about his physical strength.

The murmurs were a faint cackle. A reminder prodding at her: we're here, and we're going nowhere.

'I am,' she fought her rising anxiety. 'Sure, that is.' Then she pushed herself up off the sofa to meet his lips with hers. They kissed.

Chris shifted so that he was sitting, rather than hovering over her, and she appreciated this offer of a little space. Argued with herself that she should just carry on – they'd started, so they should finish, she thought. At least, every other man she'd been with would have pushed that agenda, but Chris was looking at her, care framed in his eyes.

'Let's have that coffee,' he said. 'And take a moment.'

'You sure?' Annie arranged herself so that she was sitting beside him, rebuttoning her blouse. Suddenly aware how much skin was on show.

'Course I am,' he replied firmly keeping his eyes trained on hers. 'Besides, I'm not usually the guy who's looking for sex on a first date.'

Annie gave him an 'aye, right' look.

'Honestly,' he said. 'I've not had that many relationships. Last one was Susan Doyle. She was in my year at school?' He checked her for any form of recognition.

'No recollection of that name at all,' Annie replied, feeling a little twinge of envy for this woman.

'We were together for nearly ten years. Fell out during the first lockdown,' he added. 'Seems close proximity with only one person for weeks at a time helps the faults in a relationship show up.' He smiled ruefully. 'Who knew?'

They both laughed.

Grateful that Chris hadn't made the moment any more awkward for her, Annie got to her feet. 'Let's get that coffee?'

Chris followed her into the kitchen. She put the kettle on as he sat at the table.

'What's all this?' he asked, pointing at the pile of papers that were sitting where in most other households the condiments might be placed.

She told him about her stalled search for her aunt. The abridged version. She wasn't ready to discuss the curse just yet. And as she explained she felt a sense of disappointment at how little progress she'd made. Bridget was family, and she deserved her story to be known.

The murmurs suddenly grew in pitch. *Dead, dead, dead, dead-deaddead.*

She squeezed her eyes shut, fighting them off, working to resist the fear swirling up from her gut, ready to squeeze at her heart.

'Hey,' Chris said. 'You okay?'

'Fine,' Annie said. Then she repeated this with some added steel. 'I'm fine, honestly.' She proffered a weak smile, and lied: 'Migraine. Comes and goes. Anyway, what was I saying?'

'You'd tried to phone the nun?'

'Yeah, but it sounds like I was being fobbed off, doesn't it?'

He nodded. 'But, gosh,' he said, 'the whole thing sounds like the plot of a movie.'

'Yeah, but stuff has gotten in the way recently, and I've let it slide.'

'By "stuff",' Chris tilted his head to the side. 'Do you mean Edward Trainer and the newspaper headline?'

'They have been part of the issue.' Annie looked at him meaningfully, letting him know she had also been distracted by him.

'Oh.' He blushed slightly. 'Can't say I'm too sorry about that.' He grinned, and he looked so cute Annie suddenly had the urge to take him by the hand and guide him to her bedroom. 'But this Trainer guy.' He shook his head. 'I've been reading up on him. Quite the nasty piece of work.'

'He doesn't scare me,' she said defiantly, only partly believing her statement.

'Has he been following you again?' he asked.

'No,' she lied. She had spotted someone just that morning, on the way to the corner shop, who looked like he might have been Trainer. But he was too far away and too hunched against the rain for her to be sure.

Chris rose to his feet. Took her hands in his. 'I've only just found you, Annie.' As the kettle behind her worked itself to the boil, steam gently billowing from the spout, she felt the heat of his gaze, and his sincerity. 'I would hate for anything to happen to you.'

She took his hand, moved a step closer to the door, and in the direction of her bedroom. Maybe it would help push away the terror to give in to another kind of emotion, another kind of feeling?

'The urge,' she said with a small smile, 'for coffee has suddenly left me.'

Chapter 61

MOIRA MCLEAN – A MEMOIR

That it happened at all was an accident, Jean would tell anyone who cared to listen. Few did, for Jean had become a fearsome woman when in full flow, so people were apt to simply nod, make their excuses and walk on.

A scarf that John Campbell had offered Mary as a token of his affection had caught Jean's attention. She tried it on, savoured the silk of it at her throat and Mary didn't have the heart to deny her this small pleasure, so merely smiled, nodded and took mental note to retrieve it at some point in the future. For although they shared most things she held that particular item dear and would only allow her sister to borrow it.

A knock at the door of their crofthouse, and James McLean, a cousin, was there, wringing his hands because his wife was in labour, or so he said. The sisters knew that this was too soon so Mary, who had a talent for sensing when the time was right, was dispatched to hold her hand and soothe her brow.

Not fifteen minutes later and another knock at the door. It was John Campbell. Jean bade him enter and offered the young man a warm drink of herbs and honey, and because she was wearing his scarf, John thought he was in the company of his beloved Mary. They kissed, and Jean found she liked it. That kiss led to a more active form of affection and soon they were coupling on the sisters' bed.

By the time Mary returned, John had gone home – pleased beyond measure that he had at last made his way into the bed of his sweetheart – and not before he promised that he would persuade his mother his heart belonged to none other than Mary McLean and that they should marry before the year was out.

Thereafter, Jean contrived to present herself as Mary whenever she could. Which confused Mr Campbell no end, because the real Mary continued to refuse his physical advances, while Jean – wearing the little silk scarf – was always willing.

Before long, nature took its course and the repeated lovemaking produced a quickening in Jean's womb. She hid her bump for as long as she could, but Mary knew, without understanding by whom, that her sister was with child.

Jean was convinced by this time that she had replaced Mary in John's affections, and when next all three were together she told them both what had been happening.

The result was not to Jean's liking. John was so furious he rushed towards her with his hand raised. Common sense prevailed and he withdrew without striking her, promising that he never wished to see her ever again.

He left, and Mary fled after him, demanding answers. Jean watched from her door as Mary followed John down the glen, him on his horse, her with her skirts bunched up before her so she could run. Predictably, in Jean's eyes anyway, Mary fell. John heard her cry of pain and turned. It appeared from her limp that Mary had hurt her ankle so John had her straddle his horse and he led her away.

Gossip arrived to Jean's ears within the week, a week during which she'd seen hide nor hair of either one of them, that the couple had been promised to each other. There were rumours of a falling-out – no one was able to furnish any detail, only that it had been brief and resulted in a marriage being agreed, and that Mary would move into the young laird's home.

That her actions had resulted in pushing them together rather than apart, sent Jean into a fury she could barely contain. Anger, hot and wilful, burned in her mind and body; and so lacking in equilibrium had she become that she was certain her babies would die in the womb – for by this time Jean knew she was bearing twins. But no, the poor little mites continued to grow, and thrive, and kick.

The unfairness of it all lashed at her mind. That she should be treated so by someone she had loved dearly could not be borne, and it was in the words she had been warned about by her grandmother all those years ago – the writings of James VI of Scotland – that she would find her revenge.

The daemonologie was, she had heard at her grandmother's knee, a warning, a detailed description of how witches worked, and what the God-fearing should observe in the minds and actions of the tainted. The learnings of the king may have been a warning for some but for her it would be her dark Bible. Her road to a reckoning.

Chapter 62

Annie – Now

'So, you and Chris Jenkins are a thing now?' Lewis was on the phone. They hadn't spoken for about a week or so, which wasn't unusual for them. Often, there would be silence between them for days, and other times they'd be in touch daily. Annie liked that there was no pattern to their contact, that they'd be there for each other just as and when, but this time the gap had the feel of them being irritated with each other. And she had to admit Lewis wasn't wholly to blame.

At the mention of Chris's name she felt the dark lighten a little and a smile hover over her lips.

'Jesus. You're doing that mooning thing, aren't you?' Lewis said.

'Shut it,' Annie replied. Laughed. Savoured the joy that came from being in love. Or, more accurately, in lust. She and Chris had been with each other four times in the last week, and each time they barely got 'hello' out before they were tearing each other's clothes off.

'Is it serious, or are you just having a nice time?'

Annie heard the concern in her brother's voice, and felt herself stiffen with irritation.

'What are you trying to tell me, Lewis?'

'Just, ca' canny,' Lewis replied. 'Be careful. I don't want to see you getting hurt.'

'I can look after myself,' Annie bristled.

'Aye, well.' Lewis paused, and when he spoke again his voice was much more conciliatory. 'Chris strikes me as genuine, to be fair. In his beliefs, I mean. But he wasn't always Mr Saintly. There were rumours at school that he was, or more accurately his cousin Conor was, bringing in some coke and hash to the area.'

Annie snorted. 'Not buying that, Lewis. Chris is as straight as they come.'

'To be fair, I found it hard to believe then, and even more so now. But you know, no smoke without fire.'

'Jesus, I hate that expression. It's for folk who desperately want to believe bad stuff about someone.' There was a heavy silence on the other end. 'But I'm sure that's not what you're like,' she added, trying to retain the happy mood she was in before Lewis phoned. 'Anyway. Why did you call?'

'This big service? Has Chris talked to you about that?'

Annie thought about the last time Chris had been in her bed. After they'd made love, he'd become fairly loquacious, telling her about what the service might mean for the church and him.

'Just that they think it's going to be a big earner for them. That it might lead to more expansion in the US. He even talked about going over there and doing a lecture tour.' For a moment, Annie conjured an image of Chris on stage, in front a massive audience, arms wide, accepting the applause of his congregation. She tried to see herself, off to the side, watching, waiting for her man, and decided, surprisingly, that she liked the idea.

'Yeah, but that's more about religion as a business rather than actual missionary work.'

'Not like you to be so cynical, Lewis.'

'Just being a clear-eyed accountant, Annie. I don't think you appreciate the scale of this. We're talking possible multi-millions, and I worry that this potential new congregation of his isn't going to appreciate him having a girlfriend who's psychic. Religious fundamentalists – and let's not kid ourselves, that's the congregation he's tapping into – will not appreciate women who can tell of someone's impending demise.'

'I'm not his girlfriend.' If she wasn't that, what was she to him?

She felt herself heat with disappointment that he might not see her that way. And then chided herself for being so flaky.

'Has he persuaded you, then?'

'To go up for the anniversary service? Yeah. You?'

'I've been invited, yes, but it depends on work. Not sure I can justify two or three days off with the workload I've got.' He paused. 'But Annie...?'

'What?'

'Just ... before you commit, think about what this might mean for you. A return to your childhood home? The place where you first heard these murmurs. The place where you experienced a trauma bad enough to cause permanent memory loss. Aren't you worried about what might happen?'

'Of course I am, Lewis.' She felt her heart stutter with fear, and sweat film the palms of her hands. She set her jaw against the worry. 'But thanks for spelling it out for me,' she snapped. 'Bye.' She cut the connection before she said anything else.

Phone on the table in front of her, she sat back, deep in thought, considering his warning. Maybe that's just what she needed. To go back up to her childhood home and face her demons.

Maybe that's where the answers lay.

Chapter 63

Lewis – Now

When Lewis called Annie back after their little spat a few days before, the first thing she told him was about her failed attempt to contact Sister Theresa.

'I meant to tell you last time,' she said, 'but ... well, we ended the call abruptly. They told me she's on retreat. But I'm sure they were just fobbing me off.'

'And that was a couple of weeks ago? Maybe she's back from her retreat now? I have a day off. Let's go to Oswald House today. See what we can dig up about Bridget. I can come and collect you?'

There was a long pause, and when she replied it sounded like Annie's voice was coming from far away. 'That's ... yeah ... Come by and...'

'You don't sound too good, sis,' he said, feeling a sense of alarm. 'Would you rather I come over and sit with you?' He often sensed that Annie wasn't having a good day, but right now she sounded as low as he'd ever heard her. 'You seeing Chris today?' he asked.

'No,' she replied. Lewis detected a sound, as if she had a dry mouth and had just tried to swallow. 'He's been busy with church stuff the last couple of days.'

'When he's with you is it better?' he asked. 'Are you more able to handle the murmurs then?'

'Yeah.' She gave a gruff, self-deprecating laugh. 'What does that say about me, eh? Whenever did I need a man to make me feel better?'

'Does it leave you altogether?' Lewis was caught between

feeling pleased there was something that helped, being a little envious it wasn't him, and worrying that so soon into their relationship Chris might have some sort of hold over her. He was a good and kind man as far as Lewis could tell, but he had a past – hinted at by the rumours of him helping Conor push a little bit of drugs up in Mossgow. And surely any sort of dependence was unhealthy in a relationship, especially when it was happening so early on?

'God, no,' Annie replied, 'but being with Chris pushes it away a little, if that makes sense?'

'Look,' Lewis said, coming to a decision. 'The Oswald House visit can wait. I'll come over and sit—'

'No, no,' she replied. Her voice was so low Lewis read that she was only just holding it together. 'We need to find out what happened to Bridget.'

'But you don't sound like you're in a fit state to come with me. So, tell you what – I'll go by myself and I'll talk to you later and tell you what I find out. Okay?'

Annie agreed. But he was sure she was just too weak to protest.

*

Sitting in his car outside Oswald House, looking up at the building, he reviewed what they knew so far. It was clear from the evidence they'd uncovered that their aunts had swapped places. That Sheila, who knew she was dying, had forsworn her treatment, and likely experienced a great deal of pain, before the nuns cottoned on to her condition. All to allow her sister, Bridget, the time to achieve her freedom.

The more he thought of that sacrifice, the more it gave him goosebumps. Could he ever act in such a way? In what circumstances might he perform such a kindness?

And the more he considered it, the more he was convinced that someone must have been in a position to make the swap work. First, he considered Tracy Dobell. Trainer reported that she and Bridget had a connection. But he dismissed that theory almost as quickly as it rose in his mind, when he recalled Trainer saying that in one of the last conversations he'd had with Tracy she'd remembered the last time she spoke with Bridget.

If she told you not to go on holiday, don't go on holiday.

Tracy had taken this use of the third person as a sign of Bridget's illness. But Lewis could see that this might have been Sheila letting her guard slip, and reacting honestly in the moment. If the swap did indeed happen?

Which perhaps suggested Tracy was not the one who helped. But who? The nun, Sister Theresa?

And that was why Lewis, on his one day off, was about to knock on the door of Oswald House.

As he pushed open the front door it occurred to Lewis that he hadn't rehearsed what he would say when he met the nun again. With a shrug he decided he'd just go with the flow. His quick tongue rarely let him down.

In the reception area, a young nun stood behind the desk, wearing a smile of welcome. She was tiny and slight, looking like a gust of wind might blow her over.

'Hi.' Lewis gave her his biggest smile. 'I wonder if it's possible to speak to Sister Theresa? Is she back from her retreat?'

'Oh.' She looked surprised, as if few people ever asked to see individual nuns, rather than patients. 'Do you have an appointment?'

'No. My sister and I spoke to her a few months ago about a relative who stayed here years ago. And she remembered Sister Theresa's kindness in letters to me.' Flattery always helped, even if it was lies. 'I just wanted to meet her and say thanks, I guess.' Lewis finished with a daft-laddie shrug. 'Probably sounds strange,' he added. 'But it feels like the right thing to do.'

'Doesn't sound strange at all,' the woman said, and Lewis mentally adjusted his opinion of her age. There was a wisdom behind those eyes, and fine lines around them that he'd missed on first viewing. 'I'll see if she's about.' The nun moved to the side, and sat in front of a computer screen, and after a few clicks of the mouse picked up the desk phone and dialled. Spoke to someone. Gave Lewis a short look, then she hung up.

'She's on her day off,' she reported. 'Which normally means she's not to be disturbed. We often spend our days off in prayer and silent contemplation. I wouldn't want to offend her by breaking into that.'

'Oh,' Lewis replied. *Normally*. 'That's a shame.' And only then did he realise how much he'd hoped to go back to Annie with some concrete, actionable intelligence.

'I'm so sorry,' the sister said, then she looked at him as if reading his disappointment. 'I do know that Sister Theresa often visits the grotto at the far end of the garden on her days off; at least in the morning. If you're lucky,' her eyes darted to the clock on the screen of her computer, 'she might still be there.'

'Grotto?'

'It's a shrine, of sorts. This one to Our Lady. It's in a peaceful little corner. All the sisters and our patients love it,' she trilled. 'Follow the path to the right of the house, into the garden for as far as it goes. You'll come to a small wooded area. Go through the gate, follow the path. You can't miss it.'

Chapter 64

Lewis – Now

Lewis followed the instructions he was given, and five minutes later found himself standing before a little wooden gate. It was about waist height, painted green and standing on its own, no fence on either side, as if its only purpose was to arrest you momentarily; to offer you a moment's pause before you walked into the trees beyond.

A crow called out a warning as he stepped through. A drop of rain sparked on his forehead. A tiny white feather floated past his vision. He trod on, entered the border of the woods and felt the air change, noise muffled by a canopy of leaf and walls of bark.

He felt the downward slope of the path in his knees, and walked on for a couple of minutes before it levelled off, swooped to the left, and before him, at the centre of a cluster of ancient fir trees, stood a small construction with a statue of Our Lady within its stone arch.

The stones were worn smooth, countless raindrops having sloughed off their rough edges. Here and there moss and lichen coloured the stone, but the statue itself looked pristine, as if it had just been placed there moments before.

Our Lady was around five feet tall, covered head to feet in white robes. Only her hands and face were visible. Her hands, steepled in prayer, and her face, serene in supplication; saying the world's burdens were hers and she was glad to shoulder them.

Lewis looked around, and saw no one, so he took a seat on a bench placed off to the right, under the boughs of a little hawthorn tree.

After some time he looked at his watch and tried to calculate how long he'd been waiting, but he couldn't remember when he'd arrived. He took out his phone, but just as he pressed the button on the side to activate it, it died on him.Swearing to himself he slid his phone back in his pocket. A breeze lifted, sighed in his ear. Feeling a growing chill, he pushed his hands into his pockets and braced himself for the wait.

Birdsong resumed. The branches above him swayed in the wind. He could smell wet loam and slowly decaying leaves. He heard a trickle of water, but couldn't work out where it was coming from.

As he waited, hoping that the nun at reception hadn't sent him on some fool's errand, he began to worry about the various tasks he had to do. The clients waiting on work back from him and the upcoming financial-year-end rush that all accountants simultaneously dreaded and appreciated.

After a time, his mind settled. The sounds and scents serving to soothe him. He couldn't remember the last time he'd been in nature without there being a purpose to it rather than just being present. He'd been so busy, so full of the things he had to do for the Jenkins that this was the first proper time out he'd had for an age.

Eventually, deciding Sister Theresa wasn't visiting the grotto that day, Lewis got to his feet and sent a rueful thank-you to the little nun. But as he turned he became aware of a presence; footsteps. A spark of sound as a foot lit on a couple of pebbles. A sigh.

A woman spoke. 'Still here then?'

'Aye,' he replied.

'I've been expecting you,' Sister Theresa said. 'Well, I was expecting the girl, your sister.'

'She's ... busy.'

'C'mon,' she said, and walked over to the bench. 'Need to take the weight off. Old age brings with it a bunch of unwelcome friends.'

They sat. Lewis watching her as she folded herself down onto the wooden slats.

'Sorry about the long wait,' she smiled. 'Given the kind of place we are and the kind of people who come here, if someone unknown arrives and appears agitated, we send them down here, give them time to calm a little before we speak to them.'

'The other nun,' Lewis looked back up towards the house, 'thought I was agitated?'

'Excitable. Or merely strange,' the nun replied with a small smile, and Lewis could see she was pulling his leg.

Sister Theresa blessed herself as she looked over at the statue of Our Lady. 'Would you believe I modelled myself on her? Dear Lord, you could hardly credit the vanity of it. For that alone my soul will spend a couple more decades in Purgatory.'

Lewis said nothing. Nodded. He knew when to remain silent.

'I'm sure you will have heard of us religious types, and the wholly nasty things we get up to. You're probably expecting me to damn myself to the very gates of hell with whatever words trip out of my mouth.'

'I expect nothing, other than the truth.'

'Ah. The truth.' She squinted at Lewis, then looked towards the statue, gave a little nod. Crossed herself, and an expression flitted across her face suggesting she was willing to deal with whatever came next. That she was ready.

'Holy Mary, Mother of God, I could murder a cigarette right now. You don't have the bad grace of being a smoker, do you?'

Lewis smiled, suddenly liking the woman. He shook his head. 'I had other bad habits as a teenager.'

'Glue-sniffing and the like?' she smiled, letting him know she was pulling his leg again. 'Ah sure, whatever they were, I'm certain the good Lord forgave you.' She'd seemed ready to unburden herself when Lewis noticed her make the sign of the cross, but now it felt like she was dragging the moment out.

Branches above them lifted and settled in the breeze. A lone bird sang out. A plaintive note. A call for an act of contrition.

'Your aunt Bridget scared me, you know.' She crossed herself, right hand tapping her forehead, briefly hovering over her heart before touching her left and right shoulders. 'Scared the bejesus out of me.'

Chapter 65

Lewis – Now

They were side by side on the bench, facing the statue of Our Lady. Sister Theresa turned towards Lewis ever so slightly, so that their knees were almost touching.

'I've often thought of her. Bridget. Wondering where she was.' Pause. 'How she was. She wasn't a well young woman when she was with us. That was why I was so worried when I discovered the swap.'

When was that? Lewis wanted to know. If the alarm was raised, was any effort made to find Bridget? He had so many questions.

'But I was already compromised,' the nun said, 'so, when I realised what had happened I was afraid to say anything.'

'Compromised? How?'

'Eleanor. The sister? She was your mother, right?'

Mystified as to where the nun was going with this question, Lewis answered, 'Yes. Why?'

'Maybe "compromised" isn't the right word.' The nun screwed her face up as she considered this. 'Bridget had a baby, did you know?'

'We ... eh?' Bridget was pregnant?

'First things first,' Sister Theresa said. 'Or last things, really.' She shook her head as if dismissing her own words as nonsense. 'When your aunt was discovered to have cancer, that was when we realised, or when *I* realised, we'd been duped. And of course by then it was too late. Sheila, who we thought was Bridget, was dying. And Bridget was off God knows where.'

She studied Lewis's face. 'But you know this, don't you?'

'Yeah,' he replied. 'We only just worked that out. A couple of things just didn't add up. And there was the last photograph taken of the annual fundraiser? Bridget wasn't in it, but Sheila was.'

'Poor Sheila. She haunts me to this day.' Her expression hung with sadness. 'She must have been in so much pain, but she said nothing.' She shook her head. 'She told me that she wanted to give Bridget as much time as possible to get away – and stay away.'

'What I don't understand is why the family wasn't alerted,' Lewis said. 'Did no one try to get in touch to let us know that this had happened, and that Sheila was dying?'

'Of course we did,' she replied. Indignant. 'The only person we could find was Eleanor, your mother. And she didn't want to know.'

'The baby,' Lewis said, while mentally pushing his reaction to his mother's callousness to the side. 'You said Bridget was pregnant. What happened to her baby?'

Sister Theresa jumped abruptly to her feet. Smoothed down the front of her skirt and looked directly into Lewis's eyes. 'I've said enough.' She turned away and walked determinedly back up the path towards the big house.

'Wait a minute,' Lewis shouted after her. 'You can't leave it like that.' He charged after her, overtook her and blocked her path. She reared back, as if frightened, and Lewis held his hands up to show she was in no danger. 'You know something. You have to tell me.'

'The only thing I have to do is to go back inside and make myself a nice cup of tea. I've given you enough of my time.' Her eyes softened. 'Let's just leave it at that, eh, Lewis?'

She walked past him. Lewis kept astride her now, his mind working furiously, picking at everything he had just learned, and pulling at the threads of things left unsaid.

'Bridget had a baby. She wouldn't be allowed to keep it, I don't think, while living in a place like this.' He looked up at the house, imagining bringing up an infant here. 'Either it was adopted or one of her family would have taken it.' He thought about his grandmother. He didn't know much about her, but his mother had alluded to her church upbringing and strong family values. 'My mother was pregnant at the same time...' He heard a change in Sister Theresa's breathing. 'Oh, I'll bet my grandmother made Mum take the baby. What's one more child, eh?' he asked. Then. 'Oh my God.' He held a hand before his mouth. 'I always believed us to be twins.' He stepped in front of Sister Theresa once more. Her eyes darted around him, studiously avoiding his gaze in case, he judged, she gave her thoughts away.

'What did Bridget have?' he insisted. 'A boy or a girl?'

Theresa shook her head slowly. Supressed a cough. Coughed some more. Her coughing built until she was all but bent double. Once it subsided she picked a hanky from her pocket and wiped her mouth. There, on the pristine white, flowered a large clot of blood.

'Oh,' Lewis said.

'Yes,' Sister Theresa replied. Then she exhaled slowly as if releasing her breath in a gentle mist might be kinder to her lungs. 'Look, young man,' she said eventually, 'I will confess to knowing things. Stuff that I swore to keep secret.' She paused. Smiled. 'But there's no one left to protect, is there?'

Wondering where she was going with this Lewis could only shake his head.

'Bring your sister next time,' Theresa said, her eyes soft with entreaty, and her mouth a hard line of self-acceptance. 'And I promise I'll tell you everything I know.'

Chapter 66

Annie – Now

When Chris arrived to take her up to Mossgow, she was so relieved to see him at her door that she threw herself into his arms.

Once they'd disentangled themselves he asked, 'Has it been a tough few days?'

Feeling small, but arguing with herself that she could afford to be vulnerable with this man, she nodded. 'It's been...' emotion pulled her voice into a low croak '...not good.'

'I'm here now, honey,' he replied and pulled her into his arms again, and with her head on the heat of his chest, she felt rather than heard him say, 'I'll keep you safe.' He guided her towards the sofa and they both sat. 'Why don't you tell me what's been going on?' he asked.

'Don't we need to get going?'

'No rush,' he smiled and reached for her hands. 'I can't help but feel there's a little more going on.' He paused, leaving a silence for her to fill.

She began tentatively, worried that he might judge her and find her wanting on some level. 'This psychic thing? The *Herald* talked about it?'

'Yes?'

She felt his attention laser focused on her. He was preparing to listen. Really listen.

'I hear this noise. These voices. There's no pattern to them. They come and go.'

Aware that her heat had risen and her forehead felt damp, she pulled her hair to the side. Could she tell him this? Could she trust him with it? And looking into his eyes she could see her answer. There was no guile there. Nothing but love, and care, and affection. So she detailed her curse, how it told her when people were going to die, how it had affected the women in her family, and how terrified she'd been lately that she might be losing her mind.

He pulled her to him again, speaking low and slow, his voice a soothing as she cried.

'You've been holding all of this in?' he asked after she'd calmed a little.

She nodded. Leaned back. 'God, I must look awful. Puffy eyes and snot.' She wiped her nose with her sleeve.

'You couldn't look more gorgeous to me right now,' he replied. 'And does it help? Has it helped when you're with me?'

Annie held a hand up, thumb and forefinger slightly apart.

'If that means only a little, I'll take that,' Chris replied, looking pleased. 'And is your memory of your time up in Mossgow still a blur?'

She nodded. 'But it's time I faced whatever my mind is protecting me from – whatever happened up there.' She sat forward now, chin up.

'I can only say that if I'm ever faced with some crisis' – Chris reached for her hands, pulled them to his lips and kissed them – 'that I deal with it with as much courage as you're showing right now.'

'You don't think I'm crazy?' she asked, hope that he was accepting her – warts, curse and all – sparking up like a pilot light in her chest.

'Unusual? Yes.'

She mock swatted at his shoulder and laughed, and found that her laughter was the first genuine version she'd heard from herself for a while.

'Crazy, no.' He smiled. 'I'm not going to pretend that many people in my congregation wouldn't be disbelieving, even wary of you, but, Annie Jackson, you are an amazing woman, facing up to a trial with real courage and I can't wait to get to know you even better.'

❋

In the car, and aiming for the motorway and the drive north, Annie stole a look at Chris. He was so obviously pleased with his new car, Annie had to almost bite her lip to stop herself laughing. He practically purred whenever Annie asked him any questions about the gadgets in the cockpit.

'It is very nice, to be fair,' Annie said, while relaxing back into the soft cushioned leather of the passenger seat.

'It's just a car,' Chris replied, aiming for humility, and failing. Besides, thought Annie, if he really wanted to be humble he could have settled for a basic Ford or something rather than a top-of-the-line Audi. 'Anyway,' he said, while reaching across to lightly squeeze her knee, 'I'm so glad you agreed to come up to Mossgow for the celebration.'

Annie didn't reply, she simply looked out of her window, watching the scenery unfold, and acknowledged that she was about to revisit her childhood home for the first time. A thought that gave her a stab of unease. Her mind was hiding her memories from her for a reason; might going back there bring them all back?

'Hey,' Chris said, as if sensing her thoughts. 'If it's too much, we can head back.'

'No,' she replied, shaking her head. 'I'll be fine. I'm ... fine.'

'I get it,' he said. 'The first time back since you were a kid.' He sent her a small smile of support. 'The brain is a pretty smart engine,' he added. 'It will be hiding from you the things that you don't need to know. And the things it judges you need to know will be revealed when you have the strength to deal with them.' He squeezed her leg again. 'If at any time you feel unsafe just let me know and I'll bring you back down to Glasgow.'

'No, you can't. You've got—'

'I'm serious,' he said. 'The memorial service isn't going out live, so I can play with my time a little. Don't worry about me.'

Annie smiled her thanks at his thoughtfulness. 'It's time I went back.' With an effort she roused herself into good cheer. 'I spent a large chunk of my life up there and it's mostly a blank. It can't all have been bad.'

Chris smiled. 'You had great neighbours.'

'Were Danni and I great pals?'

'Yeah,' he replied. 'Lewis and I played together and stuff, but we weren't close like you guys were.'

'That's nice,' she said. 'I have this sense Mum was such hard work and that it must have been great to have someone to talk about that with. I'm not sure Lewis would have been much help; he won't hear a bad word said against her.'

'Mothers and sons, eh?' Chris said.

'I haven't spoken with Lewis for a couple of days,' she said. 'When's he coming up?'

'Oh,' Chris shot her a look. 'I doubt he'll manage it actually. There's been a bit of a financial cock-up in the books, and I've asked him to look into something for me. It's going to take him the whole weekend to get it sorted.'

They fell into silence, eyes ahead as the large car ate up the miles. Rain pattered against the windscreen, and the wipers smoothly cleared it away. There was nothing but their breath and the whoosh of the tyres on the tarmac road.

But there was also a rising feeling of trepidation. Despite her attempts to allay any concerns Chris had for her, she was feeling worse with every mile they drew closer to her childhood home. Why had she agreed to this? Should she ask him to turn around, as he offered, and take her back home?

No, she decided, there was a good reason for her going back up to Mossgow. She couldn't help but feel it would do her some good, no matter how difficult it might prove to be.

'Are we there yet?' She forced a joke.

Chris laughed. He looked around. 'Any of this scenery standing out to you?'

Annie gazed around. 'Nope. How close are we?'

'Only a couple of miles to go. We're almost at Loch Morvern, and Mossgow is at the head of the loch.' He nodded his head to Annie's side of the car. 'On your side is Martyr's Hill.' Annie looked upwards. Amber-leafed trees studded the hillside. At the top stood a slim, stone tower as tall as a house.

'We were a bloodthirsty lot back in the day. I'm glad religion isn't quite so contentious these days.'

The road straightened and a stretch of water appeared before them.

'Loch Morvern,' Chris announced, a note of pride in his voice. 'Isn't it beautiful?' The sun chose that moment to edge out from behind a cloud, kissing the hilltops beyond in gold and silvering the still surface of the water.

'Wow,' Annie said, attempting to meet Chris's enthusiasm with some of her own. She waited to see if her mind would present her with sights or sounds from her past. Nothing. She exhaled with relief.

They passed one house, then another, then a row of four white, linked cottages set back from the road. Chris slowed at a bend, the road swooped to the left, with the loch on the right, then it was a low walled bridge and the stretch of road that led to the greater bulk of the homes that made up Mossgow and the church complex.

As they crossed, Annie studied the low wall of the bridge, her heart a heavy thud in her chest, wondering if this was the bridge and corner her mother had failed to negotiate that fateful day all those years ago.

'Oh,' Chris broke the silence, as if he'd suddenly just remembered something. 'I don't want to set tongues wagging. I'm sure you'll understand.'

'Sorry?' Annie asked.

'I've booked you – well, Danni has booked you – into the local hotel rather than have you stay with us. The Lodge on the Loch? You might remember it?'

She was staying at the hotel? Annie felt a twist of fear. How would her curse react? Wasn't this where she'd warned Jenny Burns about the red car? Could she deal with it without Chris's strong arms around her? She turned to face him, smiled and nodded. What else could she do? If Chris felt he had to protect his congregation from the fact that he was a fully functional young man, then who was she to argue. Besides, as the idea of having some time on her own settled in her mind, Annie considered that might prove to be for the best. At worst, if she did lose it there would be no one there as a witness. And at best, she could brace herself and prepare should an onslaught of memories burst into her mind.

Chapter 67

Lewis – Now

Mind in turmoil, Lewis drove back to his flat. Once inside he sat in front of his computer ready to jump into the work that Chris Jenkins had asked him to do for the church. The request had the feel of overkill. The tax authorities had already been given most of this information, but he could see that Chris was covering his back, and besides, he was the client. And the customer was always right? ... Right?

It meant he couldn't go up to Mossgow for the service, which was too bad. It also meant he couldn't be there for Annie. God knows how she would react to being back there. Would she be able to deal with any memories that presented themselves to her? She had told him that things weren't quite so bad when Chris was around – but, once again, he wondered whether that was really a good thing at this early stage of their relationship? Would she be better off here with him, looking into the facts around Bridget's disappearance?

The visit with Sister Theresa played over and over again in his mind. What did she know? What on earth would she tell them that would let them get to the truth? Was Bridget the mother of one of them? Were he and Annie cousins and not siblings? If that was the case that would take some getting used to.

Annie might be mightily pissed off with the woman who'd raised them as her own, but if one of them wasn't hers, would it change Annie's opinion of her? Taking on a child was the act of a person of good heart and strong character.

An image of his mother rose in his mind. He felt her hand on his shoulder. A boy receiving a well-done message for something. He couldn't recall any more detail, but it was a good moment, and one that told him he was loved. Why couldn't Annie see there was good in the woman who raised them?

With a shake of his head he opened the files Chris had emailed him and began to examine them.

A few minutes later, there was a knock at his door. Loud. Insistent. With a sigh, he pushed himself away from his desk and went to answer, thinking he could do without the distraction.

He opened the door, half expecting it to be a parcel delivery.

'Lewis. Hi.' There was a man on his doorstep, hand in the air in greeting.

'What the hell, Trainer?' Lewis said. 'What are you doing here?'

'I just need a quick word—'

'You have a bloody nerve,' Lewis interrupted. 'You're looking for Annie again. If you don't quit I'll have you locked back up so quickly—'

'Chris Jenkins,' Trainer interrupted now, his voice raised. 'This pastor guy? You need to look into him. He's not what he seems.'

'Oh, fuck off, Trainer,' Lewis said, and moved to slam the door shut, but Trainer stuck his foot in the gap. Lewis stumbled back a half-step; was Trainer threatening to force himself in?

He pulled himself upright. He was in his own home. He shouldn't be cowed by this guy. Ignoring his suddenly dry mouth and racing heart, and the thought that Trainer was a convicted killer, Lewis stuck his chin out. 'Get your foot out of my doorway, or I'm calling the police.'

'Just let me say this and I'll be gone.'

'What?' Lewis crossed his arms, planted his feet wide. What was this guy's game?

'Conor Jenkins? He's in the same halfway house as me. He wants to speak to you and Annie.'

'He does?'

Lewis was reminded of the times that Chris wasn't available to play because his big cousin was in town. From memory, Conor wasn't the most pleasant boy to be around. There was an afternoon when Conor and his parents visited the Jenkins next door. Chris, Conor, and Lewis were in the garden kicking the ball back and forth. For most of the hour or so they were playing, Conor had one hand in the pocket of his jeans and a scowl on his face. Every word out of his mouth felt like a jab aimed at Lewis.

'Fucksake,' Conor had mumbled eventually. 'Fucking kindergarten or what?' Then he'd looked Lewis up and down. 'Hey, loser,' he said. 'Why don't you fuck off back to your own garden and leave the grownups to chat.'

Feeling the spite rising from the older boy, Lewis had found himself relieved to have an out. Whenever Conor was in town thereafter, he was happy to leave him and Chris to their own devices.

'I'm not surprised that arsehole ended up in the same place as you, Trainer,' he said now. 'He was a spoiled brat back in the day...' He wondered what Conor had done to end up in prison, but he curbed his curiosity. 'I had no interest in talking to him back then, and even less now. So why don't you get your foot out of my doorway and piss off.'

'But...'

Lewis stared Trainer down. 'Fucking leave.' Lewis plucked his phone from his pocket. Stared at the screen. 'Wonder what the number for the local police station is?'

Trainer shook his head. 'Just. Watch that pastor.' He lifted his foot out of the way, and with relief, Lewis slammed the door shut.

Moments later the letterbox flap opened, a piece of paper floated onto his doormat. 'My number,' Trainer called through. 'In case you change your mind.'

'Not happening,' Lewis shouted back. Ignoring the piece of paper he made his way back to his computer, mind set on continuing his work.

✳

A couple of hours later he made a coffee then sat and stared at the files on his computer screen. Nothing was registering anymore. He couldn't wipe from his mind Trainer's expression while he'd been standing in his doorway. There had been a certainty there. A naked and urgent need to arrange this meeting.

Should he have heard him out? Could there be something in what he'd said about Chris – that he wasn't what he seemed?

He brought up the church's Facebook page and skimmed through the posts, not even sure what he was looking for. They focused on the anniversary, the latest Sunday service, and a slew of inspirational memes about Christianity and its message for a better and more meaningful life.

All of the posts had a great deal of engagement from their audience. Lots of 'amens' with the hands-in-prayer emoji. More than a few with 'greetings' and people mentioning the country or town they were from. As Lewis suspected, many of them were from the US and Canada, but there were comments from lots of places throughout the UK, including Scotland.

Lewis continued to run down the page, noting how the comments had grown in number since the page opened. He found one of the earlier posts. It was a recording of a Sunday service, the link to the YouTube page frozen on an image of Chris in his robes, arms wide, face up to a beam of light that illuminated his features in a very flattering manner.

He found himself shaking his head. This didn't chime with the boy he remembered all those years ago. As far as he could recall, when it came to church attendance Chris had mostly just gone along with the demands of his domineering father. Had Chris eventually had some kind of epiphany? What had happened to change the boy he knew to the man he saw in that image?

Similar comments to previous ones he read were listed below the post:

Excellent service with a definitely meaningful message. Thank you. Peace and blessings.

May God bless all.

And from one particularly zealous follower he read: *Greatest man in history named Jesus. Had no servants, yet they called Him Master. Had no degree, yet they call Him Teacher. He committed no crime yet they crucified Him. Share if you believe.*

Fair enough, thought Lewis. Whatever gets you through the day.

Then, further down a comment that didn't chime with the rest.

He's a fake, you morons.

With eyebrows raised in interest, Lewis read the name of the comment's author.

Conor Jenkins.

With a heightened pulse Lewis clicked on Conor's name. When his page came up it was mostly empty. Conor's last post was from the time of the pandemic, warning people that masks were ineffective and that this was all an experiment by big business and their shyster politicians to keep the little people under control.

Only a handful of photographs were on show. He scrolled through.

It took a long minute before the importance of one of the pictures leaked through. In the background was a rounded hill, with a monument on top. In the foreground, two young men, one more of a boy really. Conor and Chris Jenkins. They were several inches apart, and there was a stiffness there, as if neither wanted to be too close to the other. But they must have been in concert about something – both had their arms crossed, and legs crossed at the ankle, while they leaned against the bonnet of a small car.

A small, red car.

Chapter 68

Annie – Now

Heart a hammer in her chest Annie walked into the reception area of the hotel. She stole a look over her shoulder and saw the rear brake lights of Chris's car shine as he stopped at the junction on the way out of the hotel grounds. Could she run out there and catch him? Despite her assertions, now that she was here – in her past – she wanted nothing more than to tear back to Glasgow.

Too late. She watched as Chris's car merged into the traffic and drove away.

With a slow tread she made her way to the reception desk, taking in the excess of tartan and deer antlers on show.

A man seated behind the desk rose when he saw her. He was looking at her as if he'd seen a ghost.

'Annie Jackson?'

Annie looked at his name badge, which read *Harry Burns, Manager*. Right. Jenny's father.

'Jings,' he said. 'You've hardly changed, dear.'

Harry Burns walked out from behind the desk, his hand extended, a bright but tired smile on his face, and Annie thought he looked like a man who carried his own personal haunting around with him. 'I saw the name on the bookings, and didn't add it up.' He shook his head. 'Was it the newspaper article?' He took her hand and shook it.

'Sorry?'

'Oh, you're not here to...' His face flushed, and then his expression sagged with disappointment.

'I'm here for the Church of the Everlasting Christ,' Annie replied. 'Pastor Jenkins...' It felt so strange using Chris's formal title; a man she'd seen naked on several occasions, a figure of religious respect. 'The anniversary service.'

'Ah, that,' Harry said, with the tone of the terminally unconvinced. 'I thought. Well, I hoped...' Whatever he was going to say next got lost in a nervous hiccup. 'You were lucky to get a room, Annie. The anniversary has seen a pretty impressive rise in business.' His lugubrious features formed a weathered smile. 'Your pastor might be young but he can fairly rile up a religious fervour in the devoted.'

Annie looked around for an escape. 'If I could book in? Get my room key?'

'Of course.' Harry gave a small bow. 'I'll just...' He walked back behind the desk, stared at the computer screen for a moment, mouthed something to himself and said, 'Room 213.' Then gave her directions to her room. 'Will you be wanting to book a table? I'd suggest you do, Annie. We are very busy.' He coloured. 'I already said that, didn't I?'

'Yes,' Annie replied, adding as much kindness to her tone as she could muster. Despite her deep and growing misgivings about where she was and why she was there, on her own, she was painfully aware that the man's nervousness was down to his desire to ask her if she could help in any way to solve the defining question of his existence: what happened to his daughter?

※

She made it to her bedroom, threw her small suitcase on the bed, and put on the small TV in the corner for some background noise. She plucked her mobile phone from the pocket in her jeans. Checked the number of signal bars. One. That figured. Then she noted that she'd had four missed calls. Two from numbers she didn't recognise, and another two from Lewis. She pressed redial for Lewis and nothing happened. She looked at the front of the screen again. No bars this time.

A knock sounded at her door.

It could only be one person. He must have changed his mind. Her heart warmed through with relief, affection and gratitude, to an extent that surprised her. She really was falling for this guy. A smile stretching her face, she checked her hair in the mirror and rushed to let him in.

Chapter 69

Lewis – Now

The red car.

Jesus, the red car. Was this the car that Annie warned Jenny Burns about?

No. It couldn't be. That would make Chris a killer, and whatever the man was he wasn't that.

Lewis had to speak to Conor.

He called the number Trainer had left for him. No answer.

He phoned Annie.

No answer.

He closed the lid of his laptop and threw himself back in his chair. He was reading too much into things. He was attaching importance to a random picture, and a very common car. Any number of people would have had a red car around that time. The one in the picture must have been Conor's, because Chris would have been too young to drive.

He felt his eyes grow heavy. He looked at the time on his phone. It was six-thirty in the evening. A couple of hours on the church files, then bed, then he'd spend the next day on the files, and drive up to Mossgow the following morning, despite having decided not to go. He would surprise Annie and keep an eye out just in case Chris was up to something.

But then he recalled Annie's irritation. Her entreaty to him to let her look after herself.

The red car.

Nope. He just couldn't see Chris being caught up in something as horrible as a missing girl. He was too homely, too in thrall to his beliefs, too *nice*.

Conor, on the other hand? He was presently in a halfway house; the same lodgings as Eddie Trainer, a convicted murderer. Maybe he was the bad one in all of this.

But then … could Chris be involved in something with his good-for-nothing cousin? Chris was now earning a lot of money. Cash tended to bring out the worst in the arseholes in your life. Could Conor be looking to exploit an old relationship? Set Chris up and bribe him? By all accounts Conor was in dire straits, so such a scenario could well be plausible.

He rubbed at his forehead. He was overthinking, and tired. But he now had a way to find some answers.

❊

At the halfway house he and Annie had traced Trainer to a few months previously. Lewis knocked on the door and asked to speak to Conor Jenkins.

He was kept waiting for ten minutes before the man himself appeared.

'Lewis Jackson? When they said you were here…' He pointed vaguely behind him. 'Man, you've changed from that wee wimp I used to bump into up in Mossgow.'

Lewis knew Conor was only four or five years older than him, but he looked as if the age difference was nearer twenty. His face was lined, cheeks sunken, his hair a lifeless and greasy brown and reaching to his shoulders. Lewis tried, and failed, to reconcile the man in front of him with the youth he'd known.

'Hey,' Lewis said simply. Now that he was here, he was unsure as to what he should do next. 'Is there somewhere quiet we could talk?'

Conor nodded. 'There's a quiet corner in the lounge.' He pointed to a wide glass door.

Wondering how Conor had ended up in such an establish-ment, Lewis followed him into a long, wide room filled with tables and chairs. A few other men were scattered around the room. Conor nodded at a couple of people, waved at another, while guiding them to the far corner, by a window. He sat on a small armchair and pointed at another for Lewis.

Lewis took a seat, and looked around. 'You wanted to see me?' he asked.

Conor bit his lip. Nodded. 'Trainer spoke to you, aye?'

Lewis looked around the room again. 'Is he here?'

Conor slumped in his chair, hands clasped in his lap. 'No idea where he is mate. That guy's a law unto himself. He's gonnae get himself into bother one of these days.' Then he peered into Lewis's eyes, and Lewis read a spark of intelligence there. 'What did Eddie tell you?'

'Nothing, to be honest,' Lewis replied. 'I didn't want to listen.'

Conor responded with a gruff, humourless laugh. 'He has that effect on folk.' He grew serious again. 'He's got a thing about your sister, man. Never stops talking about her. I was you, I'd be following that cunt everywhere, making sure he didn't lay a hand on her.'

Lewis felt his heart give a twist of fear. 'She's fine. Annie can look after herself.'

'You sure about that? I wouldn't want that on my conscience, knowing I could have done something to stop him.'

'Nah, not buying it. If he's an actual murderer, why is he so intent on proving his innocence?'

'Are you really that naïve, Lewis?' Conor leaned close. 'Everybody in this place tells you they were innocent. We're just a group credit card away from ordering T-shirts saying *It Wiznae Me, Your Honour*.' He leaned back. 'And as for Trainer? Bet you didn't know he broke into your sister's flat?'

'He did what?' Lewis shot forward in his seat, his mind sparking thoughts of violence towards Trainer.

'Aye.' Conor nodded grimly. 'While she was sleeping in her bed, by the way. Came up with some bullshit that he was looking for clues to see if she really was this psychic woman he'd heard about. Don't know what he could have been looking for – some tarot cards or a fucking crystal ball?' He grinned, and Lewis felt the urge to slap it off his face. 'Does she have a Ouija board?'

'Shut up.' Lewis felt himself tremble with worry for Annie. Where might Trainer be right this moment?

'Anyway, if you didn't listen to Trainer, how did you find me, and why are you here? Want to hear what I've got to say, after all?'

Lewis tore his thoughts from this fresh worry about Annie. 'I do some work for Chris's church, and I was looking through their Facebook page when I saw a comment you'd made. And I also came across the picture of you and Chris in front of a red car.' Lewis studied Conor for a reaction.

'The red car,' Conor replied, his eyes narrow, his expression inscrutable. 'Your sister still coming up with psychic shit?'

'Did you see the newspaper article?'

Conor rubbed at his chin. 'Chris's old man freaked out about that stuff back in the day. I remember him going on about witches, saying they should all be burned. Your sister really got him going, man.'

'Why would...? I think you owe me an explanation,' Lewis said.

'I loved that wee car,' Conor said. 'My pride and joy it was.' He stretched his legs out, and Lewis noted his tattered and stained sports shoes. The Conor he encountered as a boy would never have been seen dead in them.

Conor saw his stare and, eyes full of self-loathing, said, 'How the mighty are fallen, eh?'

Lewis studied the other man, wondering how to respond. Was Conor looking for some kind of sympathy, because he didn't feel able to offer any.

'Did you have anything to do with the disappearance of Jenny Burns?' he asked.

Conor exhaled. 'First things first, Lewis.' He leaned forward.

'You might think you know me, but you don't. What do you re-member about those days back in Mossgow?'

'Your parents owned the big house and the estate. You visited Chris now and again. Acted like you'd rather be anywhere else.'

'I bet I came across as a right wanker.'

Lewis didn't see the point in pretending otherwise so he nodded. 'Chris and I sometimes played together. Watched foot-ball, exchanged comics, that kind of thing. But whenever you were visiting he didn't want to know me.'

Conor sniffed and looked like he wanted to spit. 'Tells you everything you need to know about that prick.'

'I can't remember seeing you in a red car,' Lewis said, trying to get the conversation back on track.

Conor's shrug told Lewis he didn't have an answer for that. 'I didn't often come and pick Chris up, to be fair. We mostly met at my house. His old man would bring him over when he wanted a drink and a blether with my parents.' He paused. 'Although, it was more like when he *wanted* something from my parents. Uncle Dennis wasn't the chatty type.'

Lewis was getting impatient now. Did Conor just want to com-plain about his family? 'What exactly did you want to talk to me and Annie about?' he said.

Conor titled his head back, then let it slump forward. His eyes dimmed in and out of focus. Was he on something? Lewis didn't think an establishment like this would permit the taking of drugs, so what was going on with the guy?

'I killed someone.' He exhaled, shame weakening his voice. He met Lewis's gaze. 'No, not in the red car.'

'You killed someone?' he asked, noting the difficulty Conor had in saying those three words.

'He was a good guy. My mate,' Conor said, his eyes heavy with regret. 'We were fighting over a hit, would you believe? He wouldn't let me go first. I was desperate, so I hit him with the first thing I could see. Which happened to be a half-brick. And he ...

died.' He rubbed at the right side of his face. 'He was a good guy.' He leaned forward, his hands between his knees. 'I already said that. Not my finest moment,' he added. 'Before I tell you what you need to hear, you should know this...' He held his hands out. 'Everything you see of me in this moment is as a result of what happened back then.' He paused, chewed on his lower lip. 'I'm a fucking wreck, and our Chris is head of a church and making millions. What does that tell you?'

'I won't know what it tells me until I have the whole story,' Lewis replied.

'Mossgow?' Conor said, as if Lewis hadn't spoken. 'I hated the place. Yeah, I came across as a spoiled brat, but I loathed going home. Three hours on shitty roads from civilisation? The arse end of nowhere? The only thing that made it bearable was getting my hands on some shit beforehand and then watching Chris show me how tough he was.'

'By shit, you mean drugs.'

'Yes,' Conor replied. 'The olds were too busy to, you know, raise their own kid, so I was put out to boarding school in Edinburgh. Fucking hated it there as well. Everyone was a bully, but drugs were easy to get a hold of in the city and that made it okay.'

Lewis opened his mouth to interject. He realised that Conor was building his part, trying to make himself appear more sympathetic, but Lewis needed to push him towards talking about the importance of that red car; he knew his sister was with Chris as they spoke and he needed to know if she was in any danger.

But then he questioned his source. Was Conor really trying to unburden himself, or had he watched as Chris and the church grew rich and decided he wanted to derail them. There was a bitterness studded through everything he said.

'Save me the self-serving crap, Conor. What's with the red car? Did you guys have anything to do with what happened to Jenny Burns?'

'Okay,' Conor said as if bracing himself for the moment when a long-held secret was aired. 'This one time, I drove up to Mossgow in my new car for a family get-together. My dad's fiftieth, and Mum had this huge party organised. So, you know, much as I wanted to blow the whole thing off, I kinda had to be there.

'But as soon as I could, I made my apologies and persuaded Chris to come along for a drive. With the thought that we would park up somewhere and get high. Chris knew about this wee lay-by surrounded by trees an' shit where no one would spot us. As the only son of a church elder he couldn't be seen to be so delinquent, so we took our stuff away from prying eyes.'

'I didn't know Chris was into drugs,' Lewis said. 'I mean, there were rumours that you guys could get your hands on some stuff, but I put that down to gossip.'

Conor raised his eyebrows. 'He wasn't really. He was just so weak-chinned he wanted to appear tough and more worldly. So, anyway, on the way to Chris's hideaway, just as we passed that big hotel, we saw a young woman walking along the loch road.'

'Jenny Burns?'

Conor nodded. 'She was a year or so older than Chris, and he fancied the pants off her. Normally he wouldn't risk the rejection, you know? But this night, with the drugs in our pockets, me down from the big city, driving my new car, Chris felt he couldn't fail to pull.

'I drew up beside her. She was walking on the passenger side of the car, so Chris rolled down his window, and asked her if she wanted to get high. She, I have to say, jumped at the chance.'

Conor leaned forward on his elbows. Licked his lips. Looked at Lewis, and out of the window. Shadows loomed in the dark of his eyes; shadows, and enough regret to weigh down any man's soul. Regret, and loathing.

'That prick,' he said. 'You just have a think about those two boys back then and what's happened to them since.' Lewis could see that Conor was about to try and absolve himself somehow; offer some sort of amelioration.

'What happened next?' Lewis said, insistent now.

'Think about it,' Conor said, stuck on his own mental track. 'One of those boys' – he pointed at his own chest – 'is so riven with guilt he's in and out of prison, and on and off the drugs for the rest of his life. The other...' he paused meaningfully '...becomes a man of the cloth.'

Chapter 70

Annie – Now

Annie opened the door to see Eddie Trainer holding a hand up.

'We need to talk, Annie,' he said.

Alarm sparked in every cell of her body. She slammed the door shut, put the bolt on, and cursed herself for not looking through the peephole first. She leaned her back against the door, bracing herself for his knock.

'I'm sorry, Annie.' His voice came at her in a strangled half-whisper. 'I don't mean to scare you.'

'I'm calling the police, Eddie,' she shouted, her pulse hammering in her neck. 'How the hell did you know where to find me?'

'Don't call the police. At least until you've heard me out.'

Annie resisted the urge to shout for help. 'I've got my phone in my hand. I'm dialling.'

'Annie, please, you need to listen to me. I'm not here to hurt you, I swear.'

'So says the man that's followed me for a hundred-odd miles.'

Silence.

Then footsteps getting nearer, while another set of footsteps drummed as if moving away.

Annie put her eye to the peephole. There was no one there.

At first. Then a familiar face.

'Danni,' Annie exclaimed as she opened the door.

'Pleased to see me?' Danni asked with a look of bemusement.

Annie stepped outside her door, looked either way along the corridor. There was no one there.

'Did you see a guy?'

Danni shook her head. 'Are you okay, Annie? You look rattled.'

'There was someone at my door. Remember that guy who was outside the café that time? Trainer? You must have scared him off.' Annie looked each way again, but still could see no one. 'You sure you didn't see anyone when you were walking along the corridor?'

Danni held up her smartphone in reply. 'I was checking my emails,' she said with a self-deprecating smile. 'Can't ever turn off.' In her other hand she carried a large and bloated plastic bag. 'Going to ask me in?'

'Sorry. Sure,' Annie said, and stepped back into her room. Danni followed.

'Got a corkscrew?' Danni pocketed her phone and pulled a bottle of wine out of the plastic bag.

Now that her pulse was recovering, Annie was able to note her disappointment that it wasn't Chris standing there with a bottle of wine in his hand.

'From where I'm standing' – she squinted at the bottle – 'that is a screw top.'

'Such a pro,' Danni laughed. 'Thirsty?'

'Of course,' Annie replied.

'Glasses?'

'Probably,' Annie replied looking around the room.

'Bingo.' Danni tracked across to a mini bar, set the glasses she found there side by side, cracked open the bottle, poured, and handed a glass to Annie. 'Hope you don't mind drinking red wine out of a water tumbler.'

'To be honest, I'd drink it out of a farmer's welly right now.' Annie held a hand to her throat. Had she imagined Eddie turning up at her door like that?

Danni laughed. 'Good to see you haven't taken the huff at my brother's thoughtlessness.'

'I know.' Annie sat on the edge of the bed, her fright over Eddie still trembling through her. 'Who takes their girlfriend away for a few days and then leaves them on their own in a hotel?'

'A two-faced religious type, that's who,' Danni replied, sitting down with a grin.

'What happened to family loyalty?' Annie asked, trying hard not to show how rattled she still was.

'I'm only saying what he would say himself. He knows there's a contradiction at play here, but things are going so well with our various congregations and we don't want to jeopardise that.' She shook her head. 'People can be so judgemental. They forget that the heads of their churches are people too. We all have a mix of gifts and problems, don't we?'

Danni prattled on about their plans for the filming, the size of the audience, how many countries might tune in, and how it might lead to a US tour.

'Oh, that reminds me.' She picked up the plastic bag that she'd deposited on the floor by her side. 'What size shoe are you? We're about the same height and I'm a size six.' She reached inside the bag and pulled out a pair of walking boots and a brown quilted jacket.

Annie looked at her. 'Yes, I'm a six too. What are they for?'

'Turns out the sound crew have messed up. They've sent for a part, a lead or something, that is crucial by the way, but it won't arrive until late tomorrow afternoon, at the earliest.'

'And?'

'A window of opportunity has opened up, so to speak. Chris wants to take you up into the hills to his favourite spot.' Danni performed a little seated jig. 'So exciting. He's organised a proper picnic and everything. Champagne and sandwiches. It's like something out of a romantic movie.'

'Wait? He's what?'

'He's never even taken me up there,' she mused. 'Now, promise you won't let on. I was just supposed to drop off the boots and the jacket. But you know me. I can't hold my water.' She looked dreamily into Annie's eyes. 'I've never seen him like this over a woman. He talks about you *all* the time. He's besotted.'

'What are you trying to tell me?' Annie sat back. Her mind presented her with an image of Chris down on one knee. 'Oh my God.' She held a hand to her mouth. She didn't know how she would react if Danni's reading of the situation was correct. 'But we've only known each other, really, for such a short time.' She was enjoying his company. She appreciated how being with him gave her the energy to fend off her fears about the murmurs and about her sanity – but marrying the man?

Was she ready for this? Did she love him? Was it fair to impose the full version of her onto him? How would she be able to manage those times when the horror of the murmurs became too much?

'Nothing. I'm saying nothing,' Danni said, after hinting at a whole lot. She moved a hand across her mouth and made a small locking-key motion at the corner of her lips. 'All you need to know is you're going for a picnic, with a hot young man, to a beautiful spot in the hills. A lost ruined village, or something.' She beamed. 'How romantic is that?'

Chapter 71

Lewis – Now

Conor slumped in his chair, long, thin legs stretched out in front of him. He swallowed. Scratched at his neck as if the consequence of his sin was burrowed deep in there. 'Jenny,' he said. 'I'll never get her face out of my mind.'

'What happened? Lewis asked.

'We ... we parked up...' He exhaled sharply at whatever memory had presented itself. '...And took some drugs.

'She took too much. Classic rookie mistake, but we were too out of it to notice. And by the time we came round from our own highs, Jenny was...' His head moved from side to side as if he was weighing up his words; which might cast him in the best light. '... She was unresponsive.'

'Didn't you think to get some help?' Lewis wanted to grab Conor by the throat and throttle the story out of him. 'What did you do with her?'

Conor shook his head again, slowly. Eyes downcast in sorrow and shame. 'It was too late, man. She was gone.' He licked at his lips. 'Christ, I could do with a drink.' He sat up, straight-backed now, as if preparing to accept his responsibility in the events that followed. 'We panicked. We only wanted to get high, and this poor lassie was dead. It was Chris's dad who came up with the idea of hiding Jenny up among the ruins.'

'Dennis Jenkins did what? And what ruins?'

'A lost settlement kinda thing. It's so remote that most of the people who live in the area have no idea it even exists. It was emptied during the Highland clearances. The folk turfed out, their roofs set on fire so they couldn't go back, and the land turned over to sheep.'

Lewis had to stop himself from interrupting. He wasn't stupid. He knew about the clearances.

'I heard later that they had plans to turn the spot into a tourist attraction, but Uncle Dennis, with the help of my dad, put a stop to it. He argued that the church and its history should take precedence when trying to attract people to the area. To this day, apparently no one knows it exists, and we thought by the time she was found, if ever, nature would have done its job, and the cause of death would be inconclusive. Young woman goes walking in the hills, too much booze in her blood. Gets lost, falls, hypothermia sets in. That kind of thing. Happens more often than you think.'

'What about her family, you arsehole?' Lewis demanded. 'They've been going through hell all these years, not knowing what happened to their daughter. All they had was my sister's mention of a red car. You didn't think for a moment that you should have put them out of their misery?'

'What do you think I'm doing?' Conor bristled. 'I'm trying to make amends now.'

'Yeah, too many years too late, you dick. And it looks more like you're trying to get your own back on your cousin.'

Conor's face shifted as his lips curved in a weak smile. 'There is that,' he admitted. 'I've had a lot of time to think,' he added. 'And it boils my piss; his holier-than-thou act, and all that money he's earning while I'm' – he stretched his arms out to indicate the place he was living in – 'a fucking mess.'

'How did Chris's dad get involved?' Lewis demanded.

'When we realised Jenny was dead, Chris panicked. We hid Jenny in some bushes, then he had me drive to a spot where we knew we could get a signal on my phone. Chris called Uncle Dennis and he came out and helped us...' he trailed off a little '... hide her body.'

Lewis could imagine Dennis Jenkins' self-serving justifications. The girl was dead anyway. Nothing could be done to help her, but the boys could be saved from the repercussions of this night, rather than have their lives ruined.

Lewis wondered if even then, old Mr Jenkins had an eye on Chris running the church. Even if that wasn't the case, he could still have wanted to protect his son, and his future prospects, from the consequences of the truth about Jenny's death coming out.

'Where exactly is Jenny buried?' Lewis asked, hand bunched into a fist, wanting nothing more than to slam it into Conor's face. That poor girl. Her poor family. That could have been Annie.

'There's this spot. The hills around it bunch together in almost a horseshoe shape, and in the valley below them there's all these ruins. About a dozen rectangular buildings, I guess. Most of the walls aren't even waist high. On the other side of a wee river – there's stepping stones to cross it – a tree has sprouted up from the middle of one of the houses. We buried her there.'

'How could you...?'

'Young and daft and terrified.' He looked at Lewis, his eyes accusing. 'Easy for you to get all judgey. You weren't there, mate.'

'That's the best you can offer?'

Conor ignored Lewis's question. He shifted in his seat as if deciding on whether or not to say more. He licked his lips.

'But then this woman turned up. Said she saw us carrying the body from the other side of the loch. Demanded to know what we were doing. She was going crazy, saying she was going to call the cops. She recognised Uncle Dennis. Said she would make sure everyone in the town knew what had happened.' A strange light shone from his eyes. He looked over at Lewis so intently that Lewis became spooked.

'What?' he asked.

'I'll never forget that woman's face,' Conor said. Then stared again at Lewis. 'Did you guys have other family staying up there? The resemblance is...'

'What? Who was this woman,' Lewis asked, feeling a charge. Something else of importance was being revealed here. 'What happened to her?'

'Uncle Dennis. It ... Man, it happened so fast. One minute she was shouting at us, the next...'

'What? The next what?' Lewis demanded, when Conor's silence went on too long.

'He swung at her with the shovel.' Conor's eyes were staring into the distance, his expression heavy with recrimination. Eventually he spoke again. 'We buried them together.'

'Jesus.'

'That's not all though,' Conor said, rubbing at his chin, his eyes darting all over the room. 'When me and Chris lifted Jenny to put her in the ground, she gave this little groan.'

'You what? You didn't bury her alive, for fucksake?'

Conor ignored him. 'We panicked. Dropped her.' He crossed his arms, and held everything tight as if he'd suddenly grown cold. 'Then, just as calm as you like, Uncle Dennis, he ... he...'

'He what?'

'Just as calm as you like,' he repeated. 'Uncle Dennis straddled her, there, on the ground.' He paused, licked his lips. 'And then strangled her until she stopped kicking.'

Shock burst bright and hard across Lewis's chest. 'Oh my God.'

For the first time in several minutes, Conor's eyes lifted and he met Lewis's gaze. 'As sure as I'm sitting in this shithole, that man had done that before. Nobody could have ... It was like watching the guys that used to go hunting with the old man. How they would dispatch a pheasant. It was just that cold, and efficient.' He shivered. 'I haven't been able to get the sight of it out of my head ever since.' He paused. 'If I was a betting man, I'd be laying odds that glen is full of bodies.'

Chapter 72

Annie – Now

On her second glass of wine Annie allowed herself to pretend that she was relaxed. In truth she was feeling agitated. The murmurs were restless, howling in her mind like a pack of starving wolves coming ever closer.

'So,' Danni began, eyes wide. 'If he does, you know, pop the question...' It was clear to Annie that she'd been dying to ask.

'Oh, c'mon, Danni.' Annie fought to stay present in the conversation. 'It would hardly be fair for the sister to know before the brother.'

Danni threw herself back on the bed theatrically. Then sat up with a grin. 'Bad move,' she laughed. 'I'm drunker than I thought.' She made a swooning movement with her head. 'Have to say though – Chris?' She raised her eyebrows. 'I've never seen him so happy.'

'Really?' Annie felt a swirl in her gut and a little warmth leaked from there into her chest. She sat with that for a moment, and she wasn't sure whether she should appreciate or distrust the emotion. 'That's lovely and all that, but we barely know each other.'

Jenny Burns died. She died. Is deaddeaddeaddead.

An image of the young woman from her past inserted itself into her mind's eye.

Go away, leave me alone. Annie screwed her eyes shut.

'Excuse me?' Danni asked, a concerned expression on her face.

'What?' Annie asked, donning a look of innocent enquiry. Had she said that out loud?

Danni narrowed her eyes, then after a beat allowed her enthusiasm for the subject at the forefront of her mind to take over. 'Fifty-year marriages have been built on less.' Danni crossed her legs. 'Okay. What do you want to know about him?'

Annie really needed her guest to leave her alone right now, but she shook her head with a smile and managed to reply, 'Don't know. Anything. Everything.'

Danni laughed, then began to talk fondly about her brother, how he'd been a great support to their mother when their father had his stroke, how he'd really stepped up as a brother when both parents died.

'What really impressed me,' Danni continued, 'and I guess I'm biased, is how he came out from under Dad's shadow after the stroke.' She studied Annie's face. 'I don't know if you remember much about Dad, but he was a difficult man. Withdrawn, demanding, harsh – very harsh on Chris in particular. Quite nasty, if I'm being honest.' Her cheeks pinked as if she was slightly ashamed to be spilling family secrets. 'I don't want to say too much, but a lot of boys would have been crushed by that kind of constant criticism, or would have turned to the drink, but Chris' – she beamed – 'took it all on the chin – did that turn-the-other-cheek thing, and came out the better man.'

The voices became too much. The pitch. The dark energy. Then came the images in her mind. Women in water, girls in cars, peoples' faces frozen – eyes large, mouths open so wide she worried their lips would split, showing jagged wounds in the corners...

Jenny Burns' face changed from fully fleshed to nothing but bone. There in front of Annie's eyes, the flesh and skin, muscle and nerve, were laid bare, and all the while Jenny pointed a skeletal finger. *You could have saved me*, she accused. *You could have saved me.*

You, you, you, youyouyou.

Annie covered her face with her hands.

Tomorrow, tomorrow, tomorrowtomorrowtomorrow.

Annie's breath arrived in uncontrolled gasps.

Die. Die. Die. Diediedie.

'Annie, what on earth is wrong?' Danni asked, urgency in her voice. Annie didn't need to look at Danni's face to know that she was frightened.

'Please leave, Danni,' she managed to lift her face from her hands.

'But, Annie. You're not well. Something's...'

'Just fucking leave!' Annie screamed.

※

Annie's head felt thick with fog when she came to the next morning. Fractured images from the night before presented themselves in her mind. Trainer's face as he tried to persuade her of something. Would that man ever give up? Thankfully, he'd been chased off by Danni...

A memory of slamming her door shut on the woman came to her. And before that, Danni staring at her, wearing a shocked expression.

Dear God, Annie groaned. Danni will have called her brother last night and told him what a sick woman she was. Annie felt a grudging little lift at the prospect. That would save her the job of dumping Chris. He was clearly too good for her. What kind of man would be able to put up with her and her madness?

Miraculously she had slept, for a time.

But her dreams had been so bad that she woke up a short time later, and stayed awake for much of the night, all but vibrating with fear under her covers.

A woman had been there, in her dreams, tall and slim under a heavy, woollen shawl, long hair blowing in the wind, a sea loch and an expanse of heathered hills in the background. Somehow, Annie knew her name was Mary. And she was the first in a long line of women – one desperately unhappy face blending into another. Every set of eyes were Mary's eyes, and they were all equally full of guilt and shame and regret, and an unquenched need for forgiveness. Then their faces became stuck in a tortured, frozen scream. For they knew madness was their punishment – but also their escape.

Padded walls.

Sightless eyes.

Bodies so drugged they could only obey the brain's most simple of commands.

That was her future.

That was all of their futures.

Because only when they gave into the madness would they know peace...

Her phone vibrated an alert on the bedside table. With trembling fingers she picked it up and read a text that had just come in:

Morning, babe. Fancy a walk this morning? I have the perfect place. Very romantic. Wear something warm and waterproof. Pick you up in an hour. Xxx

After the danger and terror of her dreams, this notion of normality seemed surreal.

Her stomach twisted with the realisation. Chris was going to propose to her. Perhaps Danni hadn't told him about last night, after all.

Shit.

She couldn't do this. She should just turn him down. Now, she thought as her fingers hovered over the phone screen. Send him a reply saying she was feeling ill. A migraine or something. That would do it.

But that wasn't her. She wasn't into avoidance. She'd spent her life facing up to whatever difficulty was presented to her, and she wasn't about to stop. She would find a way to tell him – before he actually got down on one knee – that she enjoyed being with him, but it was early days in their relationship. That his devotion to his church was impressive, but she wasn't sure she could accept being second best in the life of the man she was going to spend the rest of hers with.

Besides, now, when she was battling with doubts about her sanity, wasn't the best time to be making such a big decision about her future. Especially given she wasn't sure that she had one.

Feeling a little better now that she had worked out how best to approach her outing with Chris, Annie showered, dressed, and managed a quick breakfast before another text pinged on her phone:

I'm at the road-end when you're ready. Can't wait to see you! Chris xxx

Chapter 73

Lewis – Now

After leaving his meeting with Conor the previous evening, Lewis had sat in his car for a long while, trying to soak in what he had just learned. So much of it horrified him: the callous disregard for the girl who died, and for the suffering of her family, and then the murder of the woman who tried to intervene.

Then there was the way Conor looked at Lewis as he told him about the woman who tried to stop them. A woman, who, judging by Conor's reaction, looked very much like Lewis.

He and Annie knew that Sheila had come up to visit them in Mossgow. Did that mean that Bridget, once she'd escaped from the care home, had done so as well? If she had, what on earth was she doing out in the hills that day?

He shook his head. No. That was too much. He couldn't take it in. It was a coincidence. That was all.

Jesus.

Identity of the murdered woman aside, it did all have the ring of truth, and that meant Annie was falling in love with the son of a callous murderer. What impact did seeing his father kill someone so casually have on the young Chris?

Annie could well be on her own with him right now.

He called her mobile. It went straight to voicemail. He called again, with the same result. Shit. Answer your phone, Annie. He left a message:

'It's Lewis. Call me the instant you pick this up.'

He then thumbed out a text with the same message.

He then remembered the mountain of work that Chris had given him just the day before he was set to go up to Mossgow.

His stomach dropped. Was that a ploy, to allow Chris to be on his own with Annie. But why? What was the endgame here? Was Annie in danger right now? Aside from the fact she was falling for a heartless human being? How else could he describe the man? Connor had the right of it: he had spent his life medicating himself against the horrors of that day, while Chris had become the head man in the local church. What kind of mindset promulgated that outcome? But, giving the guy the benefit of the doubt, might it have been atonement for a guilty conscience?

One thing he knew for sure was that the work Chris asked for was going to have to wait. He was going up to Mossgow.

*

The next morning, as he drove through the streets, Conor's assertion that Lewis bore a resemblance to the woman his uncle Dennis had murdered nagged in his mind. He checked his phone was connected to the Bluetooth in his car, and dialled Oswald House.

'Can I speak with Sister Theresa, please?' he asked.

'May I ask who's calling?'

He gave his name, and to his surprise, moments later a familiar voice came online.

He explained that he'd found something new – something serious. That Annie may well be in danger. 'This poor woman was murdered in cold blood.' He paused. 'I'm heading up there now. I know you said you could only tell me what you knew if Annie and I were together, but this changes things. Is there any chance that Bridget could have gone up to Mossgow when she escaped from Oswald House?'

There was a long silence on the other end of the phone. Long enough to prompt Lewis to ask, 'Sister Theresa? Are you still there?'

Then came the sound of weeping.

Chapter 74

MOIRA MCLEAN – A MEMOIR

Several years passed, and Mary and Jean only ever saw one another from a distance; on market days, holidays and Sundays and the like. And from that distance Jean was able to count the children Mary produced from her marriage to John Campbell: first a set of girl twins, followed by a boy. Jean herself never married, but she did have brief relationships with a couple of men, both of whom deserted her, unable to deal with her acid tongue.

Jean herself had the twins – a boy and girl, Isobel and Andra – beautiful children who made her heart sing, followed by a girl she named Jeannie.

She had all but forgotten the words of warning from her grandmother – 'One of you will betray the other, and her very body will be thrown to the flames' – and gossip reached their parish from other parts that evil was abroad and foul things happening, all the work of Satan, and that brave men were doing God's work by tracking down the devil's servants and burning them at the stake. Jean was reminded of her sister Mary and how she had won the heart of John Campbell. She had been certain that had been through the aid of the dark arts. What more had her sister learned since then? How much more evil did she harbour in that cold, stone soul if hers?

So convinced and fretful did she become of her sister's fall into wickedness that whenever someone mentioned some foul event, she whispered in their ear the name Mary Campbell.

Like the seeds her grandmother planted all those years ago, her whispers became murmurs that grew into rumour, and filled the air until they finally reached the ears of Mary herself.

＊

Mary Campbell had not forgotten the dire words of their grand-mother, and she grew certain of the source of the whispers – for who else had become so cold and embittered, and cared so little for her that they would endanger her in that way.

Life had changed for Mary since her marriage to John. As wife to the laird, even one of such modest means, she had responsibilities and an image to uphold, so, regretfully, she had forsworn the old ways and adopted the habits of a Christian wife and mother. Her love for her husband had only grown stronger over the years, and her children were an extension of that love, and when she heard the murmurs that cast doubt on her Christian values she grew fearful. Very fearful indeed.

For it was known throughout the land that witchfinders were at large and deemed very successful in their work – torturing people to obtain a guilty verdict and then putting them to the fire. Should they hear that Mary Campbell was such a woman, the consequences would be grave.

The truth was that although she didn't ever practise the old ways she still had what she described as her feelings, where she could sense that someone was ill and how she might assist them. She rarely acted upon these messages, and when she did her words would be so care-fully measured that the person concerned would think the idea and knowledge came from their own mind.

John had word from a cousin in the lowlands that many, many people – mostly women – had been found wanting in the most ter-rible ways and suffered greatly, and deservedly, as a result. Worried for his wife, he determined that he should visit Jean and warn her to be silent about the twins' past practices. Mary counselled against it, sure his message would fall on ears of stone, but John insisted.

On his return he told her what had transpired. First, Jean had tried to seduce him, and when that failed she'd laughed at his request for her silence. Then she'd told John about her and Mary's childhood, about their learnings from their grandmother and their gifts.

'Your wife is a witch, John Campbell,' she'd said. 'What's more, I'm certain she used the dark arts to win your love, and I'll see to it that she burns before God and our people, if it's the last thing I do.'

John begged Mary to tell him the truth; was she so afflicted? Knowing that even if John loved her more than life itself, he held himself to higher values and would comply with any dictates from the crown, she lied. She denied everything, saying she'd learned naught but the use of herbs in minor ailments from their grandmother and that it was Jean who exhibited the otherworldly abilities. Don't you remember, she asked, that it was Jean who confounded you all those years ago and persuaded you to lie with her?

John was thus convinced. His mind often strayed back to those meetings in the old croft house – so Jean must have bewitched him, it suffered no other explanation.

Given his position in the community, John had the ears of important men in the region and the loyalty of the people, and when the crops failed and the men came back from the sea with empty boats, and when a two-headed lamb was born, his was the explanation that people heard.

Mary was astonished at how quickly everyone turned against her sister. And even more astonished when their attentions turned to her twin children, Isobel and Andra. She quailed at the thought that Jean might soon end up on top of a pyre, but steeled herself against softness.

The whispers grew, hard eyes and pointed fingers followed. The murmurs of hellacious acts built until the air was ripe and ready for the appearance of the witchfinder. At his very first session, her sister, Jean, was accused, and tortured until she confessed, and was subsequently found guilty.

Her worst crime, the witchfinder preached, was that she not only practised witchcraft herself but that she taught it to her oldest children, for who couldn't see their unearthly beauty and silent communication, and consider them to be anything other than spawn of Satan himself. They were also tortured and tried, and found guilty.

All three were strangled before the pyre – there in front of that white, circular church – and once dead their bodies were thrown onto the flames until they were naught but bone, teeth and ash.

Chapter 75

Annie – Now

It took a moment for Annie to recognise Chris. He looked different somehow behind the wheel of a Toyota Yaris. In fact, it wasn't until he beeped his horn that she realised it was even him.

She walked across the car park towards him, every step deliberate, doubt-ridden, and a study in courage. Wanting nothing more than to run back to her hotel room and burrow under the covers, she nonetheless determined she would face up to whatever was coming next. Her life, she felt, had been one long stream of horribly difficult moments. From a mother who didn't love her, to the crash that killed her, then the subsequent suicide of her father.

And now this curse, these murmurs.

As soon as the thought hit her mind, she heard a howl and cackle.

How had she gotten through all of that? How would she get through this?

By putting one foot in front of the other, never backing down, and facing each new challenge and upset with grit and grace. By getting back up onto her feet and mentally dusting herself down. A wise woman – Mrs Mac – once told her 'the only way *to* was *through*', and that was a lesson she'd learned herself a number of times over the years.

Facing up to the ultimate challenge of her life – saving her sanity from the horror she was living with every day – was going to be another huge struggle. And whether Chris was going to be part of that was still up for grabs. But looking at him in that car, his smile, his evident care, she found, to her surprise, that she certainly hoped he would be.

Annie climbed in and took a seat. 'Where's the Audi?'

'That's my city car,' Chris answered. 'And for distances. I keep this one for driving around Mossgow.'

Annie nodded. 'And I guess seeing the pastor driving around in a massive motor doesn't give the right look of humility.' She clunked her seatbelt in place.

'Am I that obvious?' Chris laughed. He studied her for a moment. Her heart surged in response. Maybe Danni had reported back and told him his girlfriend was a crazy person. 'Sleep okay?' He reached for her hand. Gave it a squeeze.

Either Danni hadn't called him, or she had and Chris had decided to ignore whatever she said. Annie debated whether or not to give him a hard time for leaving her on her own in a strange hotel room, and decided that as he was being kind, so would she. 'The wine helped,' she lied.

'Provided by Danni I expect?' Chris replied as he drove off.

'Have you spoken with her this morning?'

Chris shook his head. 'I noticed a missed call from her. She must have called late last night, when I was in bed.'

Pressure squeezed her forehead, she groaned and held a hand there.

'No sympathy,' Chris said with a grin. 'Hungover?'

'Only a little,' she replied. Two lies within minutes of each other. Not a good way to start off a life together, she thought.

'Nothing that a wee walk and a picnic in the country won't cure.'

'Yeah,' Annie said. She looked around, suddenly feeling a weight of concern. A *wrongness*. 'Where exactly are we going?'

'Just my favourite place in the whole world,' Chris smiled. 'Back in the nineties the forestry guys found this lost settlement up in the hills, in the next valley to Mossgow. Everyone who lived there had been thrown off the land in the clearances, and all record of the place had been lost. Can you imagine? This place where people had thrived for a hundred years or so, suddenly emptied, and completely forgotten about until fairly recently?'

'That's crazy.'

'The spot is just beautiful. The valley floor is split by this little meandering river, and there are the remains of small croft houses either side. The people would have been protected from the worst of the Scottish weather by the curve of the mountains behind them. And there's this wee loch,' he grinned.

'Sounds amazing,' Annie said. She looked back towards the hotel, and her bedroom. As difficult as her night had been, for some reason she felt she would be safer back there.

She looked over at Chris. He was grinning at her, and she allowed his open pleasure at the thought of whatever he had cooked up to allay her fears. This feeling of foreboding was simply a hangover from a horrible night, wasn't it?

Annie did have a future, and that was Chris. He was good for her.

She was sure of it.

The other women in her dream had felt so real, but they were merely a figment of an overwrought imagination. In the warmth and light of a new day she could see that. Besides, she thought, if they were real, none of them had a man of principle and kindness on hand to help them deal with whatever was going on. Whatever *this* was.

'Wait till you see the place. You'll love it just as much as I do.'

He sped up on a stretch of straight road, the loch on one side, a row of houses on the other. Then he braked as a bend came up.

A bridge appeared, a low wall on either side, and before it a road sign.

Memory flashed and buzzed.

A scream.

A loud bang.

Water. Cold. So cold.

Her mother's voice. 'I do love you, Annie, but...' Whatever else she said was lost in a whoosh as the car hit the water.

In the moment, Annie slapped a hand down on the dashboard. Screamed at Chris to stop.

He did so, pulling in at the roadside.

Annie's head was in her hands. A crushing sense of doom pressing down on her.

'Baby,' Chris said. 'It's okay. You're safe. You're with me.' He unclipped his seatbelt, edged across so that he was closer to her and pulled her into a hug. 'Let the memories come, Annie. Whatever they are we'll help you deal with them.'

Chapter 76

Lewis – Now

Once she managed to compose herself, Sister Theresa asked Lewis if he could stop by Oswald House. There was something she wanted to show him.

'I'm sorry, Sister,' he replied. He looked at the clock on his dashboard. 'Annie's about three hours away. I need to see her and satisfy myself she's safe. Can't you just tell me what you know?'

'There are some things that I can only tell you if your sister is there too,' she insisted. 'But—' She broke into a coughing fit. When she started to speak again, her voice sounded weaker, further away. 'I can tell you...' She started to cough again. After she managed to compose herself, she said. 'Where are you?'

Lewis explained.

'Right. This is a short detour on your way up north. You mentioned a placed called Mossgow? Then you need to see what I have.'

He made a decision. What would ten minutes hurt? Chris Jenkins' dad might be a murderous piece of scum but that had happened when Chris was a kid. Maybe that was what drove him to becoming head of the church? In some way he was atoning for the terrible things he'd witnessed in the past?

For sure, Annie had to know what Chris's father had done all those years ago, and he had to be the one to tell her, but surely she was safe from him? He wasn't going to invite her up to his church celebration and then cause her harm. What would be the point in that? He'd demonstrated that he was a clever man, and perhaps even callous, if he'd managed to ignore who and what his father was, but to invite her to an event Lewis knew about, and then hurt Annie? That would take some sort of deranged psychopath.

Chapter 77

Annie – Now

Annie had never experienced a silence like it. As soon as they entered the forest, the air stilled and the birdsong dulled. She'd been in louder empty churches. Moss grew everywhere, halfway up the trunks of the trees, over fallen ones, and over rocks, everything was coloured in a fecund, vibrant green.

Chris was just ahead of her, striding up the path, a heavy black rucksack on his back, head up, sure of his place in this world. Annie lengthened her stride in an effort to keep pace with him.

He stopped at a fence, opened the gate and paused to let her pass through in front of him.

'Such a gentleman,' she said.

'I have my moments.' He smiled, examining her face. 'You okay?' he asked, concern clear in his tone.

'For the millionth time, I'm fine.'

She wasn't. Ever since the bridge her mind had been assailed by memories. Fractured moments presenting themselves out of sequence, none of it making any sense. She looked up at him, read his need to help and mustered a smile.

Her father in the car, turning to her to offer a wink of reassurance.

The pastor's hideous smile – long, yellowed teeth like a row of coffin lids.

A neighbour pointing, murmuring – should have been burned at the stake.

Burn, burn, burn, burnburnburn.

At the bridge Chris had offered to postpone their trip, but

Annie was adamant they should continue. But a memory of the moment before they'd gone in the water sang a low song of worry through every cell in her brain: it was no accident, she was certain. Her mother had deliberately steered off the bridge and into the water.

She shivered.

'Are you sure?' Chris asked, again.

'Yes.' She faced him, forced down any thought of her mother, reached up, put a hand on the back of his neck and pulled him towards her.

She pressed her lips against his. Hungry. Needing something to throw the dark mood out of her mind. She gave into her heightened pulse, lined his body with hers. Felt him harden in response.

'Whoa,' he said when she let him go, his eyes bright with lust. Then he looked beyond them. 'Hold that thought.'

Another twenty yards, and they were through the other side of the woods, then crested the top of the hill to see the valley floor ahead of them, and beyond, a ridge of hills forming a protective semi-circle at the far end of the valley.

A bird called, and Annie looked up to see the giant wingspan of a golden eagle as it soared the thermals, hunting its prey.

'Wow,' Annie said, hand over her heart, welcoming a moment's relief from the whispered torture going on in her mind. 'Picture-book perfect.'

Chris pulled her into a hug, and pride was evident in his voice when he spoke. 'Pretty special, eh?'

The sun chose that moment to edge out from behind a cloud, its soft light warming her face. She breathed in deeply, and felt her anxiety swirl and tighten in her gut. Let it, she thought. If Chris was using this as a way to propose to her, she was now in the mood to listen.

Annie scanned the view, looking for the ruins Chris had mentioned earlier, but way down to her left, a stretch of water glinted, catching her eye. On the banks facing into the loch she spotted a small white building. They were at some distance from the cottage, but she could see that the roof was intact. This was no ruin.

'Imagine living there,' she pointed, feeling her heart lift, and the murmurs gave off a quite different sound from what she was used to; an almost plaintive note. She sat with that for a moment. What was going on there? Were they pushing her there? If so, could she trust them? They'd been nothing but punishing since they started. Why this change, and why now?

'It's empty as far as I know,' Chris winked, intruding into her thoughts. 'Want a weekend cottage?'

'On a nice day, it's ideal, but getting down there would be a trek in the winter.'

Chris chuckled. 'There's a road in, I believe. Not much of one, to be fair, but still, a car could make it in, no problem.' He stepped forward. 'Anyway,' he pointed to the right. 'Our path is downhill from here and it's that way.'

The way down the other side of the hill was harder work than the way up. There wasn't much of a path, and it was strewn with boulders of varying sizes, slick with mud and moss, huge puddles, fallen trees, and then more steep parts, where it seemed every step was going to lead to her slipping and falling.

The footing then became more solid and she was able to walk, taking in the scenery around her, without looking for any hazard that might cause a fall. The cool breeze on her face and neck were welcome after her exertions.

The sound of water grew louder, and they came to a stream, two strides wide, with a large, flat-topped boulder in the middle. They crossed that with ease, and Annie noted a large heap of boulders on the bank. There was no shape to them. It was as if the wall they had been part of had been dismantled, rock by rock, and the material then heaped into a large cairn. Ferns grew out of the side, and the ever-present moss tucked itself into ridges and crevasses.

'Nearly there,' Chris said, pointing. Annie looked in the direction of his finger, and saw a wall about waist height, a break where a door must have been, and a higher section that might have once supported beams for a roof. But there, in the middle of the rectangle, sprouted an oak tree, its branches draped with ribbons of lichen.

Run, a voice urged. *Runrunrun.*

Annie shook her head, as if to dislodge the words.

'You okay?' Chris asked once more.

She nodded.

They soon reached the spot, and Annie took a step inside what would once have been a tiny home, and saw that between the giant roots of the tree a blanket had been lain, and on that sat a champagne bucket, a silver-foiled bottle top jutting proudly from the centre.

'Mr Jenkins,' Annie smiled, ignoring the twist in her gut, and turned to him. 'I do believe you've already been up here today.'

'Like it?' he smiled tentatively, and for the first time that morning Annie sensed an uncertainty from him.

'Love it,' she said, and allowed herself to be guided under the canopy of leaves to sit on the blanket. 'Thank you,' she said. 'It's beautiful.'

Chris knelt before her, his face sombre. Her heart missed its beat. Her stomach roiled. God, she thought, it's happening. Did she want this? Really want this? A bright brush of panic worked its way up her neck to her face.

The voices built. Laughing, mocking. Surging. Urging. *Runrunrun.*

She squeezed her eyes shut, determined not to give into them, to stay in the moment. Their intent was nothing but poisonous, whereas Chris only had her best interests at heart. When Danni had put the thought of a proposal in her head, she was sure that it wasn't what she wanted. But now. Here and now, the voices a clamour in her mind, and the flesh and blood of Chris on his knees before her, there was only one answer. He was her way back. He could be her sanity.

Hahahahahahaha. The murmurs pulsed. The sharp edge of their harmful intent tore at her mind.

'Quiet!' she shouted.

'Sorry?' Chris rocked back onto his heels.

'Not you...' she said. 'Not you.' Her pulse a rapid din in her neck she reached out to him, put a hand out to stroke his face, in what she hoped might be a gesture of reassurance.

But when her skin lit on his, pain burst across her forehead. Pressure built in the back of her neck. Her vision swam. Daylight flickered, died, returned. His face blurred into an electric storm. Then reformed into a skull.

The sound built and built in her mind. A buzzing. A group of voices murmuring, faces leering, eyes staring, fingers pointing, the noise growing, growing, growing until all that was left was a lamentation, and the promise of never-ending terror.

Chapter 78

Lewis – Now

Lewis stepped out of his car onto the pebbled drive at Oswald House. No sooner had he closed the door behind him than he became aware of a woman walking towards him. A nun. She was carrying a small package. She was a tall woman, lean, her black robes fluttering behind her in the breeze like a flag.

'Lewis?' she called.

'Yeah,' he replied. 'I'm here to see—'

'I know,' she interrupted, her face an essay in sorrow. 'Sister Theresa is unwell. Gravely so, I'm afraid. But she asked me to give you this.' She handed him a padded envelope.

'But I just spoke to her. Is she okay?'

'She's not been okay for some time, Lewis.' The nun gave a little nod. 'But she has taken a very sudden turn for the worse. I'm Sister Abigail. I've been a friend of Theresa for many, many years. In there' – she patted the parcel now in Lewis's hands – 'you'll find a letter that she just dictated to me, which details what she knows of Bridget Bennett's last whereabouts. There is also a more detailed letter explaining everything she knows about...' her expression clouded before she continued '...your family situation. And Sister Theresa was quite insistent that you only look at that when you and Annie are together.' She peered into Lewis's eyes, and he suddenly became aware just how tall this woman was. 'Am I understood?'

'Well – yes,' Lewis replied, thinking the woman's stern expression was unwarranted.

At this she softened. 'It's a difficult time for all of us, Lewis.

Sister Theresa has been a mainstay of the place for many years. I don't know how we'll get on without her.' She put a hand over her mouth. Then she gave another little nod. 'I wish you well, young man.' And without another word she walked away.

Somewhat discomfited, Lewis turned back to the car, opened the door and sat down. He put the envelope on his knees. Looked up at the house, and wondered just how Sister Theresa was at that moment. Was she even still alive? She hadn't sounded well on the phone, to be fair, but not at death's door.

He opened the envelope and pulled out a couple of sheets of typed paper. The first was addressed simply, *Lewis*.

And as he read, he heard her voice and felt a growing sense of sorrow.

All those years ago your aunts chose the moment for their sub-terfuge very carefully. They knew we were busier than ever, that we were getting a new intake of nursing interns, and that I had just begun a fortnight's leave.

Nonetheless, the moment I stepped back inside your aunt's room I knew that something was awry. But it was the next time I was in her room that I realised what had happened: that the sisters had swapped places. They were very alike, but not so alike that someone who had spent time caring for Bridget would be fooled. But they had both grown their hair in the same, long style, and Sheila was practised at hanging her head in such a way that her hair obscured most of her features.

Of course I confronted her; demanded to know what was going on. At first she ignored me, then she insisted I was mistaken. And she did this so forcefully that I almost believed her.

Then when I wouldn't give up, she changed tack and persuaded me to maintain my silence. A silence I have kept to this day.

When Sheila persuaded me of the reasons for the swap I could do nothing but go along with them. My thinking was that this was such a tragic family, if at least one of the sisters could be happy then that would be divine providence.

Sheila had been up to Mossgow to visit you children just a few weeks before they changed places. As part of her trip there she located a cottage that she had visited as a child with her grandmother. It was left to her years before and she never got round to visiting. I can't remember the exact location, but she said it was up in the hills, on the shores of a small loch. It needed a little work, apparently, a new kitchen and the like, but it was wind- and water-tight. Bridget could stay there and judge the lie of the land – make sure she wasn't going to be carted back to hospital, before she introduced herself to you.

She'd agreed that she would send Sheila postcards now and again. Nothing that could give away her location, but containing enough to let Sheila know she was doing okay.

Only one postcard arrived. And we never heard from her again. By then Sheila's illness had progressed and she couldn't look into it. Before she died she made me promise that I would locate Bridget and make sure she was okay. But I couldn't find her. It was like she'd dropped off the face of the earth.

Chapter 79

Annie – Now

The change in Chris's demeanour was alarming. Once the skull face receded, a strange, cold light filled his eyes, his jawline tightened – indeed, the entire musculature of his face changed, became harder. It was as if a mask had fallen off. This wasn't the man she'd come to know and love. This was someone else entirely.

'What did you just see?' he asked. 'Was that newspaper article correct? Can you see into the past?' He got to his feet and towered over her. 'Do you know where the bodies are buried?'

Bodies?

Bodies.

New voices joined the tumult in her mind. Accusing, panicked, reliving the moment they realised they were going to die.

No, no, no.

They screamed an endless note of fear and confusion in her mind.

Annie scrambled to her feet, almost tripping over a root, but managed to right herself in time. 'What on earth are you talking about?' But she knew. She knew with a certainty that horrified her. They were all around, begging to be found. Bones. Beneath the very earth on which she stood. Many, many, many bones.

'You know, don't you?' he demanded.

'Know what?' Annie tore her eyes from the horrors around her feet.

'You can't pretend,' he insisted. 'I saw you at the bridge. And now. There. The way you looked at me. With pure fear in your eyes.'

Annie held a hand up. 'Chris,' she warned. 'You're scaring me.'

He stepped back, shaking his head, tears now filling his eyes. 'It was an accident. All a mistake. Dad's dead now anyway. But I can't allow you to spoil everything I've worked for.'

Annie grew cold as she watched him, fear for what was around her changed to fear for herself, for her own physical safety. There was a difference in him, an edge she struggled to understand. But one thing was growing clear: she was in as much danger now as the dead people who surrounded her had once been.

'Then that bloody woman appeared from nowhere. She went for Conor. She was going crazy. Dad had to step in.'

'Chris, let's...' She took a step towards the break in the wall they'd entered the enclosure through. Then another. She needed to create some distance between them. 'Let's just go back to the car. Get back to the church.'

He was crying. His hands over his face. Mumbling. 'I don't want to. I can't. I'm not my father's son. I'm not my...'

'Yes,' Annie said as she was forced to halt, feeling a large root at her heel, and knowing if she took a wrong step, the fast step that her mind was screaming at her to take, she would trip. 'You're not,' she repeated his words. 'You're a different man altogether. You're kind...'

He looked up. Stared. Suspicion coalesced in his eyes, became certainty.

The murmurs sang a loud note of horror.

'You do know,' he said.

He lunged: caught her easily. Pulled her by the hair. She twisted, fell back, and desperately, fear sharp in her mind, fought to get back on her feet. They collided. A tangle of limbs. He fell on top of her.

'No, Chris, no.'

His hands were around her neck. He was crying. Shaking his head. His eyes stark with fear, horror, and certainty. 'I can't let you tell everyone. I can't let you go. I have to kill you. I have to.'

Chapter 80

Annie – Now

Her vision dimmed. She struggled with her hands, her legs, fighting for purchase. Fingers feverishly searching for a weapon. A rock. A branch. Heels furiously scrabbling for a hold. Fighting for her life.

'I'm sorry,' he was saying. 'So very sorry.' As he spoke his grip tightened. His weight on her heavier and heavier.

'Chris. No,' she croaked. 'No.' She would not give in to this man.

'Die. Just fucking die, will you?' His face was full of the knowledge of what he was doing, retreating from it while giving in to his need to see this carried through.

Annie felt herself weaken, the movement of her arms and legs slow. Sparks lit across her vision. Air. She needed air so desperately.

As her sight failed, memories burst into her head. All of her life, every event prior to leaving here for the city with the McEvoys rolled across her mind in an instant. Her entire childhood laid bare. In perfect order. A sequence rolling forward from her earliest memory to now, this moment, when the man she thought she was falling for was trying to kill her.

No, she screamed.

No.

Air. She needed air.

She was in a bath. About four years old. Her mother had left her on her own when the phone rang. Annie stood up to reach for a toy. She slipped. Fell. The side of her head crashed against the metal of the taps.

Air.

Couldn't breathe.

Hands on her small arms, pulling her out of the water. Her mother crying, holding her to her chest. What happened? she cried. You could have drowned.

Annie desperately tried to suck in some oxygen, but Chris's hands were too tight around her neck.

Then just before the crash. Her mother shouting at her, saying she loved her, truly loved her and despite her foretelling the death of Pastor Mosely she'd do what she could to protect her from the people at the church. That she was not to pay any attention to them. If she was frightened of these voices, the murmurs, they'd get her to a doctor. There were all kinds of medications available now. The cottage. Sheila was right about the cottage. They'd get her up there right away.

They were approaching a bend. From her mother's reaction Annie knew there was something wrong. Something terribly wrong.

'The brakes,' her mother cried. 'The brakes aren't working.' Annie saw her mother's left knee pumping up and down.

The bridge loomed. They were going too fast.

They hit the low wall, then the water. It was cold. So very cold.

'No, Mummy, no,' Annie begged her. Clawed at the door. Clawed at her seatbelt. It released. She opened the door. Fought her way to the surface.

Then she was lying on the shore, cold, wet, terrified, her ears full of manic laughter, and a sense that she was to blame for her mother's death. If she'd paid attention to the murmurs she could have saved her life.

As she felt herself drifting away from her body, seeming to float above herself, she knew why she'd lost her memory all those years ago, why her childhood was a blank. Guilt. It had been too painful to bear, so her brain had done what it could to protect her.

Because her mother's death had been her fault.

An urgent need to breathe ... and she slammed back into her body.

'No, Chris. No,' she croaked now, batting ineffectively at his face, at his hands, hands that gripped her neck tighter and tighter, aware that her strength was failing, and that she was on the edge of death.

Chapter 81

Annie – Now

Annie was weak. So terribly weak. The pressure on her neck so strong. Her limbs barely moving now. Then she became aware of movement beyond them. A shout. The outline of a man, approaching fast.

Did she know him? Yes, she knew him.

'Eddie,' she wheezed. 'Eddie.'

He was wielding something, and as she watched he drew it back and brought it down hard. A loud banging noise, and abruptly Chris fell to the side.

Air. Sweet air.

Desperately, she filled her lungs, managed to push herself up into a sitting position.

'Eddie,' she said, looking up at her saviour. 'Thank you,' she said. 'Thank you. I don't know what I would have done if you hadn't ...'

He was standing over Chris, peering down at him, the enormity of what just happened playing across his face. Annie looked at his hand. He was holding a branch as thick as a man's thigh.

Then she dared to look over at Chris. Her lover, the man who'd just tried to kill her, was on his back, arms crucifix wide, blood blossoming from the side of his head, a lifeless stare in his eyes.

❋

Trainer helped her to her feet. She was panting, adrenaline an electric tingle in her arms and legs, but her mind was partly disconnected, as if this was all happening to someone else; a stranger.

She felt a wave of nausea, and took a step away from Chris's body.

'He's dead, isn't he?' she asked, looking up at Trainer. He was pale, his mouth hanging open, eyes full of the horror of what he'd just done.

'I didn't mean to kill him.' He looked down at the large stick he was still holding, and dropped it as if it was on fire.

'He would have killed me, Eddie,' she said. 'If you hadn't...'

Eddie stumbled back. Leaned against a wall, as if he was suddenly weak.

'I'll say it was me,' Annie asserted. 'In self-defence. He chased me. Tried to strangle me. I found the branch.' She shivered. 'And I hit him with it.'

'But...' Eddie protested.

'You can't stay, Eddie. You're a convicted murderer out on licence. There's no saying how the authorities are going to translate what happened here.' She paused. 'I'm sorry I didn't give you the time of day back at the hotel. But what the hell are you doing here?'

'I wasn't stalking you. Honest. I met Chris's cousin Conor at the halfway house, and when he heard about my story, he said I should look into the people up in Mossgow. That he knew stuff that would send people to prison for a very long time.'

'Really?' Annie looked over at Chris, and turned away again quickly. To think she'd fallen for the man. 'Like what?'

'The red car you warned Jenny Burns about when you were a kid? Turns out it was Conor's.'

Annie was back in that moment in The Lodge, looking for Aunt Sheila. Heard the warning spill from her mouth, and watched as Jenny all but sneered at her. She felt her legs tremble. The pain in her throat throbbed. The murmurs hissed in her ears. If only Jenny had listened to her.

'Dear God.' Annie looked from Eddie to Chris, then away from them. She felt a souring in her gut, and the muscles of her jaw twisted. 'I need to get out of ... I can't look at him for one more second. I think I'm going to be sick.'

Eddie took her by the hand and led them out of the confines of the former dwelling and guided her to a large rock on the river bank. They sat.

After a long moment, while she took long breaths of fresh air into her lungs, she coughed, then looked at Eddie. 'You were saying?' she croaked.

'Oh. Aye.' Eddie took a moment to gather his thoughts. 'Chris and Conor were on a mission to go somewhere quiet and get high on the drugs Conor had brought. As Conor tells it, they were driving by the loch and saw Jenny – who Chris fancied by the way. They stopped, offered her a lift and asked if she wanted to join in. Jenny was well up for it. But she...'

'She what? Tell me, Eddie...'

'She overdosed. Conor said they only realised what was happening when it was too late.'

'She died like that?' Annie searched her visions for confirmation. 'But what happened to her body? Why wasn't it found?' She paused for a moment. 'They hid it, didn't they?'

Eddie nodded. 'Chris's dad, Dennis...'

'Mr Jenkins?' Her old neighbour loomed large in her mind. She shuddered.

'Conor says he's the one. He's the one who was really dangerous. In their panic, the boys phoned him. He came to help, and made them bury Jenny. But she was alive and...'

'Wait. She was still alive...? You said she died.'

'They thought she was dead. But she came to, apparently, when they were about to put her in her grave.'

'Oh my God.' Annie's hand shot to cover her mouth. 'They buried her alive?' Her murmurs sang an urgent, tuneless note.

'No. Worse than that.'

'What could be worse than that?' Annie didn't know if she could handle any more of this – horrified that the man she was falling for had behaved like this as a teenager.

'Dennis Jenkins. The more I think about it, Annie, he's the one.'

'What happened?'

'I'm not sure what the sequence of events was. Conor was a bit woolly on that. But a woman appeared out of nowhere, and start shouting at them. Said she recognised Dennis Jenkins from the church and she was going to get the police.'

'Barely anyone knows this place even exists,' Annie insisted. 'Who would be up here?'

Laughter, bright with mania surged in her ears, and Annie sensed this was important. Who was this woman? An instinct made her turn her head in the direction of the little white cottage she'd seen earlier, further down the glen, by the little beach and loch. The roof was just visible from her vantage point and when her eyes lit upon the small building, her murmurs picked up again. But, as before, in a change from their usual tone, they issued an almost pleasant sound. To Annie's mind it seemed like a kind of longing.

'Did Conor know who she was? Where she came from?'

Eddie shook his head. 'Dennis swung at her with the shovel. Killed her. Then strangled Jenny to make sure she *was* actually dead and buried them both in the same hole.'

'Dear God,' Annie whispered. 'Dennis did that?' A memory. His eyes on her. Assessing. Cold. His index finger leaving a trail of shivers on the inside of her right wrist. A mother's warning. 'There's something not right about that man,' her mother said. 'I don't want you in that house. If you must play with Danni do it our garden – not theirs.'

'He's our guy, Annie. I bet he was the one who killed Tracy.' Annie nodded, sensing he was right. 'Conor said he could never get the image of it all out of his head, the way his uncle Dennis just calmly killed both of these women.'

They sat in silence for a long moment, Annie trying to assimilate what she'd just learned, and how close she had come to dying.

If Eddie had been one minute later...

The enormity of everything she'd just learned, along with the attack on her by Chris was almost impossible to hold in her head all at the same time.

And then there was a mind full of fresh memories.

She felt like she might burst.

'I can't...' She began to cry.

'Hey.' Eddie put a hand on her shoulder.

'To think I entertained the idea of marrying him.' Annie wiped at her face with her sleeve. She looked back towards the tree and the heap of stones beyond where Chris lay. 'He's dead, right? You checked his pulse?'

Chapter 82

Annie – Now

Eddie's face was full of horror. 'You want me to go back over there and check?'

'Don't you think we should? What if he's still alive and needs medical attention?'

'I don't know if I can.' Eddie's face had grown even paler.

'I can't do it.' Annie shuddered. 'But if there's a chance he's alive we need to get him help. And then he needs to stand trial for what he tried to do to me. And what he helped do to Jenny Burns.'

'Aww, man.' Eddie rubbed at his head. He half turned in the direction of the ruin in which Chris's body lay.

'You have to, Eddie,' Annie said. 'Besides, if he does recover, maybe he knows something about the other women his father targeted.' She left it unsaid that Tracy could be one of them.

Eddie looked at her. Bit his lip. She could see his hands flex in and out of fists. 'Okay.' He turned and trudged over the uneven ground, then he was inside the ruin and out of her sight.

As Annie waited, she hugged herself, thought of that last moment when Chris's hands were around her neck. Then the blessed relief when Eddie's strike came. Did she really want Chris to be alive? If he was could she ever be anywhere near him again?

She heard rapid footsteps, and Eddie was back in sight, bent over, hands on his thighs, and retching. He spattered the heather and grass at his feet with vomit. Then he turned to Annie, wiped his face, shook his head, and made his way over to her.

He stood by Annie, his expression grim. 'I had to touch his

neck. For a pulse, you know?' He shuddered, his eyes betraying a mix of guilt, horror and relief.

'Here,' Annie patted the rock by her side. 'Have a seat.' She gripped his hand briefly.

Eddie merely smiled at her. What else was there to say?

They sat in silence, each bearing the weight of their responsibility for what had just happened. However bad he was, a man had just died.

Annie's mind drifted to the family: the Jenkins. 'Danni,' she said. 'She put the idea in my head that Chris was bringing me up here to propose. Do you think she knew about any of that stuff about her father?'

Eddie shrugged. 'What sense do you have of her? Was she involved in any way?'

Annie reviewed her interactions with Danni. 'No,' she said. 'I'm pretty sure she had no idea that her brother had that possibility of violence in him.'

'From what Conor Jenkins said about the father – about how matter-of-fact he was about strangling Jenny and burying both bodies – it's hard to imagine that any child growing up with a parent like that would not be damaged in some...'

A thought occurred to Annie. 'Why now? Why did Conor wait until now to spill the beans?'

Eddie shrugged. 'He said he was terrified of his uncle Dennis. Then he was in and out of jail and thought no one would listen to him, but then when he saw Chris making all this money, on the verge of fame and big things, he thought he needed to call the guy out. Let people know who he really was. And Conor hadn't wanted his parents to be even more disappointed in him than they already were. But now they're gone, he said, so...'

They were silent for a long moment.

'How did you know to follow us up here, Eddie?'

'Remember that day you all were eating in that café in the West End?'

'Yeah?'

'I wasn't stalking you. Honestly. I just happened to be walking past. Saw you all in the window, and the way that guy Chris was looking at you...'

Annie thought about that afternoon. Their first meeting as adults, and how the spark of their connection was lit that day.

The murmurs set off in a cacophony of mocking laughter.

'I've been around a lot of bad men in my time, Annie, and there was something about the way he was looking at you while you weren't paying attention. This cold, detached stare. Gave me the shivers.'

Annie felt herself tremble at Eddie's words.

'Seeing that, combined with all the things that Conor told me, I thought I should keep an eye on you these last few weeks. And Chris. That's why I followed you up here yesterday and tried to speak to you. Then this morning I waited outside the manse, saw Chris leaving in that wee car of his.' He paused. 'I followed. Saw him pick you up, and kept a tail on you. Nearly lost you at one point.' His eyes widened in horror at the thought of what might have happened. 'But doubled back and saw his car crest a hill, just in time.'

She edged closer to him on the rock and pulled him into a hug, trying to keep a control on her emotions. 'I don't know what I would have done if you hadn't turned up.'

Eddie sat back. Blushing. 'Aye. I'm sure you would have sorted him out. You were well up for him. You put up one hell of a fight, missus.'

Annie merely smiled. They both knew he was lying.

'I couldn't forgive myself if you ended up in prison again.' She pushed him. 'You need to vanish.'

'Okay. Okay, I will. But listen: I've been thinking about everything Conor said, and what Chris did here today ... I'm sure now that Dennis killed Tracy. He must have.' Eddie looked around as if searching the silent hills for a clue of some sort. 'Promise me you'll get the authorities up here and get them digging.' His voice cracked with emotion. 'Our Tracy is up here. I'm sure of it.'

Chapter 83

Annie – Now

Down in the town, after the paramedics had given her a full assessment, and she'd given the police her statement, Lewis arrived. One of the policemen had phoned him at Annie's request, to find he was on the road and headed in their direction.

The moment Annie saw him drive into the car park of the small local police station she found herself swamped with emotion. Her head and her heart were a roiling mess of anger, fear, relief, and she ran to Lewis as he stepped out of his car.

His eyes widened as he took in her appearance. 'Your face,' he said, hand up but wary of touching her. 'And your neck. Shit. Look at that bruising. Are you okay?'

'Jesus, are you a sight for sore eyes,' she replied.

They hugged. Holding each other for a long minute.

Once she'd calmed down, they sat in the car and she went over everything.

Annie told him how when she was fighting Chris off, struggling to breathe, certain that she would die, Eddie Trainer appeared with a huge branch in his hand and hit Chris over the head.

'Where is he?' Lewis asked as he looked around. 'I need to give him a fucking big kiss.'

'He was never here,' Annie replied. 'He's out on licence and could easily get himself arrested. I thought the police would be far more likely to buy the story that I was on my own and I acted in self-defence if I didn't mention Trainer at all. We've been seen in public, Eddie and me. In a newspaper headline no less. There's every chance they would have read more into the situation. I couldn't take that chance, so I sent Eddie packing. And of course, I haven't said a word about him to the detectives I spoke to.'

'God, yeah,' Lewis nodded. 'Quick thinking.'

'And there's something else. I think Chris's attack ... Maybe even being close to ... Well...' She trailed off, the thought of those moments stopping her throat.

'Annie? What are you trying to say?'

She breathed in deeply through her nose. 'My memory is back.'

'Wow,' Lewis said, eyes wide. 'What do you remember? Everything?'

Annie nodded. 'It's all there. Isn't that amazing?' She smiled now. 'It's a strange, but wonderful feeling. Without it, I always felt like I was somehow faulty, you know? But it's daunting at the same time. As if there are deep waters out there and I'm just dipping a toe in.'

'Annie, that's wonderful.'

'Shame I had to be almost killed for it to happen, eh?' She reached for Lewis's hands. 'There's something you need to know. Mum – me saying she tried to drown me, once in the bath and again at the loch?' She shook her head slowly. 'She didn't do either. She tried to save me. I don't know what made me think the opposite. All that anger I was holding as a teenager, maybe. I was so angry that they both left us, you know? And then there were the murmurs, on top of a fragmented memory. All of that in a pathetic little stew, maybe?' Annie felt the wrongness of that, emotion built and she gave way to a little sob.

'Hey, sis,' Lewis said. 'Don't torture yourself. The human psyche is a wondrous, crazy thing. Who knows why we say and think the things we do.'

'But Mum did love me. You need to know that. Now that all my memories are back, my real memories, I can see she was a good mother.' Annie wiped at a tear. 'It's just a shame I didn't appreciate that and let her know that I knew.'

'That's life as a parent, Annie. And as an actual, normal human being for that matter. Few of us get to know how we are appreciated.'

'How did you get to be so wise, brother?'

'I read books and I know stuff.' Lewis winked.

At that moment a car swooped into the car park, and they saw a grey face in the back seat. When Danni saw them she barely reacted, her eyes skimming over them as if they weren't there.

'Do you think she knew what Chris's plans were?'

Annie shook her head. 'The only person who knew what Chris was planning was the man himself.' She was back in that moment, Chris's eyes large as he reacted to what she said. He was convinced she knew more than she did; that her psychic ability had presented her with the facts of that fateful day all those years ago. 'It can't be a coincidence that he only sought me out after the newspaper article appeared. As you've told me many times, there was a lot of money flowing into that church. I think he feared Eddie's prodding would lead me to somehow discover what really happened all those years ago. The first headline was all about me and Eddie's quest for the truth, wasn't it? The second could have been – in Chris's mind anyway – that he had been complicit in the murder of two women. And all that power and cash he had would have disappeared.'

Lewis put a hand to his head in shock. 'You think he planned to bring you up here and kill you right from the start?' He crossed his arms. 'God. I feel terrible. I was complicit in all of this. I was so intent on getting a big account for the practice, I noticed nothing.'

'Hey, don't blame yourself, Lewis.' Annie gave his hand a squeeze. 'Sociopaths can be very convincing.'

'You think he was that bad? A sociopath?'

'He needed to know what I knew. And he needed to protect himself from whatever he thought I knew. That means murder was on his mind from the very beginning.' Annie became aware that she was shaking as she spoke, so she tucked her hands under her arms. A throaty chuckle in her mind's ear let her know the murmurs were mocking her. 'The fact that he also got to play at being the romantic was merely a bonus.'

Annie watched as Danni was let out of the back seat and escorted into the police station. Her head was high, but Annie could detect an aura of shock coming from her.

'She's in denial right now. She can't quite believe her brother almost turned into a cold killer, and she's blaming us – well, me – for his death.'

'You can tell all of that from just a quick look at her?'

Annie managed a smile. 'An educated guess. It's how my mind would be working if the roles were swapped and *you* had tried to kill *her*.'

Chapter 84

Annie – Now

'Are the police finished with you?' Lewis asked, after Danni had disappeared through the door of the police station and they'd sat quietly for a while, digesting everything Annie had just said.

'I can go back to Glasgow, they said. And if they need anything else, they'll get in touch.'

It would be dark shortly, but they decided that it would be best just to go home. All talked out, they were mostly silent for the first hour of the drive.

At one point Lewis took a hand from the steering wheel and gave hers a squeeze. 'I can't believe how brave you are. Most people would be a gibbering wreck after all of that.'

'Trust me, there is a part of me that's gibbering right now.'

'I mean it, Annie. You've got a bad habit of doing something well and moving on. Next!' he exclaimed. 'Take a moment to give yourself a giant fucking pat on the back. How you've had the strength to deal with everything...' The power of his emotion stopped whatever he was about to say next.

'Thanks, Lewis,' Annie said. 'You're right. One of the things that kept me going? Remember what Mrs Mac used to always say whenever we were dealing with something tricky?'

'The best way *to* is *through*,' Lewis said, and they took the moment to share a fond smile. 'However, I don't think she had a family curse and a homicidal maniac in mind when she came up with that, do you?' He laughed.

'Did I tell you about the little cottage?' Annie said after a moment. 'It was in this lovely wee spot I could see from the hill.

Right on a little beach by the loch. And the murmurs? When I saw this place, it was like they ... I'm struggling to find the right word, but it was as if they approved of the place. Like they wanted me to visit.' She paused. 'I can't help but think – that woman who turned up? The other one that Dennis Jenkins killed. Might she have been from there?'

'God,' Lewis exclaimed. 'I think I have the answer to all of this.'

'What?'

'There's so much I haven't been able to tell you while you've been up here.'

'What, Lewis?' Annie sat forward. 'Spit it out.'

'Right. Hang on.' Lewis looked ahead. 'We're nearly at a...' He put his indicator on, slowed down and navigated his way into a lay-by. 'Don't think I should be telling you this while I'm driving,' he said, slowing to a stop.

'Really?' What on earth did Lewis know?

'Sister Theresa.' He pulled the handbrake on. 'Remember that day I visited her without you? I was going to drive you across but you were feeling like shit?' He shifted in his seat so that he was facing her.

'Not really. I think I was in such a bad place for a time that nothing else got through. Why, what did she tell you?'

'First, that we were right about the two sisters swapping places. It was only when Sheila's condition became clear – the cancer – that the nuns knew they'd been duped.'

'Poor Sheila.' Annie thought again of the sacrifice her aunt had made for Bridget. What strength it must have taken to do such a thing.

'But before that, they found out that...' Lewis paused. He raised his eyebrows and his chin dropped to emphasise the importance of what he was about to tell her.

'What? Cut the dramatics, Lew. What?'

'Bridget had a baby.'

'She had a what? When?' Of all the things Lewis might have said, that was not one she'd even considered. 'Bridget? A baby?'

'The dates coincided, or were pretty close with Mum's pregnancy.' He pointed to himself, and then to Annie. 'And...' He paused again. 'I don't know how to tell you this, Annie.'

'Just bloody tell me, Lewis.'

'The family decided that Bridget couldn't keep it. Sheila was away with the army a lot, so that meant...'

Annie rushed to finish his sentence, her mind snapping through all the implications and alternatives: '...Mum took over. One of us is Bridget's child!' She held a hand over her mouth in shock. 'That means, what, we're not twins, we're cousins? Oh my God, Lewis. This is...'

'Mind-blowing.'

'Which of us?'

'Don't know.'

'What do you mean, you don't know? Didn't you ask?'

'Of course. But that's when Sister Theresa clammed up. Said she needed to see us both at the same time and then she'd tell us.' He paused. 'But then she was worried she was too ill and she gave me a letter that apparently explained it all, and I wasn't to open it until you were with me.'

Annie, barely listening to her brother, bowed her head, covered her face with her hands, and exhaled. 'I don't think I can take much more today.' She looked over at Lewis. 'What on earth did they tell Bridget? They can't just take a woman's baby away from her.'

'They did though.' Lewis gave a sad, little shrug.

'What did she go through in that place? The murmurs, her baby ripped from her arms. And she only got out all those years later.'

Instinct sang, facts slotted into place.

'She came up here.' She gasped. 'The cottage.' She looked out of the window, into the distance, her mind placing her back on the hill looking down at the small, white building.

'That's what Sister Theresa told me,' said Lewis. 'There was a cottage, owned by our family.'

'It must be the same place. It totally makes sense. How many little white cottages are up in that area?'

'Well, loads, probably,' Lewis shot her a half-smile.

'I was told about it, by Mum...' She reached across and grabbed her brother's hand. 'It has to be the same place. Why would the voices' – she pointed at the side of her head – 'react like that when I saw it?'

'Mum told you? What, back then?'

Annie nodded. 'Sheila told Mum about it when I went to see her at The Lodge that day. Then Mum mentioned it when ... before we...' She couldn't say that it was when they drove off the road into the loch.

'Ah right,' Lewis said. He paused for a moment to allow all of the information to sink in. 'Sister Theresa told me that Sheila inherited it and she wanted to pass it on to you. The plan was that Bridget was going to move in, and once she'd settled was going to seek us out. Introduce herself to us.'

'Oh my God,' Annie said, with her right hand over her heart.

'Apparently, Bridget was going to send Sheila postcards...'

'The postcard in the pack. Signed B,' Annie exclaimed.

'Yeah, I'm thinking the image was of one of the beaches up in the area. People are always saying the white sand, and clear, blue waters look like somewhere more exotic.'

Annie thought for a moment. 'But there was only one postcard.'

Lewis nodded. 'Sister Theresa said Sheila only ever received one. And after she died there were no more. She said she tried to locate Bridget to let her know Sheila was dead, but that...'

'What?'

'That it was like she'd dropped off the face of the earth.'

Annie shook her head slowly. Sorrow a weight on her limbs she never thought would dissipate. 'That woman. That was her. The one who tried to intervene – that *must* have been Bridget.'

Lewis nodded, his expression grave.

'It all makes terrible, awful sense,' he said. 'I've thought it all through. The timings work. That cottage belongs to the family. She was here around that time. Unless there was another woman out there, in that glen, who else could it be?'

'The poor woman.' Annie began to cry. 'She escapes that institution only to...'

'And poor Sheila. Her sacrifice was for nothing.'

'It's just too much, Lewis. It's too much.' Annie put her head in her hands and cried.

'Hey,' Lewis said, trying to console her. 'We don't know for sure it was Bridget. It *could* have been someone else.'

Annie wiped at her cheek. Her murmurs sounded a mocking, grating tone, like the hinge on a rusted gate sawing back and forth in a gale. 'It was her, Lewis. I just know it.'

'But we won't know for sure. Not until the police get up there and search the place for bodies.'

'And there could be more than even we realise,' Annie said. 'Eddie's convinced himself that Dennis Jenkins was prowling this area for years, picking off young women. And he's certain that Tracy is one of his victims.'

'It can't be a coincidence. Tracy going missing in roughly the same area,' Lewis said.

'If it's true, how many women has he killed? Jesus.' Annie shook her head, trying to dislodge the image her mind presented her with: various sets of bones within the roots of the old oak tree. 'And we have to be thankful that he had his stroke all those years ago, otherwise how many other poor women would have been targeted?'

Silence took over for a few minutes, until Annie spoke again.

'Did you say something about a letter? The one you weren't to open until we were together?' she asked.

'I've got it here.' Lewis patted his jacket pocket. 'Want to read it?'

Annie shook her head. 'I don't think I can take any more shocks today. Do you mind if we wait?'

'It's waited this long. Another day or two won't cause any harm.'

'And what about Sister Theresa? Is she that bad? Is the letter insurance – in case she doesn't survive to tell us what's in it?'

Chapter 85

Eleanor – Then

The words the obstetrician used made no sense – while at the same time, as they reached her through air fogged with dread, the dead weight in her belly grew heavier and heavier. A numbness rose from there and spread upward, squeezed at her heart with chill fingers before a cold tingle reached her jaw and her brain.

'You said ... the what?'

'You shouldn't be on your own, Eleanor,' the woman said. 'Where's your husband? Do you have any family that can come and pick you up?'

'I'm fine,' she said, the words delivered with a voice that seemed to come from someone else. Somewhere else. 'I'm fine.' She shook her head. Nothing made sense. The woman was talking. Always talking. Eleanor put up a hand; a pale, trembling stop sign.

'As agreed, we'll get you in first thing Monday and induce labour,' the doctor said. 'That way you get the weekend to say your goodbyes to baby.'

'Monday,' Eleanor repeated, surprised that her jaw could move enough to allow her response. Aching hand to her swollen belly, she looked down at her spread fingers there, back to the doctor. 'You're telling me my baby is dead?'

The pregnancy had followed all the usual markers, all the milestones reached in textbook fashion, but then last week, a baby that was a big kicker stopped kicking. In a panic Eleanor contacted her doctor. And here she was, being told the worst possible news.

The doctor offered a tight smile. 'We'll give you something to help you cope over the weekend. Is there someone you can call?'

'My husband...' Eleanor waved a hand in the air. She wanted to say that he was away with work. On a course. But the words and meaning were stuck. She screwed her eyes shut. Tried her tongue again. 'My baby...?' She could phone the pastor. He would know what to do. What she should say. How she should be. Because this woman in front of her, with the earnest face and small hands, just wasn't making any sense.

Pastor Mosely arrived within the hour. Only when she saw him sitting outside in his car did the importance of what she was just told hit her.

The next thing she was aware of was that he was looming over her. The stone steps at the hospital entrance cold against her cheek.

'Eleanor,' he said, his eyes full of understanding and compassion. 'Let me get you back inside. The staff—'

Eleanor sat up, her head spinning. 'No. No,' she said. She couldn't go back in. Couldn't ever go back inside there. They wanted to take her baby from her.

'Your husband's away, isn't he?' Mosely asked. 'You shouldn't be on your own at a time like this. Where should I take you?'

'My car...' She pointed vaguely in the direction of the car park.

'You can't drive,' the pastor said. 'We'll get someone to pick up your car and drop it off home. In the meantime – family,' he said as if just arriving at a decision on her behalf. 'I'll take you to your mother's. A woman needs her mother in a time like this.'

❋

When they arrived at her mother's house, an ambulance was parked at a strange angle, as if rushed there, and it was being loaded with a woman lying prostrate on a stretcher. A neighbour, Mrs Hendrie, waved frantically at Eleanor when she saw her.

'Your mum,' she said and pointed towards the ambulance.

✳

Delia Jackson had collapsed in her garden while tending her roses. Mrs Hendrie found her there, curled up as if asleep, face in the dirt.

In the hospital, by her mother's hospital bed, Eleanor could scarcely believe that she was so quickly returned to such an establishment. Holding her mother's clammy and trembling hand, she struggled to make sense of everything that had happened in the last few hours. Struggled to weigh up one potential grief against the other. Which should demand most of her attention? She'd never felt so lost. It seemed that every thought that rose in her mind came with a thousand others, none of them reaching a cohesive, coherent whole.

'Brian,' she mumbled. 'Someone needs to call Brian.'

'I called,' Pastor Mosely said. He was by her side. Her guardian. She sent him a smile of love and appreciation. 'I spoke to his boss and they're going to get him on the next train home.'

'It's too much,' she mouthed. 'Too much.'

'The good Lord,' he said putting a hand on her shoulder, 'only burdens us with a weight he knows, in his infinite wisdom, that we are able to carry.'

'He does?' Eleanor searched his eyes for surety – a rope cast into a roiling sea, a handhold to safety and security, and sense.

'He does,' Mosley asserted. 'Life is but pain and suffering. You *will* endure. You have the strength of ten women.'

Suddenly, her mother stirred. Tried to sit up, but was so weak she fell back onto the pillows.

'Bridget?' Delia asked, eyes barely open. 'I knew you'd come.'

'No, Mother. It's me. Eleanor.' Even now, she thought, it's never about me. She was sure her mother's face sagged with disappointment when she realised it was, indeed, Eleanor who was by her side.

Delia licked at her lips. 'Bridget can't ... not there,' she said.

'What? I thought you approved,' Eleanor said. 'You said it was the right place, the only safe place for her.'

'I don't mean her. I mean...' Her eyes flicked towards the pastor. 'Who's he?' she demanded, her tone one of fear. Then, recognition.

'You?'

'This is Pastor Mosely,' Eleanor replied. She turned to the pastor and offered him a smile of reassurance. 'I told you about him, and the charity work we're doing.'

'You horrible, foul man. How could you take advantage...' This outburst caused Delia to weaken, and she fell back onto her pillow, momentarily robbed of the ability to speak. Then she rallied. 'Get that awful man out of here.'

'Mum, you're making no sense. This is Pastor Mosely. He has been very kind, very supportive—'

'Leave,' Delia demanded, her eyes cold. 'I can't even bear to look at him.' She turned her head to the side.

'Mother,' Eleanor said. 'How can you be so rude. Pastor Mosely has been very, very kind.' Her voice broke, and she reached for the pastor's hand.

'Leave,' Delia repeated, her voice falling to a whisper.

'Mother.'

'It's okay.' Pastor Mosley got to his feet, his expression one of care and understanding. He stretched out and briefly touched Eleanor's shoulder. 'I'll go and get myself a cup of tea.' He left.

'The baby,' Delia said. 'Bridget can't have it there.'

'Mother.' Eleanor's anger rose. She tried to speak calmly. 'You're making no sense.' I'm the one who is pregnant, she thought. *Was* pregnant. Was still pregnant?

Delia's eyes bored into Eleanor's. She couldn't bring herself to look away.

'You must take it,' Delia said, and as she did so she reached for and held on to Eleanor's hand. Her grip crushing. Where she got the strength in that moment Eleanor had no idea.

'Bridget's baby. She can't have it in there. And it's best it stays in the family. Sheila's all over the world with the army, so it has to be you.' She stopped talking as if marshalling her strength. 'You must take it, and if it turns out to be like her, you'll know what you need to do.'

'Mum, what on earth are you talking about?' Even as she asked the question, Eleanor knew the answer. In her mind, she saw Bridget in that bed, hand over her own stomach.

Bridget was pregnant and, by the looks of her, not too far behind Eleanor. And it that was true, who might the father be? Her mother's words, and her reaction to the pastor pushed through her confusion.

An electric charge ran through Eleanor's heart. 'You're telling me the father is...' She couldn't, wouldn't, believe that Pastor Mosely had taken advantage of her sister. Bridget was lying. Nothing that came out of her mouth could be trusted. She was a sick, young woman. Pastor Mosely was a good man. A kind man.

'But Mum.' She struggled to find the words. 'You're asking the impossible of me. I've just been to the ... for an emergency scan.'

Her mother wasn't listening. Her eyes were distant, in another room, with another daughter: 'If it turns out to be a girl like Bridget, you'll know what you need to do.'

'You don't know what you're asking me to do, Mother.' For a moment Eleanor tried to raise the right words, to tell her mother what she'd learned just that afternoon. That her own baby was no longer moving. 'No longer viable' were the words used by the doctor. The coldness of it still rang through Eleanor's mind.

With grim certainty Delia met Eleanor's eyes. 'Promise me, won't you,' her mother pleaded. 'If Bridget has a girl you will do what you need to. This curse can't be allowed to continue.'

Eleanor jumped to her feet, hand to her belly, and stepped back from the bed.

'You can't seriously be asking me to—'

'Deadly serious,' her mother replied. 'And it's all been arranged. You will bring Bridget's child up as your own. Lawyers, social workers, the staff in the hospital all know you will be taking the baby – and they'll tell Bridget the child died, and if you ask me that's a kindness.'

'But that's so cruel.'

'Would you have her committed to such a place and forever pining for her child, with just the occasional visit? No, that's no life at all. For the wean or her. She'd never get better, even supposing she can. This way she gets the grief out of her system.'

'Oh, dear God.'

'You'll do it for the family. You have to.'

'But Mum, there's the father, whoever he is. Doesn't he get a say in this?' She refused to believe what her mother had alluded to earlier.

'You're moving back up to Mossgow?'

'Back up? You're confused, Mother.'

'You won't remember. That's where we're from.'

'You're making no sense, Mum.'

'My mother fled there to escape the curse, but it seems it followed...'

'How about I get you a drink? Mmm?' Eleanor asked trying to shift her mother's mind elsewhere.

'You felt a draw, didn't you? A pull? As soon as that man mentioned Mossgow, you felt it, didn't you?' Her mother's hand reached for her.

'Whatever you say, Mum,' Eleanor replied. But the thought slid in, one that she fought. She had felt something. And it had happened as soon as Pastor Mosely mentioned the name of the place he was going to.

Her mother fell back on the pillow, exhausted.

'Mum.'

The flesh of her face sagged. Her eyes were half open.

'Mum?'

The machine she was attached to sounded a loud beep. Then another.

Then a long solitary note announced Delia Bennett's passing.

Eleanor sat by her mother's bed, stunned to silence, tears for her mother's passing stalled by the events of the day that swirled in her mind – a dark mist of grief, loss, betrayal and hate. How could she contain all of that and remain sane?

Chapter 86

Annie – Now

As soon as she got out of bed the next morning, Annie phoned to find out what had happened to Sister Theresa.

'She has rallied momentarily,' the nun she spoke to told her. 'I think it was because she wanted to be sure that you were okay, dear.' A heavy pause. 'But I'm afraid she doesn't have long on this earth.'

'Is she able to have visitors?' Annie asked.

After the nun went to check – the answer was yes, but to Annie and Lewis only.

❋

Walking along the corridor that led to Sister Theresa's room, Annie asked Lewis, 'Have you opened the other letter?'

'I've got it with me,' he replied. 'But it's still sealed. I thought whatever Sister Theresa had to say would be better coming from her rather than a piece of paper.'

Sister Theresa was propped up on a mountain of pillows. She seemed to have lost a huge amount of weight and created barely any bulge in the quilt that covered her from her neck to her ankles.

She smiled when she saw them, and lifted a hand from its position over her heart to wave at them.

A nun was standing at the other side of the bed, like a guardian. 'Are you sure you're strong enough, Sister?' she asked, casting a glance of warning at the siblings.

Sister Theresa reached for the nun's hand, and gave it a squeeze.

'This has been a long time coming, Sister Claire. It's not only necessary, it's my dying wish to speak to these two, and try and right an old wrong.'

'Dying wish,' Sister Claire repeated. 'There will be no dying on my watch.'

'Isn't that for the good Lord to decide?' Sister Theresa coughed. 'Now be off with you. There must be other poor souls more in need of your attention.'

With a few more grumbles and a look of warning at Annie and Lewis, Sister Claire left the room.

'Dear God, save me from the attentions of the over-zealous,' Theresa smiled. Her face was pale, but her eyes sparkled with good humour. This reassured Annie. There was a strength in this woman that she could only hope for when her end was nigh. This thought was accompanied by mocking laughter: Annie was being chided by her murmurs, but on this occasion they were less harsh with her, playful even.

'You read the letters?' Theresa asked.

'Just the one that talked about Bridget and the cottage,' Lewis replied.

'I've seen it,' Annie said. 'The cottage. From a distance. It looked lovely.'

Theresa coughed again and the look of pain on her face made Annie ask, 'Are you sure you want us here?'

'Don't worry, dear,' she replied. 'When it gets too much I'll just give myself a dose of this.' She indicated a little device by her hand that Annie guessed would provide pain medication. 'You've been in the wars, I hear.' Sister Theresa's face was full of concern for her.

'How did you...?' Annie looked to Lewis. 'Did you tell her?'

'No, dear,' Theresa said, and pointed to a TV on the far well. 'You were on the news.'

'I was?'

'Anyway,' Sister Theresa said. 'It's time you two learned the truth.'

Chapter 87

MOIRA MCLEAN – A MEMOIR

As I, Moira McLean, sit here, struggling to finish writing my recollections by candlelight on All Hallow's Eve, I fight to remember every last word learned at my grandmother's knee. At times, on these pages, I may have lapsed into hyperbole, or even melodrama, and of course I am unable to repeat what was said and by whom verbatim, but believe this: the substance of what I say is true. Frighteningly so.

I'm keenly aware of the depths to which I have fallen, and the bitterness and spite that clings to every cell in my body. It is in that spirit I have sought to be fair in elucidating both sides of the story. But who would not be burning with bitterness had they lived through what me and mine have, and ended up where I sit now. I can hardly countenance that many of my clan have sought passage to the New World while I, considered too old to risk such a voyage, sit by an unlit hearth in a Glasgow slum.

The iniquity is too much to bear. For most of my life the air was scented with heather and brine, the sounds that filled my ears were those of birdsong, children laughing, and the occasional huffs and groans of our livestock, and every sunrise and sunset came to you over the mountains like a gift from on high. Now? My ears are assaulted daily by the rough, guttural slang of the impoverished city-dweller, the smoke of industrial fires scours my lungs, and I dare not list the foul smells that permeate the air in case the reader suffers the nausea I feel every waking second of every single day.

But I must bear it if I am to give witness in full to the events of my life and the strength of feeling that resulted in me spewing a curse into the Highland air.

After Jean, Isobel and Andra were tortured and murdered, Jean's surviving child, my grandmother, Jeannie, was spirited away by a cousin, Duncan McNeil and his wife. They were rightly disgusted by what had happened and vowed to protect Jeannie from the same fate.

They knew of a distant and remote glen, only two days hence on foot, but one that was located at the far end of a little-known mountain pass, where no one would think to look. A river ran through it and into a small loch teeming with salmon and brown trout. The land thereabouts could be tamed to produce crops and to feed animals, and the mountains that ringed it in a horseshoe shape would protect them from the worst of the Highland storms.

Their first home was a very rough affair, no more than a roof of fern and fir thrusting out from the flat top of a giant rock. But they soon managed to construct a more permanent homestead, down by the loch, and over time they were joined by others fleeing from the persecution of the church and state until they had enough to call themselves a village: Anlochard. Which translates from the old Gaelic into 'the high loch'.

Duncan proved to be an able farmer and a wise one, for he saw that potatoes would have a yield much greater than that of oats – four times as much he argued – oats being the favoured crop for most crofters in those parts and in those times. And it was the success of his crop that provided the seed for the end of Anlochard.

We could only remain hidden for so long. The outside world would have to intrude at some time, for they had to have stone to build better homes, and as the community grew there was a responsibility to provide an education for the bairns, and much more besides.

A solid crop on year three of living in Anlochard meant there was enough to sell at the market and the profits raised after another two years of this brought us to the attention of the people who actually owned the land on which they lived and worked.

The landowners were a hapless bunch, always on the verge of financial ruin and therefore more than happy to raise some rent from a successful crofter like Duncan, and this arrangement lasted for a long time, even for a good few decades after Duncan himself died.

But then one too many debts were taken on, the latest laird took lodgings in Edinburgh to mingle with men of means, but the added costs stripped what little assets he held, and then the main crop that had helped to sustain his family for decades – kelp – tumbled to the lowest prices ever known. There was nothing for it but to sell the land. The new owner? The granddaughter of Jean's twin sister, Mary Campbell, a beastly woman given the name of her grandmother. A most loathsome woman has never been sired.

It is said that many of the Highland landowners suffered under increasing debts in those parlous times, but for me to give credence to that as an explanation for what happened next would require a degree of sympathy I simply cannot muster.

Campbell appeared one spring morning on horseback. Accompanied by the minister from Mossgow, and her factor, a fat-bellied bully of a man called Patrick Young.

I was sitting on a stool by my door, taking the air, when Campbell stopped by. Deigning to dismount, she shouted down at me to say that the rent would be increased forthwith, and should we fail to pay we would be out on our ears.

She had no idea she and I were kin, and I was not of a mind to inform her. If I had been a younger woman I would have pulled her from her horse, put her over my knee and given her a good spanking. Instead, all I could do was glare and give her a piece of my mind.

I would like to report that she was chastened by my ill humour, but instead she gave a cold smile, said, we'll see how you fair when your lands are turned over to the sheep. Then she turned her horse and slowly made her way out of the valley.

One month later, they returned, this time with a gang of enforcers. Me and mine were thrown out of our homes, allowed only as much of our belongings as we could carry in our arms, and to ensure we wouldn't sneak back in the night, our houses were set ablaze.

Which brings me back to the curse – and in the cold half-light of a Glasgow tenement, many miles from where I once lived, I regret nothing.

Where I sit, I have nothing but the paper and ink I write with, and a lighted candle to help me finish my tale.

I have lived a good life, a long life, a mostly Christian life, but I feel the old words and the old hurts murmur the length of my veins, fuelled by a virulence and malignancy without end. That the Campbells should continue to be the source of my family's ills is something fate could not have decreed. It is beyond imagining – and can only be the work of some foul sprite and as such must be answered.

The first curse needed the power of the open air, the loch, the mountains and the glen to gain potency. I've added strength to that every night since, fuelled by the hate that fills my mind.

I am anger, I am malice, I am the black and sharpened nails that tear at your soul, Miss Campbell, and you and yours will never know peace.

For even unto the grave I will never stop.

Chapter 88

Annie – Now

'Bridget had twins,' Sister Theresa said without any preamble. 'It was thought at the time,' she heaved a sigh, 'that it would be best to tell her the children had died shortly after.' She shook her head at the horror of that. 'And Eleanor agreed to take them both.' A pause. 'You both. After being persuaded to by her mother. On her death bed, no less.'

Annie shook her head in confusion. 'She was told we were dead? How callous was that? And what about—?'

'Eleanor's own pregnancy didn't carry to term. She lost her child.'

The siblings sat in shocked silence.

'Mum lost her...' Annie shook her head again. Even after all she'd learned over the last while, this was almost too much to take in. She and Lewis were twins after all: only they were Bridget's not Eleanor's.

'I should have told you when I first met you,' Sister Theresa said. 'I'm so sorry. I might have died without you knowing any of this.'

Her sadness at this thought was so clear that Annie couldn't help but take the woman's hand. 'You did what you thought was the right thing,' she said. The nun's hand was an insubstantial thing with no more weight than a small collection of feathers.

'What about the father? *Our* father. Did Bridget ever say?'

Theresa opened her mouth to speak, but paused, as if the burden of the words was too much for her. Then: 'Your father, was ... the pastor. Pastor Mosely.' And she watched, her eyes moving from Annie to Lewis as the implications of this hit home.

'Mosely was our father?' Annie thought about the man from her childhood, that hand on her head as he prayed for her salvation. Had he known?

She shuddered. Then exchanged glances with Lewis. He looked as dumbfounded as she felt.

'But how? When would...?'

'Bridget told me that she found solace in that church in Glasgow, only a short time before Eleanor came across it. And she'd fallen under the spell of the pastor there.' Sister Theresa's expression soured with disgust. 'He asked her to go up to Mossgow with him, but that didn't happen because she ended up in hospital. And then he turned his attention to Eleanor.'

Annie exhaled sharply. 'What a creep.'

'We have no idea whether Eleanor was treated in the same manner as Bridget...' Sister Theresa said.

Now that her memory was restored Annie was able to think back to the moments of interaction she'd seen between the pastor and her mother. 'For sure there was an emotional attachment. From what I can remember she doted on his every word.'

'People like him make me sick. Taking advantage of their position like that.'

'Maybe that was why Bridget tried to commit suicide.' Annie considered how Bridget might have felt, being used like that. 'Perhaps it was nothing to do with her premonitions.' Her emotions were all over the place as she processed this information. While feeling guilt for entertaining the thought – she was nonetheless encouraged that this might not be her ending after all. If Bridget endured the murmurs, so would she.

'It was tantamount to sexual abuse,' Theresa said. 'A man in that position, with a vulnerable young woman. Think about the shame that attends these kind of events. Must have been quite the burden for a young woman who was already greatly troubled.'

'And what about the paperwork?' Annie thought out loud. 'If Bridget gave birth to us, and Eleanor was given custody, surely there would have been legal stuff completed? You can't just hand over another woman's babies; sister or not.' Annie told Theresa about the briefcase and its contents. 'There was nothing there to give us a clue into any of this.'

'Correct,' Theresa said. She closed her eyes briefly, as if she was gathering just a little more strength. 'It was all above board. Social workers and lawyers all putting their tuppence in. If there was nothing there to see, I'm guessing Eleanor, or the man you believed to be your father, destroyed the paperwork. Maybe, as far as she was concerned, you were her children.'

Annie nodded, and considered her previous beliefs about the woman who brought her up, her certainty that she'd tried to kill her, and the truth being revealed in that moment when Chris had his hands around her throat.

Finally, Annie could accept that she had been loved.

Chapter 89

Annie – Now
Three months later

Before they went inside, Annie and Lewis walked the periphery of the small cottage. It was a square building, one window, one door in the front, with two windows and another door lodged into the back wall of the building.

Off to the side, under a fir hedge, sat a wooden garage. The window on the side was thick with dirt. Lewis wiped a clean circle in it to look inside. When he did he called to Annie, and they both noted the small jeep inside.

'A Suzuki three-door. Cool. Wonder if it still goes?' he said.

The garage had seen better days, but from what they could see, the cottage looked solid and intact, the roof tiles, from where they stood, all looked in place. Annie took in a hedge of trees and wondered if that had sheltered the house from the elements all these years.

A low fence bordered the back garden, which had, at a guess, the same footprint as the house. And there was a little gate in the middle, with a path leading to a small beach on the lochside.

A breeze lifted the loch surface into a ripple of tiny waves, sunlight glinted diamonds, and a call came from above: the high keen of a bird of prey on the hunt.

Once they'd surveyed the exterior, only then did they attempt the key in the door to see what was inside the house. The wooden door was swollen with damp, but with a hard shove they managed to push it open and enter the little cottage.

Twenty years of dust layered the meagre furniture inside. A pair of armchairs either side of a wide, cold fireplace, a sofa against the far wall, and under the window to their right a small table and two plain, wooden chairs.

The only light came from the open doorway they were standing in, so Lewis stepped across to the closed shutters in front of the one window. They creaked in protest as he opened them.

'Just look how thick these walls are,' he said as light filled the room. 'Must be a good two feet thick.'

'I can't believe this is ours,' Annie said as she walked in behind Lewis. 'I can't believe any of this, to be fair.' She closed the door behind her. The draught sent up a cloud of fine dust particles, swirling and dancing in the light.

The scent of air dulled by time filled her nostrils. Her murmurs sounded in her mind and she fancied they suggested the weight of a tomb and a tragedy of lost expectations.

Annie was carrying a small bundle in a paper bag. With reverence she sat it on the table, then moved to the door in the far right-hand corner of the room, which was open enough that Annie could see it was the kitchen. The other door, on the left, must lead to the bedroom, and a bathroom.

She walked into the kitchen and opened the shutters in there too. Then looked around. It was very basic. A sink under the window, a short wall of kitchen units, with empty spaces where an oven, fridge and washing machine might sit.

'Looks like she'd only just moved in,' Annie said, her mind filling with sadness. She opened a couple of the unit doors, and found a pair of dinner plates, soup plates, and coffee mugs, all in the same plain, white china. Another door opened to reveal a box of cereal and a packet of teabags.

She turned away, met Lewis's eyes and together they walked to the other door and pushed it open.

A double bed sat in the middle of the room, the mattress still wrapped in plastic, and a bag of what Annie guessed might be some bedding sat on top. At the foot of the bed lodged two suitcases and a large sports holdall.

Annie felt a tear slide down her cheek. 'She hadn't even properly moved in. She hadn't even unpacked.'

The word 'Mum' was a solid block at the back of her throat.

Lewis looked at her, and as if he'd read her mind he asked, 'You still struggling to get used to what Sister Theresa said?'

And she was back in that small room, the old nun on the bed, her face wreathed in apology, being told who their mother really was.

'And what about knowing Mosley was our real dad; we haven't really talked about that.'

'Do we really need to?' Annie asked. 'He was the sperm donor. Any arse can do that. He deserves no more attention than the dirt under my fingernail. The disgusting creep.'

Lewis nodded in agreement. 'Dad was our dad. And Mr Mac.'

'No more needs to be said, brother.' Annie cocked a half-smile. With that she lifted one of the suitcases and put it on the bed. She zipped it open to find a pile of clothes inside: underwear, two pairs of jeans, some ankle socks, a heavy wool, navy cardigan, and a couple of plain white T-shirts.

'God.' She moved to sit on the bed beside them. 'This was all Bridget had in the world.' She started to cry. At the waste. At the ruined hope of a new beginning that these items detailed. At the thought of how Bridget must have been so excited at the prospect of meeting the children she'd last seen when she'd given birth to them, and was told that they'd died shortly after.

'Hey,' Lewis said, sitting beside her and pulling her into a hug.

'Poor Bridget. She must have been terrified at the prospect of facing up to Mum – Eleanor – and Dad. But equally determined to get to know us.'

'But before she could do any of that she saw Chris, Conor and Dennis Jenkins carry a body up the hill.'

Annie looked at her brother and could see that his eyes were full of moisture, but his mouth was a thin line of anger.

'I wish Chris Jenkins was alive so I could be the one to kill him – all over again,' he said.

'Get in line, mate,' Annie replied, while wiping the tears from her face. 'What I don't understand is how this place remained un-discovered. Did no one notice that the person who moved in had disappeared?'

'Well, Bridget arrived quietly, and by the looks of it' – he nodded at the luggage – 'didn't unpack. Didn't even have a chance to introduce herself to any of the locals. And this place is so out of the way I'd be surprised if any of the natives even knew that it existed.'

They sat for a long moment in silence, each of them lost in their own thoughts.

'Is it time?' Lewis asked, looking towards the paper bag Annie had placed on the table under the window.

Annie nodded. 'It's time.'

Together they walked over to the table, Annie reached inside the bag and pulled out a little wooden urn and a wreath, which she handed to Lewis.

'Did you get an invite from Eddie for Tracy's service?' Annie asked.

Lewis nodded. 'It's at their local church, yeah?'

Annie weighed the little urn in her hand, considered what it contained. Bone reduced to nothing but ash. 'At least he'll be able to properly grieve for poor Tracy.'

'I haven't been watching the news the last couple of days,' Lewis said. Annie on the other hand had been gripped by it – watching the facts unfold as more and more bodies were uncovered throughout the site of the lost settlement.

'They've only been able to identify Jenny, Tracy and Bridget so far,' she said. 'There are another four bodies – as yet unnamed.'

'Bloody hell. Who would have thought that our neighbour, Dennis Jenkins, was a killer hiding in plain sight for all those years.' After a pause Lewis continued. 'What's Eddie been saying about all of this? He must be relieved he's been vindicated.'

'He's feeling a whole lot of stuff. Relieved that his innocence has been asserted, sad that Tracy has been lying in an unmarked grave for all these years. Upset at the waste of both their lives and those of their parents.' Annie paused in reflection. 'We forget it's not just the deceased who suffer, it's the people who loved them as well. Imagine the living grief of not knowing what happened to someone you loved with all of your heart? And being tortured by that never-knowing, every moment of every day.'

The search for victims had been a difficult one. The site was so large it had taken weeks and weeks to go over it, and the authorities were careful not to say that their only suspect was Dennis Jenkins. Now that Chris was dead – as far as the police and the media were concerned, at the hands of Annie Jackson, the psychic no less; and how the press had loved that – they had no way of knowing what Chris's involvement was. And Danni was denying all knowledge, defending her brother with as much energy as she could muster. She had become an online hate figure– how could she not have known? people asked. So she'd fled the country.

Outside, they made for the curve of sand at the edge of the loch. There, under a hawthorn tree, they paused. Annie looked around, at the wind-ruffled water, the fall and climb of the surrounding hills, and the ever-steady trees. All was silent apart from the wood pigeons, who cooed their content from the surrounding evergreens. Head up to accept the warm kiss of the sun on her skin she said, 'I think Bridget would have loved living here.'

'Aye,' Lewis replied, and in that solitary syllable she could tell he was choking up.

'Mrs Mac was an admirable replacement, but it would have been lovely to meet and get to know our real mother.'

This time the emotion was too much for Lewis and he could only nod in mute agreement.

And there, with the wind as their witness, while the evening sun looked on and the surrounding hills acted as sentinels, Lewis crouched down and placed the wreath on top of the water, giving it a little push so that it sailed out into the open loch.

With a sigh and a tear at the desolation of her past, an expectation of hope for her future, and a moment's gratitude that the death murmurs had quietened to a discordant hum since she'd been attacked by Chris and found her home in this little cottage, Annie offered the remains of their mother, Bridget Bennett, to the deep waters of the loch.

She removed the lid, held the urn high and upside down until the ash began to slowly fall. The murmurs became like a sighing wind in her mind and the many cascading pieces of ash spread out, suspended, floating all too briefly as they caught the rays of the falling sun, making them sparkle in the breeze like a galaxy of a million miniature stars.

Epilogue

Annie – Now

Whenever Annie approached the cottage she could sense a change in the murmuring. Whenever she stepped on to the path to the little dwelling it went from a jarring, urgent, harrying tone to a more melancholy one, and once inside the door it changed to a gentle hum, as if the spirit who inhabited the curse was content – as if the building itself provided some sort of solace.

Consequently, Annie travelled here from Glasgow most weekends – and had even started to look for a job in the surrounding area. There was a little café on the jetty at Lochaline that was looking for staff. She'd met with the owner when out for a walk one day, they got chatting and decided that they liked each other. It would soon be tourist season and the owner was thinking that she could do with the help – maybe three days a week, she'd suggested.

That was a good start, and would allow Annie time to move in to the area and make her permanent home there.

'Is it good for you to be hiding out up there?' Lewis asked. 'Especially when so many young women died a little further up the glen.'

'I'm perfectly safe,' Annie said. She sat with that statement in her mind and felt the truth of it. 'That's all in the past.'

Lewis had popped up to spend the weekend with her – bringing a futon in the back of his car, and constructing it under the front window of the living room.

'A futon,' Annie chuckled. 'Whoever heard the like?'

'It's somewhere for me to sleep – and it rolls up into another sofa. Ideal.'

He looked around. 'Have you worked out what jobs are needing done to make the place more of a home?'

'I need some appliances in the kitchen, and then I'll be set,' Annie replied. 'I'm using a wee camping stove at the moment.'

'What about the chimney?' Lewis asked as he stepped nearer, and put a hand on the stone of the chimney breast. 'You had a fire yet?'

'Not yet,' Annie replied. 'I don't know whether to get one of those log-burner things, or get someone out to make sure the chimney is clear.'

'Either would work,' Lewis said. He ducked his head into the fireplace and looked up the chimney.

'See anything?'

'Not sure what I'm supposed to be looking for, to be honest,' Lewis replied with a grin, stepping back. As he did so his foot wobbled on a loose flagstone on the hearth. He tested it, shifting his weight back and forth. 'Want me to have a look at this?'

'Yeah, right,' Annie laughed. 'When did you ever learn how to safely set a hearth stone. You'll probably make it even more wobbly.'

'True.' Lewis got down on one knee. He tugged at a corner of the stone.

'Don't make it worse,' Annie warned.

'Might be safer – less of a trip hazard if you just lift it now, and then get somebody in.' As he spoke he lifted up one corner. 'Hey,' he said as something caught his attention. 'There's something here.'

'There is?' As Annie asked the question she heard her murmurs lift from silence into something resembling a sigh. 'There is,' she said definitively.

Lewis looked up at her. 'What's going on?'

'Lift it up,' Annie replied.

He did. They both examined the space underneath. 'There's a package. Wow. Wonder how long that's been there?' Lewis took out an object the shape and size of a hardback book, wrapped in a piece of hessian sacking. He handed it to Annie.

With reverence, Annie put a hand inside the sacking and pulled out something wrapped in wax paper.

'What is it?' Lewis asked.

'Feels like it's been waiting for me,' Annie said. She teased open the wax paper to see a red, leather-bound notebook. Her murmurs sounded a note of pleasure. She felt a charge of excitement. 'This was left here for me.'

'But how?' Lewis asked. 'Even from where I'm standing it looks like it's pretty old.'

'Lewis,' she chided softly. 'Surely you realise by now that nothing that happens around me obeys the normal rules of the universe?' Annie opened the first page. 'It's getting dark,' she said. 'Put the lamp on, please?'

Lewis did, and they sat side by side on the futon-sofa.

Sitting comfortably, Annie began to read out loud.

'"A curse is a difficult thing to master..."'

Acknowledgements

Those readers who know the hills and lochs of Ardnamurchan will know that I have taken some liberty with the geography of the area. Where bad things happen to people in my books I prefer not to have that tethered to a real place.

I did however spend a fruitful few days writing and walking up in the Ardtornish Estate. I would heartily recommend it, and would like to extend my thanks to the staff there for their warm welcome and care.

Huge thanks to my technical advisors on health matters: Simon McCormack and Ashleigh Manchester. Thanks also to Kenny Dunlop for his botanical knowledge, and to Douglas Skelton for his help with the history of the area. All errors are mine alone.

They told me to say that.

As always, big appreciation to all the peeps on the crime scene – fellow authors, reviewers, bloggers, booksellers, book-festival organisers and readers – this can be a lonely job at times and your support and enthusiasm is what helps to keep this author going.

And, last but not least, Team Orenda: what can I say – they are small in number but mighty. In particular to Karen Sullivan for her unending support, and West Camel for his eager eye, and patience – this book is so much better for their attention. My huge thanks and appreciation to the whole team for their ongoing support and belief in the worlds I create within the pages of my books.